Murder Leaves
Its Mark

Murder Leaves Its Mark

A HAWAI'I MYSTERY

VICTORIA NALANI KNEUBUHL

A LATITUDE 20 BOOK

UNIVERSITY OF HAWAI'I PRESS
HONOLULU

Library of Congress Cataloging-in-Publication Data
Kneubuhl, Victoria N. (Victoria Nalani)
    Murder leaves its mark : a Hawai'i mystery / Victoria Nalani Kneubuhl.
      p. cm.
    "A Latitude 20 book."
    ISBN 978-0-8248-3545-3 (pbk. : alk. paper)
    1. Oahu (Hawaii)—Fiction. 2. Detective and mystery stories. I. Title.
    PS3561.N418M88 2011
    813'.54—dc22
                                                    2011004671

University of Hawai'i Press books are printed on acid-free
paper and meet the guidelines for permanence and durability
of the Council on Library Resources.

Designed by Josie Herr

Printed by Sheridan Books, Inc.

MONDAY

SPRING 1935

MINA BECKWITH sat wrapped in a terrycloth robe on the veranda of her bungalow after her morning swim. Her long, wavy dark hair was still wet, and she could feel the salt water drying on her skin, leaving behind a vague prickly sensation. Engrossed in reading the morning editorial in the *Honolulu Bulletin,* she reached for her tea. Warmth rose from the cup as it neared her lips, and she breathed in a small, aromatic wave of steam before she took a sip and read on, her anger smoldering with every line. When she finished, she threw the newspaper on the floor. The sound startled an innocent mynah bird who had been scrounging for crumbs on the deck. He flew quickly to the safety of a nearby tree. With a furrowed brow, Mina ate her toast and jam while staring out at the waves breaking over the reef. She couldn't understand why most of the wealthy and privileged people in Hawai'i chose to ignore what to her seemed so obvious. She hated feeling this way first thing in the morning, but she was a reporter, so how could she not be angry and ashamed after reading a slanted, prejudiced editorial in the newspaper she worked for?

Her home was on the beach, just past Diamond Head Crater, tucked away on two acres in a little area called Ka'alāwai. An unoccupied bungalow, a mirror image of hers, sat directly across the way, separated by a spacious hau tree arbor. The second bungalow belonged to her identical twin sister, Nyla Forrest. Nyla and her husband Todd lived up on the mountain ridge of Maunalani Heights, not far away, and rarely used their beach house. There were a few other houses that lined the beach, both cottages and grander homes with gracious island gardens, but because the lots were fairly large, one had the illusion of seclusion and privacy. The shoreline was a lovely stretch of white sand bordered on the east by the Black Point lava flow and on the west by the cliffs of Diamond Head. Though Waikīkī was just around the bend of the old crater, Ka'alāwai seemed miles away from the activity of the tourist hive, with its glamorous hotels, well-heeled visitors, expensive restaurants, and money-sharks, attracted by the smell of new business opportunities, big and small.

Mina stared at the newspaper lying on the floor but made no move to pick it up. A slight breeze was sweeping away the stillness of the morning and rustling the heart-shaped leaves of the hau tree. She watched as one of the hibiscus-shaped flowers that had begun as a bright yellow blossom, but was now faded to a deep maroon, dropped from the tree, swaying and twirling away from the trellis toward the ground.

As she walked inside, she kicked the newspaper into the corner. She called her sister Nyla, then sat down at her typewriter, wrote a succinct letter, signed it, and placed it in a white envelope. She took a shower and dressed in a very smart forest-green linen suit she'd bought in San Francisco, an outfit that perfectly enhanced her pale green eyes and honey-colored complexion. She swept up her dark, shoulder-length hair and pinned it in place before she put on her hat, and just as she had finished applying her lipstick, she heard her sister's car in the driveway.

"Hey," said Nyla as Mina stepped into the Ford Victoria sedan, "you look dressed to kill."

"And I feel like murdering someone, too," Mina said. "It's a shame it's illegal. Did you bring the empty boxes?"

"Yes, ma'am." Nyla pointed to the back seat. "And I made a lunch reservation for us at the Royal Hawaiian. Is that fancy enough for you?"

"Perfect," Mina said with a smile. "Let the fun begin."

They drove up the long driveway that led to a residential lane, and from there it was only a short distance to the wide road that ringed Diamond Head. Soon they were on King Street and headed downtown. It was June in Honolulu and a light breeze, sun, and drifting clouds shaped the day. It had rained the night before and the mountains stood out, clean and clear, a green cutout against the sharp blue sky. Mina watched a streetcar headed in the opposite direction, loudly clanging its bell at a jitney just in front of it. Independent drivers drove the jitneys, and they cruised the streetcar routes looking for fares. One of their strategies was to get in front of a streetcar and hustle groups of already waiting passengers. The streetcar drivers had a running feud with the jitney drivers and accused them of stealing fares they felt were rightly theirs. People waiting for the streetcar would often opt to take a jitney, as the drivers would accommodate their riders by going off the main routes, and the fare wasn't much more.

Nyla pulled into the parking lot at the newspaper building. "Are you sure you want to do this?" she asked.

"Absolutely," replied Mina as she took out a pair of dark glasses from her purse and put them on. "Maybe I should be wearing gloves. Do you still always carry that extra pair around?"

"Always," said Nyla, as she pulled open the little door on the dashboard and took out a pair of white gloves. "That's why we have glove compartments."

Mina put them on. "Are you coming in? You don't have to, if you don't want to."

"Are you kidding?" Nyla returned. "I want a ringside seat. You know, even though I might not be comfortable announcing it in public, I do agree with you."

"All right, then, grab the boxes."

Before they entered the building, Mina paused at the entrance and looked up at the three-story stucco edifice with its arched glass windows and red-tiled roof. "The Honolulu Bulletin" was officially emblazoned in big, brass letters over the doorway. She sighed, shook her head, and walked in. She took Nyla to the second floor and into a large room where her fellow reporters were busily working at their desks. They all said good morning, hardly looking up, until they saw Nyla begin to pack Mina's things in one of the cardboard boxes, while

Mina herself marched out of the room with the white envelope in hand. She quickly returned and began helping her sister. They had almost finished clearing out the desk when Christian Hollister, the editor and owner of the newspaper, came striding into the room. Hollister was a tall, lean, handsome man in his early forties, and even though he had been born and raised in the islands, with his straight blonde hair and wire-rimmed glasses he had the fresh look of an East Coast Ivy League Yankee. His visits to the newsroom were always an event. The typewriters in the room fell silent and all eyes turned toward him as he walked directly to Mina's desk.

"I've just read your letter," he said to Mina. "I think you're making a big mistake."

"I don't think so." Mina continued to clean out her desk and didn't look at him.

"Look, you can't be serious about defending these people. They're mainland thugs out to ruin our way of life."

"I don't think trying to get people fair wages and decent living conditions ruins anyone's way of life," she answered. "And I think it's unethical of this paper to continually echo the views of the business interests."

"Your family's business, the Island Ironworks, made money from the sugar and pineapple industries, just like mine." Hollister's voice was just shy of accusatory.

"All the more reason we should, at the very least, present the other side of the trade union issue. And it's not our family business anymore. It's been sold, remember?"

"These people are radicals. Some of them even subscribe to communism. They're here to make enemies out of employers and employees. We don't need unions here. We've done just fine without them."

"Maybe *we've* done fine without them, but when was the last time you visited a plantation camp?"

"Why do you think those people came here? Because their lives were much worse in their own countries!"

"That is no excuse to treat human beings like slaves!"

"Look, there's no reason to get irrational about this." His calm voice was tinged with a fatherly superiority.

"I don't think I'm being irrational. Do you think I'm being irrational, Nyla?"

"Oh, no," Nyla answered, smiling. "You're just really angry."

"That's right," Mina agreed. She looked directly at Christian Hollister and spoke in a very even voice. "I'm angry at what I believe is an immoral and unprofessional editorial policy of this newspaper, and that's why I'm quitting."

Nyla and Mina presented quite a picture as they sat in the elegant dining room of the Royal Hawaiian Hotel. It would have been difficult to tell them apart had it not been for their distinctive hairstyles—Nyla wore hers short and perfectly waved while Mina kept hers longer, sometimes put up in a twist, but more often simply pinned back, away from her face.

Mina shrugged. "Well, now I'm officially out of a job."

"Don't worry, the Beckwith Trust will save you," Nyla replied as she eagerly perused the menu.

"Ah, yes, the good old Beckwith Trust to the rescue. How much do you think we're worth now?"

"Together or separately?"

"Separately."

"At least a million." Nyla watched her sister over her menu.

"That much?"

"Yep. Maybe more. You could ask baby brother. He could tell you exactly."

"Does it ever bother you? Having so much money?" Mina looked intently at her sister.

"Not really; does it bother you?"

"It bothers me that there are so many people in the world with nothing," Mina answered.

"The estate gives thousands of dollars every year to charity."

"I know. We're responsible *and* charitable, but . . ."

"Even if we weren't rich, it would still bother us that some people in the world had less than we did because . . . that's just how we are, Mi."

"In that case"—Mina removed her gloves and turned to the waiter, who had just come up to their table—"we want a bottle of champagne and some oysters while we decide what to have for lunch."

"Oh, geez." Nyla rolled her eyes. "I can tell this is going to be a lunch to remember."

"Now that I'm not working and I know I'm worth a mint, I could have champagne for lunch every day if I wanted." Mina fiddled with her fork on the white linen tablecloth.

"Maybe you can help me with my new job," Nyla said.

"You have a job?"

"Don't sound so shocked. It's only temporary."

"What in the world are you doing?"

"I've been hired to redecorate the conference room and the sitting room at the Burnham and Robbins offices on Merchant Street. Tessa Burnham asked me to do it. Well, I should say, she got her father, *el presidente*, to hire me. Their company has lots of money, and they're willing to spend it to make the place look classy."

"I thought you were finished with decorating."

"Well," Nyla said with a sigh, "I thought so, too, but after a couple of years of women's meetings and keeping house, I realize I've missed it."

The waiter returned and began an elaborate ritual with an ice bucket and the bottle of champagne. "Let me guess," said Mina. "Tessa got you to invite her and her father over to your house, and he took one look at your place and hired you on the spot."

"They did come over," Nyla replied, smiling, "but I think he wanted to hire me because Tessa told him about me working for Syrie Maugham. Never mind that I was fresh out of college, and it was only for a year." Nyla chuckled and shook her head. "Island people are so obsessed with any mainland connection. It's pitiful."

"I don't know if Syrie Maugham had anything to do with it, but you are very good at what you do, and he's lucky you said yes."

"I learned some things working for her," Nyla mused. "One of the most important was that we have our own style here. It's a different aesthetic. I couldn't put it into words, but I know it when I see it, and you do, too, Mina."

"Are you ever sorry you gave it all up?"

"What? New York? Syrie Maugham? The glamorous life of decorating for the wealthy and famous?"

"All of that."

"No," Nyla answered. "I'm like you, Mina. I want to see my life go by here."

Mina watched as the waiter filled their champagne flutes, and when he was finished, she raised her glass. "Here's to the beginning of your new job and the ending of my old one." They both sipped the golden, bubbly liquid.

"Remember how Mommy used to complain about Amanda Burnham? I hope for your sake she doesn't interfere."

"Tessa said if her mother bothered me, to just let her know and Mr. Burnham would rein her in."

"Is Tessa still a social worker?"

"She majored in social work, and now she's on several boards of charitable organizations. She thinks she can do the most good that way."

"She probably can, with all her connections," said Mina. "I remember Tessa had an older brother and a younger sister. Wasn't there something a while ago about the sister? What was her name?"

"Hester, and yes, there was something. She was always out of sorts—angry, sad, and melancholy, and scared about everything. I think she tried to kill herself. It was all hushed up, and they sent her away somewhere for a year or so. I think she had some kind of treatments. Tessa is very protective of her. What are you going to have?"

"Hmm," said Mina. "I think I'll have the shrimp curry soup, a salad, and the mahimahi." Mina suddenly held the menu up in front of her face. "Don't look now," she said, "but I think that's Clyde, a guy from the advertising and classified section of the newspaper. I wonder what he's doing here?"

"For heaven's sake, Mina, don't be silly. What does it matter what he's doing here?" Nyla turned and observed the man speaking to the maître d'. He turned, looked in the direction of the sisters, and walked out, with the maître d' following him. "He's gone, so you can lower the drawbridge."

The chilled oysters appeared perfectly arranged on the half shell, and the waiter refilled their champagne flutes. They both ordered their lunch, and after the first oyster, Mina completely forgot about Clyde. Their table was placed near a pair of open French doors, and they sat facing each other with a backdrop of Diamond Head, curling waves, surfing beachboys, and a sharp horizon. All of the guests who wandered into the dining room, except for one couple on their honeymoon, too absorbed in each other to notice anything, found their attention drawn to the vivacious sisters, who were oblivious to everything but their food and each other's company. They worked their way through each course, and Nyla watched as Mina had a little too much to drink. She said nothing, as she knew it had been a difficult, and probably sad, decision that Mina had made this morning. Two hours later, they asked for the check.

"The check has been taken care of," the waiter informed them.

"Who did that?" Nyla looked around the room for someone she might know, but saw no familiar faces.

"The gentleman said to tell you that Christian Hollister sends his best wishes and compliments."

"We don't want him to pay for our lunch," Mina told him. "We want to pay for it ourselves."

"I'm afraid it's too late," the waiter said as he cleared their dessert dishes. "He left cash. Would you care for some coffee or tea?"

"No, thank you," said Mina, trying not to show her anger.

"None for me, thank you," Nyla added, and the waiter seemed all too happy to leave them alone.

"Damn him," said Mina. "He must have had Clyde follow us, and I bet he left so much money that the waiter is in for a huge tip."

"Oh, don't be so hard on Christian." Nyla leaned forward. "You know he's got a huge crush on you."

"I do not know that." Mina looked away.

"Well, his girlfriend Lamby Langston sure knows it. She always looks daggers at you whenever you're in the same room."

"Let's get out of here," Mina said.

Mina insisted they walk to the car through the tropical gardens of the hotel, so they could stop and admire the old coconut trees. They were what remained of Helumoa, the famous old grove of over ten thousand palms planted by Kakuhihewa, one of O'ahu's most revered and celebrated ancient chiefs. Mina always thought of the trees as a group of lonely old Hawaiians, out of place and stranded at a garden party on the lawn of the swank pink hotel, with its tiki torches and striped awnings. She gazed up at the fronds swaying back and forth and took it as a sign of agreement.

Nyla drove and Mina watched out of the open window as the beach and the surf flowed by. They drove to the end of Waikīkī and began to round Diamond Head. The road rose up along the cliff, and Nyla pulled off the road just past a lighthouse, where there was a beautiful view overlooking the sea. An offshore rainsquall was passing toward the west. Mina looked over at the lighthouse, with its lens behind the glass windows, and the pretty green lawn surrounding it. Perched on top of the cliff, it seemed like a storybook lighthouse, as if there should be some significant tale to go along with it.

"Why are we stopping here?"

"Just looking," Nyla answered.

"Oh," said Mina in a small voice.

"Our grandfather built the mechanism for that lighthouse. Did you know that?" Nyla laughed.

"Jesus," said Mina. "Daddy only reminded us every single time we drove by here."

"Because it's the thing he likes most that his father built."

"And rebuilt, don't forget the rebuilt."

"How could I ever?" Nyla said with a sigh.

"I think it would be fun to live in a lighthouse. I could have a new career as a lighthouse keeper and prevent shipwrecks."

"I'm serious about you helping me with this decorating job," said Nyla. "I really do need you, and it would only be a month or two."

"What do I know about decorating?"

"Don't pretend you don't have great taste and style."

"I hope the pay is good."

"I bet it's more per hour than you ever made at the paper." Nyla enjoyed bragging a little.

"Are you charging an outrageous fee?"

"Of course; it gives the impression that I know what I'm doing."

"What was the older brother's name?" Mina asked.

"What older brother?"

"Tessa and Hester. Their older brother. I remember I used to think he was so handsome in his polo gear."

"Oh, you mean Shel," Nyla said. "He's their half-brother, Sheldon Lennox. Their mom was married to Winston Lennox, but he died when Shel was a little boy. Then she married Henry Burnham. Are you okay?"

Mina frowned. "Not really, but I will be."

"Ned will be here in exactly a week," Nyla said, as she started up the car.

"Ned who?" Mina burst out laughing.

"You're just impossible." Nyla shook her head. "I'm taking you straight home."

Once back at her bungalow, Mina fell asleep on the pūne'e in her living room. When she woke up it was already dark, and she had a slight headache. She took a couple of aspirins, had a shower, put on her pajamas, and went into her bedroom, where she took a new photo album with a wooden cover from her closet shelf. Tucked into the album were two unopened envelopes of photographs she had picked up from the Kodak processing shop the day before. She sat on her bed and opened one of them. The first picture was one she had taken of Todd and Nyla on the ship S.S. *Monterey* as they were leaving Honolulu. The second picture was one that Todd had taken of her and Nyla only a minute later. They stood smiling, leaning against the ship's rail, with their leis and bits of broken paper streamers. Aloha Tower loomed behind them as they sailed away to Sāmoa to visit Ned Manusia and his family. Edward Manusia—or Ned, as he was called—was an old friend of Todd and Nyla. Mina had worked with Ned to solve a series of murders earlier in the year, and they were now romantically attached. Ned was a brilliant writer, born in Apia, Western Sāmoa. When he was seven his father died unexpectedly, and he and his British mother had moved back to England. He was now a celebrated playwright who also sometimes served as an "unofficial agent" for his government. He was very fond of his Sāmoan grandparents and Apia, and often visited them.

The next picture Mina looked at was taken from the deck of the ship as they entered Pago Pago Harbor in American Sāmoa, the first stop before sailing on to Western Sāmoa. The harbor was long and wide, curving like a river away from the open ocean, with steep mountains on either side rising sharply from the sea. On the port side an old white house clung to the top of a little cliff of rocks, and Mina had captured its solitary and careworn look with her camera, as surely as if she had painted its portrait. There were other pictures, too, of their arrival in Apia—of Ned Manusia's family and the island of Upolu. There were snapshots of Todd and Nyla, and a very touching picture of Ned and his grandparents standing on the front porch of their family home. Mina decided she would have it enlarged and sent as a gift to Ned's grandmother. Mina studied her pictures, as she was trying to improve her photography skills. Some of them she had taken pains to try to compose and had given careful consideration to the quality and angle of the light. Then she began to place them in her photo album, keeping them in order, arranging them pleasingly on the black pages, and neatly sticking down the corner inserts for each one. She picked up a photo of Ned standing outside a *fale* in his lavalava, with a flower stuck behind one of his ears, and she laughed and thought about the first day she'd actually met him at the Bishop Museum. He'd strolled into the room that day looking so handsome in a suit with a matching vest and a tie, and with his British accent it seemed like he had just stepped out of an English country drawing room where he had been discussing Proust. But here he was in her picture, equally handsome but dressed like a native, about to help the village men remove a cooked pig from the umu. She had watched him laughing and joking with the others in Sāmoan, knife in hand, as he carved up the steaming meat for serving. Ned would be returning to Honolulu soon, on his way back to England. The thought of seeing him again made her feel both excited and anxious. She was always afraid of what he might ask her, or expect from her, but at the same time, she acutely missed his company. She forced herself not to worry about her feelings and concentrated on the photos. When she next looked at the clock it was nearing midnight, and she put her things away and went to sleep.

2

TUESDAY

THE NEXT MORNING Mina awoke to an unexpected phone call from her brother-in-law, Todd Forrest, who also happened to be the detective in charge of homicide for the Honolulu Police Department. He asked if she would come to his office that morning to talk about something. As she hung up the phone, she thought about how her relationship with Todd had changed over the last year after she and Ned had helped him out of the messy affair of the portrait murders. He was now respectful, even kind, to her. And she had become more tolerant of him when she learned about the troubled past he'd tried so hard to leave behind. She wondered what he wanted to talk about and then remembered something about the annual Policeman's Ball. It was an affair to raise money for charity, and a few weeks ago he'd asked if she would volunteer to write up some publicity announcements for them.

Mina heard a car come rattling down the driveway. Looking out her bedroom window, she realized it was Tuesday, the day Mrs. Olivera came to clean and Mr. Olivera did the yard. As their old truck came to a stop, she saw a fluffy-looking black dog jump out of the back. Not wanting to appear too lazy, Mina scrambled out of bed, dressed quickly, and went to the kitchen just as Mrs. Olivera was coming in the back door.

"Oh, good morning! You not at work today?" Mrs. Olivera's round face looked surprised to see her. "You not sick, I hope."

"Good morning." Mina yawned and smiled. "I'm taking a break from the newspaper."

"Oh!" Mrs. Olivera could not disguise her surprise.

"I'm going to help Nyla with one of her decorating jobs."

"Oh, your sister told me all about the job she has for Burnham and Robbins." Mrs. Olivera worked for Nyla the other four days of the week. "That's good you two will be working together. Now, did you eat breakfast? You sit down and let me make you something."

"You don't have to—"

"No, now sometimes I make breakfast for your sister. You sit." Mrs. Olivera was already getting the eggs out of Mina's Frigidaire. "And here," she said, lifting out a paper bag from the basket she'd carried in. "I brought a whole bag of *malasadas*. You can have some with your coffee. They're nice and warm."

Mina knew that Mrs. Olivera could tell something unpleasant must have happened at the paper, and this was her way of trying to offer comfort and help. So Mina decided to sit passively at the kitchen table and let Mrs. Olivera feed her. And she had to admit, she did feel better when she bit into one of the sweet and yeasty Portuguese doughnuts and watched the cute black dog happily bound around the yard. The dog suddenly stopped and looked pointedly in her direction, and just before he ran down toward the beach, she could have sworn he smiled.

It was late morning when Mina crossed the street at Merchant and Bethel and stood in front of the police station. The cream stucco building reminded her of a Spanish castle, with its tiled roof and its oversized dark doors surrounded by ornate cornices and finials of red sandstone. The little curved balcony that faced Bethel Street looked like the perfect backdrop for a princess in distress to stand in and wave a handkerchief. Mina climbed the narrow stairs to Todd's corner office on the third floor and knocked on the side of the open door.

Todd looked up from his pile of papers. "Hey, Mina." There were moments, like this one, when his smooth face and wide, open smile looked thoroughly boyish. "Come on in and close the door."

"Is this a secret meeting?" she asked as she walked over and looked out one of the windows onto Merchant Street.

"Yes. You want some coffee or anything? I was just going to get a cola; do you want one?"

"Please."

"Be right back."

Mina watched people going by on the street below. There were a couple of businessmen in suits talking intently as they made their way toward Bishop Street. Two elderly Japanese women dressed in pretty kimonos and carrying shopping baskets crossed the street and walked up Bethel. Another woman selling flowers from a wicker baby buggy rested on the stairs in the front entry of the old post office. She took out her coin purse and began to eagerly count her money. The buggy sitting next to her was a profusion of carnations, roses, calla lilies, gardenias, and red ginger.

"Watching the parade?" Todd asked as he entered the room.

"Looks like it could be a big distraction," Mina commented.

"It's great if you need to think," he replied as he opened the bottles of cola and handed her one. "Sorry, no straws or glasses."

"I can take it straight," she said, laughing, and sat down on the old sofa that was up against the wall to the left of the window. There was also a little coffee table and two easy chairs, a cozy corner where Todd questioned people when he wanted them to feel comfortable. The people who were questioned at his desk were the ones he wanted to make uncomfortable. Todd came over and sat in one of the chairs.

"Are you making plans for the Policeman's Ball?" she asked.

"Yes," he answered, "but that's not what I wanted to talk to you about."

"So what *did* you want to talk about?"

"Nyla told me about you quitting the paper. I bet they're sorry to lose you."

"I just can't be there," she said. "Not when they write editorials like they have been."

"I understand," he said.

"Do you?" Mina gave him a very direct look.

"I came from a working-class neighborhood in Chicago. I know what it's like for people who have to scratch for decent pay and decent working conditions."

"Sorry," she said. "I didn't mean to sound like a witch. Although to tell you the truth, when I think about the paper, I feel like one."

"Are you serious about helping out Nyla with her job?" Todd took a sip of his cola, but didn't take his eyes off her.

"I told her I would help her," she answered, "but I don't intend to make it a career—decorating, I mean."

"I'll take that as a yes." He put his cola down on the table.

"It's a yes," she said. "But I bet you didn't ask me here to talk about my employment situation."

"I did, in a way." He frowned. "I wanted to ask you a favor."

"What kind of favor?"

"An unofficial police business favor."

"Really?" She tried not to sound too excited. She was so happy she was wrong about the Policeman's Ball.

"It happens," he continued, "that you're going to be in the right place at the right time."

"And where is that?"

"In the offices of Burnham and Robbins. There's a problem that I need someone to keep an eye on. Mr. Henry Burnham has received some threatening letters. Last week he told the chief about it, asked his advice, but he doesn't seem to want any real intervention. The chief called me in and asked if there was something I could do, unofficially. "

"How bad are they?"

"The first two were accusatory; they make vague threats, but the last one that arrived two days ago was very specific." He shifted uncomfortably in his chair.

"A death threat?" She ran her index finger around the rim of her cola bottle.

"Very close," he said. "There are certain things in the letters that suggest the writer is privy to information that only someone close to Burnham would know. So the writer either has to be someone close to him, or is being informed by someone close to him. I'd need you to do a little very discreet, firsthand observing, and since you're going to be working in the building with Nyla—I couldn't believe it when she told me last night—I was hoping you might do me this little favor."

Mina took a sip of her cola and said, "Well, if you want me to do this little favor, I guess you better show me the letters."

Todd went to his desk and brought out three envelopes. "They were all mailed in Honolulu," he said. "No prints on the envelopes or letters." He passed them to her. "The typewriter could be any one of hundreds in the islands. It would take us years to test them all."

She opened the first one. They were all typed on the kind of plain white paper sold all over town.

> *Burnham:*
> *Someday you will pay for keeping people in servitude and slavery while you wallow like a pig in your wealth. Mend your ways before it is too late. There are many in our brotherhood, determined to bring change. This is a warning. And we know all about your pretty little secretary.*

The second letter read,

> *You have the opportunity to do what is right. People are not animals to be chained to hopeless poverty for your profit. While you see your wife and daughters squandering money, think of parents who have to watch their children go hungry. We are serious, unless you help the laboring class, there will be consequences.*

The last letter was the most disturbing.

> *We know what you did at the Haleʻiwa Plantation. We know how you are pressuring workers to discourage organizing. How you hire spies. How you KILL. How you conspire with the press. How you pay off the police. How you dictate from your ivory tower. You have had fair warning so now you will suffer the consequences. You had better prepare for the judgment of your maker—an eye for an eye.*

They were all signed with a big, black X.

"X," Mina said. "When did these arrive?"

"They started in April. The first two were about three to four weeks apart. The last one was yesterday." Todd paused. "I don't know," he continued. "Could be idle threats, could be a blackmail setup with the secretary angle, could be a real nutcase out for blood."

"What does this mean: 'how you kill'?"

"I have no idea," he said.

"And what did Mr. Burnham say about the secretary business?"

"Nothing, of course." He smiled.

"Of course," she repeated. "But he was worried enough to come to the police."

"He came to the chief. They're pals. This is not an official investigation, remember?" He took a sip of his cola. "I never even talked to Burnham. Everything I'm telling you is second hand, by way of the chief."

"Did Mr. Burnham have any suspicions?"

"You know how scared all these guys are about the unions, especially after the general strike last year in San Francisco. He thinks most likely it's some union organizer or sympathizer trying to scare him."

"The writer would certainly like us to believe that, but they're definitely not written by a plantation worker. Any plantation worker who could write like this wouldn't be working on the plantation."

"It would have to be someone in the upper echelon—one of the mainland transplants, maybe."

"Don't you think there's something a little wormy about these letters?" She frowned. "In my mind, it doesn't quite fit with the idealism of trade unions."

He looked out the window. "Yeah, you're right, those union guys are anything but wormy cowards."

"So you want me to keep my eyes open, quietly snoop around?"

"Exactly. And there's one really important thing." He looked serious. "Do not tell Nyla anything! I don't want her involved in any way, or the whole thing is off."

"I understand. I won't breathe a word."

When Mina left Todd's office, she found she had over an hour to kill before it was time to meet Nyla and their friend Cecily Chang for lunch at one of their favorite restaurants in Chinatown. Cecily lived with her parents in Chinatown, where she and her mother ran an antiques and fireworks business. Mina walked out of the police station and crossed Ala Moana Boulevard to a little landing on the water that faced Pier 12. There was no ship tied up to the dock, and the harbor waters lay calm and unusually quiet. She looked down into the water just off the landing at the large blocks of hand-cut coral that lay just below the surface. They were the last remnants of a fort built by Kamehameha I in 1816 to protect his harbor. The fort had been dismantled in 1857, and the blocks brought here to make a seawall that had now fallen away. As a child Mina had been fascinated with an artist's painting of the old fort, with its red-roofed buildings and the Hawaiian flag flying high up on a pole. Her Grandma Hannah remembered the blocks in the water and had made a special trip to bring Mina here to see them. She stared down into the blue-green water, watching the moorish idols and bright yellow angelfish swim around the forgotten blocks, which were strewn carelessly like petrified sofa cushions across the shallows. She felt relieved and calm as she stood looking into the water, as if these remains from both a historical and a personal past anchored her in the present. She had to admit that she felt uncertain about the future, and maybe a little regretful about quitting a job that had meant something to her.

She turned, crossed back over the boulevard, and decided to walk up Nuʻuanu Avenue. The tall stone buildings on either side shaded the street from the morning sun, and she felt a slight chill as she walked along. She was so absorbed in her thoughts that she almost tripped over a man's legs that were sticking out from one of the narrow alleyways between the buildings. As the man rolled over on his back, she saw blood streaming down over his mouth. He moaned and clutched at his right side, and Mina glimpsed two other men running toward the other end of the alley and disappearing around the corner.

"Oh, my God! Jack!" Mina recognized Jack Carstairs, the young man who was the purser on the *Monterey* when she had sailed back from Sāmoa.

Dazed, he looked up at her. "Who are you?"

"Jack," she said, bending down to help him. "It's Mina Beckwith.

We were on the *Monterey,* remember?" She helped him to sit up. "Do you think anything is broken?" She took out a handkerchief and dabbed at his bleeding nose and lip. "Shall I call an ambulance? The police? Did they rob you?"

"No!" He waved his hand. "No police. No ambulance." He took a few deep breaths. "I don't think anything is broken. I'll be okay."

"You men can be so stubborn." Mina shook her head in disapproval. "Keep your head back until your nose stops bleeding."

"Mina," he mumbled after a few minutes, "I'm sorry I didn't recognize you."

"Don't even think about it."

"Is my face a mess?"

"Let's see, your lip is cut and swelling, your nose is not in great shape, and I'd say you're going to have a real shiner. I really think you should go straight to the doctor."

"No, no doctor." Jack lay there and stared up at the sky, then finally asked, "Do you think you could help me stand up and walk over to the Mermaid Café? It's just around the corner, and I have friends there."

She managed to get him to his feet, and as he leaned against her, they slowly hobbled back down to the boulevard, turned right, and a couple of short blocks later arrived at a stone wall with a small, arched sign above an open gate that said "Mermaid Café." Inside the gate was a little grass yard and a two-story wooden building painted off-white with a long porch that spanned the front of the ground level. There were several round, rough wooden tables on the porch, where a few customers were sitting. They stared at Mina and Jack as she helped him through the two swinging screen doors. Above the entrance doors were several whimsically carved and painted mermaids. The inside was decorated with potted plants and several other carvings, including one of a vivid, life-sized mermaid that caught Mina's attention for a moment, just before a woman came rushing toward them from behind the counter.

"Jack, who did this?" She was an older woman with unnatural, but not unbecoming, bright and wild red hair. She spoke in a gravelly voice and appeared to be in her late forties or early fifties. "Duncan, get out here," she called back to the kitchen.

A man came out wearing a slightly soiled white apron over his T-shirt and khaki pants. He was big and had several nautical tattoos on his arms. "What the—Jack, who got you? Maggie, get the boy some ice in a towel," he said, as he walked Jack to a table and sat him down.

"I dunno," said Jack. "They could have been Burnham's goons. They told me to stay away from the Hale'iwa Plantation, and to stop stirring things up on the waterfront."

"Sounds like fat-cat Burnham." The man turned to Mina. "Who are you?"

"This is Mina," Jack said. "She found me in the alley. She and her sister were on the *Monterey*. Mina, this is Duncan Mackenzie."

"And I'm his wife, Maggie," said the woman, returning with a towel full of ice.

"Those bastards, did you get a look at them?" Duncan asked. "We could send—"

"I don't know who they were!" Jack interrupted, and gave Duncan a frown.

"Are you saying the Burnhams may have sent those guys after Jack?" Mina looked at Duncan.

There was an awkward and guarded silence. Mina sensed that the two men had just thrown up a conspiratorial wall, and she was definitely on the outside. Everyone averted their gazes.

Finally, Maggie cleared her throat and said in a very polite voice, "Can we get you something, Mina? A cup of coffee? A Coke?"

"Yes," Duncan chimed in, trying his best to sound affable. "How about a sandwich on the house for helping our friend Jack here?"

"No thanks," said Mina. "I should be going. I'm meeting someone for lunch. I hope you'll change your mind and see a doctor, Jack."

"I owe you one, Mina." Jack mustered up a small smile.

Maggie smiled also. "It was nice to meet you."

"Bye now," Duncan added.

As she left the café, Mina was sure they were relieved she was gone and sure they were about to have a very interesting conversation. She had the strangest feeling about the morning's events that she could only describe to herself as uncanny. They were so closely connected, and so close in sequence that it made her feel both excited and amazed, and a phrase that her college roommate, Armine, had quoted in one of her letters ran through Mina's mind: *It's a poor sort of memory that only works backwards.* It was something the White Queen in *Through the Looking Glass* had said to Alice. Mina wanted to stop and catch her breath, to sit and think calmly, to pull the threads together, to remember what Armine was talking about in her letter, but she realized that now she was more than a few minutes late, and she walked as fast as she could up Maunakea Street. Nyla and Cecily were already seated when she entered the restaurant. As soon as she took her seat, Cecily signaled the waitress, who wheeled over the cart filled with steaming baskets of dim sum, and they chose several.

"Sorry I'm late," Mina said as she nearly collapsed into her chair.

"Where have you been?" Nyla complained. "We're hungry."

"She's hungry," Cecily said with a laugh. "I'm starving—for anything that isn't French."

"Is your father still enthralled with everything French?" Nyla asked.

"I'm afraid it might be a permanent case of Francophilia." Cecily sighed. "And he used to make the best Chinese food. I really want to have Chinese food at my wedding reception, but I don't know how I'm going to convince *mon père.*"

"And the twenty-fourth of July is just around the corner," Nyla said. "Mina, you look so flushed. What have you been up to?"

"I've had a very interesting morning, packed full of adventure." Mina knew she shouldn't have said it as soon as it came out of her mouth.

"Starting at my husband's office?" Nyla asked nonchalantly.

"How did you know that?"

"I called your house and Mrs. Olivera told me."

"Oh." Mina realized she must have mentioned where she was going to Mrs. Olivera.

"What did he want?" Nyla eyed her sister suspiciously as she helped herself to a dim sum.

"Sorry, I shouldn't have said anything." Mina looked down at her plate.

"I'm your older sister—"

"Only by a few minutes," Cecily reminded her.

Nyla frowned. "I'm your sister. Cecily's our best friend. You've always said we shouldn't have secrets."

"He made me promise." Mina put her napkin on her lap and smoothed it out.

"Oh, I see," Nyla responded. "Don't tell me. My husband thinks I'm too weak and delicate. His little wife needs protection, but her smart, capable sister can be treated like a grown-up. I might as well just get up and go home to play with my dolls."

"Come on, Ny," Mina pleaded.

"If you were me, exactly how would you feel?"

"Pressure plus guilt—you really know how to get what you want, don't you?" Mina tapped the table with one of her chopsticks.

"I'm impressed." Cecily put her elbow on the table and leaned her face against her palm as she looked at Mina.

"Okay, but you have to be sworn to absolute secrecy. I could be in big, deserved trouble if Todd ever found out."

"Sworn," they both whispered.

Over several baskets of dim sum and several glasses of lemon Coke, Mina told them everything.

"That Jack Carstairs drinks too much," Nyla said. "I saw him on the ship, plastered, more than once. He wasn't on duty or anything, but he was pretty drunk. I didn't realize he was pushing trade unions."

"Lots of those sailor types, the merchant marines, are for the unions. Lots of them are socialist, too." Cecily helped herself to a fried *mochi* ball. "They have a regular network, and the Mermaid Café is their headquarters. Duncan and Maggie are like the Ma and Pa of the club, and they make great fish chowder, to boot."

"How do you know these things, Ceci?" Mina asked.

"I grew up in Chinatown, close to the docks. I know all kinds of things." Cecily winked.

"Well, the businessmen here are certainly frightened of the unions getting a foothold in the islands," remarked Nyla. "If they weren't a threat, things like this wouldn't happen."

"They were always on the alert about unions," Mina said. "But that general strike in San Francisco made them realize how powerful the working class can be when they get together. I'm sure the sugar industry will go to great lengths to keep workers apart and unorganized."

"Mina, you sound like a Bolshi," Nyla said, laughing.

"Yes, comrade," Mina answered, "and it's time to infiltrate the citadel of capitalism posing as the bourgeois decorators."

"Oh, God!" Nyla looked at her watch. "We should get going. We're supposed to meet Tessa and her father at the Burnham offices in just a few minutes."

"Oh, I meant to tell you," Cecily said. "I just got a premium collection of island paintings on consignment—a Tavernier, a Strong, some Hitchcocks. I won't show them for a day if you want to have first crack at them."

"If I want to? Are you kidding? I'll try to get Henry Burnham to come by with me today or tomorrow at the latest," Nyla exclaimed as she and Mina stood to leave.

"And if you hear any good gossip about Jack Carstairs, let me know," Mina added.

"I'll ask around," said Cecily. "Now *I'm* curious."

The Burnham and Robbins building stood on Merchant Street. It was a four-story structure with a bluestone façade built in the early part of the century. A dark green-and-gold striped awning hung over the two swinging glass doors lined with brass at the entrance. The doors opened to the sleek, polished floors of the foyer in the center of the building. Inside, the thick walls that separated the foyer from the street created immediate silence. On the right was a French bakery where a woman in a little black uniform with a white apron and cap moved seamlessly behind a counter, while pearls and diamonds glittered from the windows of a small jewelry store on the left. The intricate gold-leaf frame of the elevator doors faced the street, and to its right a wide marble staircase with a dark, ornately carved wooden banister wound its way to the upper floors. Hundreds of cut crystals dangled from the chandelier in the center of the ceiling. It was a world away, thought Mina, from the Mermaid Café, just down the street.

"You do all the talking." Mina spoke in a hushed voice to her sister. "I'm just your assistant."

"Anything you say, Sherlock." Nyla giggled as she pressed the round black button to call the elevator.

The sisters stepped out of the elevator on the fourth floor and into the lobby of the executive offices of Burnham and Robbins. The company offices also occupied the two lower floors, but the upper management enjoyed the lofty top floor. Though the furnishings in the room looked expensive, they were far too heavy for this dark and windowless room, and Mina understood immediately why Nyla had been hired. The receptionist behind the desk took their names and asked them to wait. A few minutes later, a young blonde woman came out to greet them. Mina thought she must have been in her mid- to late twenties. A little plump, but not fat, she had a slightly blowzy look that was not unappealing.

"Mrs. Forrest," she said, smiling, "if you could just come this way. Miss Burnham called to say she would be a few minutes late. She asked that you wait in the sitting room."

"Thanks, but please call me Nyla, and this is my sister Mina. She's going to be helping as my assistant. I'm terribly sorry, but I've forgotten your name."

"Oh, I'm Gwen," the young woman said. "Gwendolyn Reed. Mr. Burnham's personal secretary."

"How do you do, Gwen?" Mina shook Gwen's hand, noticing that she couldn't be any older than Tessa. She wondered how many other employees at Burnham and Robbins knew she was sleeping with the boss. The person or persons who wrote the letters certainly knew.

The large sitting room had a view of the harbor, two sofas that had seen better days, a scratched, cracked, out-of-date coffee table, and a round koa pedestal table in urgent need of refinishing. Glass doors opened out to the patio, making the harbor and all of its activity more immediate. With only two ceramic pots growing neglected bougainvillea, the outdoor space looked bare and unused.

"Can I get you anything while you wait?" Gwen asked.

"Is anyone in the conference room? I'd like to show Mina if it's not being used."

"No, please, go right in," said Gwen.

Nyla opened double doors in the middle of the west wall and walked through to a room about the same size as the sitting room. It also opened on to the same patio and had a similar view of the harbor and Aloha Tower. There was a large table in the center of the room with drab, overstuffed chairs that made the room feel weighted down. The dark-colored carpet did not help.

"The ceilings in both these rooms are pretty high," Mina commented.

"Makes it hard to light," Nyla said. "Fortunately, during the day, there's lots of light from these windows."

"It's certainly austere." Mina ran her finger along the table.

"Yeah," Nyla agreed. "Looks like a man chose everything."

"In a hurry," Mina said with a laugh. "This place really *could* use some artwork."

"Don't we know it." Nyla looked up at the bare walls. "I can hardly wait to see what Cecily has. This could be fun, don't you think?"

"Nice view." Mina was gazing out at Aloha Tower and the harbor as her sister came and took her arm. "Remember the first time Daddy took us up in the tower?"

"I never thought a building could go up so high," Nyla said, looking out at the view with her sister. "Ned's ship will be docked right there."

"So it will."

"Are you happy about it?" Nyla asked quietly.

"I'm trying not to think too much about it."

"You know he's head over heels, Mina."

"I just can't rush into anything. He lives in London. It's a world away."

There was a sudden flurry of activity in the sitting room as the Burnham girls and their mother entered, laden with packages. Mina first saw Amanda Burnham framed by the connecting doors of the conference room in a shaft of afternoon light. She was a slim woman with blonde hair cut and curled close to her head, so it almost looked as though she was wearing a shimmering cap. Her face was finely formed, and her brows arched delicately over her large blue eyes and long, dark lashes. She had a pale, flawless, even complexion, high cheekbones, and rosebud lips colored with a deep red lipstick. Amanda was looking down at the boxes she had just laid on the koa table when she lifted her head and turned, catching and holding Mina's gaze from across the room. As she flashed a dazzlingly hypnotic smile full of aloof, elegant beauty, Mina suddenly felt a stab of apprehension. She thought she heard Tessa saying something, and Amanda quickly looked away and spoke to her daughter, and in another instant Mina's uncomfortable feeling evaporated.

"Nyla, I'm so sorry I'm late." Tessa Burnham came striding into the room to greet them. "Mina, how nice to see you again. I don't know if you remember, but at Punahou I was a year ahead of you and your sister."

"Of course I remember you, Tess." Mina gave her a little hug. "You used to sing so beautifully in chapel."

"How nice of you to say so," Tessa said with a warm smile. Tessa was tall like her mother, with a head of dark-brown curls. There was a friendly cheerfulness about her that Mina instantly liked. Tessa took them both by the hands. "Come along and meet Mummy and Hester."

Amanda had laid out their boxes on the koa table and insisted on showing Nyla and Mina everything they had purchased. She took a cashmere sweater from its box and was showing it to Nyla, going on about how she was going to wear it this fall on their trip to San Francisco. It was a rich chocolate brown with a mink shawl collar. "Tessa dear," Amanda called out, "tell the girl to bring us some tea and a few pastries from the bakery downstairs. I just love the custom of afternoon tea. Don't you, dear?" She smiled at Nyla as she opened the next box. "Now, this lovely little frock is for Hester. She's so stubborn about her clothes, and hardly ever listens to my advice. Don't you think this would look adorable on her?"

"Yes, it's very pretty."

"You see, darling," Amanda said to her daughter, "I'm not the only one who says so."

Hester looked away, like a lost dog. Mina calculated that Hester must now be at least twenty-one, but she still had the look of a teenager. She wore her thick, reddish-brown hair pulled back in a single braid that went halfway down her back. As she sat on the sofa, she alternately played with the end of her braid or scrunched up her face and pushed her sliding glasses back to their proper place on the bridge of her nose. Instead of the sinewy, fashionable appearance of her mother and sister, her body looked stocky in its expensive but rumpled clothes. Mina sat down next to her.

"I don't think we've met before, have we Hester?" Mina asked. "You were younger than we were, so we must have missed each other at school."

"I remember seeing you and your sister before," Hester said, "because you're twins."

"What are you doing these days?" Mina sensed Hester's shyness, and tried her best to sound kindly.

"Oh, I help in the garden. I like plants. I ride my horse, and do dressage. I like reading." Hester looked mostly at her lap as she spoke.

"I like to read, too, and I love riding," Mina said. "Our father runs the Uluwehi Ranch on the Big Island."

"A ranch? Really?" Hester's eyes brightened slightly.

"Yes, the ranch was in the family, and we went there every summer when we were kids. That's where I started riding. My father took it over some years ago. It's a great place."

Soon Gwen brought in a tray with the tea things and placed it on the coffee table, as the koa table was strewn with Amanda's purchases.

"No, no," Amanda scolded when she saw Gwen put the tray down. "On the larger table."

"But—," Gwen looked at the mess on the table.

"Clean it up, dear, that's what you're paid to do." Amanda looked exasperated.

"Come on, I'll help you," Tessa volunteered, and began to clear away the boxes for Gwen.

No sooner was the table cleared and the tea things moved, when Amanda ordered Gwen to serve each person a cup of tea and offer them pastries. When Amanda received her cup, she made Gwen pour her another one. "You've put far too much milk in it," she complained.

Mina was working hard to control her temper, and just as everyone was feeling extremely uncomfortable and awkward at watching the purposeful humiliation of Gwen, she noticed Sheldon Lennox leaning against the wall, arms crossed, observing the scene. His straight, brownish-blonde hair was parted on the left and fell rakishly toward his right eye. Mina couldn't tell how long he'd been there.

"Is she torturing you again, Gwen?" The young man smiled and shook his head. "Run along now; I'll manage her."

A sassy smile replaced Gwen's sour expression, and she left the room with a definite toss of her head and a little swish in her hips.

"Sheldon, why defend that little upstart?" Amanda was looking down at her left hand and twisting her diamond wedding bands.

"Mummy, you really are a piece of work," he said.

"Oh, Shel, darling, don't be cross with me. Come here and give me a kiss. Is the car ready?"

Sheldon obeyed and knelt beside his mother, giving her a little peck on the cheek. "Now look what you've done, Mummy," he said as he brushed off his mother's lap with his handkerchief. "You've gotten crumbs on your beautiful skirt. What will the lovely Beckwith sisters think?" Sheldon gave Mina a mischievous wink.

"Who?" Amanda asked.

"These ladies you're having tea with. I'd love to get reacquainted with them." Sheldon stood up and shook Nyla's hand. "I haven't seen you for so long. I can't tell which is which, or I should say who is who," he said, laughing.

Tessa laughed also. "Guess. If you're right, Shel, you can have the last profiterole."

"Hmm," he said, looking at Nyla's hand. "I'll guess this is Nyla because she's wearing a wedding ring, and I know she's married. So you must be Mina, or should I say M. Beckwith, lady reporter?" He took her hand and made a little bow.

"Good deduction," Mina said with a laugh. "I think you've just won a profiterole."

"Elementary, my dear Mina," he said. "And as another clue, I'll remember your sister has short hair and your hair is longer."

"That's how most people tell us apart these days," Nyla said.

"Shel, is the car ready?" Amanda had an impatient little edge in her voice.

"Yes, Mother," Shel answered, without looking at her.

"Good," said Amanda. "I want to go now. You and Hester help me gather up these things. Tessa and these ladies have work to do."

After Amanda, Hester, and Sheldon had left the room, Gwen came in to take the tea things away. Although Mina, Nyla, and Tessa helped her gather the cups and plates on to the tray, Gwen avoided eye contact with all of them and wouldn't say a word.

"Poor thing." Tessa shook her head as Gwen left the room. "Mummy can be such a trial, but I can't say little Gwen hasn't asked for it."

"Asked for it." Mina echoed Tessa's words, pretending she didn't understand.

"I think she and my father are, you know, extra chummy," Tessa whispered.

"Oh, I see."

"Is it for sure?" Nyla asked.

Tessa simply nodded her head.

She spent the next hour with Nyla and Mina efficiently going over particulars and answering questions about the job. As they moved from space to space, Nyla asked what the main function of each room was, how often it was used for various activities, what her father wanted to see changed in the rooms, and how she saw the rooms being used in the future. They ended up outside, with Tessa telling them that the patio was hardly ever used now. She and her father wanted to see it spruced up for receptions or company gatherings. Nyla suggested that the sitting and conference room doors could be widened so that when opened up, all three places would flow together for entertaining. She said she would like to come back tomorrow with Mina to take measurements of the rooms, but before they left, she asked if Tessa would show her the other rooms on the floor.

"I just need to get an idea of the décor in general. I want everything to be somewhat harmonious."

"Oh, of course," Tessa said. "I should have thought of it myself."

Tessa escorted them through the entire floor, and ended the tour in a comfortable room where Gwen had her desk, in a small reception area just outside Henry Burnham's executive office. Gwen was applying some color to her lips, and when she saw the women enter she put the mirror and the lipstick away, but not too quickly, as if to show she didn't care what they thought of her.

"Can I help you?" Gwen asked, then rubbed her lips together to work in the color more evenly.

"We want to see Daddy's office," Tessa said. "Is he with anyone?"

"No," Gwen replied, "but he's on the phone."

"Good," Tessa answered. "Let's go right in."

Gwen rose, about to protest, but Tessa had already opened the door and was barging into her father's office. Mina and Nyla hesitated outside the door, but when Tessa called out to them to come right in, Mina looked at Gwen, shrugged, and followed her sister into the room.

The office was large, with beautifully polished wood floors and an oversized oriental carpet. Once through the doors, Mina saw Henry Burnham's desk directly facing the door. He was on the telephone in an animated conversation. He waved, then swung his chair around so that he was facing away from his visitors. On the left, Mina noticed another door that she guessed led conveniently to the conference room. Very useful, she thought, for a grand entrance by Henry into a meeting. Tessa was already showing Nyla a painting that hung on the wall. It was a portrait of her grandfather, one of the founders of Burnham and Robbins. Mina joined them. At first she quietly listened to Tessa talk about how Robbins had been bought out early on, but then she drifted a little closer toward Henry's desk. She stopped in front of a photo of some Punahou High School athletic team, she thought maybe a track team, and pretended to be absorbed in it while she strained to hear what he was saying.

"Well, I understand that, Mr. Goldburn," he said, "but I can't honestly say I'm sorry to hear it. Your client is a known troublemaker. I don't know why you would want to represent someone who is suspected of being a socialist, maybe even a communist . . . I didn't say it justified anything. All I'm saying is that I'm surprised at your choice of clients. It couldn't be good for your practice . . . No, Mr. Goldburn, that is not a threat. I am not that kind of person. That was merely my personal opinion. I should also tell you that I am not surprised to hear that someone has roughed up your client. I know some people here who don't take well to his kind of interference. He should be more careful. It would be a shame if something worse were to happen to him . . . No, I do not condone violence, Mr. Goldburn, and I find that accusation insulting. Look, I've taken time away from very important business matters to talk to you about this. If you are in any way implying that I personally, or our company, had anything to do with your client's misfortune, then I will have to contact my lawyers. And if you or your client makes any such inferences publicly, you both will find yourself in a libel suit that you won't be able to get out of. Oh yes, and you can tell your client that his cowardly letters don't scare me one bit . . . Oh, you don't? Well, he'll know what I mean. Now if you don't mind, I have better things to do. Good day." Henry swung his chair around and hung up the phone.

Mina had sense enough to recognize the closing words of the conversation and quickly whisked herself back to Nyla and Tessa as they were examining some Chinese pieces on one of the shelves. Nyla was particularly interested in an unusual pair of green ginger jars. They were about ten or twelve inches high and had a delicate cabbage-leaf pattern that resembled majolica. Tessa was telling Nyla that they were either late nineteenth-century pieces, or perhaps made early in this century. Seeing that her father was off the phone, Tessa called him over.

"This was made for export. I believe they're late nineteenth century. I thought they were quite striking." Henry had left his rough conversation behind and was now all charm and polish. "And you are obviously Nyla's sister," he said, taking Mina's hand and giving it a little squeeze.

"I've been hired as her assistant." Mina smiled. "I'm here to make sure she doesn't go over budget."

"Then you'll have my full support, Miss. Or is it Mrs.?" Henry asked.

"It's Miss Beckwith. But I like Mina much better."

"And how is your father Charles? Still happy with his cattle and horses?"

"He loves the Big Island. Whenever he leaves, he can't wait to get back."

"He was such a fine businessman," Henry said seriously. "I was surprised when he sold everything and took up ranching."

"He's always been a paniolo at heart. We're just lucky he never ran away to ride in a rodeo circuit."

"Well, now, Nyla, I've been thinking." Henry turned, took Nyla by the arm, and walked away toward his desk. "I might like to add this office and Miss Reed's to your list of projects. It's been this way for years, and I'm thinking I would like to have a new look. Of course, we would adjust your compensation. I have a few things I'd like included. What do you think about a small bar area in here?"

As Mina watched her sister speaking to Henry, she wondered if his desire for a new look had something to do with his young secretary. She found herself thinking that Amanda must have married him for his money. Henry was not bad looking, but he was not the type to send anyone's heart soaring. He was of medium height and build. His hair was graying, and he sported the kind of mustache that Clark Gable had made fashionable. He was obviously capable of protecting his company's profits and therefore his wealth, but, as Mina knew, so were most of the men of his class. He was safe—a safe bet for Amanda. More than once Mina had heard about Amanda's first husband, wild Winston Lennox—how he drank and carried on, how he died from a heart attack that no one saw coming. She'd even seen a picture of him once—Winston on his polo pony with a little toddler in front of him on the saddle. It must have been Sheldon. Winston had looked like a movie star, with his square jaw and thick, blonde hair. His image and reputation were a Honolulu legend. He was said to have been someone with genuine magnetism, someone with an unforgettable presence—a far cry from the conservative man of commerce who was now discussing with her sister whether or not the carpet in his office should be changed.

Mina left Nyla talking to Henry about his office and gave Tessa a ride to the Burnham residence on Judd Hillside. She picked up some lamb chops for her dinner, then headed home in hopes of a swim before dark. It was after four o'clock when she pulled her Packard coupe into the driveway. She was just opening her front door when the black dog that she'd seen with the Oliveras in the morning came bouncing around the corner of the house to greet her. She went inside and closed the dog out, but he sat attentively at the door, wagging his tail. Inside, Mina thought about calling the Oliveras, but then remembered they didn't have a telephone. She would have to wait until the morning to reach Mrs. Olivera at Nyla's house. When she went back outside for her swim, the dog was waiting and followed her to the beach. She sat down in the sand, and the dog plunked himself down a few feet away and watched her. He was a medium-sized male with floppy ears and a black, fleecy coat with a few white markings on his chest. He looked like a stuffed toy come to life. She had never seen a dog quite like him before, and wasn't sure if he was a pure breed or a mix. He lay there looking up at her with his soft brown eyes.

"Okay, mister, come here." Mina patted the sand next to her, and the dog edged over. "You're a little charmer, all right," she said as she petted him, "but unless you like to swim, you're going to have to wait here."

To Mina's surprise, the dog followed her right into the water and swam comfortably beside her for almost an hour. Back at the house she rinsed him off with the hose, dried him with a towel, and told him to stay on the porch. She showered and then fed him a couple of scrambled eggs and some leftover rice. After she had cooked and eaten her own dinner, he was still right by her front door, wagging his tail, and whenever she looked his way, he cocked his head. She finally decided to let him in.

"This is just for tonight, buddy," she said sternly, "and then you're going back."

The dog looked up at her and came into the house. He found a spot in the living room and politely watched her as she made a cup of tea. When she sat down, the dog came over and curled up near her feet. She listened to the sound of the waves, sipped her tea, and felt the soft coat of the dog warming her feet. Again the phrase came to her—*It's a poor sort of memory that only works backwards.* Then she remembered. Her friend Armine had written and used that phrase to recount a conversation she had had with her mentor, Dr. Jung. The doctor had told Armine he was developing a theory about two or more events occurring spontaneously in a person's life—events without the same cause, that were connected by meaning. Mina remembered being confused by Armine's explanation and the theory, but now she felt she knew exactly what Armine was talking about. She had been called to Todd's office to look at those letters supposedly connected to the union organizers, and then a few minutes later stumbled over Jack Carstairs, one of the union spokesmen. Yes, she could see that the whole day had been composed of a tangle of events connected in some way by a larger meaning. Next came Henry Burnham on the phone with Louis Goldburn, a lawyer well known for supporting trade unions, and it was obvious that they were arguing over Jack's beating. It was also obvious that Jack *did* believe the attackers had been sent by Henry, and that Henry *did* believe Jack and his friends were behind the threatening letters. Then there was the Burnham family. They seemed to know all about Henry and his secretary. Mina remembered the secretary and the way she alternated between meekness and defiance. She knew that all these people, personalities, and complicated situations must be connected to a greater scheme, but what that might be, what the true meaning might be, was still somewhere in the future. When Mina finally got up and headed toward the bedroom, the black dog followed her, lay on the rug next to her bed, and promptly fell asleep.

3

WEDNESDAY

THE NEXT MORNING Mina was dreaming that her hand was in a bucket of warm water. She woke up and saw the fluffy, black-faced dog licking her fingers. As soon as she sat up, he sat back, wagged his tail, and made a soft bark.

"So I overslept," Mina said to him. "I have a lot on my mind."

She got up and opened the back door for the dog, who ran out behind some plants and returned before she had time to finish yawning and rubbing the sleep from her eyes. The two of them went back to the bedroom, where Mina laid back on her pillows, reached for the phone on her bedside table, and dialed her sister's number. Mrs. Olivera answered, and Mina explained about the dog.

"Oh, I'm so happy you found him," Mrs. Olivera exclaimed. "We went looking all over for him. We couldn't tell where he jumped out of the truck."

"He's a sweet boy."

"Yes," said Mrs. Olivera. "We try to find a good home for him."

"He's not yours?" Mina looked down at the dog, who was looking back at her.

"Oh, no," Mrs. Olivera said sadly. "Our landlord says no dogs. He belonged to a nephew of my husband's who worked on a ship. He came to port here and left the dog when the ship sailed."

Mina felt a twinge of uneasiness. "I'll bring him up in a little while."

"Oh, thank you, my dear. I'm so sorry for the trouble. I give you to Nyla; she wants to talk."

"Mina? Are you coming over?" Nyla sounded excited. "I have to talk to you. Have you eaten? I'll make breakfast."

Mina made another phone call to Todd and told him all about yesterday's events. "I wish my detectives could find out so much so fast," said Todd.

"Beginner's luck."

"I told you about being in the right place at the right time," Todd began, "and now there's another opportunity coming up. Nyla's going to spring it on you. Apparently the Burnhams have invited you to spend the weekend with them. I hope it's something you can do."

"Oh, God," was her only response.

She changed her clothes, grabbed a cup of coffee, gave the dog a piece of cheese, then loaded him in the car and started for her sister's house in Maunalani Heights. She drove around the old crater of Diamond Head, through the neighborhood of Kaimukī, and then up Sierra Drive, the long, winding road that led to the top of the hill. She passed the small vegetable and flower farms on the lower slopes and, a little higher, the carnation farms that scented the air with a delicate perfume. The dog was behaving so perfectly that she rolled down the windows and let him hang his head out in the cool breeze. The wind lifted up his floppy ears, and they stuck out like soft little wings.

She pulled the car in to Nyla's driveway, let the dog out, and paused to look at the view. Her sister's house was at the top of Maunalani Heights, and she was always amazed at how far you could see from this vantage. Diamond Head looked green at this time of the year, after the winter and spring rains, but soon it would start to fade to its summer brown. The ocean glistened all the way to the horizon, and the clouds moved quickly to the west. She could see past Honolulu and out towards the ʻEwa plain and the Waiʻanae Mountains. Though the heights were close to the city, they felt so quiet and removed. There weren't very many houses in the neighborhood, but sooner or later it was bound to become popular. *Maybe,* she thought, *I should buy myself a piece of land up here before it gets too expensive.*

As she scanned the view, an unbidden image of Amanda Burnham came to her. She could see Amanda's face, her porcelain skin and penetrating stare. She was like a statue come to life, Mina thought, and she wondered what was underneath those perfect features and that thin, cold smile. Such a contrast to her daughters: Tessa, who seemed practiced at making people feel comfortable, and Hester, who looked like she had never had a comfortable day in her life.

"Mina, stop daydreaming out there," Nyla called from the back door. "Let's eat."

"Come on." Mina ruffled the dog's head. "I bet you could use some food, too."

Mina sat at the long wooden table in the middle of the kitchen while Nyla poured pancake batter onto a hot griddle. There was a bowl of fresh fruit for Mina to start with, and a pot of hot tea. Mrs. Olivera had lured the dog outside with a bowl of what Mina thought was canned sardines and a little rice.

"The dog is going to have bad breath after that meal," Mina remarked.

"Mrs. Olivera is so happy to get him back. Apparently this nephew works on a freighter. I can't remember what he did on the ship, but he came into port and borrowed about thirty dollars from Mr. Olivera, saying he would pay him back as soon as he got his paycheck. Then he sailed off without paying up, and left the dog with a note tied to his collar saying, 'Sell me. I'm worth at least thirty bucks.'" Nyla flipped the pancakes.

"That dog is worth thirty bucks?"

"Yep," Nyla said, nodding. "It's a—Mrs. Olivera, what kind of dog is that?"

"He's a Cáo de agua." Mrs. Olivera was just coming in the door. "That's a Portuguese water dog. They're dogs that help the fisherman. They herd the fish, bring in nets, swim between ships, and things like that. They used to have plenty back in Portugal, now not very many left. My grandfather had these dogs. I don't know where Joseph got this one, but my husband's family are all fishermen in Portugal, so maybe one of them gave him the dog. But as I say, they are very hard to find now."

"I've never even heard of a Portuguese water dog," Mina said.

"Me either," Nyla said, as she sat down with two plates of pancakes. "Want some liliko'i butter? I made it myself."

"You made liliko'i butter?"

"Yes, and don't worry, I made you a jar." Nyla laughed.

"So, do you have a buyer for the dog, Mrs. Olivera?" Mina asked, as she spread liliko'i butter all over her pancakes.

"Oh, but I don't like him," Mrs. Olivera said, as she started taking care of the dishes from the pancake preparation. "That Mr. Freitas wants to buy him, but he's not nice to his animals. I saw him beat one of his horses once. That horse was never the same. He broke his spirit, you see. I don't like that man. I told my husband, let's not sell the nice dog to him. But if no one else comes along, we'll have to. Such a sweet dog—not even a year old, still a puppy. I hate to do it, but thirty dollars is so much money for us." She looked like she might cry.

Mina watched Mrs. Olivera start on the dishes, then suddenly stood up and said, "I'll be right back, Ny. I need to get something from the car."

When she came back, Mina handed a check to Mrs. Olivera. "He is *not* going to go to Mr. Freitas."

"Oh, holy Mary and Jesus bless you." Mrs. Olivera looked at the check and then gave Mina a hug. "You make us so happy to know he'll have a good home. And you know, he's a good watchdog, too. He barks if a stranger is coming—very good for a woman who lives alone. Now don't worry when he needs a bath. We'll give him one when we come over, and we'll cut his hair and trim his nails for you, too. Oh, thank Jesus he is not going to Mr. Freitas."

"Does he have a name?" Mina sat back down to her pancakes.

"His name is Ollie. Joseph said he named him after the fat man in the funny movies."

"So, Nyla," Mina said as she reached for more liliko'i butter, "is Ollie going to be allowed in your house?"

"He can come in the kitchen," Nyla replied, "but I don't want dog hair all over my house."

"But you know," Mrs. Olivera said, turning to Nyla, "the Cão de agua, they don't shed their hair like other dogs; no hair to clean up. It's a blessing."

After breakfast the sisters went for a walk. There was a trail across the street from Nyla's house that wound through an ironwood forest and out onto a promontory that looked into Pālolo Valley and toward the spine of the Ko'olau Mountains. They found a rocky outcropping to sit on and enjoy the view. Ollie sat down right between them. The green outline of the mountain range rolled along, and the high peaks spilled dramatically into the valley below, like a Japanese brush painting on a scroll. There was a gentle wind blowing over the ridge from the north, making the sunlight pleasant, but not too hot.

"Well, Ollie," Nyla said, "aren't you lucky that Mina rescued you from the clutches of wicked Mr. Freitas?"

"I can't believe I just did that." Mina sighed. "That was even more impulsive than quitting my job."

"He's cute as a button." Nyla cuddled the dog. "I bet he was smuggled off the ship and didn't go through any quarantine."

"Oh, no," said Mina. "I didn't even think about that."

"I guess it doesn't matter as long as he doesn't have rabies or anything."

Mina laughed. "I'll just have to keep a close eye on you, Ollie, in case you start foaming at the mouth."

"So," Nyla began, "what did you think of the Burnham clan? Isn't Amanda Burnham right out of a Greek tragedy?"

"A regular Clytemnestra."

"Tessa is really a sweetheart," Nyla said. "I think she keeps the family peace."

"I feel a little sorry for poor Hester," Mina said. "She's such a mismatch with her mother. And she doesn't look like she has the cheek to stand up to her."

"Tessa said she's really had to look out for her sister, especially since her breakdown."

"I can't believe that Tessa told us about the secretary," Mina said. "I mean, it seems like something they would want to hide."

"Maybe she thought it would be better to hear it from her instead of someone else." Nyla leaned back against an upright rock and looked at the sky. "Forewarned and all that."

"Maybe," Mina said. "Sheldon seemed to be enjoying the whole scenario, although I'm sure he didn't know if *we* understood it. If you were Gwendolyn Reed, would you keep yourself in a situation like that?"

Nyla yawned. "No, but maybe she needs the money. What about Sheldon? Isn't he handsome as ever?"

"Isn't it interesting that no one ever remembers I was married once? Sheldon told us apart by your wedding ring and said he remembered that you were married." Mina paused, picked up a rock, and threw it down and over the outcropping. "I guess no one remembers because Len died so soon after the wedding."

"What was it?" Nyla searched her memory. "Eight months? Nine months? And then, you did take back your maiden name."

"I guess I wanted to forget it, too."

Mina didn't like to talk about her first marriage to Leonard Bradley. They had gotten married right after college and moved to the Big Island so Len could manage their family ranch. When a car accident took his life, she moved back to Honolulu and almost never mentioned Len or their marriage. Mina could tell her sister was hoping she would say more, but she retreated into silence and looked at the view.

"Guess what?" Nyla finally said. "Henry Burnham has invited us out to that old Hale'iwa Hotel for the weekend, as in starting tomorrow afternoon. Can you go? Todd can't go; he has too much work, but he said he wouldn't mind if I went as long as you could go, too. Henry's arranged this little party for Hester's birthday. He's having a train car fixed up and everything. We're all going to go out on the train. Isn't it fabulous?"

"Tomorrow is awfully short notice."

"Come on, I'm sure Todd wants you to spy on everybody. I could help you. It would be so much fun."

"Nyla," Mina said, "I don't know if 'fun' is the right word to describe spending the weekend with the Burnhams. But it would be a chance to ride the train and stay at the old hotel. Isn't it a beach club or something now?"

"It's a private club with charter members. Henry Burnham has got it to himself for the whole weekend. I guess there's a small staff to look after things. Remember when it was a real hotel, and Mommy and Dad took us out there on the train?"

"We wore those little white dresses with the matching hats," Mina recalled. "And the train stopped near Ka'ena Point and everyone took pictures. Yes, I remember the hotel and beach that summer, and the sea turtles. That was one of my best summers. I wonder if that grandfather clock is still there?"

"We'd be coming back on Sunday in the late afternoon."

"In time for Ned's ship on Monday."

"See," Nyla said, "it's perfect. You have to say you can go."

"Only on one condition," Mina replied.

"What condition?"

"You have to call Mr. Burnham and ask him if I can bring Ollie."

"I'll ask him this afternoon. I'm taking him to Cecily's to look at some artwork."

4

THURSDAY

THE TRAIN DEPOT stood at the cusp of Chinatown, in the hub of Honolulu, just across the King Street bridge that spanned the Nuʻuanu stream. Palm trees framed the entrance to the classical Mediterranean building with its red-tiled roof, thick stucco walls, and a four-sided clock tower that now said one o'clock. Mina sat on one of the benches in the breezy arcade and through the high arches watched the train pull up with the special car that was to take them to Haleʻiwa. Ollie lay curled at her feet on the cool stone floor, oblivious to the hustle and bustle around him. She smiled as he looked up at her and scratched at his new leather collar just where it was clipped to the leash. He didn't seem to mind being on a leash at all, although it hardly seemed like he needed one. He always came as soon as she called him and wanted to go where she was going. The trip really hadn't begun yet, and already Mina was feeling the kind of drowsiness that comes with being on vacation. Nyla was fussing with her camera on another bench while Henry Burnham and Emil Devon supervised the loading of the luggage. Emil was a new protégé of Henry, hired, she had heard, by the Hawaiian Sugar Planters' Association and doing research at their experimental station in Makiki. Emil had the distinct and swarthy look of a gypsy and an attractive but dark aura. Mina vaguely remembered meeting him somewhere before. Henry kept checking his watch, and Mina guessed he was getting anxious, as none of his immediate family had arrived, and all the other guests were present. They were supposed to leave the station at one-thirty. Gilbert Burnham, Henry's brother, was looking at a sports magazine, *43* while his wife Helen sat engrossed in her knitting. They both looked so fresh and well groomed, so tan and healthy, so understated and fashionable—the kind of people that might be picked out to represent a wholesome American couple. Their son Alfred was showing his new wife Prudence a mounted map on the station wall that charted all the train routes, pointing out the one they would be following today. His younger brother James walked back and forth along the track, looking over the locomotive and asking the engineer questions. Tessa and Hester finally arrived, and Henry announced that they would be boarding the train in about twenty minutes.

Mina decided to take Ollie across the street to 'A'ala Park so he could stretch his legs before the long ride to Hale'iwa. Hester was already taken with Ollie and insisted on going along. Mina let her hold Ollie's leash. In the park Mina noticed a group of men gathered around on picnic blankets at the far end. She thought she saw Jack Carstairs and his friend Duncan among them. The men were of different nationalities, mostly Japanese and a few Filipinos, but all were definitely laborers by the look of their clothes and their tough posture. Mina pulled her sun hat down to shade her face a little more.

"Let's walk this way," she said, steering Hester toward the gathering.

"Ollie is one of the cutest dogs I've ever seen," Hester said. "I wonder if I could get Daddy to find me one, though I'm sure Mummy would never allow a dog. We're going to have horses this weekend. I hope you'll come riding." She sounded like she expected Mina to say no.

"I wouldn't miss going riding," Mina assured her. "Let's take Ollie by the trees over there so he can pee."

Mina got close enough so that she could definitely recognize Jack and Duncan. She could hear Jack's impassioned voice saying something about how the longshoremen in the San Francisco strike stood like a beacon to workers throughout the world, and she saw Duncan passing out leaflets to the men. Other curious people in the park were starting to gather around them. They all looked serious. This was pretty bold, Mina thought, having a meeting like this in broad daylight so close to town. Most organizing was done in secret, and workers in general were reluctant to be seen in public listening to people like Jack for fear of reprisals by their employers. Not wanting to be recognized, Mina turned her back to them and asked Hester to let Ollie sniff around the trunk of a monkeypod tree. After a few minutes he relieved himself, and they started back to the station.

"I didn't see your mother with you," Mina said.

"Shel drove her out there this morning. Mummy said she didn't want to ride the train because it gives her a headache."

When they got back to the station, Henry invited everyone on board. It was a luxurious car that had been built for the original owner of the railroad. His son maintained it in superb condition and lent it out only to a chosen few. Automobiles and streetcars had replaced train travel in Honolulu, and the locomotives were now used primarily for hauling cane and pineapple, but this car was kept for special occasions, as a reminder of the elegance of the nineteenth century and the days of the monarchy.

Large, swiveling armchairs upholstered in rich, red velvet lined both sides of the car. The interior was paneled in koa, and the floor was carpeted with Persian rugs. Three chandeliers hung from a ceiling that was inlaid with ivory and ebony in a sinuous vine and flower pattern. At one end was a galley, and at the other, two convenient lavatories. Three attendants in crisp, white uniforms greeted the members of the party as they stepped on board. Mina and Nyla chose chairs next to each other, with Ollie settled comfortably between them. When everyone was seated, drink orders were taken, and as the train's whistle blew, they pulled slowly away from the depot. Mina looked back toward the park and saw that the crowd around Jack and Duncan had grown.

She couldn't remember how long it had been since she had been on a train in Hawai'i, and the one time she had made the trip all the way to Hale'iwa had been that childhood journey so long ago. The sickly sweet smell of ripe pineapple permeated the car as they passed by the warehouses and canneries in Iwilei, but before long they were away from the city, skirting the edge of Pearl Harbor, with its great dry dock and wireless station. The lochs of Pearl Harbor lay calm and still, with Ford Island floating in the middle. In the distance she saw the sloping rise of the Wai'anae Mountains. Slow-moving shadows swept over Kolekole Pass and the flat table of Mount Ka'ala, changing the hues of green from light to dark while above the clouds moved like crumpled white sheets floating across a bed of brilliant blue.

Near Pearl City they passed some rice fields, where Mina saw Japanese women working in rice paddies and a water buffalo patiently pulling his plow through the mud, but most of the vista was an endless sea of waving sugarcane that stretched up into the central plain between the Ko'olau and the Wai'anae mountain ranges. Past Pearl Harbor were the flat lands of Honouliuli. Then the train passed directly through the 'Ewa Plantation, and they were closed in by more cane on either side. Mina was stirring her iced tea with a swizzle stick as she leaned over to Nyla and whispered about how she saw Jack Carstairs in the park at what looked like a meeting about trade unions.

"I'm surprised he's so bold about it," Nyla whispered back. "I mean, he just got pounded."

Mina shrugged. "I guess he believes in what he's doing. I wonder if any of the Mr. Burnhams saw them on their way to the train." She gave her sister the same smile she used to when they were about to sneak a drink at one of their parents' parties.

"I want you and Ned to come to dinner on Monday night," Nyla said. "No excuses. I think the ship gets in before noon, so he'll have plenty of time to get settled in the bungalow. Mrs. Olivera is going to clean it tomorrow. Everything will be all fixed up for him."

"I wonder how long he'll stay this time." Mina's voice dropped off as she looked out the window.

"Well, if you gave him the right kind of encouragement, he might stay forever," Nyla answered. "I saw how happy both of you were in Sāmoa."

They said nothing more, for the train was leaving the 'Ewa plains, and after climbing a small hill the Pacific suddenly spread out before them as the tracks unfurled like a ribbon along the shoreline of the leeward coast. Rolling waves washed up the long expanses of white-sand beaches or broke over shelves of black lava. The Wai'anae mountain range towered to the right with its dry and weathered cliffs—a stark contrast to the lush, water-soaked Ko'olau range. These mountains had always looked older and more secretive to Mina, as if their craggy faces were wiser and more stalwart than their greener Ko'olau brothers on the opposite side of the island.

The train hummed through Nānākuli, then passed the Wai'anae Plantation and Pōka'ī Bay. At Mākaha it slowed down so that everyone could have a good look at the bay and the two men who were fishing from an outrigger canoe. Past Mākua, at a beach nicknamed Yokohama, the train pulled off on a spur. The attendants quickly got out and set up a table and chairs under two large umbrellas on the beach. They set out salmon, egg, and cucumber sandwiches cut in little triangles with no crusts. There were fresh strawberries, green grapes, pineapple, cheese, and bread. A silver ice bucket with several bottles of champagne stood in the center, surrounded by crystal flutes. The wind had died down. Stillness settled over the afternoon, and the only sounds on the lonely beach came from the rhythmic movements of the ocean and the occasional cry of a seabird.

Beyond this place the mountains reached right out into the sea. A path for the railroad tracks had been hewn along the cliffs through clever engineering and hard physical labor. Mina remembered the beach was called Yokohama because of the Japanese workers who had camped at this spot while building the tracks—a labor, she reflected, that resulted in great wealth to some and only survival wages to others. High clouds now blanketed the sun, and the ocean reflected the calm paleness of the sky. No one said much. After the closeness of the train car, people seemed to want to spread out and wander the beach in solitude. One of the attendants brought a bowl of water for Ollie, who eagerly lapped it up.

The champagne spread a hazy layer of lethargy over the afternoon, and they all climbed back on the train as if ready for a nap. But once the train began to move and fresh air flowed through the car, the dramatic scenery claimed everyone's attention. The rough walls of the cliffs on one side looked as though they were almost within arm's reach, while on the left the ground dropped away into the sea. As the train wound around the rocky precipices, Mina surveyed the glassy water, wondering if Ned's ship was sailing over water as smooth as this. She laid her head against the plush velvet and felt the world of Honolulu, with its busy industries, streetcars, shops, and workdays, fading far behind her. Soon the train left the narrow cliff tracks and crossed through sand dunes that swept down to an exposed lava headland. This was Kaʻena Point, the western tip of the island, and the carriage rolled slowly to another stop so that people could take pictures. This was a place of merciless sun, arid and windblown, with little rain. No trees grew here—only shrubs, vines, and other plants that clung close to the earth, needing little water for survival. This was an unusual day at Kaʻena, as not a single leaf stirred and the perpetual sound of the wind through the brush was markedly absent. The cloud cover had thickened and grayed, making it seemed much later than three-thirty.

As Mina took in this dry finger of the island that pointed toward the western horizon, she remembered what Grandma Hannah had told her about Kaʻena. Hawaiians believed that after death the soul wandered until it found its way here. Somewhere nearby was a white rock called Leinaakaʻuhane, and from that place the soul leapt and fell into the realms of Pō—worlds that are dark and unseen by the living. In Pō, her grandmother told her, there were many different places a soul might end up. *What a journey that must be,* Mina thought, *to leave the body and this world behind, to take a leap and fly into the unknown.* Ollie looked up at her, whined a little, and paced back and forth on his leash.

Nyla's warm voice brought Mina out of her thoughts. "Okay, turn around and smile. You too, Ollie." Nyla's camera box clicked. "You look so serious. Is everything all right?"

"Remember what Grandma Hannah told us about this place?"

"Jesus, Mina, don't remind me about stuff like that. Especially when the sky is all dark and scary like this. Come on, let's get back to our seats." She grabbed her sister's arm and pulled her toward the train.

The last part of the ride took them along the beaches and coral shores of Mokuleʻia, with its shady groves of ironwood trees, and then through more cane lands and to their final stop at the old Haleʻiwa Hotel, on the banks of the Anahulu River on the northern shore of the island.

Mina stepped off the train behind her sister. Across the river the old hotel stood, somewhat worse for wear in its faded coat of white paint, but still poised and endowed with more than a little grandness. While the bags were being unloaded, the party left the train stop and strolled toward the hotel. A footbridge, in the Japanese fashion, with rails of driftwood twisted together in an artistic pattern, curved over the Anahulu and made a picturesque entry from the train depot. Mina and Ollie trailed behind the others in the soothing light of the late afternoon, and once on the footbridge, Ollie became transfixed by the languid flow of the water and the fish that floated just beneath the glassy surface. Several sampans, bobbing ever so slightly on their watery beds, were tied to the banks. Mina looked out to where the river merged effortlessly with the sea and thought she might like to go for a walk on the beach before dinner.

As they crossed the long, grassy lawn, she stopped and looked up at the dowager hotel. The main entrance was a wide and curving portico supported by white pillars with the now faded word "Haleiwa" centered overhead. Wide, cool verandas surrounded the first floor. On the second floor the roof of the portico served as a deck, and Mina recalled standing up there as a child, looking out to sea and over the river, in one of her princess fantasies, pretending that the hotel was her castle and she was overlooking her own domain. On either side of the deck were two symmetrical gables, and the sides of the building swung out and around like elongated turrets or the rounded sterns of a ship. The roof was shingled in red. Mina remembered that the rooms were all on the second floor and that there were also four cottages on the grounds. She thought she had seen one on the bank of the river as she crossed the bridge, and now as she looked into the coconut grove off on the left edge of the lawn, she thought she saw two others. To the right of the long lawn was a dense growth of trees and low shrubs, providing a border of privacy for the once exclusive hotel. Though it was overcast and cloudy, she felt a welcoming coolness as she stepped up under the portico and walked down the expansive wooden-floored veranda to the tea table that had been laid out for their arrival.

During tea Tessa explained where everyone's rooms would be. Mina and Nyla were sharing an upstairs room with a view of the ocean. Mina listened discreetly and learned that Tessa and Hester were sharing a room nearby. Amanda and Henry, as well as Gilbert and Helen, were in cottages, but the rest of the party was scattered on the second floor of the main building. Mina guessed that the arrangements were designed so that the older couples could get some sleep in case the younger people decided to stay up until all hours.

Mina and Nyla went upstairs to their room with Ollie in tow. It was a large and airy space with high ceilings and tall, wide windows that let in the sea air. Mina put her things in drawers, hung up her dresses, lay down on the soft white coverlet of her bed, and, although she was thinking about walking on the beach, immediately fell asleep. The next thing she felt was Nyla gently shaking her.

"Wake up, Mina, or you won't have enough time to dress for dinner."

It was just twilight, and the crickets had begun to chirp. Mina showered, and while she was dressing she watched her sister sitting in her muslin slip in front of the vanity, fixing her hair. The warm glow from the lamps cast soft and subtle shadows over Nyla and made her hair glow like dark honey. Mina thought about how many hours she and her sister had spent together getting ready to go out—parties, proms, dates, and dinners—over the span of so many years. She thought about how they had witnessed each other's bodies as they grew and changed, along with their taste in clothes, their hairstyles, and the boys and men in their lives. Nyla was brushing and twirling her short hair into little curls.

"Why, Mina, what's the matter?" Nyla turned to her. "You have such a strange look on your face."

"I was just realizing how much you mean to me, Ny."

Nyla studied her sister for a moment, got up, and gave her a hug. "I can't imagine this life without you in it, either. But what's really up? What is it? Your job? Ned?"

"I don't know." Mina sat down on the bed. "It's everything: leaving the paper, not knowing what to do next, and Ned. You know I feel so attached to him, but the thought of another commitment—I just don't know if I'm ready. But . . ." She looked out the window at the evening sky.

"But," Nyla repeated.

"But I guess I don't want to lose him, either." Mina said it as if she were just realizing it for the first time.

"Is he pressuring you? Has he asked you to make a choice?"

"No, not really."

"Then don't worry about it. Just let things happen." Nyla went back to doing her hair. "You don't always have to know exactly what to do. Ned's a grown-up. He's not going to make any demands, and he certainly wouldn't want a commitment from you that was half-hearted."

"Half-hearted." Mina's laugh had a touch of cynicism. "That's me, Miss Half-hearted. Maybe that's all I'm capable of now. I'm sure you knew I wasn't happy being married to Len, even though I never said anything."

"You didn't have to say—to me, that is."

"I felt smothered so much of the time, like I couldn't breathe, like I might go crazy."

"I could see that," Nyla said, "but I don't think anyone else could."

"What really bothered me," Mina continued, "was that Len never even noticed. He was blind to how I really felt. I've never, ever said this out loud, but if he hadn't died, I might have had to break his heart and leave him, just to save myself."

Nyla was quiet for a time before she said, "Hey, you don't really know what would have happened. If he had lived, maybe you could have talked about it and made some changes, but he didn't live, so there's no way you can know. But this is now, and everything is different. You're a different person. Ned's a different man, and you know yourself a lot better—well, except for one little thing."

"What's that?"

"You could never be a half-hearted person, Mina. Trust me on this one."

A woman shrieking on the lawn interrupted their conversation. "What is she doing here, Henry?" Amanda Burnham's voice penetrated the otherwise peaceful evening. Ollie, who had been sleeping near Mina's bed, jumped up and barked.

"Ollie, quiet," said Mina as she ran to peer out the window.

"What is it?" Nyla rushed over to look, too.

"I'm not sure; can you see? Oh-oh. It looks like Gwendolyn Reed just arrived."

"I could kill you, Henry Burnham. I could just kill you!" There was no mistaking Amanda.

"This could be an interesting prelude to a drama," Nyla said with a giggle.

"You mean a French farce," Mina replied, smiling.

After she had dressed, Mina took Ollie down the rear stairway and around to the back porch. Two young girls sat on the stairs just outside the kitchen door that led to the garden. They were pretty Asian girls, obviously sisters, in their early teens. One wore her hair in braids and looked slightly older. The younger-looking one sported a pair of jaunty pigtails. They were both wearing matching overalls with different-colored blouses, and Mina was reminded of the outfits that she and Nyla had sometimes worn when they were younger.

"That's a really cute dog." The younger-looking girl jumped up, and Ollie ran over to her. "Oh, he's friendly, too."

"Come here, boy," the older girl, still sitting, called. Ollie went right to her and gave her a big lick on the face. "Hey, I think he likes us."

"I wish we could have a dog," the younger girl said with a sigh. "What's his name?"

"Ollie," Mina answered, smiling. "What's yours?"

"Oh, I'm sorry." The older girl jumped up. "My name is Tamiko, and this is my sister Michiko. Our parents are the innkeepers here at the hotel. We're pleased to meet you, and if we can help you in any way, please let us know."

"Well, hello, Michiko and Tamiko; I'm Mina," she said with a laugh, "and you can help me by just relaxing."

"Thanks," said Michiko. "Our mother says we have to watch our manners with the guests. What kind of dog is Ollie?"

"He's a Portuguese water dog," Mina answered. "And I think he's a little hungry. I was hoping I could find him something to eat from the kitchen."

"I'll go," Michiko volunteered. "I'll ask my dad. He's cooking dinner."

"So your dad is the cook?" Mina asked Tamiko.

"Our dad does the cooking, and our mom keeps the house. We have to help."

"Do you mind that?"

"No," Tamiko replied. "It's kind of boring out here, plus we get to meet all the people."

Michiko came back with a bowl of meat scraps and a big beef bone. She put it down for Ollie. Although Mina assured the girls that Ollie would be fine on his own, they insisted on keeping an eye on him for her while she went to dinner. Ollie contentedly tucked in and didn't mind at all when Mina left.

She walked around the wide lanai to the front entrance. On her way to the parlor, she passed the old reception area standing directly across from the once magnificent staircase that led to the second floor. Under the angled light of a desk lamp, Gwen Reed was seated, reviewing some papers, while Henry Burnham stood over her.

Henry heard her footsteps and looked up. "Oh, Mina. Go on and join the others for cocktails. I'll be right in. Just some urgent business to take care of."

Mina smiled and walked toward the parlor, stopping at the tall grandfather clock. Its face, with the large Roman numerals and the whimsical sun and moon faces in the corners, was exactly as she remembered. She listened for a moment to the steady rhythm of its ticking before she moved to the edge of the parlor to survey the scene. The rich island-wood paneling looked less worn in the evening and gave the room a radiance that Mina liked to imagine was a carryover from the luminous lives of the trees, who had given up their existence in the Hawaiian forest for this human dwelling. The furniture was decidedly left over from the Victorian heyday of the hotel, but its solid old character and faded upholstery only added to the shabby charm of the room. Tatty Oriental carpets delineated cozy seating areas on the dark, wide-planked teak floors. Potted palms were placed around the room and framed the floor-to-ceiling windows that opened to the now dark lanai and lawn. But underneath all its vintage décor the room exuded an air of sadness, as if it would always be lonely for its own youth.

Everyone was already gathered and having cocktails. Tessa and Nyla had found some records and an old gramophone. They dusted off one of the records, wound up the ancient machine, and the sounds of the tango filled the room. Suddenly, from behind, Sheldon whirled Mina around, and she found herself swept across the room, doing her best to match his flair for the dance. They all laughed when the music slowed and faded like a deflating balloon. In a gallant gesture, Sheldon rewarded Mina with a gin and tonic for her indulgence. Amanda, Gilbert, and Helen were sitting a little apart in deep conversation that Mina guessed centered on the presence of Gwen. Hester and her young cousin James were examining the contents of a cupboard that appeared to contain board games, cards, and some old children's toys.

On a large table, Mina spotted a faded scrapbook and went to look at it. There were pictures of people and families that went back several decades, and she sat, content to pore over the mementos and comments of past visitors. Nyla, Sheldon, Tessa, and Emil Devon were talking around a coffee table. Mina wasn't quite sure, but she thought Emil looked at Tessa with more than a little interest. As she turned the pages of the guest book, she found a picture of two twin girls standing in front of the hotel in white dresses next to a beautiful Hawaiian woman. Her mother's natural radiance shone clearly in the faded black-and-white image, and Mina ran her fingers over the old photograph, hoping she could connect with some of that familiar light. She went to her sister and said in a low voice, "You have to go and have a look; there's a picture of us with Mommy."

Mina sat down in her sister's vacant place.

"You are coming for the ride tomorrow, aren't you, Mina?" Tessa asked. "We're going out to Waimea Falls and then down to the beach for lunch."

"I wouldn't miss it," Mina answered. "Will you be riding as well, Emil?"

"I was invited to go shooting with Henry and Gilbert, but to tell you the truth, I've never seen the falls, so I'd much rather go there—if there's a horse for me, that is." Emil looked a little conflicted.

"Don't worry," Tessa assured him, "there are horses for anyone who wants to go."

"I just hope your father wasn't counting on me going hunting," Emil added.

"Don't worry about that, either," Tessa said. "My father likes everyone to do as they please here."

"Including himself," Sheldon said with a laugh. "He likes to do as he pleases here."

"Shut up, Shel," Tessa warned. "If Mummy heard you . . ."

"She can't hear me," Sheldon retorted, "and anyway, she'd love an excuse to have a royal fit. Now, don't mind us, you two," he said, turning to Mina and Emil. "We always talk about Mummy and Henry like this. And Tessa deserves a martyr medal for peace making."

"Oh, Jesus, Shel," Tessa said, "we all deserve martyr medals. I can't believe he brought Gwen out here. Maybe it actually is something important."

Henry finally appeared. "Sorry to have abandoned you all," he announced.

"Can't go anywhere without the little secretary, can you?" Amanda did nothing to disguise her disgust.

"It was an important real estate transaction, dear," he answered calmly. "But the papers are signed, and she's on her way back to town. Our weekend won't be interrupted again."

"Real estate transaction?" Gilbert shot Henry a look of alarm.

"Nothing to worry over." Henry dismissed his brother's question. "I was told that dinner is ready, so we should all go into the dining room."

Dinner began smoothly. They started with a cold cucumber soup, followed by a plate of tempura vegetables, and Mina was delighted that the main course was fresh 'ōpakapaka, lightly sautéed in butter.

Mina could feel Amanda seething all the way from the other end of the table, but then she saw that Emil's conversation had distracted the unhappy wife. The young man's attention transformed Amanda into a goddess of charm. Mina also took note of Tessa, who was surreptitiously keeping an eye on her mother and Emil. Gilbert remained silent during the meal, and a little sullen, but Helen, who was seated next to Mina, asked her intelligent questions about her schooling and her work. She was surprised to hear that Mina had left the newspaper.

"Is this permanent, or will you be going back?" Helen asked.

"I'm not sure," Mina answered. "I just need to do something different for a while." She had no intention of discussing her reasons for leaving.

"Well, I'm sure Christian Hollister is a very sorry man," Helen said, "and we are, too. We've admired your writing, haven't we, Gil?"

"What's that?" Gilbert's mind was clearly miles away.

"Mina has left the paper," Helen told everyone. "M. Beckwith won't be writing for Christian Hollister anymore."

"Wonderful man, Christian Hollister," Henry chimed in. "He's doing a great job as an editor."

"Not bad on the polo field, either," Sheldon commented.

"He's really given those union thugs a what-for," Henry continued.

Tessa put down her fork quietly. "Daddy, unions aren't all that bad. They can help poor people sometimes."

"That's rubbish, dear. When you say things like that, it's like saying the big employers, like ourselves, don't care about their workers. Do you think we want our workers sick and unhealthy? How would we stay in business with an attitude like that? We provide for our workers. We give them housing, a clinic, and the opportunity to put food on the table for themselves and their families. These are people who can barely speak English, who don't know how to function in our world. They don't know about loss and profit and what it takes to keep an industry going. We know how to take care of our people without any outside interference. Those organizers aren't even from here. They know nothing about the islands. All they want to do is to create animosity between management and workers—to stir up bad feelings and resentment. We should line them all up against the wall and shoot them."

"Goodness," Nyla spoke up. "I hope there won't be any shooting."

"It's just a figure of speech, my dear," Henry said kindly. "The only things that will be shot are the pheasants and the turkeys. Promptly, tomorrow. Right, James?"

"Right, Uncle Henry," James said, beaming.

"But Daddy," Tessa persisted, "unions offer a way for workers to express their needs to their employers. If employers were really concerned about the needs of their workers, there wouldn't be any union movement."

"Oh, Tessa," her father began. "I know you social-worker types are all concerned for the poor people, and that's very kind of you. But we're in a Depression here, and the sugar industry holds up the economy. It's more complicated than just worrying about poor people."

"It should be everyone's worry," Tessa murmured.

Mina was sure that underneath Tessa's cool, sweet exterior a swamp of anger and resentment must be brewing. She'd seen it so many times before—fathers and mothers who took great pains to see that their daughters got excellent educations, and then turned around and patronized their ideas and their intellects even when they were making perfect, logical sense. How could Tessa or anyone else in her position not be seething inside?

"You need to be more realistic, darling." Henry kept on. "People have to learn to take care of themselves. They have to be responsible for their mistakes and learn from them. In my book, there should be no free rides. Handouts don't teach people anything. You've been protected all your life, so you don't understand these things."

Tessa said nothing further, but she glanced over at Emil, who, Mina observed, had gone red-faced and rigid as he pretended to listen to Amanda go on about her career as a fashion model in San Francisco.

After dinner, dessert and coffee were served on the lanai. The men gathered in one corner and smoked cigars while the women made small talk. Mina leaned against the veranda railing, thoroughly enjoying an almond cookie. Amanda strolled over and stood next to her. She looked out across the lawn in a distant silence for a few minutes and then turned to Mina.

"What is it like for you, to be an identical twin?" Amanda's voice was soft, almost kind.

"In what way?" Mina had heard this question a million times.

"I mean, are you close? Do you share thoughts and feelings, things like that?"

"Sometimes we do, yes, but we're not in constant communication, if that's what you mean."

"It must be nice to feel so close to someone," Amanda mused. "But I suppose it could cause confusion sometimes."

"Confusion?"

"Yes," Amanda said, chuckling. "Didn't you ever have a boyfriend who fell in love with both of you?"

"There was a boy," Mina replied with a smile, "in the seventh grade. He used to send both of us these little love notes, and we mercilessly teased him by sometimes pretending we were each other. He got so confounded, he gave up."

"No adult triangles?" Amanda arched her eyebrows.

"We may look alike, but we have different personalities and interests. Nyla's choices have never been my type, and vice versa."

"I knew some twins once." Amanda's voice seemed far away. "They were . . ." She stopped herself and frowned. "What I would really like right now," she said in a voice more like her old self, "is a tumbler of brandy. Do you want one?"

"No thanks," Mina said. And Amanda strutted across the veranda as if she were on a fashion runway.

Mina went to change and gather up Ollie for a walk on the beach. They crossed the footbridge and walked past the little depot, over the tracks to the white crescent bay. The folding waves fanned out along the sand, and the beach smelled faintly of seaweed. She walked for a while with Ollie and then sat down to look at the night sky. The cloudy skies of the afternoon had cleared and the constellations stood out against the black backdrop of space. Memories of her girlhood trip here came flooding back, and she remembered lying out on the lawn in front of the hotel one night, staring up at the sky with her mother, who pointed out a hazy band of light that stretched across the dome of night and told her it was called the Milky Way. Ollie made a soft growling noise, and Mina immediately sat up. A figure was walking toward her on the beach.

"Sheldon?" Mina called out, just to be sure.

"Good eyes," he replied. "Are you wanting to be alone?"

"No, please, there's lots of room for one more."

"It gets tiring listening to the men talk about business. What were you ruminating about out here by yourself?"

"Actually," Mina began, "I was remembering coming here with my family as a little girl."

"Was it a pleasant memory?"

"Yes. We all liked being together. We had a happy childhood."

"Where are your parents?"

"My father lives on the Big Island. He manages the ranch. My mother died some years ago."

"Did you get on? With your mother?"

"I know it's more fashionable to not like your mother, and it's not like she was perfect or anything, but she was someone special, and she genuinely loved us more than anything."

"Not like my mother, huh?"

"Your mother loves you," Mina answered.

"My mother loves the idea of me—she loves the idea of having a handsome young man-about-town for a son. 'Genuine' would be a totally foreign concept to her. She has no idea who I am."

"And who are you, Sheldon?"

"Well," he answered, laughing, "I have no idea, either."

"You know, when I was here as a girl, I thought there was a Japanese garden somewhere."

"It's still here," said Sheldon. "It's in the back of the hotel, over to the right. I could show you, although we won't be able to see much in the dark."

"I don't care," said Mina. "I just want to know where it is."

As they walked back toward the hotel, Mina asked Sheldon if he noticed Emil's strained reaction to Henry's comments about poor people.

"You mean when he got to the part about how handouts were bad?" Sheldon shook his head in disdain. "That was so callous. I can't even believe Emil is working for Henry at the Sugar Planter's Association."

"What do you mean?"

"Well," Sheldon began, "you know Emil lost his father a few years ago, right after the stock market crashed."

"Yeah, there was some kind of hiking accident, wasn't there?"

"Right. He was hunting deer with some friends up on Moloka'i. He fell over a cliff."

"That's what I heard," said Mina.

"A month or so before that, he came to Henry. He'd taken a bad hit in the crash. He was out of cash and his business was about to go under. He and Henry had been friends since high school, and he asked Henry for a loan, just to tide him over, until his cash started flowing again. It wouldn't have been a big deal for Henry, but he refused. He told him it was against his principles to lend money, especially to friends. Then a few weeks later, Devon was dead. Lots of people think it wasn't an accident, that maybe he jumped over the cliff on purpose. His life insurance left his son and widow in a decent financial situation. There's nothing anyone can prove one way or the other, but still, you have to wonder."

"That *was* an insensitive remark to make in front of Emil."

"Like I said, I'm glad he's not *my* father," said Sheldon. "Well, here's your Japanese garden, but you can't see much in the dark."

"No, but now I know exactly where it is." Mina could barely make out the pond and the little bridge she remembered. "Let's go back," she suggested. "I hope they haven't taken away the tray with the almond cookies."

Mina sat on her bed and ate the almond cookie she had brought up to the room. Nyla was sleeping peacefully, and Ollie had found a cozy spot in the middle of a throw rug. Outside, the wind had picked up, and through her window the stars dotted the sky behind the dark silhouettes of the palm trees. She decided to go downstairs for one more cookie. One of the girls had shown her where the cookie jar was kept in the kitchen. As she walked down the wide stairs, a gust of wind swept up through the old hotel and made it creak, and then all was quiet again. When she got to the bottom of the staircase, she saw a light coming through the door of the room just behind the old reception desk and heard loud, arguing voices.

"You know how much that place meant to our mother and father. How much it means to me. How could you do that without even consulting me?"

"You're too sentimental, Gil. That estate is worth thousands and its upkeep is horrendous." She recognized Henry Burnham's voice.

"Some things are worth more than money, but you'd never know what they were, would you?" There was more than bitterness in Gilbert Burnham's voice.

"As I said, someone has to be practical."

"You had no right to do that."

"I had every right. I control fifty-one percent of the company."

"I'm going to stop that sale." Gilbert's tone scared Mina.

"Over my dead body," Henry retorted.

"Yeah, maybe it will be," Gilbert fired back.

As Gilbert stormed out of the room, Mina had to drop back into the shadows to avoid being seen. She quickly made her way to the kitchen and found the jar of almond cookies as she thought about how there were certainly a lot of people who might threaten Henry Burnham who had nothing to do with trade unions.

5

FRIDAY

MINA WOKE EARLY the next morning, and while Nyla was still asleep, she took Ollie out. In the gauzy morning light she went again to look at the Japanese garden. The garden was contained and separated from the rest of the grounds within a high mock orange hedge and appeared to be very well tended. Close behind the south side of the hedge grew a tall monkeypod tree that spread in a canopy over half of the garden. In her bare feet, Mina immediately felt the Japanese grass, with its tickly, prickly little blades. The grass grew in pleasing humps and miniature hillocks that visually transformed the landscape into a faraway place, removed from the tropical reality on the other side of the hedge. A sinuous pond curved across the center of the garden, resembling a flowing brook. She remembered that there were several natural springs in the area and supposed that this pool was fed by fresh water. A miniature stone pagoda stood to one side, and a narrow wooden bridge crossed the pond almost at the center. The paint was peeling from the bridge, but Mina could see that at one time the rails had been an aqua blue, with touches of white and orange for contrast. It was just big enough for one person, and she tested the wood with her foot before she stepped onto it.

From the middle of the bridge she looked into the pond and saw several gold, red, and white koi gliding through the lily pads and the reeds. The trees planted in the garden were trimmed in sculptured shapes, and next to the pond, in a few places, were pebbled areas nicely raked and decorated with curiously shaped standing stones.

Mina crossed the bridge and went to sit on a stone bench under one of the trees. She sat quietly and watched as Ollie explored the garden. Once he discovered the koi, he ran along the banks of the pond, tracking their movements. An Asian woman came into the garden with a little bowl of rice and began to feed the fish.

"Good morning." Mina smiled and walked over to her.

"Oh, good morning," the woman said cheerfully. "I never saw you sitting there. You up early, no?"

"I had to take the dog out."

"Nice dog. My daughters told me. They love every kind of animal."

"Yes, I've met them," Mina said. "They're lovely girls. They seem so bright."

"Oh, yes, they too smart for their own good sometimes. My name is Masami, my husband and I work here, long time now. He's Chinese, so my girls are Japanese and Chinese, mixed up." She chuckled. "Everybody thinks we funny kine because I'm Japanese and he's Chinese, but I say, mind your own business, we very happy couple. You see, my first husband died young. Then I met Tong Yee. He's single, no more wife. I made sure he no more wife back in China, too. Some Chinese men like that, you know. You going ride horse this morning?"

"Yes," said Mina, "I was hoping one of the girls could watch out for Ollie, my dog, while I'm gone."

"Oh, sure, sure," the woman said. She threw a handful of rice in the water, and all of the koi rushed toward it and began eating, swishing their tails and churning the water.

"This is a beautiful garden," Mina commented. "It's so peaceful."

"You like it?" The woman didn't wait for an answer. "I try to keep it nice. When I first came here, oh, so many weeds! The trees need trimming and the pond, so pilau, but slowly, I fix it all up. Remind me of home, you see. I have little bit Japan-place here in Hawai'i."

"You've made it very beautiful."

"I happy this place make you feel good," she said softly, with pride.

"Have you lived in Hale'iwa for a long time?" Mina asked.

"Yes, long time now. We used to work plantation. Hard work, yeah? So when our contract finish, we look for other work. We had small plate-lunch place in Hale'iwa, but then this job comes up and it's much better for us. We take care of everything—cook, clean, take care of the yard. Good work for our family, and they give us small house, too." She threw in the rest of the rice, and Mina watched as the koi once more devoured the food.

"My name is Mina." She smiled.

"I know, my daughter tells me. She say you write for newspaper. She cannot believe. She says, 'Mama, I want job like that someday.' I see you with sister. She's twin?"

"Yes," said Mina, "we're twins."

"I born like you too, but my sister die after three days," Masami said with a sad smile. "I always wonder, what would she be like? Now, you need anything here, you ask me or my children. Come to kitchen and I give you something for dog."

They left the garden and walked toward the back of the hotel and the kitchen. It was still early, and morning quietness prevailed. As they got close to the kitchen stairs, they could see Gilbert Burnham on the back veranda. He was dressed for hunting and checking his rifle, a sour look on his face. Mina went inside and sat down in the parlor. She worried about Gilbert and Henry going hunting together after the argument she'd heard last night. Guns and anger could be a lethal mix. But when she remembered that Gilbert's young son James was accompanying them, she relaxed a little. Surely, no matter how angry he might be, Gilbert would never do anything to his brother in front of his son.

They drove in two cars across the Anahulu Bridge, with its rainbow-shaped arches, and down the highway. After no more than half a mile, they turned inland and arrived at the corral and stable. The horses were saddled and ready to go, and a handsome, elderly Hawaiian man who was introduced as Puna assigned everyone to a mount. Tessa had arranged things so that he knew in advance how much riding experience everyone had. Tessa, Emil, Alfred, and Prudence were given gentle horses, while Sheldon, Hester, Nyla, and Mina were riding younger, more spirited steeds. Puna packed water and snacks in bags on his own horse, and they all set out for Waimea. They doubled back, crossed the highway, and rode along the shore. The day had become fine and sunny, with a slight offshore breeze. The sea and the waves brought out the playfulness of the horses as they trotted and galloped over the sand and along the water's edge. Mina saw that Hester transformed into a happy and confident person in the saddle. If there was a rocky spot on the beach, Puna guided them up through the ironwoods, and just before they reached Waimea, they turned inland and followed the road and the railroad tracks skirting the cliff that bordered the bay.

They paused for a moment to look over the beach and the stream that flowed from the valley into the sea at the other end of the bay. Far beyond the stream an abandoned quarry tower, once used for rock crushing, stood out like a bewildered stranger, looking out to sea. Waimea was feared for its high winter surf, but it was early June and the beginning of summer, so the bay lay calm and placid as the strong late-morning sun warmed the drifted sand. They rode down and over the bridge, then turned up to ride inland along the stream. Mina saw Tessa stop to talk to some of the Japanese farmers who still worked the land here. There was a small contingent of them living near the mouth of the valley where the stream ran shallow and wide. Farther on, the valley narrowed and split into two separate canyons.

Puna led the party on his horse, a little ahead of the rest, and Mina was positive that she heard him softly chanting as they rode into the forest. Through the brush along the stream, she thought she could make out faint traces of ancient agricultural terraces. She knew that at one time this valley had been the home of powerful Hawaiian priests, including Hewahewa, Kamehameha's famous kahuna nui. Her eyes scanned the valley walls that were reputed to be laced with hidden burial caves. Everyone rode in silence, as if they all perceived the residual presence of the former valley dwellers who had lived, worked, and died on this land. While those ancients had been gone for many decades, it felt to Mina as if they had just stepped out for a minute or two and might return at any moment and wonder what these strangers were doing in their home. As they plodded along under the shadows of the tall trees, sunlight filtered through from above and dappled the trail with bits of light. Soon they heard the sound of the waterfall, faintly at first, then louder and louder, and then the trail ended, and they rode out into the sunlight in front of the falls and its wide pool.

Mina guessed from the sun that it was a little after noon. Puna tied the horses in the shade. Alfred and Prudence wandered downstream while Emil and Sheldon climbed up the falls and went to have a look at what lay farther upstream. Mina and Hester lay sunning themselves on the edge of the pool, while a little ways away Tessa and Nyla appeared to be caught up in a serious conversation. Mina thought that Tessa looked somewhat distressed.

"Are you having a good birthday?" Mina asked Hester.

"Oh, yes," Hester replied. "It's so nice to be away from—away from everything."

"Let's swim up to the falls and let the water rush over us," said Mina.

"Can you stay by me?" Hester asked. "I can't see very well without my glasses."

The greenish water was much colder than Mina expected. Not only was Hester half blind without her glasses, but she couldn't swim very well, either, so Mina had to watch her very carefully. Halfway across the pool Hester got scared and wanted to turn back, but Mina talked her into going on. Once they reached the rushing waterfall, they found that there were rocks to stand on. Hester squealed with delight as the cold water poured over them. When they had had enough, they dived forward and drifted back to the bank of the pool. Emil and Sheldon stood perched at the top of the falls. Mina looked up at Sheldon and realized why she had been attracted to him when she was younger. He had his mother's finely cut features and something else—there was a certain brightness about him, like a polished new penny.

"Do you think Shel will jump?" Mina asked Hester.

"Yes," she answered as she adjusted her glasses. "He's always been a daredevil. My father doesn't like him that much, you know."

"Why not?"

"Well," Hester spoke confidentially, "I guess he thinks Shel should be different, get a job or something, and not just play around all the time. But Shel has a trust fund from his own father, so there's nothing my father can do about it."

Mina smiled. "Still, it's nice for Shel—that he has his own money, I mean."

Just then, Sheldon leaped off the cliff and out over the pond, soaring through the air and making a big splash in the water. As he surfaced, he looked back up at Emil standing on the cliff.

"Now poor Emil will have to jump, too, even if he's scared," Mina commented.

Sheldon swam around the pool, waiting. Finally Emil also jumped, and when his head emerged from the water, Mina guessed his smile was one of relief more than enjoyment. Nyla joined them in the water, as did Alfred and Prudence. Tessa came and sat next to Mina and Hester, and Mina saw from the side that underneath Tessa's dark glasses her eyes looked a little puffy, as if she'd been crying. After everyone finished swimming, they remounted the horses and rode back to the beach.

Mina and Nyla volunteered to help Puna secure the horses in a spot he had chosen, a little ways back from the beach and close to the stream.

"You girls," Puna said, smiling, as he tied up one of the horses, "you Hannah Keola's granddaughters?"

"You know our grandmother?" Nyla asked

"That's where you get your looks from." Puna winked at them. "She broke everybody's heart in the old days."

"How did you know her?" Mina gave him a suspicious smile.

"You try ask her," Puna replied with a laugh. "See if she tells you. She's still married?"

"She's a widow," Nyla said. "But I wouldn't get any ideas. She lives on the Big Island on our father's ranch."

"You never know." Puna gave her a mischievous look. "Us old cowboys still get plenty charm."

As the two sisters walked back to join the party on the beach, they passed Tamiko and Masami, who were watching the vehicles. Amanda and Helen had driven in a sedan, followed by Masami and Tamiko in a truck with the food and beach equipment. They had their own little picnic basket and were eating their lunch on a blanket they had spread out under a tree. Tamiko was dressed in her blue work overalls and a white T-shirt, with a little bandana tied around her neck for decoration. She had Ollie on a leash, but he bounded away from her at the first sight of Mina.

"Sorry, Mina," Tamiko said. "Michiko had something to do, and I didn't want to leave him alone."

"No, it's fine," Mina assured her. "I'm glad you brought him. He can come down to the beach with us."

The sisters walked on, and the beach and bay opened up before them. A few white clouds drifted above and stood out in stark contrast to the bright blue depth in the sky. Ollie began to wince and whine a little because of the hot sand on his paws, so Mina and Nyla picked him up and carried him down to the shoreline, where the sand was wet and cool. Once near the water, he bounded back and forth, ran a few circles around the sisters, and headed straight for the water.

Nyla laughed and shook her head. "That dog is very peculiar."

Three large umbrellas were set out on the beach. Amanda and Helen sat on chairs under one of them. Amanda, who was wearing a large-brimmed sun hat and a kind of diaphanous Greek-looking toga over her swimsuit, was fanning herself with a red Chinese fan, while Helen had her nose in a book and appeared oblivious to her surroundings. Everyone else was talking and helping themselves to the sumptuous spread that Tamiko and Masami had laid out before discreetly retreating to the background. Mina grabbed a sandwich, an apple, and some cookies and went back to watch Ollie.

Soon Sheldon was at her side, handing her a glass of cool lemonade. "It's hot out here," he said.

She smiled. "Thank you, Shel. That was very thoughtful."

He smiled back. "That's me, thoughtful Shel. Your dog seems to be having a great time."

"He's funny, isn't he? I think he adopted me because I have a house on the beach."

"He's a lucky boy. Too bad you have a boyfriend; otherwise you might adopt me, too."

"How do you know I have a boyfriend?"

"I always check up on beautiful women who pass through my little sphere. They didn't exactly say 'boyfriend.' They said 'interest.'"

"Oh, really?"

"Really," he echoed.

"Did you find out anything scandalous about me?"

"The juiciest thing I found out," Sheldon said as he threw a couple of little pebbles into the sea, "is that you told off Christian Hollister and walked off the job. Very impressive, Mina."

"I guess the coconut wireless is still in full operation." Mina lay back on her elbows and watched Ollie, who was now on the beach chasing sand crabs.

"So what's this famous playwright got that I don't?"

She looked at him over her dark glasses. "A grandfather with hereditary peerage."

They stared at each other for a moment, then burst out laughing.

Amanda seemed to appear out of nowhere. "Oh, Sheldon, darling," she said, "take your dear mother for a walk on the beach. Mina won't mind, will you, dear? You've got your little dog to keep you company."

"Of course I don't mind," Mina answered politely.

"I'd love to walk with you on the beach, Mother." Sheldon gallantly took his mother's arm.

Mina was sure she detected a little tension in his voice, but once they started down the beach they were smiling and laughing, so she reasoned that she must have been mistaken. Still, she thought, Sheldon could probably use a day off from his mother. Ollie came up to her, cocked his head to one side, made a polite, soft bark, and whined a little.

"Okay, you shameless little beggar," Mina said. "I'll go swimming with you."

It was nearly four when they got back to Hale'iwa, and Mina felt she needed to call Todd with an update. She thought about using the house phone, but she was wary of others picking up the extensions and listening. To be extra safe, she decided to walk to the little town and use a pay phone. Her sister insisted on going along, and Ollie bounced around at their side. As they walked up to the dusty road that was just a few yards from the Anahulu Bridge, Nyla paused and looked back over her shoulder, wanting to make sure no one was around.

"You wouldn't believe what Tessa told me when we were at the falls," she said with excitement.

"It looked like she'd been crying," said Mina.

"She's really upset and angry with her father. Apparently this Japanese man had been talking about trade unions to the field workers in Hale'iwa. Then he went missing on Saturday, and two days ago they found his body up in the Wai'anae Mountains in a gulch. The official announcement from the police is that he fell and died, but some of the men who found him said it looked like he'd been worked over."

"Oh, Jesus," Mina muttered.

"It was in the newspaper. Didn't you read about it?"

"No." Mina frowned. "I haven't been reading the newspaper."

"Well, get this—Tessa heard her father talking to someone on the phone that Saturday night saying things like, 'I told you just to rough him up, damn it. I just wanted you to scare him, that's all.'"

"That gives getting away with murder a whole new meaning. Did she tell you the man's name?"

"It's Shimasaki. She didn't know his first name. He had a wife and a kid. The community out here is pretty upset about it, too."

"I guess I better tell Todd, but we'll have to pretend she told the story to me, not you."

"Got it." Nyla gave her a mock salute.

Across the wide dirt road was a wooden storefront and a pay phone, but Mina decided they should walk a little farther away from the hotel, so they ventured up the street, past the little bank building, to another group of wooden stores. The one-street town lay still and tired in the afternoon light, and the weathered board-and-batten buildings stood like thin-skinned boxes with their single-wall construction and wide glass windows. The sisters stepped up from the street onto a wooden-plank walkway that fronted a store and a barbershop. A tin-roof overhang brought them into the shade. Mina could see only one customer getting his hair cut while several other men sat around talking as the barber did his work. They walked into the store next door and looked at the merchandise in the big standing glass cases. The other items were on shelves that rose from the floor high up toward the ceiling. Everything smelled a little dusty. It was dark and quiet in the store, and only one elderly lady in a blue cotton dress sat on a stool behind the counter. She had a pile of cigars that she was counting and placing back in a cigar box.

"Yes, can I help you girls?" she said without looking up.

"Is there a pay phone nearby?" Mina asked.

The lady pointed. "Down the street. Get one outside the dry goods store."

The dry goods store was part of a two-story affair, not far up the street. It stood next to a small café that, according to the posted menu, specialized in saimin and other simple local food. Mina guessed it was probably patronized by single plantation men who ate dinner there just before they walked across the street to squander their money at what looked like a pool hall and bar. The sisters ducked into the dry goods store and were surprised to be greeted by Michiko.

"I work here on Friday afternoons and sometimes on Saturday," Michiko explained. "The Taniokas own the store and the café next door, and Friday and Saturday are their busy days, so Mrs. Tanioka goes to help there. She usually runs this store and does most of the sewing. Mr. Tanioka does the restaurant."

"Do they live upstairs?" Nyla asked.

"In the back," Michiko answered. "They have a few rooms upstairs that they let out by the night. I was just closing up, but I'll stay open if you need something."

"I was looking for the pay phone," Mina said.

"Oh, it's just outside around the corner of the store, right up against the side." Michiko walked to a window and showed her. "I hope it works."

While Nyla sat on a bench outside the store with Ollie, Mina went to the pay phone. When she got Todd on the line, she told him everything that had transpired so far. When she got to the part about the death of Mr. Shimasaki, Todd groaned on the other end of the line.

"This does *not* sound good," he said.

"I know," Mina agreed. "It seems like there's a lot of undercurrent, everywhere."

"Just be circumspect and see what else you can—"

"Oh, God, you won't believe it," Mina interrupted. "This car just pulled up in front of the pool hall across the street and let someone out. And guess who it is? It's Jack Carstairs!"

"That isn't funny, Mina."

"I'm not joking. He's out there shaking hands with these other men, and now they're going into the pool hall."

"If I said what I felt right now, I'd have to use uncouth language," said Todd. "Is there any way you can keep tabs on him?"

"Well, I'm not going in the pool hall, if that's what you mean," Mina said with a chuckle.

"No, I know you can't do that." Todd paused. "Just do the best you can. Maybe ask around about what he's doing there."

By the time Mina hung up the phone, Michiko had swept the floor, neatly covered all the fabric bolts with muslin, and was pulling the blinds down on the windows. The sisters sat out on the bench in front of the store while waiting for Michiko, who was headed back to the hotel to help her parents. Michiko appeared and joined them on the bench.

"You and your sister speak such great English." Nyla made it sound like a compliment, but she was actually curious.

"Our mother hired a tutor for us when we were in elementary school." Michiko laughed. "She says if we talk like haoles, we'll get ahead much faster."

"Your mother is very smart," Nyla said seriously.

"She's different, too," Michiko said. "Not like the other mothers, but we like her that way."

"Say, Michiko," Mina began, "did you happen to notice that man who came up to the pool hall while you were closing up?"

"Oh, you mean that union guy, Jack? Sure, he comes here off and on. He usually rents one of the Taniokas' rooms."

"How would you and your sister like to earn a little extra money?" Mina asked.

"Doing what?" Michiko brightened.

"By keeping an ear out for what Jack might be doing." Mina smiled. "I don't want you to follow him or anything; just ask around about him, and also anything that might have to do with a man who just died. His name was—"

"Shimasaki!" Michiko's eyes were sparkling with excitement. "I heard my parents talking about it. Is this for a newspaper story or something?"

Mina nodded. "Yes, it could be. But you have to be very discreet. Do you know what that means?"

"It means you have to be quiet and careful."

That night Mina lay awake in bed. The crisp white sheets felt cool and soothing on her sun-drenched skin. The slight smell of the sea and the sound of the waves breaking on the shore drifted through the open windows. Her sister lay still and peaceful in her own bed. All the things that had happened in the last week crowded into her mind one after another, the most prominent image being the look on Christian Hollister's face as she walked out of the newspaper building. Only a week had passed, and she already missed her job. The thought of not ever going back there, of not feeling the rush of trailing a good story, made her conscious of an empty place somewhere inside. She tried to tell herself it was just a phase she had to get through, a kind of withdrawal from a familiar routine, but in the back of her mind she worried that she had made a bad decision.

She got out of bed and looked out of the window at the dark lawn. The leaves of the trees rustled as the wind passed, then became still again. Ollie appeared at her side and nuzzled against her thigh. She put on her cozy terrycloth robe, opened a drawer and took out a small paper bag, and then she and Ollie moved quietly out of the room, down the wide staircase, and out into the night. She went straight to the Japanese garden. When her eyes grew accustomed to the dark, she saw the pond and the bridge as inky, shadowy shapes. Ollie ran around while Mina walked up to the pond and stuck the toes of her right foot into the water.

"Be careful," said a familiar voice. "You could be pulled into the water by a hand from the underworld." Mina turned to see her sister standing behind her, also wrapped up in a robe.

"Spying on me again, are you?" Mina chuckled. "I thought you were sound asleep."

"You think I'm going to let you sneak out here by yourself? I thought I might be missing out on something."

"Well, I do have a bag of sweet whole plum seeds," Mina confessed.

"I suspected a rendezvous with Shel, but Chinese seeds are much better."

"Shel? Oh, please!" Mina sat down on the grass and opened the bag of Chinese preserved seeds.

"You never notice, or maybe you choose not to notice, when all these men start falling for you." Nyla reached in the bag and took a seed.

"He knows I have another interest, and besides, it looks to me like his mummy wants to be his best girl."

"I'm sure it makes you all the more attractive," said Nyla as she threw the plum seed into the pond. It made little silver circles in the water.

"These people are exhausting, aren't they, with all their little rivalries and conflicts?" Mina lay back and looked up at the sky. She could see the Milky Way as clearly as she had so many summers ago.

"They are, and then there's something a little sorry about them, too," Nyla reflected. "None of them seem very happy. Well, maybe 'happy' isn't the right word. None of them seem quite right with the world."

"Maybe most people are like that," Mina said, yawning, "and we're the different ones."

"Because we have Grandma Hannah and Daddy, who really love us?"

"And Mommy, when she was alive; she loved us, too."

"Yes, she did," said Nyla as she lay back beside her sister and stared up at the moon.

Ollie emerged from the shadows to lick the sweet, sticky residue the preserved seeds had left on Mina's and Nyla's hands. Then he curled up on a tuft of grass near their feet and dozed off under the canopy of starlight.

6

SATURDAY

THE NEXT MORNING, as Mina was taking Ollie out, Tamiko ran to meet her before she got down the stairs.

"Mina," she said, "you won't believe what's on the front stairs."

Tamiko led her outside, and there on the rounded concrete stairs at the entrance to the hotel was a message scrawled in chalk that said, "HB prepare to pay for your crimes." It was signed with a big X. Mina looked down at the letters written in an oversized and almost childish hand, and a sickening feeling swept through her.

"What should we do?" Tamiko asked. "Mama and Papa are scared."

"Let's get rid of it before anyone else wakes up," Mina answered automatically. "I'll tell Mr. Burnham about it myself."

Mina looked around and found a hose on the side of the stairs. Tamiko quickly went to grab a scrub brush, and in no time the offensive message was erased and the stairs clean and dry.

"Michiko and I have something to tell you, but not here," Tamiko whispered when they were finished. "We went on an adventure for you last night. I have to help with breakfast now, but maybe you could meet us at the dry goods store at noon. Michiko will be closing up."

Mina tried to calm down, and she watched as Ollie sniffed around and did his morning business. She went back to the room and then risked using the house phone to call Todd, who had obviously been fast asleep when his phone rang.

"Just be very careful," Todd warned.

"I'll call you again, around noon." As Mina hung up the phone, her sister popped up in bed.

"What's happened?" Nyla asked in a groggy voice.

Mina told her about the message and about Tamiko having some information. Nyla insisted on going with Mina to hear what the girls had discovered.

Breakfast was a small buffet laid out on the veranda, and Mina quietly took Henry aside and told him about the threatening message. He laughed it off, but Mina could sense discomfort underneath his bravado. He thanked her for getting rid of the message before anyone had seen it.

"I'm sure it's just a prank," Henry said as he casually sipped his coffee. "Only a real coward would do something like that. Probably one of those mainland thugs."

"You think so?" Mina asked.

"I've heard one of them is in Haleʻiwa right now, stirring things up."

"Really?" Mina was amazed at how deceit sometimes came to her so easily.

"Oh, yes, my dear." Henry lowered his voice. "I have my eyes out there."

There was talk about going to Mokuleʻia Beach around three that afternoon and having a barbecue. Everyone seemed agreeable to a morning of amusing themselves until then. Tessa and Emil went off to play tennis with Alfred and Prudence. Henry took Hester and James out for a round of golf. On her way outside, Mina saw Sheldon playing bridge in the parlor with his mother, Helen, and Gilbert. Sheldon caught her gaze as she passed by and rolled his eyes as if to say he couldn't think of anything more boring.

Mina and Nyla wandered down to the river where the outrigger canoes for the hotel sat under a tin-roofed shed, and decided to take one out for a paddle. One of the gardeners helped them get one into the water, and with Mina steering and Ollie perched between them, they proceeded to paddle upstream at a leisurely pace.

The morning was so still that Mina could hear the laughter, the *whack!* of the racquets, and the bounce of the ball floating over the air from the tennis courts. It hadn't rained for a few days, so the water in the stream was clear and calm, and paddling upstream was no chore. As they went under the Anahulu Bridge, with its graceful concrete rainbow arches, several boys waved from above, and once their canoe had passed under, the sisters turned to watch as the children flew through the air all at once, hooting and screeching with happiness before they splashed into the river.

"Looks like fun," Nyla said. "Makes me wish I were eight years old again."

"You don't have to be eight years old to jump off the bridge, Ny," Mina said. "We could do it this afternoon if you like."

"Oh, right."

Beyond the bridge the sounds of the hotel and the children faded into a pastoral silence. A few homemade piers extended into the river, and lawns stretched back toward small wooden houses. The occasional rope swing hung down from a tree, always long enough to swing out over the water and drop another exuberant neighborhood child into the Anahulu. They slowed their pace to look at a huge banyan tree growing near the shore whose branches were sending down a curtain of roots to hang in the water, creating an intriguing but dark tableau along the bank. Just past the banyan the river turned, and they passed the remains of the old mission school, with its adobe walls and deep windows. They glided past the houses, and the river narrowed as hillsides rose up to become cliffs on either side. The water was getting shallow and Mina worried about scraping the bottom or hitting a rock, so they turned the canoe around and drifted back downstream to the hotel.

Just before noon they set out for the little town to meet Tamiko and Michiko. Mina thought it was odd that even though it was almost twelve and most of the stores were closing, there were still quite a few people milling around the town.

They went into the dry goods store and looked at the fabric. Nyla decided it would be good to buy something. At precisely twelve, Tamiko closed the door and pulled the front window shades while Michiko cut three yards of palaka material for Nyla. Ollie lay down in the corner.

"We're dying to hear whatever it is you found out," Mina said.

"Well," Tamiko began as she started to cover the fabric bolts with muslin, "last night after dinner and dessert were served, Michiko and I left the hotel. We usually do that, and Mom and Pop clean up and get ready for the next morning. We're only supposed to work a certain amount of hours for the hotel unless it's some special event that there's more money for. Anyway, we found out that Jack was having a meeting that night, but we weren't sure where, and then on our way home we saw a lot of people going up a lane that we pass by. And I asked one of the kids what was going on, and he said it was some boring haole guy talking to some men. So Michiko and I snuck around into the hau thicket in back of the house."

"We had to be real careful not to make any noise or break any branches," Michiko added, "but we're pretty good at it since we've been playing in hau bushes since we were kids."

"At first that guy Jack was just talking about trade unions and working people and how everyone deserved to be treated better and how people needed to band together—that kind of stuff. I think he's right, do you?" Tamiko looked at Mina.

"Yes, about that I think he's right," Mina agreed. "But then what happened?"

"Well, then they started to talk about Shimasaki, the man who died." Tamiko's expression clouded over.

Michiko jumped in. "They found him dead in a gulch. The paper said it was an accident, but—"

"Yeah," said Tamiko, "and Jack was real upset about it and said it was a lie—that Shimasaki was very sympathetic to trade unions and that it wasn't an accident, that it was murder. He said he knew for certain that the company wanted him silenced, and, well, maybe they only meant to beat him up, but he was dead now, and so it was murder. He said something should be done about it. He said they shouldn't be allowed to get away with murder."

"He was so mad," Michiko blurted. "He looked scary."

"Then," Tamiko continued, "the meeting kind of broke up and one of the men took Jack aside. They were so close to where we were hiding. I just closed my eyes and tried to breathe as quietly as I could.

The man asked Jack how he knew for certain that the company was involved, and Jack said because he had inside information from someone very close to the top. Jack made the man swear he wouldn't tell anyone about it."

"Did he give a name?" Mina asked.

"The man tried to get Jack to tell, but he wouldn't," Michiko stated.

"Okay, listen carefully," Mina said, in a way that was calculated to be calm but very serious. "*Do not* tell anyone about this. You could put yourselves and your parents in danger. Do you understand?"

The girls nodded their heads.

"Now you've done a great job of finding information for me, but from now on, no more risky situations. If you happen to hear anything more, please tell me, but don't sneak around and eavesdrop—promise?"

The girls nodded their heads again and were quiet.

"Mina, are you a real detective?" Michiko looked a little awestruck.

"She's a real unofficial detective for my husband, who's a real detective," Nyla answered. "And he doesn't know I know anything about this, so if you ever meet him, don't tell."

"No, we'll never tell," Tamiko said.

"Never," added Michiko.

Ollie stood up and was barking and growling by the door. Michiko walked over, pulled up the door shade, and then called out to the others, "Something's going on!"

A crowd of men, plantation laborers, had gathered up the street, while their wives and children lined the roadway under the awnings and overhangs of the stores. The men were milling around like an uneasy herd. Several of the women stood just outside the door of the dry goods store. Tamiko opened the door and spoke to one of the women in Japanese, then closed the door and turned to the others.

"It's the man!" she said. "The one we were talking about, Shimasaki. They're bringing his body back."

"It looks pretty scary out there," Nyla said. "I think we should stay inside."

Mina raced to one of the other windows and pulled up the shade so she could have a better view. She estimated that there were over three hundred men out there. Hats shaded their faces, and they had pieces of cloth tied under their noses and across their faces so you couldn't really see who they were. They began a low, guttural chant that sounded like the growling of cornered wolves or wild dogs, trapped and ready to attack and break free. The chanting got louder and louder, as if someone was steadily increasing the volume on a radio. Mina had the impulse to cover her ears or duck under a table. Then all of a sudden it stopped, and the crowd of men parted to let an old pickup truck through. The truck drove very, very slowly, and Mina could see a rough pine box that she knew was a coffin lying in the bed of the truck. The crowd of men fell in behind the moving vehicle. They marched silently, in a slow and somber rhythm, their raised right arms holding cane knives or machetes. Mina thought she spotted Jack, all dressed up like a worker, right out in front, leading the march. They made no sound but radiated an unmistakable anger that Mina imagined she could taste in the back of her mouth, and she felt as if at any moment the very air could ignite in an explosion of rage.

"Where do you think they're taking him?" Nyla asked.

"To the Buddhist temple," Michiko said. "It's over the bridge a ways."

They all watched, not saying anymore, as the procession continued and passed out of sight. The women who were standing on the sidelines dispersed in one smooth wave, and once again the dusty town lay hushed and lazy, like every usual Saturday afternoon. No one knew what to say about the scene they'd just witnessed. Michiko and Tamiko went back to closing up, and Mina went outside, feeling obligated to call Todd and report all the things she'd seen and heard.

Mina woke up on Mokulēʻia Beach in the light of the late afternoon. She rolled over on her towel and stared up into the clouds and brushed a little sand off the side of her face. No one else was on the beach, but she could hear shouts and laughter and the crack of a bat on a softball coming from the grassy field just behind. She remembered the heat of the midafternoon sun, swimming, and walking down the seemingly endless beach, while everyone kept an eye out for glass balls that sometimes floated in all the way from Japan. She remembered saying something to Hester and feeling a little sleepy. *I must have been more than a little sleepy,* she thought. She wondered how close Ned's ship might be now and realized how glad she would be to see him and talk to him about everything that had happened. When she had called Todd from the dry goods store, she could tell he was about an inch away from asking her to take Nyla and get the hell out of there. Images of the funeral procession passed through her mind, and she marveled that no one else in their party had seen it go by, or maybe some of them had seen it and, like Nyla and her, just hadn't said anything.

"Hey, you're awake," Tessa shouted over the naupaka hedge that separated the beach from the field. "Come on, we need you. We're one person short, and they're killing us."

"I'll be right there," Mina said with a yawn. "I just need to find a friendly bush that I can change behind."

She strolled a little way down the beach and stopped next to the hedge, where there was no one in sight. She changed from her damp swimsuit into a pair of navy pedal pushers and a white sport shirt, thankful that they were eating out here at the beach and not back at the hotel. She wasn't sure if she could endure another night of evening dress and cocktails on the veranda with Amanda Burnham holding court. She hoped they might be having teriyaki something for dinner—steak would be perfect, but chicken would do.

The baseball game was the usual males against females division, and once Mina joined, it did not go well for the men. To everyone's surprise, she was a formidable pitcher, striking everyone out in rapid succession, and even though Hester kept dropping the ball in the outfield, the women won by three runs. Amanda sat pouting in one of the cars, claiming a headache and waiting for Sheldon to take her back to the hotel.

"She had one of her embarrassing little fits, because Shel said he wanted to stay for dinner and wouldn't leave right away," Tessa whispered. "It's so unusual; he always does whatever she wants. There must be a reason he wanted to stay." Tessa winked at Mina and smiled.

Masami and the girls had prepared a really local island picnic dinner for them, with sushi rice, teriyaki steak and chicken, noodles, *nishime,* fried fish, vegetable tempura, and macaroni salad. For dessert there was a wonderful pineapple cake. They finished eating just as it was getting dark. Mina walked out to the beach to look at the night sky. A sliver of moon hung above the sea like a picture from a child's book, as the stars twinkled all around. The others came down to the sand and gathered together as Emil lit the pile of driftwood they had collected in the afternoon. Everyone watched as the sparks flew high up into the air on the breath of orange flames. Mina, looking on from a distance, saw Tessa produce a bag of marshmallows and Emil open a bottle of port. The fire made people's faces glow in a way that looked unreal to her, as if the fun and warmth was a mask that was about to crack and fall away.

"Is something wrong, Mina?"

She hadn't seen Sheldon come down from the picnic area. "No," she said, laughing, "just a morbid, passing thought."

"Well, I have to be off, and I just wanted to say good-bye."

"You're going back to the hotel?"

"Just to drop off my mother," he answered softly. "Then I'm going back to town. I have a polo game tomorrow—can't let the old team down, you know."

"It's been great fun to be here with you," she said, "and to see you again after all these years."

"It's funny how Honolulu seems so small, and still one can go for years without seeing someone one knows." Sheldon looked away for a moment and then back at her. "If only I'd had a chance to marry someone genuine and good like you."

"What do you mean?" She tried not to show her surprise.

"I mean things would be better with my stepfather and my mother. I seem to have an inability to settle down."

"It's not like you're over the hill. It just takes some of us longer to figure out what we really want. It's not too late."

"How about you? Am I too late for you?"

"Shel, you know I'm involved with someone else." She couldn't help feeling a little sorry for him, so she added, "But if I were free, you'd be at the top of my dance card."

"Just wanted to make sure." He smiled. "Well, aloha, my dear, until we meet again." He kissed her on the cheek and went to say good-bye to the others before driving off along the beach road.

7

SUNDAY

MORNING SUNLIGHT STREAMED through the windows and a slight breeze lifted the sheer white curtains. Mina knew that she'd overslept, but she didn't realize how long until she saw that the clock on the dresser said ten. As she rolled out of bed, still half asleep, and headed for the bathroom, she did manage to remember that they were leaving this afternoon. When she later emerged fully awake, freshly showered, dressed, and smelling of powder and perfume, she decided to pack so she wouldn't have to do it at the last minute. She began stuffing her things in her suitcase with reckless abandon. Most of her clothes were dirty anyway, she thought, so why bother to fold them up? She heard her sister's footsteps just outside the door and quickly snapped her suitcase shut so Nyla wouldn't see how she'd packed.

"Stuffing all our dirty clothes in little piles in the suitcase, are we?" Nyla gave her a sly look as she entered the room. Ollie, who was right behind her, ran up to Mina and licked her hand.

Mina frowned. "You're such a priss sometimes."

"No, I'm not. I've just always been neater than you are."

"Well, don't be so smug about it first thing in the morning. Besides, nobody is going to see the inside of my suitcase but me. It's not like we have to go through customs to ride the train."

"It's not 'first thing in the morning,' so you better hurry," Nyla said, looking out the window, "*if* you want to get anything to eat. Breakfast on the lawn was over an hour ago, and it looks like they've taken everything in except the coffee and the pastries."

"There isn't any group activity planned for the day, is there?"

"Thank God for small favors," Nyla answered. "We're on our own until late lunch and the train. I have no idea where anyone is and no desire to know."

"That's not quite true," Mina said, after a quick glance over the lawn. "You know Henry and Amanda are out there lounging around in steamer chairs."

"They're a little potted," Nyla warned. "Too many mimosas at breakfast."

Mina felt the sudden need for a cup of coffee and a little something to eat before she finished up her packing. She left Nyla fussing over a broken fingernail as she closed the door to their room. The hallway lay dim and quiet, and Ollie's paws made a kind of clacking sound as he walked along the wooden floor. Cool air blew up the staircase as they descended, and at the bottom of the stairs it swirled in soft currents all around the vacant rooms. Mina looked around in the parlor for some sign of the others, but there was no one to be seen, and the only sound was the ticking of the grandfather clock. Emptiness permeated the old hotel, and she stood there for a moment feeling like a solitary voyager on a silent vessel, plowing forward over the sea. She closed her eyes and listened, wondering if there might be something the old hotel was trying to tell her, now that it had her all alone in this quiet peace. When no revelation was forthcoming, she opened her eyes, took a deep breath, and walked out through the open front doors onto the wide, shaded veranda.

She saw Amanda and Henry, talking and laughing in the lounge chairs that had been moved out to the lawn. Under the shelter of a large monkeypod tree with a wide, round trunk, the sun-dappled remains of the breakfast buffet sat on a sideboard just opposite a long picnic table dressed up in white linen, with wooden benches on either side. Someone had hauled out the old gramophone, and it stood gleaming on another table like an oversized tin flower. Mina sauntered over to see what she might be able to scrounge up for breakfast. The day was fine, and the birds sang and chattered away in the trees. As they crossed the lawn, Ollie bounded off toward the footbridge, and Mina laughed to herself as she watched him begin to patrol, perched over the river, staring intently through the driftwood rails to the water below, searching for fish, then trotting along the shore, on the alert for birds. To her relief there was an urn of coffee, and it was still warm. She also found a basket of muffins and a bowl of fruit. Amanda came walking toward the gramophone, her pale-blue silk dress trailing behind her, just as Mina sat down at the table with her coffee, two muffins, a pear, and a banana.

"I hope there was something left for you, dear." Amanda seemed awfully cheerful.

"This is just perfect," Mina said as she took a sip of her coffee.

"I'm going to get Henry to perform." Amanda winked. "You wouldn't guess he was a marvelous dancer, would you?"

Amanda carefully selected a record, wound up the old machine, and placed the stylus on the spinning disc. Static strains of the Sleeping Beauty Waltz flowed out and over the lawn. Mina watched as Amanda walked back to her husband and extended her smooth white hand.

"Henry, darling, indulge me," Amanda said, smiling.

He took her hand and swept her into a graceful waltz. The filtered sunlight sparkled over Amanda's hair and dress. A sudden gust of wind rocked the boughs of the trees, sending a shower of tiny, glistening leaves cascading over the dancers. They moved in graceful unison, gliding over the lawn, Amanda's dress swaying with the music. In this perfect moment, Mina thought, anyone who saw them would never guess that they were anything but deeply in love with each other and the world—a romantic couple, waltzing under the trees beside the clear river.

The sudden crack of a gunshot from the thick brush on the side of the hotel shattered the pretty illusion. The bullet whistled past Henry's head and hit the edge of the monkeypod trunk, setting off an explosion of bark in all directions.

"Get down," yelled Mina as a second shot rang out. Without thinking, she ran toward Henry and Amanda, who were frozen with fear.

"I said get down," she screamed, reaching for Henry's arm in an attempt to get the couple to move toward the protection of the table.

She heard the next shot, then felt a tug and a sharp sting in her left shoulder. She let Henry's arm drop and stepped back, moving her right hand up to the spot that hurt. It was instantly washed in red. She heard another crack from the direction of the brush as she sank to her knees. In the distance, and in what seemed like a slow-motion dream, moving scene by scene, she saw Ollie charging from the foot-bridge. To the repeated sounds of gunshots, she saw Amanda faint-ing and clutching her head. She saw Henry stumble and fall. She looked up and saw the sun glinting on leaves and white clouds sailing over the bright blue sky. The old hotel shimmered and tilted. She thought she saw Nyla screaming and dashing down the front stairs and Tamiko and Michiko running around from the back. She heard Ollie's bark as he raced toward her. She wanted to yell, to warn them all to stay away. She tried to call out, but she couldn't make her voice work. Ollie was crying, and she felt his warm breath on her face. A single, piercing flash of pain came from her shoulder, cutting through her. And then there was only darkness.

8

MONDAY

IT WAS A dark morning at the Hale'iwa Hotel, and Ned Manusia stared out of the window at the gray sky as rain poured down from the gutters. The storm had come during the night, and the glassy river that greeted him yesterday evening was now a murky brown. It churned and moved swiftly, carrying branches, leaves, and mud under the footbridge and out to the windswept bay.

This was the last thing he had expected—to arrive in Honolulu and have a policeman greet him at the pier, to be taken on a long drive across the island to the scene of a violent crime—a crime that had left Mina lying in the bed behind him, wounded and under a blanket of morphine.

Ned thought he heard her moan slightly and turned from the window to see her stirring in her sleep. The doctor from the small plantation clinic had ordered her to rest here and advised that she should avoid making the long drive back to town for a few days. He also warned that her medication would be wearing off sometime this morning, and she might wake up to a considerable amount of pain. He had left another tablet for her and promised to come around after lunch to check up on her. Ned went to her bedside and turned on the small lamp. The light cast a warm glow over her and washed away some of the pallor in her face and limbs. Her beautiful brown hair was held off her face in a clip, and gently he brushed back the little wisps that had escaped to fall across her face. From a wingback chair he had pulled up next to her bed, he watched her sleeping and breathing, not knowing how much time had passed before he saw her slowly open

89

her eyes. She blinked several times and stared at the white sheet before she turned her head and saw him.

"Ned." Her voice came out in a hoarse whisper.

"You don't have to talk, darling." He smiled and kissed her cheek. "Are you in much pain?"

"Yes, it hurts," she managed to say. "What's happened?"

"You were hit in the shoulder by a bullet. Do you think you could drink a little water?"

She nodded and he held a glass while she drank the water through a straw. She was still for a few minutes, looking dazed and a little anxious. Ned purposefully said nothing.

"I was eating outside at the table," she finally said. "Henry Burnham, is he . . . ?"

"He's got a very superficial wound on his arm, just grazed." Ned raised her hand to his cheek.

"Was anyone else hurt?" She turned her head slightly, looking away.

"His wife is dead."

"Oh, God." She closed her eyes, leaned a little forward, and automatically tried to move her left hand to her face, which made her cry out in pain.

"Lie still now. Your shoulder is very fragile."

"I heard the shots. I tried to—"

"I know, darling, you were very brave, but there was nothing more you could have done."

She lay back again before she spoke. "It was terrible." She paused for a moment. "It was like when you dream something bad is happening and you can't get your body to move, or you can't get your voice to come out."

"You're awake!" The door opened, and Nyla rushed over and sat right on the bed, facing her sister. "Oh, Mina, I tried to get to you, but it all happened so fast. Thank God you're going to be all right."

Ollie came in the open door, put his two paws up on the bed, whined, and licked Mina's face. He then settled down on a throw rug in the middle of the room, where he had a straight view of her on the bed.

"What do you think of my new shadow?" Mina asked Ned.

Ned grinned. "I think I'd like to steal him."

"Do you think you could manage some tea and cinnamon toast?" Nyla asked. "You've been out a whole day."

"If you and Ned have some with me," Mina answered.

"Dad's called several times. Grandma Hannah is on her way as we speak, and Christian Hollister has called twice this morning," Nyla said.

"Oh, no!" Mina groaned. "I really don't want to talk to *him*."

"Don't worry, you won't have to. I'll be right back." Nyla turned to go, but stopped on her way out. "I assured Daddy you weren't in any danger of leaving us, and he said he'd come in a few days. I hope that's okay."

"Of course it is," said Mina. She waited until Nyla left, then turned to Ned. "Have they arrested anyone? Do they know who did it?"

"Yesterday afternoon they arrested Jack Carstairs."

"Jack Carstairs? I don't believe it." Mina shook her head. "Did Todd tell you what he asked me to do?"

"Yes, he's told me everything, and now he's feeling very guilty about placing you and Nyla in such a dangerous situation."

"I guess his investigation is no longer unofficial."

"No, it's not, so until further notice, you're relieved of your assignment, and you'll have to concentrate on getting better."

"Why did they arrest Jack? Did they have evidence?"

"They went 'round to question him at the place he was boarding, above the dry goods store. They found him passed out, the weapon in his room. His clothes had twigs and leaves on them, and his shoes matched some of the prints in the brush."

"Were there fingerprints?"

"The gun was a .30-30 wiped clean, and the clothes were stuffed in a paper sack, as if he were going to chuck them."

"But did anyone see him come or go?"

"The family that runs the place are Christian converts so they were all at church that morning and didn't get home until noon." Ned paused. "Are you okay? You just went a little pale."

"The pain comes in waves," Mina half whispered.

"The doctor left you a tablet for pain, but he said you should eat a little something when you take it. Take it now, and Nyla will be right up with the toast, I'm sure." He got her more water and made sure she could easily swallow the pill. "It's apt to make you feel groggy."

"I'm glad you're here, Ned, but this isn't what I had planned for our reunion." She gave him a weak smile.

"It wasn't what I imagined, either, but I'm glad I'm here too. The ship got in yesterday at noon, a bit early because of the calm sea. Todd had a car waiting for me at the pier, and I came straight away to the clinic to see you. When I got to the hotel at about four, it was chaos. There were reporters all over the place. They were asking about you. Todd's boys were very effective, warding them off. The rest of the house party was packing up and going back to town, all of them shell-shocked by the shooting and Mrs. Burnham's death. Henry Burnham was able to make the drive, but the doctor said you had to stay in bed for a few days. The news of the arrest had a very sobering effect on them, particularly Henry. He's quite shaken by his wife's death. I guess you don't remember, but we brought you here a few hours after the others left."

"How did you get me up here?"

"Very carefully."

Just then, Nyla entered with the tray of tea and toast. "There're some bouquets of flowers for you downstairs. I think one of them is from your former boss."

"Great." Mina made no effort to disguise her sarcasm.

"And, Masami made us some jasmine tea." Nyla set down the tray. "She said it's from a very special tin that belongs to her husband. It smells heavenly."

The sweet, strong smell of the tea rose from the cups as Ned poured. He watched with pleasure while Mina ate two pieces of toast, started on a third, and then asked for a second cup of tea. She spilled crumbs all over the sheets and herself, and Ned saw color and vitality bloom on her face. He sipped the perfumed liquid and wondered where such lovely tea came from.

"Some reporter from the paper just called about your condition," Nyla said. "I've told him that we expect you'll make a full recovery."

She paused and looked out the window. "It's terrible about Amanda. I didn't like her very much—well, not at all, in fact—but I am sorry she's dead."

"How are Hester and Tessa?" Mina asked.

"Tessa was busy taking care of her father. Hester floated around in a state of oblivious confusion. She said something quite odd to me, actually," said Nyla.

"What was that?" Ned's forehead wrinkled.

"She said now she would be able to have a dog. That's a little cold, don't you think?" Nyla looked both disapproving and puzzled.

"Hester is emotionally immature," Mina explained to Ned. "We're pretty sure she had some kind of breakdown a few years ago."

"Sometimes people do and say strange things after a trauma," Ned said.

"Well, Todd told me everything," Nyla stated. "He told me about getting you to spy for him, the letters, everything. Of course, I did my best to act surprised. I even pretended to be a little irritated that he didn't trust me enough to tell me, too."

"I think that medicine must be working now," Mina said. "I feel the pain fading."

"Good," Nyla said, "because Ned is going to take our tea and toast things down to the kitchen while I walk you into the bathroom and help you get cleaned up a little. You look positively frazzled."

After Ned returned the tray to the kitchen, he discovered a couple of Todd's assistants working away on reports in the old reception area and found Todd slouched on one of the frayed couches in the parlor, staring out at the rain as it swept across the lawn.

"It's a good thing we went over the grounds yesterday," Todd said. "We'd never find a clue in this rain. How's she doing?"

"Remarkably well for someone who took a bullet yesterday."

"That was a close call."

"A bloody close call," echoed Ned.

"I had no idea things would get this out of hand. I never should have asked her to help." Todd shook his head.

"Don't ever let her hear you say that." Ned frowned. "She wouldn't forgive you. If I were you, I'd tell her what a marvelous job she's done of ferreting out information, which she has, and what a brave thing she did, trying to protect the Burnhams. If she were one of your officers, you'd be giving her a commendation."

"I know, I know, you're right, but she's family, and I sent her into harm's way." Todd stood up and walked to the window. "Well, at least now she'll be out of it, and Nyla, too."

"Do you think so?" Ned leaned back and stared up at the cove ceiling. "I'm sure Mina *and* Nyla have been uncontrollable since they were two years old. I bet they're both up there right now talking about what they're going to do next. You think Nyla's just going to give up the decorating job because you think it might be dangerous? And right now, I'm guessing Mina feels more invested than ever."

"Judas Priest." Todd turned back to him. "I hope you're not leaving right away. On top of everything else, I'm going to need someone to keep an eye on them."

"I would, except for they probably wouldn't stand for it."

"Before I forget, Johnny Knight, from the theatre, phoned a couple of days ago and wanted to talk to you. He said it was important and to call as soon as you could."

"So what's next on *your* agenda?" Ned asked.

"I think I'll take a drive and talk to a luna at the plantation."

"A luna?"

"They're the overseers, the direct bosses of the field-workers. This particular one was Shimasaki's overseer. He's the guy I told you about who was found dead up in the hills. Why don't you come along and see what you think?"

"Very good. I'll just make that call to Johnny Knight and be right with you."

The wind had let up a little, but it was still raining as Todd and Ned drove toward the mill. They rolled through the little town, careful not to drive too quickly through the huge puddles that had formed on the road. There were few people out, and the dark sky and rain made

everything look a little forlorn. They passed a stately theatre built in
the art-deco style, and Ned's interest was piqued.

"I didn't notice that on the way in yesterday. That's a lovely looking theatre," Ned said.

"It's about five years old," Todd remarked. "They mostly show
movies, but I think it was built for live performances, too."

"I'll have to have a talk with Johnny about it for his little project.
He's planning to do a staged reading of one of my plays in a few
weeks, and he wanted to make sure I'd be in town. Maybe we should
do a reading out here, too."

"Bring a little culture to the plantation workers?" Todd smiled.

"Why not? I'd love to bring my play to the workers."

"You might have a very small audience. I don't know if these people go in much for the theatre. They're more the cops-and-robbers
type."

"Small audiences can be very appreciative, although I always think
it's better if there are more people in the audience than on stage," Ned
said with a laugh.

They had passed through the town and were headed toward the
mill. Clouds shrouded the Wai'anae Mountains in shifting swirls of
gray. For a few seconds Ned caught a glimpse of green, rising cliffs,
but like a magician's scarf trick, a thick veil of clouds quickly fell, and
the cliffs vanished. They passed a flat-bed truck going in the opposite direction, loaded with sugar workers huddled together, sodden
clothes stained with reddish-colored dirt. Some of them held dirty
tarps over themselves for protection from the rain. Their worn faces
were sun-wrinkled and brown and had the same look of wary resigna-
tion that Ned had seen on the faces of indentured laborers in other
countries.

"Who is the fellow you're going to question?" Ned asked.

"His name is Lars Bruhn."

"Sounds like he's from Denmark."

"Yeah." Todd grimaced. "And I think I smell something rotten. I
did a little checking up on the guy. Seems he came here from Brisbane,
Australia, by way of Fiji. He was working in sugar in both places. No
one knows where he was before that."

"He might be one of those permanent expatriates, world drifters, who like foreign countries because they can get better jobs than they would at home."

"Word is," said Todd, "he likes his booze."

"Not a big surprise. I'm quite sure I've met several people like Mr. Bruhn before. Most likely, he fancies himself a big fish in a small pond."

They were now near the mill, driving past the small wooden houses of the field-workers. Stained a dark green with white-trimmed windows, the cottages wore corrugated tin roofs that glistened in the rain. Weather-beaten chairs or benches sat on the front porches, and everything in the village looked a little tired, like a work shirt washed with age but still fit for practical use. Mango and banana trees were favored in many gardens, and Ned saw that most families tended neat vegetable patches. Some yards were not so well cared for, and unchecked weeds and grasses surrounded their houses.

Beyond the laborer's camp they turned a corner and passed a grassy park, and the neighborhood changed. Sidewalks appeared on the tree-lined street. Picket fences fronted long lawns that rolled up to smart bungalows with white siding and shingled hip roofs. Except for the occasional mango tree, the plants here were mostly decorative: yellow and pink plumerias, orchid and shower trees, alamanda vines and vivid bougainvilleas. They passed one house, larger and grander than all the rest, that Ned guessed must be the home of the plantation manager. Todd pulled the car smoothly up to the curb in front of one of the manicured residences at the end of the street. It was smaller than most of the others, but very well kept. The rain had become a light drizzle, and the drops made tiny, transparent polka dots on the car windows. As they walked up the drive, Ned had a nagging feeling about the neighborhood and all the perfect exteriors. Todd stepped up to the front door, onto a straw mat emblazoned with the word "Welcome," and rang the bell.

The door opened and Lars Bruhn, a man of medium build with very light hair, cut short as if he were in the military, invited them in. Ned had a hard time guessing Bruhn's age. The sun had tanned and weathered his face into one of those mapped masks that could have belonged to someone who was under forty or over fifty. Bruhn's solid frame suggested a degree of physical strength. He loped across the room with the ease of a big cat, and in his wake Ned detected the overly sweet smell of scented shaving lotion. The sitting room was sparsely decorated with a white rattan sofa, two matching chairs, and a coffee table. Set in the corner was a small bar with two stools. The furniture looked like it had come with the house, and Bruhn had neglected to add anything more except for the painting on black velvet hanging prominently behind the bar. It was a garish portrait of a bare-breasted Polynesian woman wearing a straw hat and a hibiscus behind her ear. With more than a little fascination, Ned stared at the painting. He found it hard to believe anyone would want such a thing on the wall.

"Ah," crooned Bruhn, misreading Ned's interest. "I see you have noticed my painting. I bought it early this year when I was in Tahiti."

"Oh, really?" Ned suppressed an impulse to smile.

"Yes, I paid practically nothing for it." Bruhn's accent was distinctly Scandinavian. "The artist was a young American, hard up for money and fond of his liquor. I acquired it for a couple of bottles of gin. Speaking of which, would you care for a gin and tonic? This rain makes one think of having a drink in the afternoon."

"Perhaps I will," Ned answered.

"Detective?" Bruhn turned to Todd.

"Easy on the gin," Todd said. "I still have some work to do after this."

Bruhn got some ice from his kitchen, mixed the drinks, and brought them on a tray to the table.

"Now, how can I help you?" Bruhn asked as he settled down in one of the chairs with his drink. He leaned back, looking very urbane in his white shirt, the sleeves rolled up to the elbow, and his matching white pants. "You mentioned something about this Shimasaki affair. I thought it was all settled at the inquest that it was some kind of accident?"

"I'm sure you've heard by now about the shooting at the hotel yesterday?" Todd began.

"Yes, it was shocking," Bruhn answered. "But I'm told you have the man in custody."

"Yes, we have *a* man in custody. It seems that one of the theories about the motive for the shooting is revenge for the death of Mr. Shimasaki. Apparently some of the workers believe he was killed deliberately." Todd took a sip of his drink and leaned back, looking at Bruhn.

"This is news to me," Bruhn commented.

"You had no idea there were feelings like this among the workers?" Todd asked.

Bruhn shook his head. "None." He picked up a box from the table and offered Ned and Todd a cigarette. They refused; he took one up and lit it.

"Was Mr. Shimasaki one of the men under you? Did you supervise him?" Todd asked.

"Oh, yes," Bruhn replied, as he exhaled a cloud of smoke. "He was a very good worker, and I was sorry to lose him."

"Do you know if he was an agitator? If he encouraged other workers to think about unionizing?"

"I wouldn't know," Bruhn said, crossing his legs and leaning forward. "I only saw him during working hours. I have no idea what he did in his spare time, but I've heard such things are going on from time to time."

"And what is it that you've heard?" Todd asked.

"Oh, nothing in particular, just talk about organizers visiting the town, workers talking among themselves. I believe most of it takes place in Hale'iwa, away from the mill. I don't pay much attention to it."

"You aren't concerned about union activity?" Todd acted a little surprised.

"That is the concern of my employers, not me." Bruhn smiled. "I am only a hired supervisor of workers."

"So you're not aware that some of your workers are accusing you of having something to do with Shimasaki's death? That many of them are very angry about it?"

"Why, no." Bruhn seemed astonished. "I was completely unaware of this. But if it is true, Detective Forrest, then it's the job of the police to see that I am protected, isn't it?"

"Well, I don't think it's come to that," Todd said, taking out his notebook and a pencil. "Now, just to review a few things. Shimasaki was found on a Tuesday and had been missing since the previous Saturday. Can you tell me of your whereabouts at the time?"

"Do I have to answer these questions, detective?" There was now a slight edge to Bruhn's voice, and he rubbed the back of his head with his left hand as he looked straight at Todd.

"No, of course you don't," Todd answered. "But it would be helpful in dispelling any frivolous rumors, and it would certainly look better for you if the investigation happens to be reopened."

"Do you think that's likely?" Bruhn took a drag from his cigarette and exhaled slowly.

"I don't know," Todd said. "It's hard to say at this stage."

"On Saturday," Bruhn began, "I always work in the morning. In the afternoon, I met with my supervisors for lunch, and then I came home to have a nap. Saturday nights, I play cards with friends here in the neighborhood. On Sunday I played golf and then went to dinner at the manager's house. It was a celebration for his wife's birthday. If you like, I can give you the names of the men I play cards and golf with. The manager, I'm sure you can confirm with him about the party if you need to."

"I appreciate your cooperation, Mr. Bruhn." Todd tried to sound sincere. "What was Mr. Shimasaki like?"

"What was he like?" Bruhn seemed a little perplexed. "I have no idea, really. As I said, he was a good worker. He was quiet and did what he was told to do. I don't know much more about my workers. I make it a point not to become friendly with them. I believe it's important to remain aloof and in a position of authority."

"I understand," Todd replied.

"I know he had a wife and a child," Bruhn added. "I have seen his wife. She is young and very beautiful."

"Oh?" Todd encouraged him.

"If you find Oriental women attractive," Bruhn said. "Do you? I know many white men don't."

Todd laughed. "I suppose I do."

"And you, Mr. Manusia?" Bruhn turned to Ned.

"There are attractive women from every race," Ned said flatly.

"I find the women of the Orient and Polynesia to be much more to my liking than women of my own race," Bruhn said as he gazed up at his lurid painting. "They are softer by nature, more pliant, and much more accommodating, if you take my meaning." He smiled.

After a short but uncomfortable silence, Todd stood up. "Well, thank you so much for your time and cooperation, Mr. Bruhn."

"Please, call me Lars."

"And thanks for the drink," Ned said as he stood to leave.

"Yes, yes," said Bruhn, "it has been a pleasure to meet both of you."

Ned and Todd walked away from the house in silence. When they got in the car, Ned looked back and saw that Bruhn had pulled open the drapes on the front window and was watching them leave.

"I don't know about you, Detective Forrest," Ned said as they pulled away from the curb, "but he's not someone I'd like to get to know."

"I'll bet he was lying through his teeth," Todd said with disgust. "About almost everything."

"That tasteless painting and those comments about the widow," Ned went on. "It seems he was hoping we would join him in some sex talk."

"I guess we made him feel like one the boys," Todd said, laughing.

"One of the adolescent boys, with spots on his face and girly magazines under his bed?"

"So I'm thinking," Todd said, shifting the car into third gear, "that I could ask the chief if you could become a consultant on this case. I know he appreciated your role in the investigation of the portrait theft."

"Do you think he'd agree to it?"

"I'd have to think of a way to convince him," Todd said.

"Would you like me to see what I can do on my end? I could make a few trunk calls to my unofficial employers and tell them I'd like to observe, firsthand, the labor issues involved in this case."

"Do you think your contacts will be able to influence the chief?"

"They won't directly, but somebody will, and most likely your chief will do just what they ask." Ned noticed that it had stopped raining and rolled down the window.

"Are you trying to impress me with your influence?"

"Only because you asked for it, sahib."

The storm that arrived so quickly had flown out to sea by evening, leaving the sky clear and cloudless. Animated conversation drifted from an illuminated corner of the old hotel parlor across the wide room and into the night. Mina had felt well enough to come down after dinner and was now stretched out on a sofa, wrapped in a deep-green silk kimono, with her feet resting in Ned's lap. Nyla and Todd sat together on a love seat, and Grandma Hannah, who had arrived in the early afternoon, was crocheting a shawl in an overstuffed easy chair. As she was not nearly so tall as her granddaughters, the chair enfolded her round form, and her muʻumuʻu of rich purple eyelet fanned out around the seat. Thick white hair, expertly rolled, framed her face in the old-fashioned Gibson look so popular during her younger days. White pearls dangled from her ears, and on her flawless brown face she wore her wire-rimmed glasses perched on the middle of her nose, so that she could look down at her work and then easily peer over the frames to talk to others. Her dainty fingers mechanically managed the yarn and the needle in an effortless rhythm.

"Mina, dear," Grandma Hannah began, "while you were asleep this afternoon, an old friend came to call."

"Is it that cowboy, Puna?" Nyla asked. "Seems like he has fond memories of you, Grandma."

"Yeah, Grandma, his eyes twinkled when he asked about you," Mina chimed in.

Grandma Hannah laughed. "We're much too old now for any mischief we might have wanted to get into." She paused and took off her glasses. "Puna told me that a certain man we used to know, Kaiwi is his name, is still alive and living nearby. Kaiwi is a very gifted healer, and he might come and see you tomorrow. I hope you don't mind. I saw him do some marvelous things when I was younger, but now Puna says he keeps to himself and hardly works on people anymore.

He must be very old. Puna's going to ask him, but he might say no. It's not for sure."

"I would like to meet him," said Mina. "I know there aren't very many like him left."

"No, dear," Grandma said with a sigh, "not very many who have his knowledge and gift."

"The doctor won't be here until the afternoon," Mina reminded her.

"Yes, it wouldn't be good if the doctor knew," Grandma Hannah agreed. "He wouldn't approve or understand. No sense inviting criticism. Well, my dears, I'm very tired from today's journey, so I'm going to bed now. I'll check in on you, Mina dear, in the night. I'm just in the next room, and don't stay up too much longer, no more than an hour. You need your rest and quiet."

After she was sure her grandmother was out of earshot, Mina said, "So, Todd, who are your main suspects?"

"Besides the most obvious one we've arrested?" Todd shifted on the love seat.

"I just can't believe he'd do something like that." Mina fussed with the tie of her kimono.

"And why is that?" Ned asked. "I don't know the fellow at all, so I'm curious."

"Well," Mina began, "because it defeats the whole purpose of his work. I mean, if he wants to promote trade unions in the islands, something like this sets everything back into the dark ages. Workers aren't going to rally around a person or a group that assassinates people."

"I agree, it's not what you'd expect from these union organizers," Todd said carefully, "but we can't dismiss the evidence, and you know yourself that he had more than one motive to push him over the edge."

Mina considered this and then replied, "So, you think he just got enraged over being beat up, thinking about the Shimasaki incident—"

"*And* possibly the continued injustices he feels Burnham perpetrates on all of his plantations," added Ned.

"And that too," she continued. "So he gets really fed up, gets a gun, comes out here, and tries to kill the evil capitalist?"

"I'm sure that's the line the prosecutor will take," Todd said.

Nyla yawned. "Jack is one of those temperamental intellectual types. I don't think he'd have the guts to do something like that."

"But if we assumed, as an exercise in speculation, that he wasn't the one, who else could it be?" Ned asked.

"It could have been anyone here. There's no shortage of people who disliked Henry Burnham." Mina looked at her sister.

"Yeah," Nyla agreed, "especially in his own family."

"There's his brother Gilbert, for one," Mina began. "I heard them arguing about selling the family estate. Gilbert made a sinister remark that could now be considered a serious threat, and if Henry were gone, Gilbert would be number one in the company. Then there's Tessa. I know you like her, Nyla, but she was awfully upset about the Shimasaki death and her father's callousness."

"What about the other two, Hester and what's his name?" Ned asked.

Nyla shook her head. "Hester is incapable of arranging her hair, much less something so complicated. And Shel has no motive. He's got his own money from his father and his rich granny."

"But do you know everything about the family?" Ned asked. "The stepson could have been mistreated, or he could be holding some kind of grudge."

"We've already checked him out," Todd said. "He was playing polo at Kapiʻolani Park on Sunday morning at the time of the shooting, in front of a crowd of people."

"Don't forget Emil Devon," Mina reminded them. "He could be nursing some dark and vengeful feelings for his father's death."

"While we're on nonfamily members," Ned interjected, "what about the secretary? Maybe he made promises to her he later reneged on. And of course, it could be *any* friends of Mr. Shimasaki, settling a score."

"I could certainly believe that, after what we saw when they brought his body back," Mina said.

"And," said Nyla, "Amanda herself had the classic motive. We even heard her say 'I could kill you' to her husband. Maybe she hired someone who turned out to be a very bad shot."

"Maybe, maybe, maybe," repeated Todd, "but Jack Carstairs has a clear motive, the opportunity, and now a pile of evidence against him."

"Where did all the others say they were at the time of the shooting?" Mina asked.

"One of the boys questioned everyone on the grounds. Masami and Tong Lee were in the kitchen cleaning up, and the girls were cleaning the rooms. Gilbert and his wife said they went back to their cottage. Devon and Tessa had gone on a walk, and Hester went into the town to see if she could buy postcards. Alfred Burnham and his wife Prudence were walking on the beach, and the boy was reading comics in his room. There's hardly any point right now in verifying their statements. But like I said, unless other very strong leads come up, I'd have a very hard time justifying any investigation into these other people, because of the evidence we already have against Carstairs."

"It's a problem with police work," Ned said. "If you have what looks like a heap of evidence against someone, you stop looking, and if you happen to be wrong, the real criminal might get away because you didn't look any further."

Todd frowned. "Looking for evidence on a hunch in this instance would look like wasting police time in the chief's book."

"Well, but you have your unofficial investigating squad right here." Mina threw Todd a satisfied smile. "Ready, willing, and anxious to go to work. Well, maybe not totally ready, just yet."

"Whether I want them to or not, right?" Todd folded his arms and looked at his wife.

"It's no use looking at me like that. I'm not giving up my decorating job or my assistant," Nyla said.

In the night, Mina lay in bed, staring out of the wide-open French doors, across the balcony and over the sea to a night sky full of stars. The scene was full of luminescent moonlight. But slowly she realized that she must be dreaming because there were no French doors or balcony in this room, and the moon was nowhere near full. She sensed another presence near her, and when she looked to her left, an old Hawaiian man sat in the chair next to her bed. He looked at her intently.

"Do you know who I am?" he asked her with his thoughts.

"Are you the one my grandmother told me about?" Mina answered.

"And do you know what this is?" He spoke gently, as if to child.

"It's a dream," she said.

"This is moe ʻuhane, a spirit dream. Our spirits are dreaming together so we can heal. You understand?"

"It seems so real," she whispered.

"This is good. Not everyone can see this way." He was silent for some time and looked at her. "You got hurt, but if we work together, you can recover more quickly."

"What shall I do?" she asked.

"You have to remember what happened to you. Don't worry, because I'll be with you this time, but I have to see how you do."

All of a sudden, the scene changed and they were out on the lawn watching the Sunday breakfast. Mina couldn't see the old man, but she felt him right behind her. She heard the sound of the gramophone again and watched as the music floated out and around the waltzing couple, in a blue mist. She heard the report of the gun, and then felt the bullet, like a furious bee. She felt herself flying through the air toward the dancing couple, and the sting in her shoulder, before everything went black. Then she and the old man were sitting on the footbridge over the river. The stars in the dream sky seemed like huge rhinestones, and the overhanging trees were odd shades of lavender. Mina and the old man dangled their feet above the water as they watched bright, glittering red-and-orange fish swimming in lazy circles and figure-eights in the moonlight. One fish had big eyes like jewels, and it looked up at Mina as it swam by.

"The wound comes from the bullet, but also from the anger of the one that sent the bullet. It ties you together. So now we pray to turn back the anger, to send it away and into Pō. If you break the cord of the bad feelings, you heal faster."

"But this fish is so strong, Uncle." She stared, transfixed by the fish with the jeweled eyes and its sinuous movements.

"Yes, it's strong and powerful, but it's bad—no good, turns to poison. Don't look at it anymore," he said to her, but she couldn't stop staring. "I said, *don't look*," he yelled, in a voice that shook the night.

Mina felt her gaze ripped away, and she was looking straight up into the night sky as the voice of the old man began a low chant that grew and spiraled all around them. The sound of his voice became a great wind. It rushed by her and through her, as she felt herself falling from a great height. She thought she saw the big, dazzling fish being swept up and away, fading into a black night. Then a thick fog of sleep crept over her, and she had no more dreams.

9

TUESDAY

"MINA, DEAR, WAKE up. It's almost noon, and the doctor will be here soon." Grandma Hannah gently shook Mina's right hand.

Mina opened her eyes to a room full of sunshine. The pain in her arm had transformed into a kind of stiffness. She looked up at her grandmother. "Grandma, I dreamt about the man. The one you asked to come."

"Puna came this morning and told me that Kaiwi said he didn't need to come, and that he would see us the next time, when we came back. I wasn't sure what he meant, and neither was Puna."

Grandma Hannah listened quietly while Mina recounted every detail of her dream. When Mina had finished, Grandma sat silent for a few moments. "You're very lucky, my dear," she said, and kissed her granddaughter's forehead. "Those things are fading away now. I'm glad you've had a small glimpse of what once was." She paused and looked out of the window. "I've always hated the word 'primitive.' Now maybe you understand why."

"There's way less pain in my shoulder," Mina said.

"The doctor will be here in a little while to look at it." Grandma Hannah smiled. "Let's hear what he has to say."

Ned sat drinking a cup of coffee at the banquette in the large and busy kitchen. Tamiko stood at the sink, washing the breakfast dishes, while Michiko chopped vegetables at a large worktable in the middle of the kitchen. A profusion of carrots, onions, green peppers, celery, scallions, and mushrooms fanned out from her cutting board. Above the center of the table, pots and pans of every shape and size hung suspended from an iron oval carefully centered, Ned noted, to be out of the way of anyone's head. A simmering pot on the six-burner stove filled the room with the aroma of warm chicken broth and an undertone of Chinese parsley. The banquette looked out over the back veranda and the garden beyond. This morning all the windows in the kitchen had been opened, and a pleasant breeze ruffled the short, white muslin curtains that had been pulled back to let in the air and light.

"We heard you went to talk to that Lars Bruhn," Tamiko said as she rinsed off a plate and placed it on the dish rack.

"Yeah, Louse Bruhn," Michiko said, laughing. "That's what people call him."

"How did you know we spoke to him?" Ned asked.

"Everyone's watching where the detective goes," Tamiko said.

Ned smiled. "And why do people call him a louse?"

"Because he's always after women," Michiko blurted out.

Tamiko nodded. "Even girls our age. Some afternoons, he just sits around town when school gets out, so he can look at all of us."

"Yeah," Michiko continued, "and once he came into the dry goods shop when I was working, and he said, 'Oh, I need someone to come and clean my house. Perhaps you and your sister would like to earn some extra money.' He thought I was by myself, but Mrs. Tanioka was in the back room, and she came out. 'You leave young girls alone,' she scolded. 'Shame! Shame on you!' she told him."

"What did he do?" Ned asked.

"He turned red and stomped out of the store." Michiko giggled.

"Now he's pestering Mr. Shimasaki's widow." Tamiko had progressed to wiping plates, using a white dishcloth that had a bunch of carrots embroidered on one end. "She's very pretty and has a baby to raise. I heard he's offering to help her pay for her husband's funeral and things, trying to get her to take money from him."

"I bet now he'll try to get *her* to clean his house," Michiko said, making a face.

"She might have to go to work in the field now," Tamiko continued. "And then he'll make her life miserable if she doesn't do what he wants. That's what can happen if you're too pretty."

"And poor," Michiko added.

Ned frowned and looked at them. "What will she do with the baby if she has to work in the cane fields?"

"The mothers tie their babies on their backs or in the front while they work," Tamiko informed him. "I hope I never have to work in the cane fields."

"I wish Mr. Louse would drop dead," Michiko muttered.

"You girls, always gossip!" Their father, Tong Yee, had entered the kitchen with a basket full of several kinds of greens.

"But we like to gossip, Daddy." Tamiko gave her father an affectionate smile.

"They learn this from mother." Tong Yee winked at Ned. "Hard to stop. I am Tong Yee," he said to Ned, "but everyone calls me Tony. They say sounds like Tong Yee so that is my American name."

"I'm Ned. Ned Manusia."

"You work with Detective Forrest?"

"Unofficially, so far. The girls were just telling me about Lars Bruhn."

"Very bad man." Tony shook his head. "Very bad man. Chase women, drink, and gamble. He play for big money, too. I surprised he not in money trouble."

"He gambles, too?" Ned asked with interest.

Tony nodded. "Oh, yes. Haole men play card game here in Hale'iwa. Not too much money. But Bruhn, I hear he play in Chinatown, too, sometime. Haole, Chinese, Japanese, Filipino, any kine man. Big money games there. Very big money, and you owe, you better pay up, otherwise you in big trouble."

"Do you think he owed anyone money?" Ned asked.

Tony looked at Ned. "I don't know that. But I know what workers say. He's mean, and they say maybe he kill Mr. Shimasaki. He better watch out. People getting mad."

"What people?"

"No can say what people," Tony said, shaking his head. "You see, I used to work like those men, too. Terrible to have luna like him."

"You're a very good cook, Tony." Ned changed the subject, knowing Tony would never name names. "Every meal here has been excellent."

"Thank you, very nice of you. Tonight I make big Chinese dinner. Doctor says Mina can go home tomorrow, so tonight I make special dinner."

"The doctor was here?" Ned brightened.

"He just leave." Tony smiled. "So you better go see your girlfriend."

Ned found Nyla, Mina, and Grandma Hannah sitting on the veranda. Nyla and Mina were on the pūneʻe and Grandma Hannah sat in a chair with her crocheting. Nyla and Mina were devouring a bowl of fresh lychee. Nyla was peeling Mina's for her.

"Hey, Ned," Nyla said. "Would you like some?"

"These are really good," Mina added as she popped a peeled fruit into her mouth.

"'Ono, as we say." Nyla smiled just before she ate one, too.

"You girls be careful now," Grandma Hannah scolded. "Don't drip juice all over for Masami to clean up."

"We won't!" they answered together in childlike voices, then started laughing.

"Do you think they're making fun of me, Ned?" Grandma Hannah smiled.

"Probably," Ned said, smiling back. "I guess you must be feeling much better, Mina. What did the doctor say?"

"The doctor," Grandma Hannah replied, leaning forward, "said that he was astonished at how fast she was healing. What did he call you, dear?"

"An overnight miracle," Mina said as she ate another lychee. "He said I could go home. So I guess we're leaving tomorrow morning."

"And they're planning a special dinner for us tonight." Ned decided to try a lychee and took one from the bowl.

"I wonder," said Grandma Hannah to herself. "Maybe I'll ring up Puna, and see if he wants to join us."

As the night was still and warm, the dinner table had been set out on the veranda. Mina and Nyla had insisted that Tony, Masami, and the two girls sit down to eat with everyone. The girls had decorated the table, and the kapa-printed tablecloth was strewn with things they had found in the garden. Fresh green banana and monstera leaves cradled the Chinese serving dishes. Sprays of bougainvillea, plumerias, and kupukupu ferns surrounded individual plates. Beach shells were artfully scattered and added to the casual, unself-conscious island effect. Light from several hurricane lamps softened everyone's features. Grandma Hannah sat at the head of the table, laughing and reliving old times with Puna. Mina was at the opposite end, with Ned and Tamiko on either side.

"I know for sure the Gilbert Burnhams weren't in that cottage at the time of the shooting," Tamiko said firmly as she helped herself to more of the lobster noodles. "I was there just a few minutes before, and the cottage was empty. I knocked about five times, and then went in the room to change the towels." Tamiko lowered her voice and giggled. "Do you think they could have been naked and hiding in the closet?"

"They don't seem like the type of couple that has that much fun," Mina said with a laugh.

"It's the quiet couples that often go in for the naughty," Ned interjected.

"And how do you know that?" Mina asked, just before she bit in to a deep-fried oyster.

"I happen to have friends in very low places, Mina," Ned said, winking.

"Tessa and Emil were supposed to have gone on a walk." Mina directed the statement at Tamiko.

"I did see him leave. He was taking a kind of canvas bag with him. But she didn't go," Tamiko said.

"And I heard them talking in the hall before they left," Michiko added. She was seated next to her sister and had been listening intently. "She seemed kind of nervous."

"Where did you hear them?" Ned asked as he reached for another piece of roasted duck.

"I heard them coming down the stairs. It was just after breakfast." Michiko put down her chopsticks and poured herself some tea. "She said something like, 'But where are you going?' and he said, 'You said you trusted me.' And she said, 'Yes, but now I'm scared,' and he told her, 'Don't worry, everything will be fine.' That's what he said. Do you think they're in love?" Michiko looked at Mina.

"I think they like each other," Mina said. "I'm not sure about love."

"Did either of you happen to see Hester? She said she was going into town for postcards," Ned said.

Tamiko made a face. "Why would she do that? Everyone knows nothing is open in town on Sunday morning."

"Is something wrong with her?" Michiko asked. "She always looks like she's afraid someone's going to hit her."

"Be quiet, Michi," her sister scolded. "That's rude."

Michiko ignored her sister. "I wish you weren't going tomorrow," she said to Mina. "Most of the people who stay here aren't nearly so nice."

"I bet people aren't going to want to come here anymore," Tamiko said. "Not after someone's been murdered."

Michiko's eyes widened. "What if Mrs. Burnham's ghost comes back to haunt us? Her spirit must be very upset."

"I'd hate to imagine what she could do if she decided to come back as an angry ghost," Mina said as she reached for a crispy *gau gee*. "Although I'm sure she'd make every effort to be the most beautiful angry ghost we ever saw."

Grandma Hannah stood up at the other end of the table and gave a little speech thanking Tony and Masami for the dinner. She asked everyone to be thankful for Mina's recovery. She then offered a toast, asking that the warmth and aloha of their evening gathering always remain between them. As Mina watched, she knew that this was her grandmother's way of wanting to dispel the darkness of the event that had transpired here, but she also knew it couldn't erase the fact that there was a killer lurking just outside their warm little circle. Underneath their happy dinner, she was acutely aware of her own personal fear, the physical and psychic residue of the trauma she'd been through, and the collective fear of all those sitting at the table, whose sense of peace and security had been shattered by the violent event. As she looked at Ned, who was now charming Masami with a story about his childhood in Sāmoa, she realized that the only way they would all truly recover was to find out who had pulled the trigger.

10

THURSDAY

THE GROUP THAT gathered at Oʻahu Cemetery around Amanda Burnham's grave was considerably smaller than the crowd that had nearly filled the Central Union Church for her funeral service. Apparently, Mina reflected, most people didn't feel obligated to be present to watch Amanda being lowered into her final resting place. The late spring sun had already fallen behind the western wall of Nuʻuanu Valley, where the old cemetery, laid out in the park-like American rural style, presided behind the city of Honolulu. In the softened daylight, an indifferent wind ruffled through the tall trees that sheltered the departed, swaying the lavender clusters in the jacarandas and rustling the fronds of the royal palms. This was one of the oldest cemeteries on the island, Mina mused, and the list of Amanda's new neighbors would read like a who's who of Hawaiian history. Mina loved this old graveyard, and on more than one afternoon she had wandered around, idly looking at its Victorian tombstones, Celtic crosses, and the carved child-angels that guarded the graves of the young. She wondered what kind of marker Henry Burnham would choose to memorialize his wife.

Several rows of folding chairs were placed on either side of the new grave, and she and Nyla had chosen seats in the very back of the set that faced the family. As the minister spoke, Mina's attention wandered toward Nuʻuanu Avenue and an old fluted stone pillar with a broken top. When she and Nyla were young, a marble dove had sat on top of it until a vandal broke it off and stole it. A story about the theft had appeared in the newspaper. The girls concocted their own version of the event and decided that whenever they passed the cemetery they had to chant out "The bird, the bird, the missing bird" or run the risk of being haunted by the ghost of the unhappy corpse that lay beneath the pillar. They so terrified their younger brother with this tale that he continued to repeat the ritual well into his teens. "The bird, the bird, the missing bird," she said to herself in a low voice, as she lifted the whisper-thin veil of her hat down over her eyes. Her sister turned to her and gave her a conspiratorial half-smile.

Mina wished she could have taken a picture of the Burnham family as they sat together, lined up in their formal black clothes, awash in grief. She thought they would make a perfect contemporary portrait of an upper-class island family in mourning. Henry stood at the side of the first row of chairs in his dark suit with a stoic and serious expression. Next to him sat Tessa, her hands folded dutifully on her lap, her eyes, in a beatific expression of hope, trained on the minister. It was such a perfect pose that Mina wondered if she'd practiced in a mirror. Beside Tessa, Hester was making a valiant effort to be decorous, sitting stone still, her eyes fixed on the ground, afraid to move a muscle. On Hester's left sat an elderly woman that Mina didn't recognize. She was wearing an old-fashioned black dress that looked vaguely Edwardian, with several strands of long pearls draped around her neck. Her veil was heavier than currently fashionable, but Mina thought she detected a pair of sharp eyes and thin lips beneath it. The old woman sat with an ornate cane in front of her, her hands draped over the handle so that the big rings over the black lace gloves were prominently displayed. Sheldon stood next to her, wrapped in an aura of disbelief and melancholy, with his right hand resting on her shoulder.

Mina felt a sharp pain flash through her shoulder as she turned to her sister. "Who is that woman next to Shel?" she asked.

"I think that's his grandmother," Nyla answered. "Mrs. Lennox."

In the second row of seats, Mina spotted the Gilbert Burnham family. She could see James shifting in his seat and Alfred and Prudence looking solemn and bored. Mina's gaze drifted over the other faces. Some she supposed might be family members, but she wasn't sure, and as she scanned the very edges of the gathering, she was surprised to see Mrs. Olivera and another woman doing their best to look unobtrusive. She pointed them out to Nyla, who was equally puzzled.

After the conclusion of the graveside service, Mina and Nyla made their formal condolences to the family, and as they threaded their way through the maze of graves on their way to the car, they came upon Mrs. Olivera and her elderly companion resting on a bench. Mrs. Olivera's friend was dabbing away tears from her eyes with a handkerchief as the sisters drew near. Both of the women wore simple, dark dresses. Mrs. Olivera carried a straw bag, while her friend's purse was a brown crocheted tote, stuffed to the brim. Both women wore small, but not identical, crosses on gold chains.

"We thought we saw you," Mina said with a smile. "I didn't know you knew Mrs. Burnham."

"Oh, no." Mrs. Olivera looked a little flustered. "I didn't know her. My friend Betty did. I came with her because she didn't want to come alone. This is Mrs. Perreira. Betty, these are the two sisters I told you about that I clean for, Mrs. Forrest and Miss Beckwith."

"How do you do?" Mrs. Perreira said in a polite but shaky voice.

Betty Perreira appeared to be in her late seventies or early eighties. It was obvious that she had been crying and that the outing had been physically and emotionally exhausting for her. Mina wanted to ask her how she knew Amanda. She thought that Mrs. Perreira probably worked for her at one time, but she held back because the poor woman looked so vulnerable.

"Where were you two going now?" Nyla asked. "Can we give you a lift?"

"We were going to take the streetcar to Kaimukī," Mrs. Olivera answered. "Betty lives there, and my husband is going to pick me up at her house."

Nyla shook her head. "No, I won't have you taking the streetcar. My car is right over there, and Kaimukī is on our way. Now, I'll take Mrs. Perreira, and you two bring her bag and umbrella." She promptly helped Mrs. Perreira stand, and walked her away.

"Oh, bless you." Mrs. Olivera beamed. "Mina," she said, as soon as her friend was out of earshot, "I was so worried about bringing her here. She was going to try to come on her own on the streetcar. Can you imagine? She's nearly eighty and her health is not good, but when she fixes her mind on something—my goodness!"

Before they dropped off Mrs. Olivera and Mrs. Perreira in Kaimukī, the sisters insisted on treating them to an afternoon sweet. They stopped at a small bakery and coffee shop on King Street famous for its coconut custard pie.

"We need a nice little something after such a sad occasion," Mina said, as they all settled in a comfortable booth.

Everyone ordered coffee with pie. The waitress returned quickly with generous servings of the house specialty and their beverages.

"Did you know Mrs. Burnham well?" Mina asked Mrs. Perreira, who now seemed calmer.

"Oh, dear," Mrs. Perreira began. "Well, I suppose it doesn't matter so much now that she's passed on." She hesitated for a moment and then said, "She was my niece, you see."

Mina was just about to take a bite of her pie, but she put down her fork in disbelief. Nyla, who had been sipping her coffee, tried to stifle a gasp and started coughing.

"I see you're surprised that I could be related to such a rich woman, but it's true, isn't it, Adele? She's my niece."

Mrs. Olivera nodded. "Yes, it's true."

"Rose Marie," Mrs. Perreira began. "That was the name she was given. She was the daughter of my brother, Antone Rodrigues. He's gone now, Jesus bless him. I thought it was only decent, someone from our family should be there to see Rose Marie buried, even though all these years she pretended we weren't her family. I'm so worried because she didn't receive the last rites from a priest, and I feel so sad that she's not in the Catholic cemetery with her family." She stopped for a moment to wipe her eyes. "All Antone's children were raised to be good Catholics. Rose Marie was baptized and confirmed at St. Joseph's on Maui, just like her sister, Marie Teresa. You were there, weren't you, Miss Beckwith and Mrs. Forrest? I read about it in the paper. You were both there when she died. Oh, I hope she didn't suffer."

"No," Mina said as she took Mrs. Perreira's hand across the table. "I'm sure she didn't suffer. It all happened very quickly." Mina could tell that Mrs. Perreira wanted to talk about her niece. "But I don't understand; I thought Amanda Burnham had no family here."

"That's what she wanted," Mrs. Perreira began. "She must have wanted a different life. She must have been ashamed of us, because we were just dairy farmers from Maui. She must have been ashamed to be Portuguese. She was such a good girl when she was younger, before Antone sent her away. She was quiet, very good at school. She always helped at the church. You see, when they got to be young teenagers, about thirteen or fourteen, her sister began to get into trouble all the time, so Antone sent Rose Marie away to California, to get her away from the influence of her sister. Even though Marie Teresa was wild, Rose Marie loved her sister, but Antone didn't want Rose Marie to be spoiled the way her sister was, you understand? He didn't want her influenced that way. He sent her to stay with our aunt in California, who was a very strict Catholic. Rose Marie stayed there, and Antone thought everything was fine, but when Rose Marie became eighteen—on that exact day she ran away, and no one heard from her again. Oh, my brother was very upset. Then one day, maybe four or five years later, Antone happened to see her picture in the paper. She had married Winston Lennox in San Francisco, and come home on the *Lurline*. Rose Marie's mother was dead, but her father tried to call her on the telephone. She denied she was his daughter and told him he must be mistaking her for someone else. She told him, 'Don't bother me anymore or I'll have my husband call the police.' Antone was heartbroken when she said these things. I suppose she didn't want her position spoiled."

"But wouldn't people find out?" Nyla asked. "This is such a small town."

"Antone kept very quiet. He only told me. I don't think anyone really knew, because who would recognize a young girl from Makawao who left when she was only fourteen? Who would know it was the same person except her father? And if there was ever a rumor going around about her, it died away. I never did hear of one. Her sister, Marie Teresa, such a wild one! Poor Antone, he didn't know what to do with that girl. Oh, they were beautiful sisters, just like the two of you." Mrs. Perreira's voice trailed off as she became lost in reverie.

"What happened to the sister?" Mina asked.

"What's that, dear?" Mrs. Perreira looked like she hadn't quite heard her.

"I was wondering about Marie Teresa, Mrs. Burnham's sister. Is she still alive? Did she know about Amanda, Rose Marie, coming back? Or about this terrible tragedy?" Mina tried not to seem too eager.

"Oh, no, she died long ago, a little while after Rose Marie came back," Mrs. Perreira replied. "My poor brother, he's dead, too, over ten years now. I think he went to watch the boy once. Rose Marie's boy. Antone was in Honolulu and saw the boy's name in the paper for a polo match. He went down to Kapiʻolani Park to the polo field. He said he just wanted to see his grandson once. Of course, he didn't say anything to him. He was always hurt by what Rose Marie did, but I know he forgave her. 'Let her have what she wants,' Antone said. 'Let's not bother her if she doesn't want us.' So we left her alone and never talked about her anymore."

"She certainly got the life she wanted," Nyla commented.

"Though we never found out," Mrs. Perreira went on, "how she met Mr. Lennox. I'm sure she didn't know him as a girl." She sipped her coffee and looked cautiously at Mina and Nyla.

"I only know what her daughter Tessa told me." Nyla stopped for a moment. "Teresa—that's Tessa's real name. She must have named her daughter after her sister."

"Oh, you see, she didn't forget us completely." Mrs. Perreira tried not to cry.

"Tessa told me Amanda's parents died when she was a girl. I think she told Tessa her father was a doctor or something. Anyway, Tessa said that Amanda was raised by an elderly aunt, and after the aunt died, Amanda went to San Francisco and became a fashion model. Winston Lennox saw her at some gala event and fell in love with her almost at first sight."

"I see," said Mrs. Perreira.

"So her children, Tessa, Hester, and Shel, don't know anything about this?" Mina stirred her coffee.

"No, I don't think so, no," Mrs. Perreira answered, sighing. "The way they were brought up, I'm sure they would be ashamed of our family, too."

The afternoon sun filtered through a raised, barred window of thick, opaque glass and into the basement jail cell that smelled musty and damp, as if water had penetrated the concrete interior and never dried out. Paint was peeling off the walls where previous occupants had scratched names, dates, phone numbers, and various unsavory words. Ned sat on a plain wooden chair across from Jack Carstairs and his lawyer, Louis Goldburn. Louis was also a friend of Mina, and he had agreed to arrange the interview. Louis had the stocky, solid look of a longshoreman or an ex-boxer with a taste for fine clothes, and Ned judged the lawyer to be about forty. Louis and Jack were sitting side by side on a green army blanket that covered an uncomfortable-looking cot. Jack was dressed in faded khaki pants and a white T-shirt. He was tall, over six feet. His hair was cut very short, and although his face was drawn and tired, his hazel eyes retained their quick intelligence. Ned thought he had the look of a worn-out child who needed a cheese sandwich, a glass of milk, and an early bedtime, and even though Ned knew Jack was about twenty-one or twenty-two, he still had the urge to take the boy's cigarettes away and give him a scolding. Louis had just introduced Ned and explained the reason for the interview.

"We're just interested in hearing your side of things," Ned began. "Perhaps there's some way we could help you, unofficially, of course."

"I'll do whatever Louis says I should do." Jack looked at his lawyer.

"I think you should talk to him," Louis said.

"You're a friend of Mina's?" Jack raised an eyebrow.

"That's right," Ned replied.

"How is she? I know she was shot." Jack sounded genuinely concerned.

"She's doing very well." Ned thought better of him for asking.

"I owe Mina one. So what would you like to know, Mr. Manusia?"

"Please, call me Ned."

"What would you like to know, *Ned?*" Jack took a drag on his cigarette.

"I've read your statement, about what happened in Hale'iwa, but I'd like to hear it in you own words." Ned did his best to sound low-key and neutral. "Why were you out there?"

"I just went out to talk with some of the men. That's one of the things I do when I'm in port. I help with the paper, the *Labor News.* I pass out pamphlets. I talk to workers. I just talk about trade unions and what they can do for people. I tell them what goes on in other places. Lately, I've been telling people about the Wagner Act that's before Congress and what it could mean if it passes. God knows, the workers in the islands wouldn't hear anything about it if we didn't go out and inform them. And there's real interest, except that most of the men here are so damned scared of reprisals." Jack grimaced and looked away.

"Like Mr. Shimasaki? Is that what you mean?" Ned said it quietly, and waited for a reaction.

Jack took out another cigarette, and his unsteady hands lit it with the butt of the one he'd been smoking. "Shimasaki-san was a good man, a smart man, a steady worker, thoughtful of his wife and child, his friends. He looked around and thought there could be a better life for everyone. He had influence and people respected him."

"Then he went missing and died," said Ned.

"Murdered." Jack's voice was bitter. "He was murdered."

"So you went out to Hale'iwa to talk," Ned continued. "When did you get there?"

"Late Friday. It was after four, anyway. I was hitching rides, and it damn near took all day to get there."

"Why don't you just tell me what happened up until the time you got arrested?"

"Well," Jack began, "I got to town. I met some of the guys. We went to the bar. There's a pool table there and we had a few games. I didn't drink anything. I never drink before a meeting. Then I went and left my duffle at the boardinghouse. I ate some noodles down-stairs, and then went to a meeting at a house there in Hale'iwa. It was in the backyard. We were talking about things for a while, and then towards the end of the meeting someone brought Shimasaki's death up. I guess I got angry and said some hard things in front of everyone. On Saturday we marched behind Shimasaki's coffin. That evening I went to the pool hall and started drinking. The place was noisy and crowded, being Saturday night. I was sitting in the corner. I was still pretty upset. I don't know how much time passed, but later on this guy comes over. Says his name is Orsino, Orsino Hood, and he acts friendly and buys me a few more drinks. We get to talking. He says he knows who I am and that he has a few guys he wants me to meet that have come over from Kahuku."

"Kahuku," Ned interrupted. "Where is that?"

"It's a plantation town, a few miles from Hale'iwa," Louis said. "There's another sugar mill there."

"So," Jack continued, "he says they just want to meet me tonight and maybe fix up a time for me to go there and talk to them. I agree to go with him, and we leave the pool hall. I'm not exactly sure where we're going. I'm just following this guy because I'm pretty blasted, but it seemed like we spent a long time walking through a jungle or something until we finally came out on the beach. This Orsino guy laughs and says something like, 'Oh, I guess we missed them.' Then he says he's got some really fine bourbon to make up for the wild goose chase, and he hands me this flask from his jacket pocket. I took a few sips of this stuff, and that's the last thing I remember until the police woke me up."

"And what did this Mr. Hood look like?" Ned asked.

"He was around six feet, shorter than me, curly dark hair, dark complexion. He had a mustache and a really bad complexion, lots of pockmarks on his face. I don't remember much more. The bar was dark. The beach was dark. He was wearing khakis, a cap, and a jacket—he looked like a regular working-class guy."

"These letters that Mr. Burnham received," Ned said, "you say you know nothing about them?"

"I don't write cowardly letters," Jack replied in disgust, "or run around scrawling threats on doorsteps."

"Do you own a gun? Can you shoot?" Ned saw that his question jarred him, and Jack gave his lawyer a nervous look.

"If you go to trial," Louis said to Jack, "it's bound to come out."

"I was in the rifle club in high school," Jack stated. "I won some competitions. But I don't own a gun, and I wasn't shooting people on Sunday morning."

"And what about the Shimasaki affair?" Ned kept on.

"What about it?" Jack snapped back.

"What do you know about his death?"

"I'm ninety-nine percent sure they killed him. I'm ninety-nine percent sure they took him out to teach the others a lesson. Burn 'em and Rob 'em want to make sure the profits keep rolling in."

"Do you know Mr. Lars Bruhn?" Ned watched him.

"I've seen the guy. I don't know him, but I know what the men say about him—that he's a cruel, sadistic snake with a taste for the ladies. And I'd bet a case of booze he had something to do with Shimasaki's death." Jack turned to Louis. "Say, Lou, did you bring me anything?"

"No, Jack." Louis sounded irritated. "I didn't bring you anything."

"God damn it, Lou!" Jack punched the mattress. "I asked you!"

Louis stood up. "Look, you better wise up, kid. Can't you see that your drinking is way out of control? Can't you see where it's gotten you? Do you seriously think you would be sitting here if you'd managed to stay halfway sober that night?"

"Don't lecture me," Jack growled back. "You're not my father, you're not my doctor. You're my lawyer."

"That's right," Louis said calmly as he gathered up his briefcase. "I'm your lawyer, not your bartender. Come on, Ned, this interview is over for now. You can waste your time on him later."

Louis called for the officer in charge, and the two men left Jack sitting in his dank cell, his face flushed with anger. They walked up the stairs and out onto the street, where Louis took a deep breath.

"The boy has a bit of a temper," Ned commented.

"The kid has a drinking problem, and he needs to dry out." Louis shook his head. "Hell, jail is probably the best place for him right now." He paused and looked at Ned. "What do think about this Orsino Hood?"

"I think we'd have a very hard time finding him—if he exists at all," Ned answered.

"So you think he's lying?" Louis' face betrayed no emotion.

"I don't know him well enough to know if he's lying," Ned replied, "but if he's not lying, I'd bet Orsino Hood was not this character's real name and that he didn't live in Kahuku. Tell me, Mr. Goldburn, do you think he's lying?"

"At this stage," Louis answered, "I have to believe he's telling the truth. Later on, well, we'll have to see what happens. What do you say we go down to the Mermaid for a cup of coffee? You could meet Duncan Mackenzie and Maggie. They know the kid real well, better than I do."

"Sounds splendid," Ned said, smiling.

As they walked down to the boulevard, Ned remembered that Mina had told him that Louis was a graduate of Harvard and had come to Hawai'i shortly after law school. Louis frequently represented the underdog. He was the only lawyer in town sympathetic to the unions and unafraid to stand up to the Honolulu business elite. His socialism and his Jewish heritage made him unpopular with members of island high society, many of whom quietly nursed an anti-Semitic sentiment. Ned had admired the way Louis handled Jack, especially his no-nonsense advice about drinking.

As they walked along, Ned noticed how quickly the neighborhood had changed in just two blocks. The solid business district of banks and offices, with its crisp white-shirt-and-tie couture, was only a stone's throw away from the cafés and bars near the wharf and the fish markets of Chinatown, where work shirts and dungarees looked like they were lucky if they got a wash once a week.

"I understand the theatre is going to do a reading of one of your plays in the next month," Louis said with a smile. "My wife and I certainly enjoyed the production of your last play at the theatre. Nyla Forrest was marvelous. They all were—even Christian Hollister, who I don't much care for in real life."

"Yes, Johnny Knight wants to do some sort of staged reading of one of my plays. I suppose he's hoping there will be an interest in having a full production next season."

"I worked in summer stock when I was in college," Louis said. "I had the time of my life. I suppose I should look into doing something with the theatre here."

"I think they're always looking for people with some background," Ned remarked. "I'll let you know if Johnny holds auditions for the reading."

"I would be interested. Here we are, then." The lawyer opened the gate under the Mermaid Café sign, and the two men stepped into the little inner yard. It was a small patch of lawn with a little grove of bamboo, and when Ned looked up at the two-story structure he thought that at one time it must have been a home. The covered patio was deserted, as it was now late afternoon, and Ned could not help but smile at the two mermaids that hovered over the doorway. As they stepped inside, there was only one table occupied, by a couple of men who were drinking coffee and sharing a plate of pastries. Ned's attention was immediately drawn to the other carvings around the room. There were several other mermaids carved from wood, painted and stained to look like weathered objects, but the most impressive one of all was a near life-size carving that resembled those seen on the prows of ships. The mermaid herself had all of the quintessential features of these sea beings—long, flowing hair, a classic, fey face, and, of course, a glistening, sinuous tail. She was gazing in a mirror and combing her hair, but there was something so human and lifelike about the carving—as Ned looked at it, he immediately felt as if there was a real woman imprisoned in the wood, and that he should help her get out. Perhaps, he thought, it was the innocent, sensitive expression in the face and eyes. It looked as though she were seeing something in the mirror that was just out of her reach, and somehow it made her plaintive and sad.

"It's pretty quiet here at this time of the day," said Louis. "There's a simple dinner offering every night that draws a crowd, but they won't show up for another few hours. The customers are mostly people who work around the docks."

"Sorry," Ned said, when he realized Louis was speaking to him. "This is such an extraordinary piece."

"Oh, I know." Louis looked at him. "Whenever I look at her too long, I get this guilty feeling, but I'm not sure why. I can't tell you how many people have wanted to buy her from Duncan, but he'll never part with her."

Just then Maggie appeared from the kitchen. "Louis, how are you?" She gave the lawyer a kiss on the cheek.

During their introduction, Ned couldn't help but notice her husky voice, which made him think she had been a singer at one time. Her voice perfectly suited the flaming red color of her hair, and when she smiled, her eyes lit up—a sure sign, Ned thought, of a genuine person. They sat down at one of the tables.

"Can I get you some coffee?" Maggie asked. "Or how about some afternoon tea? Ned, you sound like that's more your style, and Louis here is getting trained by his New Zealand wife to want a cuppa in the afternoon."

"It's an easy habit to get into," Louis agreed.

"I'll just put the kettle on and find Duncan for you." She smiled and disappeared behind the swinging doors to the kitchen.

A few minutes later, her husband Duncan appeared. He had the look of a veteran man of the sea, with his spiky crew cut, his ruddy, crinkled face, and the tattoos of an anchor on one arm and a sea monster on the other. He was a tall, strong-looking man with large hands, and Ned found it hard to believe that this big, somewhat clumsy-looking person had created the feminine wooden sculpture behind him.

"Ned is trying to see if he can help Jack out," Louis explained after their introductions. "He's a friend of Mina Beckwith, the girl who brought Jack here after he'd been roughed up."

"Uh-huh." Duncan crossed his arms and looked at Ned. "Isn't her brother-in-law a cop?"

"Todd Forrest," Ned said. "He's the head of homicide. But off the record, he's not opposed to our little independent investigation."

"You mean he's not convinced the boy did it?"

"It's my opinion," Ned said, "and only my opinion off the record, that he's not thoroughly convinced, even though the evidence against him is quite strong. And I have to warn both of you that any mention of what I've just said to anyone could bring our help to a halt, and put Todd's job in jeopardy."

"We know how to keep our mouths shut." Duncan looked serious. "I blame myself. If I'd gone out there with the kid, this never would have happened. He's smart and dedicated, but he starts drinking, and he screws up."

Maggie appeared with a pot of tea and a plate of pastries. "These are from a bakery down the street, and they're very good, especially the apple turnovers." She sat down and poured everyone a cup.

"Have both of you known Jack for a long time?" Ned asked.

"I met him about two years ago, just before I quit sailing and opened up this joint," Duncan answered. "He's a hothead, all right, but he's no killer."

"Duncan's right," Maggie joined in. "He couldn't do something like that. He talks big, but he's like a kid inside. He's one of those people who really thinks the world isn't fair, and he wants to make it more fair, that's all."

"What about this incident? The beating in the alley?" Ned looked at both of them.

"That happens to us all the time," Duncan began. "These big shots get riled because we tell their workers about trade unions, and then they send some goons out to talk to us with their fists. I don't know, Jack thought it might have been Burnham's doing, because he'd been out to Hale'iwa recently, and because of Shimasaki's death. We're pretty sure they killed him—maybe not intentionally, maybe they just wanted to rough him up, and it got out of hand. I don't know. A couple saw Shimasaki being driven away by Bruhn and some others, but they won't come forward. They're scared as hell, but we're going to keep working on them."

"Lars Bruhn," Ned repeated.

"He's a bloody sadist," Duncan said. "We heard he got fired from a Fiji plantation for being a little too enthusiastic with a whip. I think you should know that the plantation in Hale'iwa is a powder keg right now, and it's mostly because of Bruhn. Those men have taken Shimasaki's death pretty hard, and none of them believe for one minute that it was an accident. I hope there isn't any more violence, but I wouldn't be surprised if there was. It's not enough that people have to slave away for almost no money just to stay alive, but when you add physical punishment, and now death, to the mix—well, you seem like a smart man, Mr. Manusia; you see how it is. Profit comes at an inhumane price in the sugar and pineapple market."

"I'd have to agree with you," Ned said, hoping Duncan would continue.

"It's a shame Henry Burnham has controlling interest of that company. Things might be different if he and his brother were on equal footing. The brother is much more sympathetic to our side."

"Really?" Ned was surprised. "How do you know that?"

"We have our sources. We make it our business to find out everything we can about these big companies, any way we can. We keep track of their boards and their directors. We keep our ears to the ground about their politics. It's not hard to do in this town." Duncan laughed. "Everyone gossips."

"And you've heard things about Henry Burnham's brother?" Ned's interest was piqued. "I can't recall his name right now."

"Gilbert," Louis chimed in. "Gilbert Burnham. He's a few years younger than Henry, I think."

"You see, Henry has controlling interest in Burnham and Robbins," Duncan explained. "Not by much, but enough to make his brother subordinate. And from what we hear, the two don't see eye to eye on a lot of things. Gilbert is actually concerned about workers. We hear he's made personal visits to camps and talked to people, and we hear Henry has blocked his efforts several times on improving living conditions and medical care."

"That's very helpful," Ned said.

"We'll do anything we can to help Jack," Maggie said. "Poor soul, he's had it tough. His father died when he was a baby. He watched his mother struggle to support him and his sister. His mom had some crummy job in a factory, and she got sick and died when he was a teenager. He's sure it was the long hours and working conditions. That's why he's so committed. And we know he didn't write those letters to Burnham," she added. "That's just not how he operates."

"I have to get back to the stove," Duncan said as he stood up. "If there's anything else you need to know, just come back. Hell, I'll talk to you while I'm cooking, if it helps Jack."

"Thanks for your time." Ned stood up and shook his hand.

"Don't have to rush off," Duncan said. "Finish your tea and talk to Maggie." He turned and disappeared through the kitchen door.

"Duncan makes a wonderful fish chowder on Friday nights when Maggie bakes fresh bread," Louis said. "Sometimes Doris and I come here after work and eat. The setting is simple, but the food is great."

"We have one fixed meal at night, and we don't stay open very late," Maggie said.

"Do you live here as well?" Ned asked.

"Upstairs," Maggie replied, pointing. "There's a lovely view of the harbor, and there's a garage near the alley out back where Duncan does his carving."

"The mermaid here is really a work of art," Ned said.

"Duncan carves other things, but he always comes back to mermaids." Maggie smiled. "He thinks he saw mermaids once when he was at sea. Maybe that's why."

"Mermaids are supposed to be dangerous seducers, aren't they?" Louis asked as he helped himself to a second apple turnover.

"Duncan says it wasn't that way at all," Maggie answered. "He said he felt like he'd received a gift, just seeing them."

"I remember in school, reading once in Plutarch about mermaids, or was it sirens?" Ned tried to remember. "Well, I've not forgotten it because it was just the opposite of all the tales you hear about them being femme fatales. He said something about their song captivating the attention of souls after death, that the harmony of their voices inspired the binding of souls to divine love."

"That's beautiful," Maggie said with a smile. "I'll have to tell Duncan. You know, it's funny, but that's how Duncan and I met. I was singing in this club in San Francisco in a cheesy mermaid costume. He loved my voice, and it's been divine ever since."

11

FRIDAY

NED CAME ACROSS the hau arbor into Mina's bungalow with a bowl of warm scones and placed them on the dining table that Grandma Hannah had neatly set. Ned was glad to be once again staying next door to Mina in the twin bungalow owned by Nyla and Todd. They seldom used the little house and were more than glad to have Ned there. Grandma Hannah had come to stay with Mina until she recuperated and was delighted to be cooking and straightening up for her granddaughter.

"Mina will be right here," Grandma Hannah told Ned. "She slept in a little. I think she overdid it yesterday, going to the church service and the burial. She asked for tea when I told her you were making scones. I hope that's all right with you."

"That's lovely, thanks," Ned said.

"Do I smell scones?" Mina asked as she walked out of the hallway to the table with Ollie following closely behind her. Ollie walked over to Ned and gently nuzzled his leg, then placed his head on Ned's knee and peered quizzically into his face.

Grandma Hannah laughed. "Mina's always been good at identifying food with her nose, especially if it's something she likes to eat."

"Why, Mina," Ned said, smiling at her, "you're far too modest about your talents."

Mina frowned. "Grandma, don't tell him things like that. I'll never hear the end of it."

"Don't be silly, dear. Ned has very good manners," Grandma said as she got up from the table and headed for the kitchen. "Now, you two get started, and I'll be right back with the eggs and fish."

"That's right," Ned said to Mina. "I have lovely manners. I'd never compare you to a bloodhound or a truffle hunter."

"Be quiet and pour me some tea, would you?" She reached for one of the warm scones, cut it in half, and began to smear it with butter. "Now, let's see if your baking is up to par this morning," she said, before taking a bite.

"Well?" Ned asked.

"I'll spare your life for another day," Mina said. "They're delicious. They have the slightest taste of liqueur or something."

"I put a bit of rum in them," Ned replied. "A little recipe from my aunt."

"What are you going to do today?" Mina asked.

"I have to go up to the theatre and meet with Johnny about the play reading, and then I thought I would pay a visit to Uncle Wing Chang in Chinatown to see if he knows anything about this high-stakes poker game that Lars Bruhn is supposed to frequent. What about you? I hope you're planning on resting."

"I'm going with Nyla to the Burnham and Robbins offices this morning, just for a bit. Maybe I'll meet you at the Changs', and you could bring me home? Nyla has to pick up my father later at the airport, and I'd rather not drive all the way out there."

"I'm at your service, Miss Beckwith."

"What is she getting you to do now, Ned?" Grandma Hannah asked as she returned with a platter of scrambled eggs and small fillets of sautéed mahimahi.

"I'm just asking for a ride home, Grandma, so I don't have to go to the airport with Nyla. Here, try one of Ned's scones." Mina passed her the basket, then proceeded to help herself to some scrambled eggs and a piece of fish.

"It's lovely having fish for breakfast," Ned said. "Real fresh island fish, not kippers."

"It tastes great, too, Grandma," Mina added.

"I can see why Mina's been bragging about your scones, Ned," Grandma said, after she'd taken a bite of one. "I hope you'll share your recipe. These will be a big hit at the ranch."

"Can you believe that Amanda Burnham was actually Portuguese and from Maui?" Mina said between bites.

"I think the Lennox family used to have a place up on Maui," Grandma Hannah commented. "I can't remember if it was in Makawao or Kula."

"I wonder if Winston Lennox knew her before," mumbled Mina.

"If she got shipped away when she was still young, he could only have known her as a child," Ned commented. "Do you think Winston Lennox would mix with the children of a dairy farmer?"

"Not formally," Grandma Hannah said. "Violet Lennox, Winston's mother, would have forbidden it, but children have ways of meeting."

"She was at the funeral, sitting next to Shel," Mina said.

"Was she showing off her jewelry?" Grandma asked as she served herself another piece of fish.

"You know her?" Ned asked.

"We belong to the same women's organization, the Daughters of the Islands. Of course, now that I've moved away, I don't get to the meetings in Honolulu. I go to the Kona chapter." Grandma Hannah paused. "But I used to see her at every meeting here."

"I wonder if she would know anything useful about Henry Burnham," Mina mused. "Her son's replacement."

"She doted on Winston and took his death very hard," said Grandma Hannah. "He was a spoiled boy, if you ask me. Violet indulged him too much. She was always smoothing things out for him with his teachers, with other parents, and later with his spending. And the wife was the same way, I hear. She spoiled him, too. Violet thought the world of Amanda. I don't think she cared for Henry Burnham, but she and Amanda were always very friendly."

"How well do you know her, Grandma?" Mina tried to sound blasé.

"Not as well as I know you, dear." Grandma Hannah winked at Ned. "Are you fishing for some way to meet her?"

"Do you think she would? Meet us, I mean?" Mina reached for another scone.

"What do you think I should do with this girl, Ned? She's never been able to mind her own business. I guess that's why she became a reporter."

Ned shrugged. "I've given up. I just do whatever she wants."

Johnny Knight and Ned sat alone at a table in the middle of an empty stage. A desk light on an extension cord illuminated their working area, but otherwise they were surrounded by darkness. The heavy black stage curtains hung motionless, and the empty seats of the auditorium watched in silence as the two lively young men discussed Ned's play. Ned could never explain why he felt so comfortable in the void of an empty stage, why he often carried this space around in his mind and compulsively pictured things happening here, people coming and going, lives passing by. He recognized that he felt a certain reverence for the physical space when it was empty this way—this empty space where he and so many playwrights before him watched their imagination come to life.

"I think we can assemble a solid cast pretty quickly," Johnny was saying. "People will be anxious to participate."

"I hope Nyla will be interested," Ned said.

"I've already enlisted her," Johnny replied. "And Christian Hollister called me up as soon as he got wind of the reading. What do you think about him for the role of Leon?"

"He is a talented actor," Ned answered, "though I suspect he has a little crush on Mina."

"Probably because she's unattainable," Johnny said. "For him, I mean. And listen, half of the single men in Honolulu have a little crush on Mina, so you better watch your back, Mr. Playwright."

Ned laughed. "Why don't we just assemble a cast of her devotees, and you can help me arrange an accident involving all of them. We'll place them all in various spots on the stage and fly in some sandbags, right on their heads."

"A kind of modern Odysseus ending?"

"Precisely."

"Well, speaking of returns, there's a guy who recently came back to the islands. He was a great actor when we were in high school. I wanted to try to get him back into acting." Johnny was making doodles on a piece of paper as he talked.

"Who is it?" Ned asked.

"His name's Emil Devon. You've probably met him, since he was involved in that mess at the Hale'iwa Hotel."

"I met him briefly. You knew him in school?"

"We were in the drama club—Emil, myself, and sometimes Sheldon Lennox. Now there's someone who could be a wonderful actor if he had any discipline. I remember him doing Romeo in a Shakespeare showcase once. He had a reserve of passion that floored all of us."

"I haven't met him yet."

"And he was quirky, too," Johnny went on, "in an amusing sort of way. He made me up once to look like Dracula. He was very good at it, but Emil was the one for the tough-guy roles. That's why I thought he'd be perfect for Hector, if we could persuade him."

"He does have that naturally dark quality, as if he's chronically unhappy."

"He wasn't always like that, you know. He used to be the life of the party, but he had a hard time when his father died, and he went sour."

"How do you mean?"

"It was our senior year when it happened. He was mad and scowling all the time. If you asked him a question he'd just snap at you. He came to school and then he'd go straight home. His mother was hitting the bottle, so on top of losing his old man, he had to be nursemaid to Mom. He didn't join any of the clubs, he stopped playing sports, he didn't go to any of the senior class functions. I don't even think he showed up at the graduation ceremony."

"But he managed to go to university."

"I think his mom came around when she realized she was on the verge of ruining her son's life as well as her own. She started to get some help, and he went off to college."

"So things started to mend?"

"They did, but then there was another tragedy. His mother died of a heart attack while he was away at school. It was pretty sudden. He came back for the funeral, but then went back to school, and nobody's heard from him all these years. Suddenly he shows up, and Henry Burnham has given him a prestigious job with the Hawaiian Sugar Planters' Association at the experimental station. Go figure."

"And you think he'd be a good addition to the cast?" Ned leaned back, folded his arms, and looked at Johnny.

"If we can get him to do it." Johnny smiled. "Maybe I could get Sheldon, too. It would be like a little reunion."

"Do you know Louis Goldburn?" Ned asked. "He's a lawyer downtown. I think we should ask him to read for Shane."

"Really? He acts?"

"He says so."

"Great," Johnny said. "Let's try him out. It would make for some natural sparks between him and Chris Hollister. People might pack the theatre just to see that."

"Say, I passed by a gem of a theatre in Haleʻiwa," Ned said. "I was wondering if it might be possible to do a reading out there, too."

Johnny seemed doubtful. "I don't know. It's a sweet little theatre, and it would be great to do the reading for a rural audience. But it's far out of town, and the cast would have to spend the night out there. I don't think the theatre would cough up the money. We're always on such a shoestring here."

"What if you received a little donation to cover the expenses? I've always been in favor of bringing theatre to the people."

"Well," Johnny said, grinning, "with a patron of the arts behind us, I'm sure we could swing it."

Before Ned left the theater, he made a call to Todd.

"Just calling to check on my status as your temporary assistant." Ned tried to sound breezy.

"I don't know who it was that called the chief, but he was pretty impressed."

"And?"

"And so you're in, with the caveat that you keep a low profile—no talking to the press, no speaking for the department, you know."

"Easily done," Ned agreed. "And I will do my best to keep an eye on those decorators."

"So who did call the chief? Do you know?"

"Sorry, old man," Ned answered. "I'm not allowed to tell you, and neither is your boss."

"So what are you, Manusia? A British Mr. Moto?"

"Sayonara, Captain Forrest." Ned hung up the phone and smiled to himself.

"I was surprised, too," Nyla said to her sister. "Tessa called me up on Tuesday and said her father hoped we would all carry on as usual as soon as the funeral was over. Something about how he didn't want the killer to have the satisfaction of disrupting things and making him hide and cower."

"So here we are, the day after," Mina replied.

"Todd advised and offered him police protection, but he wouldn't hear of it."

"I don't think Henry's 'show no fear' approach is very wise. If I were him, I'd be worried."

They drifted out to the terrace of the Burnham building and were admiring the view of the harbor. Earlier they had met with the carpenter, who was widening the doors between the sitting room and the conference room, and the painting contractor. Both men had agreed to have their crews work all weekend. They also consulted with a furniture maker about a new koa table for the conference room and some matching pieces for the sitting room. They were just exchanging ideas about the outdoor space when Henry Burnham appeared.

"I wanted to thank you two for coming back on the job so promptly." He gave them an official-looking smile. "It means a lot to me that things keep running smoothly."

"Of course," Nyla responded.

"And Mina," Henry said, turning to her, "I haven't yet thanked you for saving me. For trying to save . . ." His voice began to waver.

"There's no need to thank me," Mina said. "One doesn't take time to think in those situations. One just acts."

"Still," Henry said, regaining his composure, "it was very brave of you."

"You would have done the same, I'm sure," Mina said.

"I hope you don't mind, but I've sent you a little gift," he said.

"But I don't—"

"No." Henry waved his hand. "I won't be dissuaded. It's the least I can do, and it's already too late to stop the delivery, so you'll just have to graciously accept it."

"All right," Mina said, smiling. "I'll let you win."

"Yes, well, I won't keep you any longer," he said. "And thank you both again for carrying on." Henry then turned and left quickly, as if he were glad to get what he felt to be an obligation checked off his list.

"I can't believe he's not protecting himself," Mina said softly as she watched him walk away.

Nyla turned away to look at the view again. "I can't believe he refused to follow Todd's advice."

It was late morning, and the blue-green waters of the harbor were bustling with activity. The boom of a freighter swung a netted load over the side of the ship, and the sisters watched as it disappeared from sight to the dock below. In the distance, a tug and barge plowed steadily toward the narrow mouth of Honolulu Harbor and the open sea, while a small sampan returning from a fishing trip bobbed its way toward the docks near the fish markets.

The Aloha Tower clock read eleven-thirty. They had just gone back into the conference room when they heard voices from the adjacent sitting room. Mina recognized Hester's childlike pitch and guessed that the other female voice belonged to Gwendolyn Reed. The door between the rooms was opened just enough so that Mina and Nyla could hear them without being seen.

"I said I was sorry you don't feel good, but if you want some tea, you have to get it yourself. I'm busy," Gwen said.

"You work for my father, and you have to do what I say," Hester retorted.

"That's right. I work for your father, not for you," Gwen shot back.

"You always did it before." Hester almost sounded hurt.

"That was different," Gwen said in a superior tone. "Your father told me to try to keep your mother from complaining."

"You shut up about my mother." Hester's voice was laced with venom.

"Why?" Gwen spat back. "Don't pretend you liked her. I know you didn't."

"Well, she was right about you. You're nothing but a cheap slut. You slept with Sheldon, and then you slept with my father. I bet you'd sleep with anyone who offered you a dime."

"So, are you jealous?" Gwen laughed, and her voice trailed off as she left the room. "Nobody would ever want to sleep with you for a million bucks."

"You bitch," Hester growled. "You'll be sorry you said that."

Mina and Nyla stayed silent as they heard someone else enter the room.

"Hester?" The voice belonged to Sheldon Lennox. "Did you say something to upset Gwen? I passed her in the hall and she referred to you as my blankety-blank sister."

"I don't know why," Hester answered innocently. "Do you think she still likes you?"

"I told you, sis, that was over a long time ago, and *I* never really liked *her*. She was just something to do."

"Do you think Daddy will marry her?"

"No." Sheldon was definite. "Don't worry about it, Hess. Men like your daddy never marry girls like Gwen. It wouldn't look good at the Kama'āina Club."

"Are you sure?" Hester had become weepy.

"I'm positive," Sheldon answered. "How was the dentist? Do you think you could manage a chocolate shake before we go home?"

"If you have one, too." She seemed to cheer up.

"Okay, let's get going," said Sheldon.

When the two of them had gone, Mina and Nyla walked into the sitting room.

"My, my, that secretary gets around, doesn't she?" Nyla said, laughing.

"So does Sheldon." Mina frowned. "I'd like to know when and how long he was involved with Miss Gwen."

"Could you believe how nasty Hester was?"

"I wonder what happened to her, what kind of breakdown she actually had."

"You mean you wonder if it was violent?" Nyla asked.

"Exactly," said Mina.

While Mina and Nyla were contemplating the terrace, Ned was talking to Cecily's father, Wing Chang, in the family flat above their business in Chinatown. Wing Chang had insisted on preparing lunch for Ned, and they sat to eat in the large country kitchen designed to satisfy Wing Chang's passion for gourmet cooking, French in particular. Uncle Wing (as he insisted on being called by younger, close friends) served Ned a perfect *croque monsieur* and a salad. He also insisted that Ned have a glass of white wine with his meal. The two sat at the wooden table in the kitchen.

"This is a delightful meal," Ned said to his host. "I haven't had a *croque monsieur* since the last time I was in Paris."

"When was that?" Uncle Wing asked.

"I think it was over three years ago." Ned tried to remember. "I went with my grandfather. He wanted to go to some kind of flower show."

"Your grandfather likes to grow flowers?"

"His greenhouses and gardens occupy most of his time," Ned answered. "He even employs a part-time botanist, along with his gardener and the assistants. You know, he loves tropical plants. I keep trying to get him to come to the tropics. I'm sure once he got here, I'd have trouble getting him to go back home."

"You might want to think seriously about that." Uncle Wing looked at Ned. "Things are not going well in Europe, and that part of the world could be very unsafe soon."

"The truth is," Ned said, "my mother and I have seriously discussed how to transplant my grandfather if things get really bad. His health is terrific so the traveling wouldn't be a problem, and he could leave the estate in capable hands. It's just a matter of knowing what will really happen."

"It couldn't be anything good." Uncle Wing frowned. "Not with most of Europe infatuated with totalitarianism and Hitler rearming Germany." He paused and took a sip of his wine. "But you didn't come today to talk about the woes of the world."

"No," Ned said, smiling. "I'm interested in a poker game."

"I didn't know you were a gambler, Ned."

"I'm not," he answered. "I'm wondering if you know anything about a high-stakes poker game here in Chinatown."

"Any special reason?"

"Someone connected to this business at the Hale'iwa Hotel is supposed to be a regular participant. I'm not sure, but I have this feeling that it somehow has some bearing on the case."

"Ah, it's one of your famous feelings," Uncle Wing said teasingly.

"That and my natural curiosity about Honolulu's dark side."

"Who is this someone, if I may ask?"

"His name is Lars Bruhn, and he works out at the plantation in Hale'iwa. Do you know him?"

"No, I don't think so." Uncle Wing seemed lost in thought for a moment. "But, yes, there is a high-stakes poker game that originated here in Chinatown. The men and very few women who frequent it are either extremely wealthy, addicted to games of chance, or both. The game floats from place to place and time to time. There are several contacts who inform those interested when and where the next game will take place. I think at first the games were always in Chinatown, but now, to elude the law, they are in different places—private residences, I've heard, or hotel suites."

"It sounds like a very sophisticated operation."

"Oh, it is," Uncle Wing assured him. "I went to one of these games once when a business acquaintance from the Orient was in town, someone my wife and Cecily buy antiques from. He had his heart set on a big American poker game, so I had to oblige him. He was very wealthy and treated me to the adventure. It was a very interesting evening. The buy-in fee for the game is quite high, and the dealer is paid as well as tipped for each hand, so the house does quite well. Also, there are women available for another fee, and there is money lending at an extravagant rate of interest. Those who borrow and do not pay back in a timely fashion had better beware. I'm told there can be serious physical damage inflicted on the transgressors or their loved ones."

"It sounds like organized crime."

"Very organized." Uncle Wing rose from the table and returned with two lemon tarts for dessert. "A new recipe," he said proudly as he placed the little plate in front of Ned.

"So how did your business friend like the evening?" Ned asked.

"Oh, he lost his shirt, but it was the highlight of his visit to Hawai'i."

"This tart is quite delicious, Uncle Wing," Ned said after the first bite. "I'm sure Mina could eat three or four of these."

"And I'm sure Cecily would join her," Uncle Wing said with a laugh. "Would you like me to find out if this Lars Bruhn still attends the games?"

"It would be a useful piece of information," replied Ned. "And only if it would be safe for you to ask—whoever you would be asking."

"It will be as safe as a baby's cradle," said a smiling Uncle Wing.

It was early in the afternoon when Ned and Mina met and drove back to the bungalows. In the car, she eagerly told him all about Hester's hostile behavior and the Gwen and Sheldon affair, and he told her about the Chinatown poker games. When they got home, Ollie came bounding off the porch as soon as they got out of the car. Grandma Hannah insisted that Mina go and rest, so Ned did a bit of writing and walked on the beach. The afternoon passed, and soon it was time to go to Nyla and Todd's house for dinner.

Mina insisted that Grandma Hannah sit in the front seat with Ned, and she and Ollie piled in the back. Her shoulder still felt too uncomfortable to drive, and she was enjoying the novelty of being chauffeured around. Ollie stretched out and laid his head in her lap. She ran her hand through the soft curls along his back.

"That dog is living the life of a royal," Ned commented as he started up the car engine. "We may have to bestow a title on him."

"He was very well behaved the whole time you were gone," Grandma Hannah told Mina. "He never whined or cried, and he let me know when he wanted to go outside. You better be careful; I'm sure your father will want to take him away to the ranch."

"N-O," Mina said. "You're my dog now, aren't you, Ollie?"

"Oh, by the way, dear," Grandma Hannah added, "Violet Lennox wants us to come over to her place for lunch tomorrow."

"What?" Mina was genuinely surprised. "How did you manage that so quickly?"

Her grandmother smiled. "I have my ways. And I don't know if I should share my professional secrets with you. What do you think, Ned?"

"I think you should ask for a fee," Ned said, grinning. "A very steep fee."

"A fine way to treat the unemployed, Ned." Mina rolled down her window halfway. "Seriously, Grandma, how did you wrangle an invitation?"

"I called her up on the pretense of asking if there was a Daughters of the Islands meeting in the next few weeks, as I was in town. She knew that you and Nyla were at the Haleʻiwa Hotel when Amanda was killed, and of course she wants to know all of the details. The more dramatic your account, the better she'll like you, dear, and if you fuss over her house and her jewelry, you'll have her in the palm of your hand. And her house and jewelry are worth fussing over."

It was almost sunset when they reached the top of Maunalani Heights, and Ned pulled the car into Nyla and Todd's driveway. Charles Beckwith, Mina's father, came straight out of the house. He was a handsome outdoorsman, weathered in a way that only added to his good looks. He made a fuss over Mina and wanted to help her out of the car. Though she didn't really need help, Mina leaned on her father's arm and let him walk her into the house. Once inside, she sat down and repeated the whole scene of the shooting and assured him that her arm was mending nicely and that she was in no danger.

"That's enough about me, Daddy," Mina said. "How are things at the ranch?"

"Oh, rolling along," he said. "The big hitch now is that Haruko informed me she wants to retire so now I'll have to find a new cook."

"Hm." Mina pursed her lips. "I think I just might be able to help you out."

Just before dinner, Nyla herded everyone out to the patio. The evening was pleasantly cool, and she had set a table outside so that they could dine alfresco. As the sky darkened, the garden lanterns cast a soft glow over the company. Grandma Hannah helped Nyla serve a crisp green salad first, with fresh sweet tomatoes and just the right amount of watercress. Once the salad plates were whisked away, Todd carried out a large pot of paella.

"Mrs. Olivera wants everyone to know," Nyla announced, "that this is her grandmother's dish. Her grandmother came from Spain to Portugal and married her grandfather."

"Handed-down recipes are usually the best," Grandma Hannah remarked.

"I think it has a little Portuguese sausage," Nyla continued, "and lots of seafood. She spent quite a bit of time making it and sent Mr. Olivera out somewhere to buy this table wine for us."

Everyone was delighted with the dish and the wine. Ned remarked on how few Americans appreciated wine, and Nyla suggested they all go on a campaign to drink more wine with dinner. It touched Ned to see that Charles paid particular attention to Mina. Watching them, Ned couldn't help but think of his own father. Old feelings of loneliness and longing washed over him, and he felt just as he had when he was seven years old, with his father recently buried. A string of events—cricket matches, graduations, and opening nights, when he would have given the world to see his father standing there, cheering him on—streamed through his mind. He sipped his wine and firmly suppressed the familiar inner scenario, and it took him a moment to realize that Charles was saying something interesting about the legendary Winston Lennox.

"We used to call him Tarzan, the wild man," Charles said, laughing. "When we were in high school, we had a spot in Nuʻuanu up in the back of the valley where we'd go and drink beer. There were all these vines hanging from the trees and Win used to like to swing from them and beat his chest like Tarzan."

"Somehow, I can't imagine Amanda married to Tarzan," Nyla said as she poured herself another glass of wine.

"Oh, he was a real ladies' man." Charles extended his glass for Nyla to fill. "And he had a penchant for working-class women. It used to drive his mother wild because he didn't like any of the society girls she was always trying to fix him up with. We were all shocked when he came home from San Francisco married to sophisticated Amanda. Of course his mother was delighted and probably relieved."

"We found out that Amanda definitely did not have very sophisticated origins," Nyla said to her father, and then proceeded to tell him what they had discovered through Mrs. Perreira.

"I'm amazed," Charles responded. "I would never have guessed."

"We aren't saying anything about it to anyone else," Mina added. "We thought it should be the Maui family's decision to tell Tessa and Sheldon."

"And Hester," Nyla added.

"That's the right way," Grandma Hannah said. "Leave it to the family. It's up to them to come forward."

"She was certainly a beauty," said Charles.

"They must have made quite a couple," Mina commented as she ran her finger around the rim of her glass.

"They looked and acted like movie stars," Charles said. "A little too affected for your mother and me. This food is terrific, Nyla. You wouldn't want to send your housekeeper over to the Big Island, would you?"

"No, sorry, Dad, no stealing Mrs. Olivera," Nyla replied.

"I know a woman who might need a job," Mina chimed in. "She would have to be trained, though. She lives in Hale'iwa. She's a widow with a baby."

"Can she cook?" Charles asked.

"I can find out, but would you hire her if she had potential?" Mina asked.

"I don't know, Mina. She'd have to be cooking for the paniolo. You know how that is."

"Are you thinking of Mrs. Shimasaki?" Nyla asked.

Mina nodded her head. "Let me call the people who know her. Who knows, Dad? She could be the perfect person for the job."

"Well," said Charles, "let's take things one step at a time. You call the people who know her, and then tell me and your grandmother what they say, and we'll go from there. I'll be depending on you, Hannah, to protect me from my daughter's enthusiasm if need be."

"Don't worry, Charles," Grandma Hannah said with confidence. "I can spot a talented cook from miles away."

"So, Todd." Charles turned to his son-in-law, who had been very quiet. "What's the latest at the station? You've hardly said a word this evening."

"Well," said Todd, "I was going to save the big news until after dessert, but since you asked, the big news is that Jack Carstairs is out on bail."

"I don't believe it!" Nyla exclaimed.

"Who bankrolled him?" Mina asked.

"It seems that his friends took up collections, and people, mostly laborers from all over the islands, not just O'ahu, contributed." Todd was quiet for a moment and then added, "The kid's made quite an impression with the people he's talked to."

"Do you know where he's gone? Where he's staying?" Mina asked.

"He's staying above that Mermaid Café with Duncan Mackenzie and his wife," Todd answered.

"Say, Mina," Charles said, attempting to steer his daughter's thoughts in a different direction. "I have to go to Maui to check out a bull at the Kilakila Ranch. Uncle Jinx has invited anyone who wants to come. Why don't you and Ned come over on the *Humu'ula*? You've never been to Maui, have you, Ned? Anyway, it's a great change from busy Honolulu. What do you say?"

"Hey, am I invited, too? Or just Mina?" Nyla pouted.

"Of course, darling," Charles said quickly. "Of course I meant you and Todd, too."

Todd chuckled. "She just means herself. She knows I can't get away."

"Then you'd be too busy to miss me, right, darling? Let's go, Mina," Nyla said. "It'll be fun. I know you love going on the freighter."

"I don't know," Mina said, frowning.

"I bet Ned wants to go, don't you, Ned?" Nyla asked.

"I would love to see something of Maui," Ned admitted.

"Well," said Mina, "only if they'll allow Ollie on the boat."

"It's a cattle boat, Mina," Nyla said. "Of course they're going to allow a dog."

"I don't know if you realize this," Charles said to Mina, "but those Portuguese water dogs are quite rare now. He's a very valuable dog."

"Are you valuable?" Mina smiled as she petted Ollie.

"If he's ever a bother to you, I'd be happy to have him at the ranch," Charles said.

"Nice try, Dad." Mina gave her father a wry smile. "But, sorry, he's mine."

12

SATURDAY

NYLA EASED THE sedan along a wide driveway, bordered by a precisely trimmed mock orange hedge. The drive ended in a roundabout that enclosed a grassy circle with a birdbath at its center surrounded by a profusion of small, pink roses. A deep, shady portico sheltered the grand wooden doorway to Violet Lennox's whitewashed Mediterranean house. The neighborhood was tucked away at the base of Round Top Drive, in a small area sheltered by the ancient volcanic cone of 'Ualaka'a. It was a quiet, older neighborhood with well-established gardens where people with money and family connections preferred to live. A Japanese woman in a blue silk kimono had already opened the door as Mina, Nyla, and Grandma Hannah ascended the tiled stairs. The woman bowed slightly and extended her arm in a welcoming gesture. She led the way through a parlor with high ceilings and timbered beams, past the dining room and its thick Chinese carpet and magnificent dining table, and out onto a loggia with a perfectly set luncheon table where Violet Lennox was installed in a dress of pale pink linen and a string of large white pearls with matching earrings, her gray hair swept up and expertly pinned. Mina thought she looked like the perfect Honolulu matriarch.

"Please forgive me for not greeting you at the door," Violet apologized, raising her walking stick to assure them she was a semi-invalid, "but the doctor has ordered me to avoid any unnecessary steps these days."

"Of course, we understand, Violet, dear," said Grandma Hannah, just before she delivered the obligatory kiss on Violet's cheek. "I don't know if you've met my granddaughters, Mina and Nyla."

"So kind of you lovely girls to come; please sit down, in whichever place you like." Violet waved her hand and then turned to the Japanese woman. "Fumi, I think we will start with the iced tea right away. It's so warm this afternoon."

With only a soft rustle of her kimono, Fumi instantly disappeared.

Mina sat facing the back garden. A rectangular fishpond with a border of grass took up most of the small backyard. Green lily pads and water lilies covered the pond's surface, but Mina thought she detected the movement of fish ever so slightly breaking the stillness of the water. Planted terraces rose up behind the house like wide steps cut into the hillside and created the effect of a private amphitheatre, with the loggia as a central stage. Mina wondered what kind of scenes had passed over this space. It was a pleasant, beautiful, and protected place, she thought, with its thick walls and polished concrete floors— the kind of place that wealthy people get to pass their lives in. Mina was startled from her thoughts when she realized that Fumi had quietly come up behind her to fill her glass with iced tea.

"This is a lovely home you have, Mrs. Lennox," Mina said as she reached for the sugar bowl and dropped two cubes in her tea.

"Thank you, darling; I've been here for a very long time." Violet seemed quite pleased with the compliment. "It's difficult to keep up such a big house, but I can't see living anywhere else. I'm a bit lonely at times, but I suppose that's to be expected at this age."

"Didn't you mention your grandson was coming to stay?" Grandma Hannah asked as she placed her napkin neatly on her lap.

"Yes, Sheldon will be moving into the cottage. He doesn't want to stay in Henry's house now that his mother is gone. And the girls aren't really his sisters, just *half*-sisters, as you know. But, I don't suppose he'll have much time for me. He's always out and about somewhere. If it's not polo, it's golf or tennis or his ponies on Maui."

"Still," remarked Grandma Hannah, "it will be nice to have him close by."

"Yes," said Violet. "But if you don't mind, I want to hear about this dreadful shooting from your granddaughters, every detail now; don't leave anything out."

Mina and Nyla once again repeated the story and everything leading up to the shooting, from the boarding of the train to the tragic events of Sunday morning. They took turns speaking as Fumi served a cold beet soup, curried chicken salad with chutney and peanuts on a bed of lettuce, and homemade rolls with butter. Violet interrupted every so often with a question, but by the time the mango bread and ice cream dessert was being served, Mina and Nyla had finished their story. Fumi stood unobtrusively in the background, waiting to pour more tea or remove a plate. Mina wondered how much of the story she was taking in and what she thought about it.

"I was so fond of Amanda, you know," Violet said, sighing. "We stayed very close after Winston passed away. Even after she married that milquetoast, Henry. I understood. She was still young and had the rest of her life to think about, but to tell you the truth, she never cared for Henry the way she cared for Winston. She told me so herself. 'I'll never love him the way I loved Winston.' That's what she told me just before she married him." Violet gave a satisfied nod.

"I've seen a photo of your son," Mina said. "He was certainly handsome."

"Oh, he was handsome, all right." Violet sat up a little straighter. "I'll tell you, he had women eating out of his hand. And I was so worried because he was always flirting with these common girls— you know, waitresses, farm girls, girls who worked in the cannery, or worse, as a maid in the hotels."

Mina cast a glance in Fumi's direction, but Fumi stood statue still, as if she hadn't heard a thing.

"You can imagine how thrilled I was when he brought Amanda back as his bride. She was so beautiful, so sophisticated. They were the most attractive couple on the island. Now, I've heard they let that Jack Carstairs out on bail."

"Yes, they have," Nyla said.

"I suppose he did it." Violet fussed with her napkin. "But there are a lot of others who don't like Henry, including his own brother. Although I can't say I blame him, after what Henry did."

"What's that?" Mina asked, trying her best to sound innocently interested.

"Why, he cheated him, that's what he did!" Violet took a bite of her mango bread. "He and his brother Gilbert were supposed to have equal control over the business, but, you see, Henry was always his mother's favorite. The father was very fair when he was alive, but Adeline Burnham, she had control after their father died. Anyway, Henry went to his mother behind his brother's back with a new will leaving a higher percentage of the business interests to himself, and a controlling interest over the rest of the estate, their family land, and such. Gilbert knew nothing about it until his mother died a few months later. I've never liked Henry. He never took any interest in Sheldon. That's why Sheldon is moving back here. He says he just can't feel comfortable in Henry's house now that his mother is gone."

"That's very understandable," Grandma Hannah said. "He and his mother were quite close."

"Poor dear." Violet shook her head. "He's a sensitive boy. Don't you believe we can sometimes feel what's happening to our loved ones, even across great distances? Now, the morning Amanda was shot, when Sheldon was miles away, playing polo at Kapiʻolani Park, his game was simply off, and I'm certain it was because some part of him felt the shock. I was there to watch him play. I like to go as often as my health allows. Do you girls like polo?"

"Oh, yes," Mina replied, smiling. "It's so exciting." She felt an ache creeping into her shoulder and hoped the lunch wouldn't go on much longer so she could go home and rest.

"The girls are expert riders," Grandma Hannah said, beaming. "They've been around horses all their lives, because of the ranch."

"Why, of course," said Violet, finishing her dessert and motioning Fumi to clear the table. "We have a little place on Maui, you know. Not really a ranch, just a country house on a few acres with a stable and an exercise ring. My husband and I bought it when we first married. We had such good times there when Winston was a boy. But Amanda hated Maui for some reason. She never wanted to go there. And now, I can't go anymore, but Sheldon uses it to raise his ponies. It's up in the Kula area."

"Those are lovely pearls," Nyla commented.

"Why, thank you." Violet smiled. "My husband bought them for me on our tour of Japan. They just seem to grow more beautiful with age."

"And you certainly have one of the best housekeepers in Honolulu," Nyla added. "Fumi is so quiet and efficient."

"Oh, I don't know what I would do without her." Violet was emphatic. "She is a jewel. But we are having so much trouble, though, finding some reliable temporary help. Getting the cottage ready for Sheldon and doing some of the very heavy cleaning, windows and such."

"I know two young girls who are looking for summer work," Mina said.

Grandma Hannah chuckled. "Mina seems to have become an employment agent this summer."

"Fumi really does need some help," said Violet.

"These are sweet, hard-working girls," Mina said, "and very honest, but the only problem is they live in Hale'iwa, so they would need a place to stay while they worked in town." The aching in her shoulder was on the verge of pain, but she was still able to manage it.

"Do you know them personally?" Violet asked.

"We do," Nyla joined in. "Their parents run the Hale'iwa Hotel or Club, or whatever it is now. They're used to cleaning and housework."

"It would be a problem," said Violet, "if they didn't have a place to stay."

"They could stay with me," Nyla offered. "I adore them, and after they helped Fumi, they could help out at our house. Our windows and walls need a good cleaning, too."

"I'm very interested," Violet said eagerly. "I want Sheldon here as soon as possible. Maybe you could give these girls a call when you get home. They are decent girls, now, not wild or unruly?"

"They are very well-behaved girls," Grandma Hannah said with authority. "Charming and unspoiled."

As Nyla drove back to the bungalow, Mina lay down in the back seat. As she tried to will the pain in her shoulder into subsiding, she fell into a deep sleep. When she arrived home, she was able to walk herself into her bedroom, where she slept again and dreamed of playing polo on her father's ranch.

It was early evening when Ned arrived at the Aliʻi Theatre. It was not far from the bungalows and sat atop a hill above the small neighborhood of Kaimukī, just behind the fire station. Ned stopped to admire the sunset. From one perspective, there was a marvelous view of Waikīkī, the city, and the side of Diamond Head crater. Turning to the right, the Koʻolau Mountains swept up against the blue and white of the sky. If one turned again, the view stretched along the curving coastline, all the way out to Koko Head. The days were getting longer, and although it was nearly six, the sky was still bright and sunny.

As he walked toward the backstage entrance off the parking lot, he saw Emil Devon and Tessa Burnham standing on either side of the door. They were standing there with their arms folded, staring each other down, and Ned thought maybe they had just had a disagreement. Because they were quiet, he thought it would be safe to walk straight between them to the door, but suddenly Tessa started in again. Ned froze in his tracks. He couldn't believe they didn't see him.

"Why don't you trust me?" Tessa shouted.

"Why won't *you* trust *me?*" Emil answered.

"I want to know where you were!"

"And I told you, it's none of your business!" His voice ratcheted up a notch.

"Look, I know you hate my father!"

"So give me one good reason why I shouldn't—," he yelled.

"I just need to know if you—," she yelled back.

Ned cleared his throat, and they both turned and looked at him, surprised that they hadn't seen him standing there. Tessa blanched slightly and Emil's face reddened.

"Excuse me," Ned said as he stepped between them, opened the door, and went inside.

The door closed behind him, and he realized he'd witnessed a very revealing conversation that he would have to discuss with Mina. He paused for a moment and let the cool, dark, windowless silence of the theatre replace the brilliant afternoon light. The irony of the space struck Ned, as it often did when he entered a theatre. It was supposed to be a space in which a mirror of reality was held up to an audience, but to do so required being completely shut off from the outside world.

He made his way along the hall to find Johnny Knight. The staff offices on one end were separated from the men's and women's dressing rooms on the other end by the costume shop. Two sets of stairs at either end led up to the stage level. One set of stairs ended in the wings of the right side of the stage and the entrance to the scene shop, while the other set ended in the wings of the left side of the stage. Off to the left of the stage was the green room, a lounge in which actors could wait between entrances and exits without having to go down to the dressing rooms. From the green room, a door opened outside to a small patio with a few chairs for smokers. Because of the fire hazard, smoking in the backstage area was discouraged, but not totally forbidden. Johnny wasn't in his office. Ned sat for a few minutes, then decided to go upstairs and wait for him on stage.

As Ned walked out onto the stage, he saw Emil sitting alone on the edge of the apron, staring out at the audience seats. A table and chairs were set up on stage for an initial reading. The scripts were all in place and the work lights already on. Ned was about to approach Emil when Johnny burst onto the stage.

"What ho! Ned, you're here!" Johnny smiled with his usual enthusiasm. "I just went for doughnuts, and there's a pot of coffee and a pot of tea on the table back there. We can't have a first read through without doughnuts."

"Heaven forbid," Ned said with a laugh.

"The others are arriving," Johnny said as he opened the box of doughnuts and helped himself to the biggest one he could find. "Louis Goldburn just pulled up, right behind Nyla and Mina. I've asked Mina to read the stage directions. We'll have to work out which ones to keep and which ones to leave out for the reading."

Before everyone got settled, Ned just managed to pull Mina aside and tell her about what he'd seen pass between Emil and Tessa, but soon everyone was comfortably seated around the table with their scripts, doughnuts, and cups of coffee, and they began to read through the play. There was a particular magic, Ned thought, in hearing your words read through the voices of others, and in watching the characters you only imagined in your mind taking shape before your eyes. Johnny had been right about both Sheldon Lennox and Emil Devon. Sheldon was a natural, instinctive actor whose subconscious immediately grasped the nature of a character and translated it seemingly without effort. Beneath Emil's restraint, Ned could sense the kind of emotional energy that would reach out to an audience and enrich his performance. Christian Hollister and Nyla had appeared in one of Ned's plays earlier in the year, so Ned was familiar with their acting abilities, and Johnny had been right about the tension between Louis and Christian. It served the play and their characters very well. Ned couldn't help but notice the glances Christian cast in Mina's direction whenever she read a stage direction, any more than he could help but notice the way Mina winced slightly when she moved her shoulder.

Two pleasurable hours passed quite quickly, and at the end of the reading everyone felt a kind of camaraderie, as if they had just taken a long drive together. Johnny gave some directions to the actors before going over the rehearsal and performance schedule. They would have only four, possibly five, rehearsals before reading the play for the public. When the rehearsal was over, they talked about heading to the Harbor Grill for dinner. Louis said he couldn't go, and so did Emil. Sheldon left the theatre and said he needed to get some gas, but that he would meet them there. Nyla went to phone Todd, who was working late, to see if he could join them. To Ned's disappointment, Christian eagerly agreed to go along. But right on cue, just as they were cleaning up, Lamby Langston, Christian's girlfriend, marched onto the stage, flaunting her expensive clothes, her striking figure, and her eye-catching blonde hair. She cast a suspicious eye at Mina, who failed to notice because she was asking Johnny a question about the script.

"There you are, Chris!" Lamby smiled a petulant smile. "I thought you were going to call me after the rehearsal. It's nearly nine and I'm absolutely famished."

"Well, you're just on time, then," Christian replied. "We're all headed for the Harbor Grill."

"The Harbor Grill?" Lamby scrunched up her nose as if she

smelled something bad, but immediately caught herself and said sweetly, "But wouldn't you all rather go to the Kamaʻāina Club? It's so much nicer."

"No," said Johnny, looking at Lamby from across the stage where he was talking to Mina, "we would *not* rather go to the Kamaʻāina Club. We're slumming it at the Harbor Grill." He immediately turned back to Mina to finish what he was saying to her.

"Oh," said Lamby, in a voice that sounded a little too sweet, "okay, that sounds like fun."

The Harbor Grill in downtown Honolulu was a working-class café and a favorite spot with local people. There were too many in their party to sit in one of the wooden booths, so they chose a big, round table in the middle of the floor. It was just after nine and the dinner crowd had thinned out, but there were still a few people in booths and single diners sitting on the red-topped stools along the counter. Christian maneuvered a place right next to Mina, and Lamby quickly grabbed the place on the other side of him. Ned thought about moving to Mina's side, but decided that he didn't want to seem worried or possessive. Johnny sat next to Mina, and Ned sat next to him, with Nyla on his right, leaving one place for Sheldon, who hadn't shown up yet.

"Did you get a hold of Todd?" Ned asked Nyla.

"No," she answered. "He wasn't available, so I left a message for him. I doubt he'll show up."

A waitress in a white uniform that looked like it had seen a hard night appeared with a tray of water glasses and passed out plastic-covered menus. She informed everyone that they had run out of the oxtail stew special. Johnny let out a sigh of disappointment, and Ned thought he saw Lamby cringe at the mention of oxtails. While they perused the menu, the waitress slapped down cutlery, rolled in a paper napkin, in front of each person. After she had gone around the table, she took out her pencil and paper and stood there, expecting to immediately take their orders.

"Separate checks?" the waitress asked.

"No," said Christian. "One check. My treat, folks."

"That's very kind of you, Chris." Nyla smiled while Lamby beamed with pride as if *she* were treating everyone.

"Yes, thanks," Ned joined in.

"Does anyone know what they want?" the waitress asked with a hint of impatience. She took their orders, and just as she left, Sheldon strolled in and took the empty seat between Nyla and Lamby.

"You wouldn't believe how long it took me just to fill the car up," Sheldon complained. "There was only one pump working instead of two, and there were three people ahead of me, and the one and only attendant worked at a snail's pace. He fussed over every tire until he was satisfied that the pressure was perfect. And, I'm sure now I have the cleanest car windows in Honolulu."

"Gee, where did you go?" Mina asked, laughing. "Sounds like a place I need to take my car to."

"What's everyone having? I'm half-starved." Sheldon immediately began scanning the menu, flagged down the waitress, and asked for the teriyaki steak plate with fried rice and tossed salad.

"How is your arm, Mina?" Christian asked in a confidential tone.

"It's much better," Mina said, although she could feel little twinges of pain when she moved it. "I think I'll be able to drive again in a couple of days. Thanks so much for the flowers. They were lovely."

Lamby heard Mina. She gave Christian a dark look and squirmed in her seat.

"Oh, they were from all of us," Christian said smoothly. "Everyone at the paper chipped in."

"I see," Mina said with a forced smile. "How thoughtful." She distinctly remembered two bouquets, one from the staff and one signed personally from Christian.

The waitress came by with two bowls of potato chips. "These are complimentary, since you have such a large group."

They all started in on the potato chips, and in no time the waitress was placing plates and bowls of food in front of them. Ned had eaten here before with Todd and enjoyed this quintessential American diner with an island twist. He had nearly finished his cheeseburger and chocolate shake, and had just ordered a slice of the diner's famous apple pie, when a young man approached the table and discreetly whispered in Ned's ear. Ned excused himself, and when he returned to the table, he apologized for having to leave.

"Would you mind taking my slice of pie with you?" he asked Mina. "Maybe you could leave it at my place when you get home."

"You'd trust her not to eat it?" Nyla said with a laugh.

"But where are you going?" Mina looked puzzled.

"I'd forgotten I have to meet someone," Ned said, a worried look on his face.

Ned thanked Christian, wished everyone a good night, and left the restaurant. Everyone else had dessert and left the restaurant about a half an hour later, extremely full and mostly happy.

"Do you know where Ned was going?" Mina asked Nyla as soon as they got into the car.

"Not exactly," said Nyla as she started the engine, "but that was one of Todd's boys that he left with, so I'd bet something has happened."

A brief rainsquall had just passed by when Ned stepped out of the automobile and into the Chinatown scene. The light from the streetlamps made the sidewalks and the road glisten in the night. Up ahead an ambulance and a couple of police vehicles were parked on the eerily empty street. Ned and his companion moved toward the group of men clustered in an untidy circle. The flash of a camera signaled the seriousness of the situation, and Ned immediately wondered who it was who lay lifeless on the cold, wet ground. A stray dog was making his way along the curb on the opposite side of the roadway. The dog stopped and scratched himself while looking directly at Ned before continuing along the wet sidewalk. Todd spotted Ned and broke away from the group to meet him. Todd's face looked pale and haggard—a sure sign, Ned knew, that there was a body.

"Jesus." Todd sucked in his breath. "I hate this part of being a cop." He took a small flask out of his raincoat pocket and took a surreptitious sip.

"What happened?" Ned asked.

"Hit-and-run." Todd looked back over his shoulder.

"And why did they call you in?"

"One of the boys who answered the call recognized the victim as someone I was interested in."

"Who is it?"

Todd shook his head and walked back toward the group, motioning Ned to follow him. The doctor stood by making notes while the photographer snapped pictures, and in the moments in between the sharp flashes of light, Ned recognized the profile of Lars Bruhn. He lay on his back, his upper torso twisted to the right and his left arm curving over his head, which was encircled with a halo of blood. His blue eyes stared vacantly into oblivion. There were no visible injuries to the rest of his body, and Ned guessed that the impact as his head hit the pavement must have instantly killed him. Thrown next to the body was an X made of crudely tied sticks. It was beginning to drizzle again, and the body was being covered with a veil of tiny raindrops.

"Did anyone see anything?" Ned asked in a low voice as they walked a few feet away and leaned into the darkness of a brick archway.

"Someone did, but we don't know who."

"Anonymous phone call?"

"It must have come in right after it happened."

"It could have been the killer." Ned sighed. "I think our Mr. Bruhn was meant to be found right away. Say, is there a pay phone nearby?"

"I think there's one just around the corner. What's so urgent?"

"I might be able to find something out. I'll be right back." Ned turned on his heel and disappeared around the corner.

When he returned a few minutes later, the body was covered and being moved on a stretcher into the waiting ambulance, and the men were dispersing. The rain began to come down in earnest as Todd and Ned made a dash down the street to Todd's car. They sat there for a few minutes without saying anything.

"Are you all right now, old man?" Ned broke the silence.

"Aw, I'm fine," Todd answered. "Now I'm just hungry."

"Did the doctor come up with anything?" Ned asked as he rolled down his window a little. Fresh air began to circulate through the interior of the car.

"Nothing we couldn't guess," Todd replied. "He hadn't been dead long. His skull was severely fractured. He probably was hemorrhaging internally. Stuff you'd expect from being whacked by a car."

"At a high speed, I assume?"

"I'd put money on that, too," Todd agreed.

"If I found you some information about this, would you be willing to protect the source?" Ned gave Todd a slight smile.

"What? Whadda you mean?" Todd frowned.

"Just what I said." Ned looked out the window and then back at him. "I might have some useful information about this, but you'd have to promise to protect the source. No statements, no further official inquiries."

"Take it or leave it, huh?"

"Take it or leave it, huh," Ned repeated.

"Jesus H." Todd shook his head as he started up the car. "Okay, Sherlock, where are we going?"

"Just a few blocks away, to the home of Uncle Wing Chang."

"I should have guessed." Todd sighed. "Oh, well, at least we'll get a decent cup of coffee, and maybe some dessert."

In a few minutes they were parked in front of a long storefront with plate-glass windows and stunning Asian antiques on display. A small sign in the bottom corner of the window read "Unusual Fireworks, Inquire Within." They walked down along the alley on the side of the store to a doorway. Ned knocked on the door, and it was unlocked and opened a few inches by Cecily Chang.

"A late-night visit from the gumshoes," she said in a low, conspiratorial tone, before she laughed and welcomed them in.

"You're working late yourself." Ned noted the lights in her office.

"I'm unpacking some exquisite artwork from Japan. Come and take a peek on your way out. There are some remarkable prints. Dad's waiting for you upstairs." Cecily pointed to the staircase just inside as she carefully relocked the door. "See you later."

Ned and Todd made their way up the stairs to the Changs' living area and into Uncle Wing's kitchen lair. The copper pots and pans hanging from a rack above gleamed, and the smell of baked apples permeated the room. There were three places set at the table. There was also cream and sugar, a plate of cheese and sliced fresh pears, and a steaming pot of coffee. Uncle Wing motioned them to sit down and served each of them a warm piece of what looked like apple pie, but much more elegant.

"It's called tarte tartin." Uncle Wing smiled when he saw the puzzled look on Todd's face. "You'll think that apple pie at the Harbor Grill is barbaric after this."

Todd took a bite and said, "How much do I have to pay you to teach Nyla to make this?"

"Anytime she wishes, I'm here to shine a light on *la cuisine française*. There is no decent cookbook in English. I learn what I can from hotel chefs, and on my visits to San Francisco," Uncle Wing said as he poured the coffee. "So, you've agreed to the conditions, Detective Forrest?"

"I don't see as I have much choice." Todd looked at both of them.

"And there's no doubt that this incident isn't an accident? A hit-and-run by a frightened driver who left the scene?" Uncle Wing asked.

Todd shook his head. "No chance. The driver left an unmistakable calling card."

"You were able to discover something?" Ned stirred his coffee and looked expectantly at Uncle Wing.

"Yes. I think it will help you in a small way, but I don't know if it will lead you to the killer," Uncle Wing began. "As you know, Todd, there is a high-stakes poker game in Honolulu that floats from place to place, and Lars Bruhn was often a participant. I happen to know someone connected to these games, and don't ask me who or how, because I won't tell you. What I will tell you is this: Mr. Bruhn was playing poker tonight somewhere in Chinatown. Sometime around nine he excused himself from the table to receive a phone call. After two more hands, he excused himself again and said that he was stepping out for a few minutes and would be back in a half an hour. As a sign of good faith, he left his winnings with the bank there, and from what I understand he was having an excellent night. He did not return. The only thing that was heard by my informant of his phone conversation was, 'Don't worry, darling, I'll be there.'"

"Sounds as if someone made an arrangement to meet him." Ned took a sip from his coffee cup. "And then killed him."

"It could be one person," Todd said, "or two people working together. If so, one of them may be a woman."

"You mean he thought he was going to meet a woman for quick sex and instead was killed by an accomplice?"

Todd nodded. "Something like that. It could be a revenge killing. Shimasaki's widow lures him out into the night, and one of Shimasaki's union friends runs him over with a car."

"Or Henry Burnham has Gwendolyn Reed arrange a meeting and then has him killed because he knows too much, and because it will take the pressure off with the workers and relieve any suspicion that may fall on himself?" Ned speculated.

"Or his brother and the wife? Or that Emil Devon and Tessa Burnham?" Todd continued.

"I hope it's some help to you," said Uncle Wing. "He was not a very good man, but no man deserves to be murdered."

"Even one who's murdered someone else?" Todd asked.

"That is my moral opinion," Uncle Wing stated. "Although I know there are many people who disagree with me."

"I'm not one of them," Ned volunteered. He had finished his tart and was helping himself to a fresh pear slice and a piece of cheese.

Uncle Wing turned to Todd. "And how do you feel about it, Detective?"

"To tell you the truth"—Todd had finished his tart and was unashamedly licking his fork—"I'm not sure. I waver back and forth on the issue. On the one hand it seems like a fair end for a heinous killer, and on the other hand it seems hypocritical to say murder is wrong and then murder someone for murdering. Not to mention the danger of executing an innocent person."

"Your answer has earned you a second piece of tarte tartin." Uncle Wing clapped his hands. "If you care for one, that is."

"If I care for one? Are you kidding?" Todd handed over his plate. "It's too bad you can't tell us who your informant is, Uncle Wing."

"Never," said Uncle Wing, as he served Todd another piece of tarte tartin. "I may want to be in on that game myself someday. I am an excellent poker player, you know."

13

SUNDAY

THE DAY WAS sunny, with a fine breeze that rolled in waves through the tall, green leaves of cane. The coupe hummed along while Ned drove and Mina gazed, lost in thought, at the sunlight and shadows moving over the Wai'anae mountain range. Ollie had curled up in the back seat and gone to sleep. Up ahead, Ned could see Todd's car. Nyla's window was rolled down, and he could just make out her elbow as it leaned into the bottom of the frame, her hand resting on the top. He could see the outlines of Charles and Grandma Hannah in the back seat. They were all headed for Hale'iwa on the ribbon of road that stretched from the Pearl Harbor area between the two island mountain ranges to the north shore of the island.

"How long do you think you'll be with Todd?" Mina asked.

"I'm not sure," Ned answered. "I know he wants to look over Bruhn's house. I don't know what else he has planned."

"Dad's excited about seeing the old hotel," she said, smiling. "Grandma's friend is a member of the club, and she's arranged it so we can have lunch and use all of the facilities. She said no one has even been there since the shooting."

He looked over at her. "People will forget."

"I hope so," she said in a soft voice. "So are there any guesses about Lars Bruhn?"

"No real leads, but it definitely wasn't an accident."

"This confuses and complicates things, doesn't it?" She looked out at the fields, which had changed from sugarcane to pineapple. "I mean, it makes it look more like it could have been some kind of revenge for Shimasaki's death."

"It looks that way, doesn't it?" Ned agreed. "But on the other hand it could be a false trail, engineered by someone who just wanted to get, and who still might want to get, Henry Burnham out of the picture. Although unnecessary murder is a drastic style of misdirection."

"Or," said Mina, "the two things could be unrelated. In crime number one, someone wants Henry dead, and in crime number two, someone else, possibly many others, want to see Lars Bruhn pay for their friend's death."

"Thinking on those lines, I would place Emil Devon, perhaps helped by Tessa, in the first category, and also Gilbert Burnham, perhaps aided by his Helen."

"What about the secretary? Gwen?"

"She could make list one," Ned replied, "but only if she was an accomplice. I feel she doesn't have the drive or a strong motive on her own. What would her motive be? Revenge for her lover not leaving his wife?"

"It's happened before," Mina observed. "So that leaves Jack Carstairs on the second list, and maybe worker or workers unknown out for payback?"

"And," Ned added, "they might be working on their own *or* they might be working with Jack, but Jack and worker or workers unknown could definitely be on list number one, too."

"So what do you think of Nyla's theory that Amanda hired someone with bad aim to kill her husband?" She yawned.

"Sounds like a bad plot from a cheap mystery."

"A cheap mystery with a villain called Orsino Hood?" She shook her head. "But what about Lars Bruhn? What was he like?"

"Let's see," Ned began, "he was a Scandinavian who liked to use a whip on his workers. He fancied himself a Lothario, and he had vulgar pictures of half-naked women on his parlor wall. He gambled. In certain quarters he is referred to as 'Louse' Bruhn. Trust me, darling, he wasn't your type at all."

Ollie bounded out as soon as Mina opened the car door. He ran around the lawn in front of the hotel and back to Mina's side as she followed the others up to the veranda. Charles and Grandma Hannah wandered over the ground floor, reminiscing about what it was like many years ago, while Michiko and Tamiko, who were supposed to be laying out the table for morning coffee, kept asking Mina and Nyla questions about their summer job and Violet Lennox until their mother chased them into the kitchen.

"We do have to go to Maui for a few days," Nyla reminded Masami. "But Grandma Hannah will be looking after the girls at our house, and Mrs. Lennox promised to have her driver pick them up and drop them off every day."

"I hope they won't be too much trouble for your grandmother," Masami said.

"Our grandmother had to deal with me and Nyla," Mina said to her, "and your daughters are perfect angels compared to us."

"I was hoping that they could stay a few extra days in town after they finish at the Lennox house," Nyla added. "I thought they could help Mrs. Olivera do the windows and the walls at my house. It's such a big job and it hasn't been done for ages."

Masami nodded. "Yes, yes. Hardly anybody coming out here all month. I think everybody scared now."

"I bet people will be back by July," Nyla said. "Todd and I have talked about trying to become members. It's a lovely place for an escape."

Mina listened to her sister and then walked to the end of the veranda, standing a little apart from the others. With Ollie at her side, she stared out toward the sea. Today it was calm and glassy. She could hear Nyla chatting away with Masami and the girls, and even though they were right there, they seemed distant, miles away. *It's a lovely place for an escape* echoed in her mind. That's what Amanda Burnham may have thought when she arrived here. *An escape. What a strange word to describe a holiday,* she mused, as if regular, daily life were a prison. For Amanda it was the ultimate escape, and now she was so far gone, she couldn't ever come back. And Henry Burnham, he almost escaped. *And I did, too,* she thought. *I came very near escaping.*

Mina felt her stomach falling suddenly and her body becoming hollow and stretched out like a shadow, as if she weren't quite there.

The thought came to her that maybe she was really dead—maybe she had died that day on the lawn, and this was just a dream, an after-death dream. She felt so light and insubstantial, like one of those clouds out there floating way up in the sky, or like a balloon cut off from its string and flying higher and farther away. From somewhere she sensed the warmth of Ned's body next to hers. He said nothing, but led her quietly to a chair in the corner, away from the others, and got her a cup of tea and a Danish. She sipped the steaming tea until its heat made her feel comfortable and solid. She took a bite of her pastry and felt the sweet taste of sugar and cream melting in her mouth. Ned watched her carefully.

"Are you all right, Mina?" He tried to sound casual but careful.

"It's the strangest thing," Mina said. "I feel like I just woke up from a weird dream. Did I look strange?"

"I saw you go a little pale," Ned whispered. "I don't think anyone noticed."

"You did," she said.

"I notice everything about you."

"I don't know why I feel so peculiar," she said, a note of worry in her voice.

"You're like a soldier, darling, coming back to the scene of a battle, and what's more, there's someone else who didn't survive the battle. You're bound to feel some kind of reverberation. It happens when we come close." His voice trailed off.

"You mean close to death?"

"Yes," he answered her. "And I'm so glad you didn't go. I don't want to have to be in a world without you."

Mina wanted to answer him, but she couldn't. She was confused and unprepared for his level of intimacy and by her own inability at this moment to understand her real feelings.

The sound of chanting pierced the air, distracted them, and directed their attention to the front lawn. Ollie jumped up and cocked his head. An old Hawaiian man, a little bent over, walking with a wooden staff, was making his way over the Anahulu River on the driftwood bridge. A shock of white hair rested on the shoulders of a simple blue work shirt that was tucked neatly into a pair of dungarees. Not a tall man, his dark brown skin folded over a slight and wiry frame, but whatever he lacked in physical stature was made up for by the volume, depth, and intensity of voice, which rolled through the air. He walked steadily toward them, chanting words of greeting in rich, dark tones, and then, in the very center of the lawn, he stopped. Then they heard Grandma Hannah's voice, chanting back in answer as she came streaming out of the house to give him welcome, and when she reached him, they embraced in the old way by touching noses and taking in each other's breath. Grandma Hannah graciously took his arm and led him up to the porch. Everyone had been so focused on the interaction between the two chanters that they failed to notice the old man was followed by the cowboy, Puna, until he stepped up to take Grandma Hannah's other arm. Surprised and delighted, she gave the cowboy a kiss on the cheek.

"Kaiwi," said Grandma Hannah when they reached the veranda, "these are my two granddaughters, Nyla and Mina."

"Aloha," Mina said politely, and as she looked into his face, she recognized the man from her dream, the one she had at the hotel, and to her surprise felt at ease with the idea.

"Maybe we met somewhere before, Mina." Kaiwi's eyes danced with delight, and his broad smile revealed a missing canine tooth. "Maybe, yeah?"

"Maybe." Mina returned his smile spontaneously, as if they shared a great joke.

Grandma Hannah politely introduced everyone else and then shuttled Kaiwi toward the comfortable pūneʻe. "Come, come," she said to him, "sit down here in the shade. Nyla, dear, bring Kaiwi a nice cup of coffee and some pastries. Puna, you're young," she continued with a laugh. "You can help yourself."

"If I'm young, then you must be teenaged, Hannah." Puna winked at her and tipped his hat before heading for the coffee.

Nyla brought Kaiwi's coffee and plate of pastries, and there was a flurry of visiting and eating while everyone sorted out what they would do before lunch. Todd and Ned had business to take care of, and Masami and Tony had arranged for Mrs. Shimasaki to come to the hotel to meet Charles and Grandma Hannah.

"Say," Kaiwi said to Nyla and Mina, "why don't you two girls come on a little holoholo with me around this 'āina, and I'll show you some things. I see you have a nice car to go in."

"We'd love to," Mina and Nyla said in unison.

"Yeah." Kaiwi winked at the girls and motioned with a slight movement of his chin toward Puna, who was engaged in conversation with their grandmother. "I guess one of you girls will have to drive, because my friend Puna has found something more interesting than going holoholo with us."

Ned and Todd stood once again before the front door of Lars Bruhn's house. They were accompanied by a clerk from the plantation office who held the key and opened the door, then politely said he would wait outside until they finished. Today the house held a noticeable silence. The air in the rooms hung stagnant and heavy, and Ned immediately went around and opened several windows. The woman in the lurid velvet painting smiled down on him once again, and this time, instead of distaste, it made him feel more than a little gloomy. There wasn't much to go through in the house. Bruhn had not been one to acquire heaps of material possessions. The white rattan sofa, the chairs and coffee table, and the bar with nothing on its shelves were the only things in the parlor. One bedroom looked as if it was never used. The closet stood empty of anything personal—only a few dingy-looking blankets and sheets lay folded on the shelves. Todd headed straight for the master bedroom, so Ned went into the kitchen to have a look around.

Painted in a dull yellow, the kitchen reflected the unlived-in quality of the rest of the house. A plate, fork, and knife sat unwashed in the wide white porcelain sink, while the faucet let out a steady drip. Ned fussed with the hot and cold water handles, but the drip wouldn't stop. The window above the sink looked out onto a view of a panax hedge, and Ned remembered he had seen some children playing in a yard the other day, setting up a little tepee using panax sticks for poles. He next opened the Frigidaire. There were several bottles of beer, a jug of water, a piece of cheese, some eggs, apples, butter, and a half of a pineapple. The food cupboard was equally bare, and it looked to Ned as if he may have eaten breakfast here, but probably went out for every other meal. He went through all the other cupboards and drawers and found nothing of interest until he sat down at the painted green kitchen table that stood in a little breakfast nook. He had almost missed the drawer in the table because it had no knob and was set flush with the side underneath the tabletop.

In the drawer were several little books. One of them was a book of phone numbers and addresses, many of them with only initials. Another was a calendar book with very few dates scribbled in, but the third was a ledger book. Glued on the inside of the cover was a playing card, the jack of hearts. The first few pages listed accounts of wins and losses by date, and Ned guessed that they must be a record of Bruhn's poker games. One game seemed very regular, probably the Saturday night game he mentioned at the plantation. He always began with roughly the same amount, between twenty and thirty dollars, and faithfully listed the amount he left with at the end of the evening. The high-stakes games appeared to occur at least twice a month, and his beginning figure was always considerably higher, averaging about three hundred dollars, and from a quick survey of these records, it looked like lady luck was not only at the table with Lars Bruhn on most nights, but she often sat on his lap. It would be more than interesting, Ned thought, to see Bruhn's banking statements.

A black string marker was stuck in about halfway through, and here Ned found a different kind of list. It was a list of loans, but instead of real names, Bruhn had assigned colors. He had loaned Mr. Blue one hundred dollars with an interest rate of 20 percent on July 9, 1934, and was paid back in increments in the next four months. There were several people he regularly loaned money to—Mr. Green, Mr. Red, and Mr. Yellow, and one person, Mr. Brown, who had racked up nearly ten thousand dollars worth of debts, not including interest, to Mr. Bruhn over the last two years.

Todd walked into the kitchen. "There's nothing interesting in the bedroom except a box of condoms and some magazines with pictures of naked men and women engaged in unusual activities." He grimaced. "Some of them aren't even women; they're just little kids.

If he was still alive, I'd want to punch out his lights. What have you got there?"

"As you would say, I think I've hit the jackpot." Ned held up the ledger. "And found another reason why someone might want to hit Lars Bruhn with a car and kill him."

Mina sat in the back seat with Ollie as the car bounced along on the dirt road. Kaiwi sat in the front with Nyla and gave her instructions on which way to go. They had driven toward Kaiaka Bay, the next bay over toward the west, and turned seaward near a school and a store, crossing over the railroad tracks. The road had then turned into a dirt track, bisecting someone's vegetable gardens, and the smell of rich soil, recently turned, filled the car. Kaiwi told Nyla to stop, and they got out and walked toward the shore where a large limestone outcropping broke the otherwise flat landscape. The formation stood about ten feet tall in a crooked but conical shape and looked like a geological relic from another age.

"This is Pōhaku Lānaʻi," Kaiwi explained. "Some of the old timers believe it floated to this place from Kahiki. If you look around, no rock like this for miles. This was a place for the fish seer, the kilo iʻa, to wait and watch for fish. If he saw a good school, he beat the rock with a wooden mallet, and the hollow sound would bring all the fishermen together with nets and canoes. Men knew how to fish in those days. Now, people not so smart. Let's go down by the beach."

Mina and Nyla followed as Kaiwi led the way. The beach arched gracefully along the shore, and the three of them sat and watched as a turtle made its way out of the water and fell comfortably asleep. The waves broke in pleasing tones on the sand while the clouds sailed overhead. Ollie ran over to sniff and paw at the turtle, who made a secure retreat into its shell.

"The fishermen," Kaiwi began, "used to be more close to the sea. It ran inside them—inside their blood and inside their dreams, too, because they kept more to the old gods, the akua, the ones that helped them. Some families kept a shark—not just any shark, but the shark that was an akua of their family. They tended these sharks. Sometimes they would go in the water and scrape the shark if it had something growing on its skin, or they would feed the shark as one feeds family. And the shark would show them where the fish was, or help them find their way home if they were blown out to sea. Sometimes the akua would send a dream about where to go and fish. You think I'm talking nonsense?" Kaiwi looked slyly at them.

"No, not at all." Nyla sounded surprised.

"We would never think that," Mina joined in.

"Lots of haole people," Kaiwi began, "lots of haole people, if you tell them things like this, they think it's nonsense."

"Not us," Mina assured him.

"Well, you know," he continued, "these akua, these 'aumākua, they had rules, you see. Sometimes if one of the family broke the rules, ate something or did something they not supposed to, the shark would come and take them away. They would have to go and sleep with the shark for a few days as a punishment. Yes, I've seen the place under water where they had to lie, and a few days later they would be returned, just like that. And sometimes, at death, the akua would come for one of his family, to take him to the sea and be changed into a shark. The body would disappear from the house or the place it had been laid to rest—completely disappear. Some of the old folks said they even seen the akua come and take a person away. People in my parents' and grandparents' generation, they said they saw these things for themselves, but things like that don't happen nowadays. We stopped that kind of worship, and then it fades away. It turns into haole 'nonsense,' because they cannot believe. They cannot make any sense of it." Kaiwi laughed. "But you two know better, yeah? Let's go now. I'm getting thirsty. You girls like root beer? That's my favorite drink." He stood up and marched toward the car.

Mina whistled for Ollie, and she and Nyla followed Kaiwi.

"He's certainly a character," Nyla commented.

"A fascinating character," Mina added.

They drove back to Hale'iwa Town and stopped at a store. Nyla jumped out, went in, and came back with three root beers and three almond cookies. Kaiwi took a sip of his soda and looked out the window at the town.

"You know," he began, "Hale'iwa is not the old name of this place. It's a name that comes from the missionaries, the Emerson family. They came over here to Waialua and put up that female seminary. They called the building Hale 'Iwa after the 'iwa bird that soars in the sky. Then pretty soon the name stuck, and now it's the name of the town."

"At least it's a pretty name," Mina said as she bit into her cookie. "I think those birds are beautiful to watch."

"Let's go across the bridge now," Kaiwi said, before he started to eat his cookie. "I want to show you something over there. You know," he added, "I think that Puna would like to go with your grandmother."

"Go with our grandmother?" Nyla asked as she handed Mina her soda to hold while she got the car underway.

"That's right," Kaiwi said. "He like go home with her."

"You mean to the ranch? To the Big Island?" Mina asked. "Did he tell you that?"

"He doesn't have to tell me." Kaiwi rubbed the top of his head. "You don't believe me; you watch."

Nyla shook her head. "I doubt if our grandmother would allow that."

"You don't think so?" Kaiwi seemed very pleased with himself. "She might, you know."

They crossed over the Anahulu Bridge and had driven a little ways beyond the river when Kaiwi told Nyla to pull over to the right. They parked the car and walked away from the road until they came to a grassy knoll that overlooked a large pond surrounded by marshy wetlands. Protected by the shade of a small grove of coconut trees, they sat down and looked over the tranquil pond. Tinged with algae, the water had a deep green glow. Reeds and rushes grew along its banks. They all sat silently for a few minutes, transfixed by the beauty that surrounded them. Ollie sidled up to Kaiwi, placed his head right next to the old man, and drifted into sleep. Mina thought she saw a large fish swimming just beneath the surface.

"This is 'Uko'a." Kaiwi spoke in a quiet, low voice. "We call this kind of fishpond loko wai nui because it's not a walled pond like the ones by the sea. Mo'oinanea led the great procession of mo'o, and she was the first to reach Waolani. Laniwahine and Alamuki came at the end, and these moʻo remained here in Waialua. This is the home of Laniwahine, the akua moʻo. Sheʻs a kamaʻāina and the guardian of these waters. Under the water here is one of her nests, and there is a tunnel that connects the pond with the sea, so when Laniwahine wishes to bathe in the sea, she just goes. You girls know whatʻs a moʻo?"

"Itʻs one of the old gods," Mina answered, "who lived mostly in freshwater places and had forms like large reptiles, like lizards."

"That is only one of the forms they can take," said Kaiwi as he stared into the water. "Laniwahine sometimes appears as a beautiful woman who sits and combs her long hair. She was worshiped and brought health and abundance to the people in Waialua, and lots of fish. One used to see marvelous fishes in this pond. A fish might be a mullet on one side and a kūmū on the other, or one side might be all silver and the other side striped. But everyone knew these strange fish belonged to the moʻo, and so they left them for her."

"Our grandmother told us that she knew people who said they had really seen a moʻo," Mina said as she stretched out on the grass.

"Oh, yes," Kaiwi agreed. "When we were young, many of the old timers said they had seen. Kihawahine, the famous moʻo from the island of Maui, was often seen there at Mokuhinia. It is said she appeared before hundreds of people. She was seen when Kamehameha Kapuāiwa died, and in 1838 many people saw her when she almost tipped over the canoe that was carrying that Christian chiefess, Kekāuluohi, to church. That would have been a good joke if she fell in the water. The moʻo in their lizard body can sometimes be as big as thirty feet, and they are black as the darkest night. Sometimes people would bring them an offering of ʻawa. When the moʻo drank the ʻawa, then they would sway from side to side in the water, like the keel of a canoe."

"I wonder where they all went?" Mina said.

"Who knows." Kaiwi looked at her. "They could still be here, only we just canʻt see them anymore. Maybe Laniwahine is listening to us talking right now."

"I hope she is," Mina said, transfixed by the water.

When Todd and Ned were leaving the house, the clerk from the plantation office told them that there were some men waiting to talk to them up in the park. He asked if they would not mention to his supervisors that he had given them the message. "I owe somebody a favor," he said, before he left. "I'm not taking anybody's side."

They drove a few blocks out of the "management neighborhood" to a small park with a baseball diamond. There was a distinct smell of fresh grass, as if the park had been mowed recently. Under a tree three Asian men sat at an old picnic table. The men were dressed in old but clean clothes. They were dark from working in the sun, and their hands looked calloused and as rough as the splintered picnic table. Even though they sat somewhat hunched over, Ned could see that they were strong and powerfully built from years of hard physical labor. They didn't stand up when Ned and Todd approached, but invited them to sit down on the opposite side of the table. No one bothered to introduce themselves, either, and Ned sensed that they were alert and on guard even though they sat quietly.

"We like talk to you about Shimasaki-san," the man who looked the oldest said. "Oh, yeah, thanks for coming to listen to us."

"We're very interested in anything you could tell us." Todd assumed a neutral attitude.

"We know that da kine, Bruhn, took him away in one car."

"How do you know that?" Todd asked.

"Because some people saw him. Only thing, they scared, so they no like talk."

"Could you tell me who they are so I could question them?" Todd continued.

"No can," the man responded. "They too scared."

Todd shrugged. "There's not much I can do unless someone comes forward."

"We just like you know," the man said. "And we know was Burnham who told him for do it." Now there was a distinct tone of disgust in the man's voice. "He tells Bruhn, and Bruhn does what he says."

"I can't do much if there's no evidence." Todd scratched his head.

"Everybody getting fed up, you know," the man continued. "We not animals. We not going do nothing."

"What does that mean?" Todd asked.

"That Henry Burnham, he only hire mean kine men for luna. He thinks we not going work unless we all scared. Stupid, him. Everyone works better when they not scared, when they know they get fair treatment, when they respect the bosses, not when they hate them. Burnham's lunas, they bad men, I tell you. If a man stays home because he's sick, they go drag him from his house and force him to work. Last month, somebody died in the field. He felt sick, but he too scared for stay home because he know they going force him. So he come work, he's sick, and then he falls over, right in the field. And look what happened to Shimasaki-san. Nothing going happen to Burnham. He can just kill somebody and nothing going happen to him."

"If someone came forward, there might be something we could do," said Todd.

"Nothing you can do. No one going believe one of us against Henry Burnham." The man looked at Todd like he was crazy.

"Do you know anything about who killed Lars Bruhn?" Todd knew very well they wouldn't say anything if they did.

"No," the man said. "But plenty people no like him. No one surprised somebody kill him. He's one mean bastard, I tell you. He *likes* for hurt people. He used to smile, you know, when he use his whip on someone, small-kine smile under his hat. No one sorry he not coming back."

"Look," Todd said, taking out a scrap of paper from his pocket and writing on it. "Here's my name and phone number. If the people who saw Bruhn take Shimasaki away change their minds, call me. Otherwise, I don't know what else I can do."

"We just like you know," the man said, "why everybody stay mad like hell. That Henry Burnham, he better be careful what kine man he makes boss over us. We not going take it. Shimasaki was one good man. We not going forget what happened to him."

When Ned and Todd arrived back at the hotel, they found Charles and Puna engaged in a serious conversation on the veranda. Inside, in the cool and quiet of the parlor, Grandma Hannah was speaking to a young woman dressed in a blue-and-white kimono. They were comfortably seated in two armchairs, drinking tea. The woman's dark hair was swept up and away from a face of fine, delicate proportion and flawless skin. Her dark eyebrows arched perfectly above her active and intelligent eyes, and as she lifted her hand to tuck back a stray strand of hair, Ned observed that she made the simple act an elegant gesture. Grandma Hannah introduced Mrs. Shimasaki to Ned and Todd.

"Mrs. Shimasaki will be coming back with me to the Big Island," Grandma Hannah reported. "It's lucky for us that she wasn't under contract to the plantation anymore."

"Congratulations," Ned said, smiling.

"Mrs. Shimasaki, I don't know if you know," Todd began quietly, "that I'm a detective, a member of the Honolulu Police Department."

She nodded. "Yes, I know this. You came when there was the shooting. Everybody knows you."

"Well," Todd said, doing his best to sound kind, "now I'm looking into another death, and it's lucky that you're here because I would like to ask you some questions."

Mrs. Shimasaki looked at Grandma Hannah for a cue as to how she wanted her to behave.

"Don't worry, my dear." Grandma Hannah looked up at Todd. "I won't let him make you uncomfortable. He's married to my grand-daughter, so I can scold him if I want to. Todd, you and Ned sit down. Don't stand there towering over us."

Todd and Ned obediently sat across from the two women on the faded brown sofa.

"Okay," said Mrs. Shimasaki. "I try to answer."

"A man was killed last night in Honolulu. I believe you knew Mr. Lars Bruhn?"

"Yes," she answered. "I knew him, and I hear he died."

"A car hit him and then drove away," Todd said.

"Yes, that is what people say."

"He was your late husband's luna?"

"Yes."

"We understand many workers think your husband died under suspicious circumstances." Todd tried to choose his words carefully.

"Yes," she replied, "many people think this. I think maybe it's true."

"I hope this isn't painful for you," Ned interjected.

"No," she said emphatically. "I am glad to talk to police."

"We've heard that many people think Bruhn had something to do with your husband's death."

"Yes." She looked at Todd. "Many people think this." She paused, looked out the window, and looked to Grandma Hannah, needing to be assured. "You sure I go work for you? You sure I leave this place?"

"Yes, my dear," Grandma Hannah said in a soothing voice. "You won't have to worry about the plantation and their overseers."

Mrs. Shimasaki turned back to Todd. "They say my husband go up to the mountain and have accident. He never went that place before. Why he would go up there? I hear somebody say they saw him get into car with Bruhn, but they scared to tell. What I can do? No can prove nothing. Everyone scared all the time. This terrible place. I happy to leave with my baby."

"I understand your husband was interested in trade unions," Todd said. "That he talked to the men about it."

"Yes," she said, lowering her head. "I told him: Don't do that. Don't say those things, but he said, no, it's for everyone to have better life. For our baby to have better life. You see, men respect my husband. They look up to him, so plantation didn't like."

"Do you think many of the men were angry when your husband died?" Todd asked carefully.

"Yes," she said, "many men very angry, but very scared, too. They think: Maybe this happen to me, too."

"Do you think any of them would want to avenge your husband's death?" Todd looked away when he asked.

Mrs. Shimasaki lifted up her head and said, "I don't know. I don't know what men do. They don't tell me. But I know they very angry."

And if they did tell you, Todd thought, *you certainly wouldn't tell me.* He was quiet for a moment, then said, "I'm sorry to have to ask you this, Mrs. Shimasaki, but where were you last night between eight-thirty and ten-thirty?"

The question didn't seem to rattle her in the least. "I stay home, take care of baby, iron clothes. That is how I make money now, wash clothes and iron. Many people walk by my house. They see kerosene light. They hear baby. They see me with coals and the iron. I work very hard—after midnight, I still working. Everybody tell you."

"Of course I remember Emil's father very well," Charles said in answer to Mina's question.

They were all gathered around the old wooden table on the veranda for a late lunch and had just begun the first course of ahi poke. Kaiwi had provided the fresh fish very early in the morning. The table was set with woven lauhala place mats, and the faded brown cloth napkins were monogrammed with the initials of the hotel using thread of a darker shade. Some of the threads had pulled out. Mint and pineapple floated in pitchers of iced tea, and little bowls of sugar cubes sat along the center next to low vases that each held several blossoms from the cup-of-gold vine that grew in the garden.

"What was he like?" Mina asked.

"He was one of the nicest people I ever met," Charles said. "It's a shame he passed away like that. He was one of those genuinely good people, not a malicious bone in his body."

"I guess he was a good friend of Henry Burnham," Nyla commented.

"Was he?" Charles asked. "I really don't remember. It's certainly possible. They traveled in the same circles. I can see how Henry Burnham would gravitate to a man like Peter Devon."

"Why is that?" Mina asked, as she ate her raw fish.

"Peter had this way about him," Charles began. "He was warm. He naturally made people feel comfortable and at ease. Henry Burnham is missing all those qualities, if you ask me."

"You think Henry was attracted to the qualities in Peter Devon that he himself lacked?" Ned asked.

"Something like that," Charles responded. "It's like when one kid on the block has a fancy new two-wheeler bike and the kid who still has a tricycle wants to hang around and be his friend."

"And what about Gilbert Burnham; did you know him?" Mina asked.

"A little." Charles wiped his napkin across his lips. "In high school he was always in Henry's shadow. Henry didn't go in for contact sports, but he loved competition. He couldn't be beat in track and swimming. He was fast. And he was great on the tennis court and playing volleyball, too. Of course college is the great equalizer; everyone goes away, comes back, and has to make it in the job world. But it seems like Henry's always been determined to keep Gilbert in second place."

"I knew two brothers like that once," Kaiwi commented. "One brother always had to be the star. He always liked to lord it over his younger brother. They went fishing one day and there was some bad weather. Only the younger one came back."

"You think he killed him?" Todd asked.

"Maybe. He had plenty anger inside him. But nobody can prove anything." Kaiwi then started in on the second course of ginger soup with shrimp dumplings. "Umm, this soup is 'ono. Nowadays, hard to find someone who can make the broth just right."

"We understand you'll have a new cook at the ranch," Ned said to Charles.

"Not right away," Grandma Hannah chimed in. "Haruko will have to train her for a few months before she can take over, but I think she'll fit into the ranch family perfectly."

"It will be a wonderful place for her to raise her child," Nyla added.

"And we have another addition to the ranch." Charles leaned back in his chair and took a sip of iced tea. "I've stolen Puna away from his present employer. He's going to be an Uluwehi paniolo by next month, and we're lucky to have him. You girls probably didn't know he's one of the best horse trainers in the islands."

Mina tried not to look too surprised, but Nyla had to quickly cover her mouth with her napkin and try not to cough iced tea onto her blouse. Mina noticed that Grandma Hannah was looking non-chalantly over the lawn with a very self-satisfied expression on her face. Kaiwi looked directly at Mina and raised his eyebrows.

Charles Beckwith, oblivious to any subtext at the table, kept on. "It's so rare that I find someone who knows what they're doing with the horses. There're lots of younger men, but Puna here has a real reputation."

Kaiwi smiled. "I'll say."

14

MONDAY

"I CAN'T BELIEVE that Daddy hired that cowboy," Nyla said as she pulled into a parking stall on Merchant Street.

"I tried to talk to Grandma about it," Mina said. "She just smiles and says she had nothing to do with it." She looked over at the Burnham and Robbins building. "I'm not sure if I'm ready to dive into the Inferno first thing in the morning."

"Come on," Nyla said with a laugh. "It's not that bad."

"Close enough," Mina answered. "Look, here comes Cecily, right on time. It's just nine."

When they entered the building, Mina and Cecily insisted on buying a box of pastries and cups of coffee from the bakery. They went upstairs and into the sitting room, now empty of all furniture except a small table and chairs. The crew had come in over the weekend, and the room stood newly painted and the wooden floors freshly polished. The double doors between the conference room and the sitting room had been expertly widened, and when opened now allowed an easy flow between the two rooms. Two large new carpets lay rolled along one wall, and several large boxes containing artwork were carefully place around the room. Cecily had seen to their delivery earlier.

After they had made short work of the pastries, they moved into the conference room, where the largest of the boxes waited for them. The room was also freshly painted, and a new, sleek koa conference table, also delivered earlier that morning, stood surrounded by simple but elegant chairs of the same rich wood.

"Wow! That's some table." Cecily ran her finger over the rich, deep-grained top.

"It was a stroke of luck," Nyla said. "Somebody ordered it and couldn't pay up."

"It looks like it was made for this room." Cecily tried out one of the chairs.

"I got it for a good price, too," Nyla mentioned with self-satisfaction.

"Now remember," Cecily said, "if Burnham changes his mind, any of this is returnable. They're such great pieces. I'm sure I'd have no problem selling them to someone else."

They carefully unpacked a long and beautifully framed piece of Chinese brushwork, done horizontally on a scroll of rice paper, laying it out on the new table. Line and paper merged in an integrated embrace to depict the shoreline of Honolulu, the Koʻolau Mountains, and the sky above. The rhythmic flow of the brushwork captured the serenity of the island landscape as seen from offshore.

"I'd like to have something by this artist someday," Mina commented.

"You better hurry," Cecily said. "He's getting on in years and I don't know how much longer he'll be able to do this. He had this piece rolled up and stashed away. To tell you the truth, I think he'd forgotten he did it. I only got to see it because his wife remembered where it was. I think he did it over ten years ago."

"How did you find him?" Nyla asked. "I've never even heard of him."

"He's a friend of my father's," Cecily said. "He used to be an herbalist in Chinatown, but this has been his passion and hobby all his life. He's never promoted himself as an artist."

They next went back to the sitting room, where they unpacked three more paintings. Nyla had strongly suggested that all of the paintings should be island landscapes, and Henry Burnham had agreed. She had taken him to Cecily's, and he had chosen a dramatic volcano scene by Jules Tavernier, a classic Diamond Head and canoe painting by Joseph Strong, and a beautiful landscape of Hilo and Mauna Kea by Howard Hitchcock. While the women were deciding where to place the Tavernier, Sheldon Lennox strolled in.

182 MURDER LEAVES ITS MARK

"I heard there was a room full of beautiful women here." He grinned and brushed his hand through his hair, looked at the Tavernier painting, and whistled. "Speaking of beautiful, how did you find this gem?"

"Someone was interested in turning their art collection into money," Nyla reported. "They had just contacted Cecily—perfect timing for us. This one is a Tavernier."

"And this one is by his buddy, Joe Strong." Sheldon walked over to look at the other painting. "Also acquired by the clever Cecily?"

"That's right," Cecily answered.

"Boy, my stepfather is going to be even more insufferable when he finds out he owns these. Has he seen them?"

Nyla nodded. "Of course. I took him over to Cecily's shop . . ." She was about to say "the day before we went to Hale'iwa," but she caught herself just in time.

"If he changes his mind, I'll buy them," Sheldon said, "even if I have to rob a bank to pay for them."

"Sorry," Mina chimed in. "I'm first in line."

Sheldon shook his head. "We'll have to play a hand of poker to see who's first, Mina."

"Listen, Shel." Mina grabbed his arm. "If you really want to see something extraordinary, step right this way."

Mina led Sheldon into the conference room to see the ink-brush painting. Just as he was admiring the delicate work, they heard loud, angry voices and crashing sounds coming from Henry's office.

"That sounds bad," Mina said. She tried the connecting door, but it was locked. "It sounds like a fight."

"Right. Let's go see what it's all about."

The pair ran through the sitting room, down the hall, and around to the reception area outside Henry's office. Gwen was standing in front of the closed door looking distressed.

"Who's in there with him?" Sheldon demanded.

"His brother!" Gwen blurted out.

The shouting suddenly turned into scuffling. Sheldon opened the door and dashed into the office. Mina and Gwen saw the two brothers grappling. Sheldon forced his way between them while yelling at them to stop. Gilbert pulled a fist back to take a swing at Henry, but instead hit Sheldon. Blood gushed immediately from his nose.

"Jesus H. Christ," Sheldon bellowed.

Slightly shocked, Gilbert and Henry both stepped back from him.

"Sorry, Sheldon," Gilbert muttered, and rushed out of the office, not even looking at Gwen or Mina.

Sheldon stumbled out to the reception area.

"Close the door, Gwen," Henry ordered.

Gwen quickly closed the door, then grabbed a handful of tissues and was about to help Sheldon when her phone rang.

"Here," Mina volunteered, taking the tissues. "You answer the phone. I'll see to Sheldon." Mina took the tissues from her and steered Sheldon to a chair. "Sit down and try to keep your head back. It'll help the bleeding stop."

"Oh, shit, does it look bad?" he asked.

"You might have a pretty cute shiner," Mina said as she tried to assess the bruise on his face.

"Oh, great, that's just great," he groaned. "Tonight is the publicity pictures for the reading."

Mina smiled. "You'll look especially glamorous in dark glasses."

Gwen had barely answered the phone and transferred the call when Henry came storming out of his office.

"Listen, Gwen, I want you to march over to Island Trust right now and get those papers from that snot lawyer," he blustered. "She was my wife, damn it, and I have a right to know about her affairs. I don't know who the hell they think they are." He turned on his heel, went back in his office, and slammed the door.

"Are you all right, Shel?" Gwen tenderly put her hand on his cheek.

"Oh, just dandy," Sheldon answered, reaching up and taking her hand away.

"I'll be right back," she said apologetically to Mina. "He'll have a fit if I don't get his stupid papers right away."

"Don't worry about it," Mina said calmly. "The patient will be fine."

"I will?" Sheldon tried to sound pitiful.

"Yes," Mina answered. "The bleeding is mostly stopped. Let's go into the sitting room, where the three graces can clean you up properly." She got Sheldon to stand up, and they walked down the hall to the sitting room, where Nyla and Cecily immediately came to his aid. Mina went to the women's lounge and came back with several damp paper towels. Nyla and Cecily had Sheldon lying on the floor with his head tilted back. They took the towels from Mina and began to wipe around his nose and face.

"Why don't you see if you can get some ice, Mina?" Cecily asked.

"From where?" Mina felt a little put out.

"Just go downstairs to that bakery. I bet they have some. Tell them someone had a little accident and it's an emergency."

"All right," Mina grumbled as she left the room.

She went first to the pay phone in the foyer just under the stairs and made a quick call to tell Ned what had happened. In the bakery, the woman cheerfully gave Mina a paper cup full of ice cubes, and just as Mina pressed the button to call the elevator, an out-of-breath Gwen came into the foyer.

"How is he?" Gwen asked.

"Fine," Mina answered. "He'll probably have some bruising. I'm just getting some ice to help with the swelling."

"I can't believe he just rushed in there like that." Gwen shook her head as they stepped into the elevator and began the slow ascent.

"What were they so angry about?" Mina tried to sound concerned.

"Henry is all for this new Management Alliance League." Gwen sounded irritated. "And Gilbert is against the company having anything to do with it."

"What is the Management Alliance League?" Mina asked.

"It's an organization of companies to fight trade unions. Anyway, those two are always disagreeing. I'm surprised they haven't killed each other." Realizing what she had implied, she quickly tried to retract it. "But I don't mean that in a real sense. It was just an expression, a figure of speech. I don't mean he would—"

"I know what you meant," Mina assured her as the doors of the elevator opened.

"Let me just give Henry his papers, and I'll be right in to check on Shel," Gwen said as she made for her office.

Mina delivered the ice and watched Sheldon as he thoroughly enjoyed Nyla and Cecily taking turns holding the ice near his nose and asking him how he felt every two minutes. He was sitting up and seemed himself again when Gwen entered the room.

"I hope you weren't hurt, Sheldon." Gwen didn't wait for an answer. "Henry wants me to apologize for the disturbance"—she sounded very official and diplomatic—"and to thank you, Shel, for trying to help. He said you could all eat lunch at the Kama'aina Club on his account. If you like, I'll call over and have them reserve a table for you."

"That would be lovely, thank you," Nyla answered immediately. "You will come to lunch with us, won't you, Shel?"

Sheldon grinned. "How could I resist?"

"We'll be there in about twenty minutes," Cecily said.

"Fine, I'll let them know." Gwen turned and left.

"She is a very odd person," Mina commented.

"What do mean?" Sheldon looked at her.

"It's hard to read her. She's hot and cold. It's hard to tell when she's really being herself."

"That's because she doesn't really know when she's being herself," Sheldon said cynically. "But she has no trouble recognizing the smell of money."

"Let's forget about her," Cecily said as she put on her hat, took up her purse, and grabbed Sheldon by the arm. "Come along, invalid. We're going to our free lunch at the Kama'aina Club, where I hope to God there is no French food!"

That evening Mina sat next to Johnny Knight in the middle of the auditorium at the Ali'i Theatre. She yawned and wrapped her sweater a little tighter around herself. Ollie snuggled up next to her and put his head in her lap. A photographer was taking pictures on the stage of the actors, and of Ned.

"Excuse me, Johnny." Mina yawned again. "I came home from a

long day of decorating with Nyla and had to have a nap. I think I'm still waking up."

"How's the shoulder?" he asked.

"It's on the mend, but it aches sometimes, and I get tired more easily."

"I guess it's to be expected," Johnny said sincerely. "We're all thankful that you're still here with us, kiddo, especially that brilliant playwright."

"Oh, yes, the *handsome* and brilliant playwright," Mina replied.

"Oh, stop bragging, cousin!" Johnny elbowed her playfully. "Just because you have the best boyfriend *and* the best dog in Honolulu." He reached over and ruffled the fur on Ollie's back.

Mina and Johnny watched the photographer snapping photos and the flash of the camera capturing people in their poses. Ned left the stage and came to join them.

"Why doesn't Mina have to do this?" Ned complained. "She's reading the stage directions."

Mina grimaced. "Now you've done it. He'd forgotten all about me."

"No," said Johnny. "I was saving you for last."

"Well, I want Ollie in the picture, or no deal."

"Listen to her," Ned said, smiling. "Give her a bit part and she's acting like a diva."

"No Ollie, no picture." Mina folded her arms and turned her head away.

"Okay, okay," Johnny agreed. "Just so long as he's not on stage for the reading. He'll steal the show."

The photographer had placed Nyla and Emil together against one of the black velvet drops.

"They make a handsome couple," Johnny commented.

"He's worked out very well for the part," Ned added.

"I told you," Johnny said. "He has that undercurrent, the stuff that truly good actors inherently have because they've suffered in their real lives. The stuff acting lessons can't buy. He almost killed a boy once, when we were in school, you know."

"He what?" Mina asked excitedly.

"Do tell." Ned leaned forward, obviously intrigued.

"That's right," Johnny continued, reveling in their rapt attention. "We were in the locker room at school. It was after some kind of practice. I think it was track. That's right, we were all on the track team. You know, Emil's parents were never really rich. I mean, they were comfortable, but certainly not filthy rich like some of the other boys' parents were. I'm sure you remember some of those types, Mina. Boys and girls who thought their family money entitled them to be disdainful and self-righteous. I don't know, sometimes I think the kids got it through osmosis from their parents. Anyway, it was right after Emil's father died. We were in the locker room, and we'd all just showered. I remember this kid had it in for Emil because Emil was always outdoing him in the pole vault. So Emil's almost dressed, and this kid starts to go on about how suicide is such a cowardly thing to do, and we can all see Emil starting to boil but not doing anything. You know, there were rumors that his father's death wasn't an accident, that he committed suicide for the insurance. Then the kid turns on him with this smug smile and says something like, 'I bet you know what I mean, Devon.' And Emil just snaps. This knife comes out of nowhere. And in one instant he's got the kid pinned up against the wall and the blade at his throat, and he tells him, 'You want to go on, punk?' And the kid's about to pee in his pants because nobody, I mean *nobody*, ever carried a knife like that at Punahou. You could get kicked out just thinking about a knife. Emil makes him apologize, and tells him if he ever breathes a word to any of the teachers or anything, that he'll find him and cut him up good. Then he looks around at us and tells us that he'll do the same to anyone who rats on him. Boy, you could have heard a pin drop in there. We all went back to getting dressed, and a few minutes later the coach comes in and asks why it's so quiet. Emil bursts out laughing, grabs his books, and leaves."

"It's terrible when you lose your father." Ned's voice was even and quiet. "You could do and say things you never imagined yourself doing."

"I was scared," Johnny said, "but I remember thinking this at the time—good for Emil. That snot kid needed a lesson."

Mina looked a little worried. "Let's just hope he's not still responding to trouble in the same way."

The photographer signaled to Mina, and she went up to the stage
with Ollie prancing behind her. When they had finished, Johnny
called the cast together. "I just wanted to let everyone know we've
been asked to do a special reading for the theatre members only the
night before opening. We had a rehearsal scheduled for that night and
the night before, so I hope it's okay with everyone. It just means we'll
push up performing in front of an audience one night."

When the reading rehearsal began it was slow going, as Johnny
had decided to give the actors blocking. They went through the first
act scene by scene, each actor writing down the stage directions and
Mina trying to record all of them for a reference. Christian Hollister asked the most questions, and although they weren't silly, he did
seem to want a bit more than his share of individual attention. Louis
Goldburn was proving to be a very fine actor, and Mina could tell it
was making Christian feel both nervous and competitive. Christian's
natural brightness contrasted sharply with the brooding Emil, but
in the context of the play, it couldn't have been better. Sheldon read
very well and actually did look very glamorous in his dark glasses, and
Mina suspected that Nyla more than enjoyed being the only female
character in the midst of a handsome male cast.

When the rehearsal was over at eight-thirty, Ned and Johnny said
they needed some time to talk. The cast dispersed except for Mina and
Nyla, and Mina had the idea of calling the Mermaid Café to see if she
could pick up some of their fish chowder while Ned and Johnny had
their meeting. She got Maggie on the phone, who said they were about
to close and would be happy to pack up four bowls of chowder and
some bread to go. They all agreed to meet at the bungalow in an hour.

Nyla stopped her car near the alleyway that led to the back of the
Mermaid Café. Maggie had asked them to come around the back, as
they wanted to lock up the front when they closed. Mina got out of
the car with Ollie, assuring her sister that she didn't need any help.
She felt a slight chill in the air as she started down the dark, nar-

row lane with Ollie trotting silently beside her. The café was only two doors down. She could see a dim light in the back entrance, but beyond that she thought she saw two familiar people at the other end of the alley in animated conversation in the dark. She approached quietly, staying close to the alley wall. She pulled Ollie gently by the collar and ducked into a doorway so she could observe without being seen. The dog looked up at her, panting softly. "Hush now, Ollie, be quiet," she whispered. The dog looked up at her and then out into the night, silent but alert.

Down the alley, on the other side of the light, she saw Jack Carstairs talking to Gwen Reed. Mina's mind raced. Gwen thrust an envelope at Jack, and he thrust it back. They raised their voices, and she could hear what they were saying.

"Keep your dirty money," Jack said. "I don't want it."

"Then why do you keep asking for it?" Gwen shouted. "I have bills to pay."

"Don't make me laugh. I'm sure sugar daddy covers everything."

"Shut up," Gwen answered. "And don't ever ask me to tell you anything again."

"It's disgusting. I don't know how you can go through with it." Jack's voice was bitter. "You don't even like him."

"I never want to be poor again, and that's what I would be if I'd stuck by you. I'm going to marry him and that's that."

Jack's voice was full of rage. "He uses people, Gwen—tramples them down and grinds his heels in. He's had a man killed, and now you're marrying him? He makes me sick and so do you."

Jack turned on his heel and stormed into the café. Gwen looked at the envelope in her hands, pushed it into her coat pocket, and walked off in the opposite direction. Mina and Ollie emerged from the shadows and walked toward the light. She heard footsteps behind her and turned to see Nyla headed toward her.

"I was worried," Nyla said. "Haven't you even gone in yet? What are you doing out here?"

"I saw something," Mina answered. "I heard something. I'll tell you in the car. When we go in, pretend we just got here. Come on, now I'm starved."

The sky was brilliant and clear as they finished their chowder on the veranda of Ned's bungalow. Grandma Hannah, who was at Mina's listening to one of her favorite radio programs, had given them a plate of peanut butter cookies she'd made earlier in the day. Mina and Nyla could never get enough of them. Ned brought out a bottle of brandy, four glasses, and two cigars. He and Johnny proceeded to puff away while they all sipped the honey-colored brandy. Then Mina, who had saved her story about Jack Carstairs and Gwen, repeated it once again for the benefit of the two gentlemen.

"This puts another twist on things," Ned mused.

"Do you suppose they were once an item?" Nyla asked. "I wonder exactly what 'if I'd stuck by you' means?"

"And I wonder what 'don't ever ask me to tell you anything again' means," Mina added as she finished her second cookie.

"Sounds like he's used to taking money from her, too," Johnny said.

"Gwen is certainly a busy girl," Ned said. "It could be a dangerous position to be in."

"Well, Jack was really angry with her for associating with Henry Burnham. In fact, I'd say he was enraged." Mina reached for a third cookie and caught the look her sister was giving her. "Don't worry, Nyla, Grandma made a whole package of them for you to take home."

"Speaking of home," Nyla said, standing up, "I better get there and get to bed. We're almost done with the conference room and the sitting room, and tomorrow I thought we would look around for some things for the terrace."

"I was going to bring Grandma up to your house tomorrow," Mina said to her sister. "Mrs. Olivera is coming, and I thought Grandma would rather be out of the way."

Nyla yawned. "Come around nine-ish."

"I think I'll be getting along, too," Johnny said. "Great rehearsal, everyone."

Ned walked Nyla and Johnny to their cars while Mina sat with

Ollie on the veranda and listened to the sound of the crickets. Ollie was a little confused by the sound. He cocked his head when they started up, then looked at Mina as if he wanted her to explain it. When Ned came back, they decided to walk on the beach. Out on the sand, with the dark sea spreading out before them, the sky seemed even more luminous. Ollie bounded around them in circles. The ocean was calm, the tide low, and the night very still. Two men were fishing in the shallow water, wading along with their spears and torches, their brown bodies illuminated by the flames.

They sat down in the sand and Mina lay back, looking up at the stars. They could see the lighthouse planted up on the cliff, blinking on and off, with the dark cliffs rolling away beneath it, and she wondered how long it would be there, this thing her grandfather had helped to create, this guiding light, this beacon in the night. She suddenly felt the need for human warmth and connection, and she reached over to take Ned's hand.

"We're close to the killer, aren't we?"

"Yes," he answered. "It's like we're driving down a road, and we know some cold and terrible place is out there, lurking around one of the corners, but we just don't know which one."

"I feel like we've all been touched by these killings, like we've all been stained."

"Murder does that," he said, lying down next to her. "It leaves a mark in your mind, like a scar. After a while you get used to it, but it's always there."

"I'm sure I'll have a scar on my body, too," she said, touching the wound on her shoulder, "a mark that will always be there."

They lay together quietly in the cool night air under the dome of the starry sky. Yes, Mina thought, there would always be terrible things in the world, but right now she was here, sharing a moment with Ned, feeling peaceful and warm, even a little hopeful, not wishing she were anywhere else.

15

TUESDAY

MINA TOOK THE wheel of her 1934 Packard convertible coupe and was conscious of the fact that she hadn't driven since the shooting for fear of aggravating her shoulder. She willed herself to relax. It was a fifteen-minute drive, she told herself, and nothing really bad could happen in such a short time. As she and Grandma Hannah pulled out of the long driveway, she could hear Ollie gently protesting being left behind. While Mrs. Olivera cleaned, Mr. Olivera had promised to find time from his yard duties to give Ollie a bath and clip his nails. Mina thought the dog could use a haircut, too, as he didn't shed and his hair appeared to be growing longer everyday. She had no idea how to cut a dog's hair, but she was sure she could figure it out with a little help from her sister. The summer weather was setting in, and Ollie would be better off with shorter hair, especially because he went swimming whenever he could.

It was a beautiful day. They drove past the town of Kaimukī and began to climb Sierra Drive to Nyla's home. When they arrived at the hilltop house, Nyla was in the kitchen. Grandma Hannah had promised to make a big pot of stew for dinner, and Nyla showed her where all the ingredients were and the big Dutch oven she had left on the stove.

Just as they had gotten into Nyla's sedan, they heard the phone ring. "Let's get out of here before I have to talk to somebody," Nyla said. "I still have to get some gas and drop something at the post office."

"How are Tamiko and Michiko doing at Mrs. Lennox's house?" Mina asked.

"Well," said Nyla as they started downhill and she shifted the car into a lower gear, "they couldn't be more enthusiastic, and they're fascinated with Fumi. Apparently she's very old-fashioned, and they see her as some kind of antique from Japan. I guess Fumi doesn't get out much, and the girls are concerned she might be lonely."

"And what about the work and getting along with Violet Lennox?"

"They say the work isn't much different from what they do in Hale'iwa. In fact, they think it's a lark to be working in such a swank home. I don't think Mrs. Lennox fazes them because they're used to all those different, some of them rich, guests coming and going at the old hotel or club or whatever it is now."

"I bet they love staying with you," Mina commented.

"They're a hoot," Nyla said, laughing. "Kind of makes me think about having kids."

"Will you, do you think?"

"You know, I've been putting it off because I wanted Todd and me to have some really good years by ourselves first. I didn't want to plunge into marriage and kids all at once. I don't think that's selfish, do you?"

"No," Mina replied, frowning, "not at all. I think it's sweet and practical."

"Yeah." Nyla glanced at her sister. "You know, hardly any other women would agree with us."

"Who cares?" Mina folded her arms. "We can march to our own drummer. It's nobody's business."

"Well, now I'm thinking I might want to, maybe. I'm trying to make up my mind."

"Aunty Mina," Mina said with a smile. "I like the sound of it."

When they finally parked on Merchant Street, they saw two police cars and an ambulance in front of the Burnham and Robbins building. A uniformed policeman stood guarding the door, asking people to move on and away from the building entrance. The officer recognized Nyla.

"Sorry I can't let you in, Mrs. Forrest," he began. "Your husband asked me to tell you to wait for him in his office. He said he tried to call but you'd already left. He's up there now with your English friend."

"What's happened?" Nyla asked.

"Sorry, ma'am," the officer replied, scratching his head. "I can't tell you that, either."

"That must have been Todd calling when we were leaving," Mina reflected as they walked toward the police station.

"Too bad we're not mind readers," Nyla said.

"Whatever it is, it looks serious."

"Doesn't it get you," Nyla said as she looked up at the bright sky, "how terrible things can be happening and the world just goes on being beautiful."

"Sounds like you've been reading Kierkegaard." Mina kicked an old candy wrapper into the gutter.

"Who the hell is that?" Nyla tweaked her sister's cheek.

"Oh, nobody, really," Mina answered. "Just another haole guy with a philosophy."

Ned was sipping a cup of coffee and looking out of the window of his bungalow, watching Mina and Grandma Hannah leave the driveway, when the phone call came from Todd. He threw on some slacks and a clean shirt, then sped for downtown.

One of Todd's young men was waiting for him in the foyer of the Burnham and Robbins building and ushered him up to the fourth floor. He was then directed into the reception area for Henry Burnham's office. The reception desk on the left side of the room stood cordoned off. The drawers of the desk were flung open and papers lay scattered around the floor. Todd sat grim-faced in a chair on the other side of the room, while a bustle of activity went on in Henry's office. Todd looked up at Ned and nodded toward the office door. Ned stepped up to the threshold and looked inside. A photographer was changing the flashbulbs in his camera, and two others Ned recognized as Todd's men hung back, waiting to go over the room. In the centerpiece of the scene a doctor knelt beside the body of Henry

Burnham, with the crumpled body of a young woman next to him. Both of them lay on their backs, blood fanning out from their hearts, with the look of absence and abandonment the physical body assumes when life has left it. Papers and files were strewn around them. All the objects from Henry's desk had been swept to the floor, and Ned noted that the small, once carefully framed photos of Henry's family had been deliberately smashed. The small act struck Ned as a particularly vicious assault on human tenderness. A huge, painted black X glared out from the wall behind the desk. He turned away, not wanting to see anymore.

"I presume that's the secretary?" he asked Todd.

"Gwendolyn Reed. The doc thinks it happened maybe around ten or ten-thirty—close-range shooting."

"It's a gruesome sight first thing in the morning." Ned shook his head. "Your wife and Mina are on their way over here."

"I'm having the guy downstairs tell them to wait in my office. I don't want them anywhere near this place. Christ, if they'd walked in here and found those poor people—" Todd turned his head away and let out an exasperated sigh.

"I wonder if the killer was looking for something, or just ransacked things for effect?" Ned looked over at the reception desk.

"We'll know more after the boys go over everything and someone comes in who can tell us if anything is missing."

"You all right?" Ned asked.

"No." Todd looked up at the ceiling. "I *told* Burnham he needed police protection. He wouldn't have it."

"He made the bad decision. You did your job. It's a shame he refused your advice." Ned waited for a moment. "Is there anything I can do for you?"

"Yeah," Todd said. "Could you handle telling Nyla and Mina? Maybe get them to go home or at least out of the way? It would be one big thing off my mind."

"Leave it me," Ned replied.

Downstairs, the officer told Ned that he'd directed Nyla and Mina to Todd's office. The station was no more than a block away, but at that moment it seemed much farther. The harshness of what he had just seen seemed to have distorted his sense of time, and he had to remind himself to put one foot in front of the other and to keep moving forward. He had a vague awareness of cars and people passing by, but everything felt like it was fading back and away, with only the sidewalk stretching out before him like a narrow bridge. In his mind he heard his footsteps as hollow reverberations each time one of his shoes hit the ground.

Yes, he thought, I was right. Murder carried a particular coldness with it that cut through one's being like a cruel winter night and left its stinging mark, a black X scrawled on a white wall. An etched image of Charon in a book he had as a boy emerged in his mind. Charon stood muscular and towering at the stern of his boat, gripping the steering oar, his hair flying in the wind, his eyes fierce and wide, while two small figures huddled under a cloak as some invisible force propelled them across a wild river. Ned imagined Henry and Gwen as the passengers in the ferryman's boat, crossing the river Styx. They shivered—dazed, disoriented, and confused as they huddled together under their blanket.

Eventually, Ned found himself standing in front of the police station, staring up at the decorative Spanish tile that framed the doorway. He glanced back down Merchant Street in the direction of the Burnham and Robbins building, then trudged up the narrow stairs to Todd's third-floor office. The door was left open, and as he entered he saw the two sisters sitting on the old sofa near the window. The morning light, softened by the surrounding buildings, streamed through the windows behind them, glazing the room, and he thought of the light in Vermeer's paintings, the way it folded through the windows, surrounded women, and filled spaces with atmosphere. Mina turned toward him, and the calm smile that illuminated her face transformed in an instant to a look of concern.

"Ned, what's happened?" She crossed the room, took his arm, and guided him to the sofa.

"Henry Burnham and his secretary were found dead in Henry's office," he said. "Shot."

Without saying a word, Nyla got up and went to Todd's desk. She pulled out a bottle of brandy from the lower left-hand drawer and a single glass. They all sat down, and she poured the first one for Ned, the second for herself, and finally one for Mina. Then she did it all again. The three of them just sat there for a while in a trance.

Mina broke the silence. "I'm glad I don't have to report this for the paper," she said as she stared into the empty glass.

"You were right after all." Nyla turned to her sister. "The Burnham and Robbins building is the Inferno."

Todd turned the sedan onto Prospect Street as he and Ned headed for the Henry Burnham residence to deliver the bad news to the family. The road skirted around the south side of Punchbowl Crater, high enough so that the city spread out below.

"Why did they call this crater Punchbowl?" Ned asked.

Todd scratched his head. "I don't know. Because it's shaped like a bowl?"

"There must be some older name for such a prominent landmark," Ned said. "Some Hawaiian name."

"Ask Hannah," Todd suggested. "She knows all that old stuff."

"People don't realize that they lose their history when places lose their original names," Ned grumbled.

Soon they made a left turn, and, going uphill, Ned recognized Punahou School and its well-kept athletic field at the mouth of Mānoa Valley. At the top of the rise they made another left turn onto Judd Hillside Road. The street wound steeply away from the main road. Quiet replaced the sound of traffic, and serenity floated over the neighborhood. Every home sat on a large lot, set back, well placed, and well hidden from the street and the prying eyes of anyone passing by. It was all part of the cultivated, exclusive atmosphere, Ned reflected, always found in the environs of the very wealthy.

"This isn't going to be easy," Todd warned as he parked the car on the street near the Burnham driveway.

"No," Ned agreed, "but look at it this way. It will be over in less than an hour."

They walked down along a thick hedge of mock orange to a wrought-iron gate that stood next to the large trunk of a monkeypod tree. The tree reached out above them in thick, sculptured branches covered in green leaves and had dropped sticky black seedpods onto the ground. Ned stepped on one and had to peel it off his shoe. The gate creaked as he opened it. They followed a wide walkway bordered on the left by a high wall covered in some kind of vine, and on the right by a slope thickly planted with ginger and ferns. The path led to a small quadrangle with the formal stairs to the house on the left, so that visitors had to pause, turn, and first view the house from this particular vantage.

They walked up the first set of stairs and across a garden terrace, and then came a second set of stairs that leveled off a few feet from an archway over a thick wooden door. Designed in the Tudor revival style, the solid, patterned stonework of the rambling first floor rose to the half-timbered second floor, with its cross-gabled roof and potted chimney. A house, Ned thought, that resembled a miniature medieval palace, a house that a king of enterprise had built for his queen.

A surprised Tessa Burnham greeted them at the door and invited them into the breakfast room. With the full light of the morning sun at their backs, the foyer and the interior of the house seemed dark and cool as it received them. Many of the Honolulu residences Ned had been in had the same feeling of calm and shade—probably a reaction, he thought, to the brilliance of the sun and the dazzling colors of the outdoors. They passed under a curving staircase through a long, silent hall lined with closed doors, and finally through a doorway near the rear of the house to a room off the kitchen with a bay window that overlooked the back garden. The morning newspaper lay open where Tessa had been sitting. Her fine china plate with the rosebud border was littered with a few toast crumbs, and the smell of bacon and coffee lingered in the air. Sheldon Lennox sat there, looking half asleep. He was also surprised at their visit, and he sank into his chair, yawned, adjusted his robe, and immediately poured himself a cup of coffee. She offered them something to eat or drink, but they declined. From the kitchen, Ned heard a bustle of activity that he recognized as the morning routine of the hired help.

"Is your younger sister here?" Todd asked.

"No," Tessa answered, "she's riding at the stables. Is something wrong?"

After Todd broke the news, Tessa gave them both a sharp, cold look, then turned away to stare out of the bay window into the well-tended flower garden. Sheldon sat dumbfounded, as if he couldn't quite comprehend what Todd had just told them. After a period of silence, Tessa turned back and faced Todd. With her right hand, she nervously began to twirl a lock of hair around and around in her fingers. Ned wondered if it was a spontaneous or calculated gesture.

"I don't understand," she spoke rapidly. "First our mother, now our father—are we next?"

"We'll see that you're well protected," Todd assured her, "however long it takes. I'll post an officer out front and anywhere else you think one might be needed."

"Really," Sheldon said, waving his hand, "I don't think that will be—"

"Oh, Jesus, Shel," Tessa interrupted. "What will this do to Hester?"

Todd stood up. "We'll leave you now, but I'll need to talk to both of you later. Oh, one thing I do need to know before I go—" Todd looked down at his feet and then back at them. "And please understand, I'm not insensitive to your grief, but I would be remiss in doing my job if I didn't ask you what you both were doing last evening."

Ned caught the quick look that Sheldon and Tessa exchanged.

"Of course we understand." Sheldon got up and stood behind his sister. He put his hands on her shoulders. "As Ned knows, I went to rehearsal and then went straight to the rooftop garden at the Alexander Young Hotel, where I drank and danced too much. It was after midnight when I left and came home."

"I went out for a drive after dinner." Tessa spoke with confidence. "I came home around half past eight. I wasn't sleepy so I sat in the den and read until quite late. I was up when Shel came home."

"Yes," Sheldon agreed, "and I called her around nine-thirty from the Young Hotel so I know she was at home."

"Why did you call?" Todd asked.

"Well, I tried to get her to come and join me," Sheldon said. "She's been feeling a little blue lately, and I thought it would cheer her up."

"Hester will tell you—oh, please give us some time before you talk to her," Tessa pleaded.

"Of course we will," Todd assured her. "You weren't worried that your father didn't come home last night?"

"No," Sheldon replied. "He sometimes spent the night elsewhere, if you take my meaning."

There was an awkward silence before Ned spoke. "I'm very sorry about these terrible events," he said formally. "You both have my deepest sympathy."

"I'll be contacting you again, soon," Todd added.

Once in the car, Todd turned and looked at Ned. "So what's the prognosis, doctor? She didn't shed a tear for her father. Does the lady have a case of shock or was she covering something up?"

"To be fair, it is a shock to find out your father has been murdered just a few weeks after your mother," Ned replied as he rolled down his window. "But suspicion is always healthy until a case is solved."

"Right," said Todd as he pulled out the choke, pushed in the clutch, turned the key, and stepped on the gas. "Let's go see how her uncle has digested the news."

"Where does he live?"

"On Kāhala Beach," Todd answered, "out past Diamond Head and the bungalows."

"Diamond Head," Ned repeated.

"And no," Todd said, shaking his head, "I don't know what the real name of that crater is, either. Come to think of it, Koko Head and Koko Crater don't sound very Hawaiian, and neither does Red Hill. Now *I'm* curious."

Their drive took them past the university and through the familiar neighborhood of Kaimukī. Wai'alae Avenue ended, and they turned toward the sea onto a narrow two-lane road that passed through pig and dairy farms.

"I guess no one ever has to ask what's being raised in this area." Ned twitched his nose and rolled up the window.

"You have to learn to appreciate our wafting island breezes," Todd said, smiling at him.

"This doesn't look like a neighborhood for a Burnham."

"We're not exactly there yet," said Todd. "Damn, I hope I took the right turn." He slowed down the car and asked a boy who was painting a fence for directions.

Soon they found themselves bouncing along a dirt road that wove through the farmland of Kāhala. Small shacks stood in the midst of kiawe trees, and little clouds of red dirt blew up here and there on the dry ground. When there was a patch of grass, it looked withered and brown. Ned thought about how abruptly the landscape changed on the island, from verdant valley to dry plain.

"Must be tough living out here," Todd commented.

"It isn't the most inviting landscape."

"It's a cheap place to live," Todd said. "And the pigs and cows seem to like it. Okay, here we are."

They emerged from the farmland onto a paved road. The smell of farm animals vanished, replaced by the salt air of the sea. The avenue ran parallel to the shoreline, and on the ocean side Ned caught glimpses of the sea, some large beach houses, and some small fishing shacks, nestled in expansive yards. Todd slowed down to check the address and parked outside one of the driveways.

"This is it. Let's park out here and arrive quietly." Todd looked down the unassuming driveway. "I guess the Henry Burnhams and the Gilbert Burnhams have different tastes."

"No pigs and cows in this neighborhood?"

"Nope," Todd said, getting out of the car. "We jump from that to this quickly in our little town. I called Gilbert before we left, so they've had a few hours to absorb the shock."

"How did he take the news?"

"If I had been playing poker with him," Todd answered, "I'd have had no idea what kind of hand he held."

The straight driveway led into a sprawling, sheltered lawn that stretched out to the shoreline. Palm trees dotted the yard, and a couple of shade trees hung over the two-story house, a Cape Cod design adapted for the islands. The first floor was raised about six feet from the ground. Under the house Ned spied fins, *tabis*, goggles, spears, bamboo spear-gun slings, and other ocean paraphernalia. Surfboards, paipo boards, a rowboat, and a six-person canoe were out on the grass, and looked as if they got frequent use. From around the side of the house two golden Labrador retrievers came bounding toward them, barking but wagging their tails and keeping a respectful distance away. Todd and Ned walked up the stairs to the wooden front door that stood open. A screen door provided only a token barrier of privacy between the outside and inside of the house, and Ned guessed that it was only closed in case a mosquito or two sought entry. It was one of the charming things about Honolulu. No one ever thought to lock their doors. Todd knocked on the side of the door frame after trying the doorbell and realizing it didn't work. Helen Burnham appeared—not at the door, but from around the same side of the house that the now quiet dogs had charged in from.

"Hello," she called up to them, shading her eyes from the sun with her hand. "I'm in back on the patio. Just come around this way."

They followed her and the dogs to the back of the house and a shaded wooden deck that faced the sea. She directed them to take a seat up on the deck while she went down and hoisted up a red flag on a pole that stood near the beach.

"That was for Gilbert," she explained as she joined them. "He's out paddling in the small outrigger. When he sees the flag, he'll know to come in. He said to apologize if you got here while he was out. I hope you understand. He just needed some time alone on the water."

"Of course," Todd responded in an understanding tone of voice. "I'm sure it was—still is—quite a shock."

"I'm making a simple lunch, and I hope you'll join us," Helen said.

"Really, it's not necessary to feed us," Todd assured her.

"Don't be silly," Helen responded. "It's no trouble at all. It's only sandwiches and some chips."

"It's a lovely spot here," said Ned, admiring the ocean and the sky.

"We have two boys, and Gilbert makes three," Helen continued. "I tried to prevent our home from becoming a beach club when we were first married, but it was a battle I could never have won, so I gave up. As you can see, this is not a showplace, and what's more, it's full of sand half the time because everyone keeps forgetting to rinse their feet before they come in the house. But we wanted our boys to have a happy, outdoor childhood, away from all the formality of the Burnham clan and the elite Honolulu circles."

"I'm sure any child would love to grow up here," Ned said, smiling at her.

"I'm not from the islands." Helen spoke in a confident but intimate voice. The tree overhead swayed slightly and shifted small patterns of light over her perfectly tanned face. A mane of sandy brown hair sparkled and curled around her shoulders. "Gilbert and I met at college. I had no idea how wealthy his family was when I married him. Both my parents were teachers, firm believers in education, economy, and modesty. I was upset at first that Gil didn't tell me about the Burnham money and power. I wasn't happy in Honolulu, but when we moved out here to the beach, everything changed. I was able to relax, to detach myself, to raise our sons, and have my own friends. I've been very happy here, and I think Gil has, too, when he gets home, that is . . ." Her voice trailed off as she saw Gilbert coming up toward the house. The dogs stood up and wagged their tails.

It was just after noon. From the shade of the deck Ned watched Gilbert Burnham striding toward them against the backdrop of a vivid blue sea, as if middle age had hardly touched him. The hypnotic sound of wind rustling through palm fronds filtered into the borders of Ned's thoughts. Something about the sound slowed down his breathing and at the same time sharpened his awareness. Gilbert's tanned, solid body glistened with drops of seawater, and Ned found it difficult to imagine him playing second best to anyone. He walked with the honest self-confidence of someone who wouldn't stand for any nonsense, much less bullying. Ned wondered if that's what happened, if Gilbert just couldn't stand for any more of his brother's injustice to himself and to the hundreds of workers under their employ. He wouldn't have been the first person to commit one or two murders for the good of the many.

"Sorry to keep you waiting," Gilbert said in apology. "Let me just rinse off and change, and I'll be right with you."

"Take your time," Todd responded.

"And I'll just be a few minutes in the kitchen getting our lunch," said Helen as she stood.

"Let me help you," Ned volunteered. He could see into their kitchen from the deck and noted the absence of domestic help.

A pleasant light filled the kitchen, and a wide, pass-through window opened onto a counter on the deck, expanding the view to the beach and beyond to the sea. The space exuded a sense of peace and comfort, and Helen moved through it with graceful efficiency. She took a bowl of tuna salad, some bread, and lettuce and began to make the sandwiches. "There're some potato chips in the bread box on the counter," she said, pointing behind him. "You could put those in that bowl there, and then pour the iced tea. The glasses are on the shelf just above."

"This is a kitchen with a view, isn't it?" Ned tried to sound friendly.

"Are you one of those men who can actually cook?" Helen looked at him and smiled.

"Yes," he replied, chuckling, "I'm afraid I am one of those."

"I wanted to make something simple and familiar for Gilbert's lunch today. I think it helps when something tragic happens—to keep the food simple and comforting."

"I'm looking forward to it myself," said Ned as he took four tall glasses from the shelf.

"Did you . . . ," she hesitated for a moment and then continued in a very quiet voice. "Did you see their bodies?"

"Yes, I did."

"It must have been a terrible, terrible thing for you to see." Her voice conveyed sadness and sympathy.

"It was."

"He wasn't a very nice person," she murmured. "Still, I feel awfully sorry for the poor girl. It's a shame she was in the way." She looked up at Ned, almost surprised at what she'd said. "I mean, that is why she died, isn't it? Because she was there? Just like Amanda?"

"Yes, I suppose so," he replied, "unless she—" Ned stopped himself.

"Unless she what?"

"You know, I shouldn't say anything." Ned shook his head. "I've no right to. I'm not the police, and I wouldn't want to say anything out of turn."

"I understand," she said. "Well, I think we're ready to put these things on a couple of trays and deliver them to the table."

The four of them ate over quiet conversation, as if the violent discoveries of the morning had left a wake of hushed propriety and politeness. When lunch was over and Helen began to clear the table, Ned rose to help her, but she insisted that she could manage. It was her way of removing herself, he supposed, from the serious conversation that ensued.

"What would you like to ask me?" Gilbert began. "I'm sure it's about the fight I had with my brother yesterday."

"That would be a good place to start," Todd said.

"We have—I guess I should say had—argued fairly regularly," Gilbert explained, "although it's been a few years since we actually came to blows over anything. Things have been building up between us. First, he planned to sell our family estate on Kaua'i without even consulting me. It's a piece of property that's been in our family for almost a century. It's not like the business needs the money. He was going to sell it to an industrialist from the East Coast just to make a connection—the place itself, our family history, it meant nothing to him." Anger flushed over his face, and he paused for a moment to take a sip of his iced tea.

"Yesterday," he continued, "was something different. My brother and I had different ideas about how our agricultural workers should be treated. Unlike most businessmen in this town, I don't feel threatened by the idea of labor unions. I think that workers who are well taken care of are good for business. There's a thought that rubs most of my colleagues the wrong way. Henry and his cronies were up in arms about the National Labor Relations Act that would allow some laborers to organize and strike. They planned to form this organization of business owners, the Management Alliance League, to put a stop to union organizing. Henry was going to make Burnham and Robbins the primary financial contributor for the organization. What that means is we would be funding spying, intimidation, strong arming, maybe even—" Gilbert stopped himself and looked away.

"Were you going to say murder?" Todd asked. "Do you think

206 MURDER LEAVES ITS MARK

he had something to do with the death of that worker in Hale'iwa, Shimasaki?"

"I don't know," Gilbert answered. "Maybe."

"Do you think Bruhn was in on it?" Todd persisted.

"I don't know," Gilbert repeated. "And it's not the kind of information Henry would ever share with me."

"You know that there're some pretty bad feelings about the incident among the men." Todd leaned back in his chair.

"Of course I know that," Gilbert answered. "I can't say I blame them." He looked off and stared at the ocean.

"So the argument you had with him was over this organization he was planning?" Todd continued.

"That's right." Gilbert's eyes left the view and focused on Todd. "I can't remember exactly what we said, but I just lost my temper, and the next thing I knew, I was going after him."

"Will you head the company now?" Todd tried to sound matter-of-fact.

"Yes, of course." Gilbert sounded unapologetic. "And I'll be shaping very different company policies, *and* we won't be selling our family estate to a mainland muckety-muck."

"I see," Todd responded. "Now, I have to ask this question, and I want you to know that it's part of my job. In fact, I'm asking everyone I interview today the same thing. Where were you last evening between say eight and midnight?"

"I was at home with my wife," Gilbert answered.

"Your boys were here?"

"No, Alfred and his wife have their own place near the university, and James was spending the night at a friend's house. They had some kind of special gymnastics demonstration last evening at school, and we let him stay in town."

"So Helen is the only one who can verify that you were here?" Todd brushed his hand over the back of his neck.

"Should I call my lawyer?" A faint smile crept over Gilbert's lips.

"No," Todd said, smiling back. "This is just routine."

"It would be useless to deny that there was no love lost between Henry and me," Gilbert said, "but I didn't kill him. I'm very sorry about the way he died *and* that he was never the kind of older brother I could be proud of."

"Well, thanks for your honesty." Todd leaned forward. "I may need to speak to you again."

"I understand," Gilbert responded.

Helen, as if on cue, returned to the deck. Ned and Todd thanked her for the lunch, and before they departed, she made them take a packet of sugar cookies. Gilbert said good-bye and retreated into the house, but Helen stayed out on the deck, and as they walked away, she watched them with a serene smile.

It was a little after two when Ned looked out of the window of Emil Devon's office at patches of sugarcane in various stages of growth. Some of the very straight rows were new green blades, like a large grass only a few feet high, while others were nearly full grown, with long stalks and blades taller than a man. The grounds of the experimental station covered a whole block in the middle of an otherwise suburban Honolulu neighborhood. Through the growing cane, Ned caught a glimpse of the high, green-slatted fence that completely surrounded the property. The offices and laboratory were in a thick, solid two-story building that fronted Keʻeaumoku Street. Ned thought the whole setup had the atmosphere of a place for secret operations, or the grounds of some kind of prison reform program.

Emil sat behind a plain wooden desk with a blotter pad and a cup containing pens and pencils. There were some books on the shelves behind him, and some folders, but for the most part the office looked bare and either unused or rigidly organized to look unused. Ned thought Emil looked so out of place here, in this sterile office wearing a white lab coat.

"Do you ever have kids coming in here to steal a stalk of cane?" Todd tried to be friendly.

"On a regular basis," Emil replied. He was quiet for a minute, then asked, "What exactly can I do for you, detective? I can only take a short break."

"This morning we found the bodies of Henry Burnham and Gwendolyn Reed. They were shot in the Burnham and Robbins building last night." Todd did not take his eyes off Emil.

Ned was sure he felt a tangible shift in Emil's mindset.

But without skipping a beat he asked, "And why are you here to see *me?*"

"I'd like to know where you were last night, where you went last night after your rehearsal." Todd kept his voice on an even keel. "This is purely routine."

"I still don't understand why you're asking me. Am I under some kind of suspicion?" His dark eyes flashed, but he showed no emotion.

"Not really, but we'd very much like to eliminate you. To be honest," Todd continued, "we've heard some stories, true or untrue, about your father's death in relation to Henry Burnham, and you were present in Hale'iwa when Mrs. Burnham was killed. We just have to make sure."

"So you're not here because you have any *real* evidence against me?" Emil cocked his head.

"No," Todd answered.

"I went home last night after rehearsal. I listened to the radio and read, and then I went to sleep."

"Did you see anyone? A neighbor? Did anyone phone?" Todd asked.

"No, not that I remember."

"I hope you're not offended," Todd said, almost apologizing. "These were brutal murders, and we have to turn over every stone."

"I understand you're just doing your job." Emil relaxed slightly. "I hope you don't mind if I relate this to my lawyer."

"Not at all," Todd said. "What exactly do you do here? If you don't mind my asking."

"I'm a botanist," Emil replied. "I study plants. I do experiments with different kinds of cane. I study plant nutrition. I look at how different plants and trees in the watershed help or hinder the water table. Growing cane takes a lot of water. I do all kinds of things. I don't know if you realize this, but this station has an international reputation, and people come from all over the world to visit because the work we're doing is so advanced. I'm very lucky to be here, and I really need to get back to the lab."

"Well, thank you for your time." Todd stood to shake his hand. "Is there a phone I could use here?"

Emil pointed. "Down the hall, where you came in. Ask the receptionist there." He turned to Ned as they were leaving. "I don't know what *you're* doing here."

"I'm an old friend of Todd's." Ned tried to sound lighthearted. "He calls on me as a consultant when he's confused."

"Well, I hope you can straighten him out." Emil cracked a small smile. "I'm not a murderer."

"I'll do my best," Ned said, nodding.

Mina swam, with Ollie never far away, trying not to tax her shoulder. The water was calm and clear, and when she and the dog emerged onto the beach the shock and intensity of the morning began to recede. After leaving Todd's office, she and Nyla had decided they needed to relax, so they gathered up Grandma Hannah and spent the rest of the day at Kaʻalāwai, close to the ocean. Mina told Mrs. Olivera what had happened and let her go home early. Nyla stayed in the water only a short time, complained about feeling tired, and was now sleeping on a towel under a hau tree. Next to her, Grandma Hannah sat on an old bedspread in a patchwork of light, looking out to sea and fanning herself with a lauhala fan. She wore a faded muʻumuʻu that had seen better days   the closest, Mina reflected, that she would ever come to a bathing suit. The sight of her grandmother sitting under the tree with Nyla unleashed a flood of memories—the three of them on their outings, going shopping, going to the circus, going to ride the streetcar, and, especially, going to the beach, with Grandma Hannah always there, waiting in the shade, ready to embrace them with a warm, clean towel after they'd stayed in the water so long their fingers were like little prunes and they were shivering. There it was again, Mina thought, the pull back to the past, only this wasn't like the coral blocks in the harbor. It was a woman, now old, with snowy hair and golden-chocolate skin, whose face carried the story of all of their ancestors, someone that she and Nyla still counted on for a warm towel.

"Come, Mina," her grandmother said, motioning to her as she drew near. "Come lie down here. I brought some kukui oil to lomi your shoulders."

Grandma Hannah sat cross-legged, and Mina lay down on her stomach in front of her and into the faint, familiar cloud of her grandmother's lavender-scented bath powder. She could feel the heat of the sand radiating through the quilt, and it made her want to close her eyes and rest, the way she did in grade school after lunch on her denim sleeping mat. She looked over at Ollie, who had found a place in the shade, dug himself a little depression, and gone to sleep.

"Kaiwi told me this would help you," Grandma Hannah said as she let the oil fall in drops on the back of Mina's shoulders. "You say if anything hurts. He said to go around the wound and try to relax all the muscles. They tense up all around a spot when there's trouble in the body."

"He's so different, Grandma," Mina mumbled.

"Yes, I'm sure he seems strange to you, maybe less to me." Grandma Hannah began to massage Mina, gently spreading the kukui oil over the tops of her shoulders, down the side of her arms, and then onto her back and neck. "But he still carries things from the past, things that are almost gone from our world."

"I hear the old folks say things like that all the time," Mina said with a sigh. "But why? Why do we have to lose everything?"

"I don't know, baby. It's a different world now." There was a trace of sadness in Grandma Hannah's voice. "The kūpuna who were entrusted with knowledge—it's their decision, to either pass it on or take it with them."

Mina felt her grandmother slightly increase the pressure of the massage, and her back, neck, and shoulders began to feel warm and pliable. She thought about Kaiwi and the pond he showed them. She felt the oil on her body and tried to imagine being a moʻo with slippery, sleek skin, gliding through the water, transforming herself at will. Shape-shifting, that's what people called it. Would changing bodies be hard and painful, or would it be like changing clothes or putting on a disguise? Her grandmother's hands began to push a little harder as her body drifted into a kind of sleep, slowing down and losing resistance while her mind stayed aware and awake.

"Kaiwi said something might happen." Grandma Hannah spoke in a hushed, calm tone. "He said there might be more."

"Did he say anything else?"

"Yes," Grandma Hannah went on, "he said through this wound, through this injury, that you were connected to the person who did this to you, connected through the pain. He said that there was anger, and you had to be careful, to recognize how people cover up their anger."

"I don't really understand that, do you?" Mina said.

"No," Grandma Hannah admitted. "Except for the *be careful* part."

"Everyone involved in this mess seems to be angry, or has a good reason to be."

"Okay, now you can turn over and lie on your back."

Mina rolled over and repositioned herself. Her grandmother spread the drops of kukui oil across her chest and arms as Mina closed her eyes and listened to the sound of the waves breaking offshore. She thought she heard the distant cry of a seabird.

"How is it? Being away from the newspaper?" Grandma Hannah carefully worked her hands around the wound.

"I don't know. I thought I was doing the right thing by leaving, and then this happened. Now I feel like I'm in a whirlpool, and I've no idea where things are going."

"You're a very good journalist, Mina. If your mother was alive, she would be very proud of you."

"It's hard for me to think it all might be over."

"It's not over." Grandma Hannah sounded very sure of herself. "You're too good for it to be over. How is your shoulder now?"

"It feels like it's melting."

"Good." Grandma Hannah sprinkled a few more drops of oil onto her hands. "Remember that story you loved so much when you were little? The one about the boys that were turned into swans?"

"By heart, I remember it by heart."

"You used to be so worried about the last little boy whose shirt wasn't finished."

"And when the spell was broken, the youngest lacked only a left arm and had in its place a swan's wing," Mina recited.

"That's what your arm and shoulder feel like now," Grandma Hannah whispered. "Soft, like a swan's wing."

As her grandmother's hands soothed and calmed her body, Mina felt herself floating. The last thing she remembered was feeling the warmth of the sun and the familiar security of being with the two women she loved most in the world, and then she was surrounded by the soft white plumage of sleep.

Ned suspected there had been some new development in the case, as Todd had become thoughtful and silent. On the way back to the station, Todd pulled the car over and stopped at Thomas Square, one of the oldest parks in the city, just across from the Honolulu Academy of Arts.

"Let's take a stroll," Todd suggested.

In the middle of the park, a high plume of water fountained from the center of a wide, circular pond that was surrounded by banyan trees. They walked along the perimeter of the square, Todd lost in thought. They ended up sitting on a bench, watching the fountain. At intervals a spout of water would rise some fifteen feet and fall back down, leaving the surrounding pond calm and quiet once again. Ned watched as a group of mynah birds hopped around looking for bugs. Their impudent behavior always amused him, and he thought about the old sea dog, Captain Stephany, a close friend of his grandfather who carried a grubby-looking parrot around on his shoulder. The captain's shirts were always soiled and smelly, but the bird was an impressive mimic, had a large vocabulary, and could recite all sorts of things. There were few people in the park this afternoon—a mother pushing a pram and a man walking two poodles.

"What's the news?" Ned asked after the mynah birds had flown away.

"Some of my guys went snooping in the alley behind the Mermaid Café, and guess what they found?"

"A gun that fits as the murder weapon?"

"What?" Todd exclaimed. "Are you a mind reader?"

"It's an obvious clue," Ned said. "This whole thing is full of the obvious—the threatening letters, the man in disguise, the weapons at the foot of Jack's bed, the X at the murder scenes. The murderer loves orchestration and is probably congratulating himself on what he thinks is clever misdirection."

"There were no prints. They're doing a ballistics test as we speak," Todd said as the fountain plume rose and a breeze blew a fine, watery mist in their direction.

"Anyone could have put that gun there." Ned stifled his frustration and tried not to sound too impatient. He knew his own involvement in the case hinged on a healthy respect for Todd's authority.

"If it's a match, I'll have to arrest him unless he has a solid alibi." Todd picked up a pebble and threw it in the fountain. "He was pretty steamed with the secretary last night. That doesn't look good, either."

"It's just too easy." Ned shook his head.

"I know it stinks," Todd said, sounding agitated, "but I have to do my job! And who knows? He could be crazy, and we just don't want to believe it because we sympathize with trade unions."

"So what's next?"

Todd crossed his arms. "Look, I can't keep making allowances for this guy, so here's the last thing I'm doing for him. I'll drop you somewhere, and if you just happen to be having coffee or something at the Mermaid Café with Louis Goldburn in an hour or so, at least the kid will have his lawyer around if we have to arrest him."

Ned studied the intricate trunks of the banyan trees, and their smooth gray, sinuous shapes looked to him like half-formed creatures, almost ready to step from one world into another. "You don't really think he did it, do you?"

"Five people have died. Things have spun way out of control," Todd said. "I don't know what to think anymore."

It was nearly four-thirty. Ned thought he could feel the eyes of Duncan's mermaid sculpture boring a hole in his back as he sat in the café and stirred his cup of tea. Jack had gone out with Maggie to buy some supplies for the restaurant, and Ned dreaded being a witness to the boy's rearrest. Across the table, Duncan sat with a grim face as Louis made notes in a small pad.

Louis stopped his scribbling and looked up. "Thanks for letting me know about this, Ned."

"You're welcome," Ned replied. "If anyone asks, we'll just say we were discussing the play." Ned turned to Duncan. "Do you think there's any chance that a group of plantation workers are responsible for this, all of these killings?"

Duncan scowled. "Anything is possible. Burnham was so callous to the misery he caused, there are hundreds of people who could have done it."

"If you know anything, and you care about Jack," Ned said, "now is the time to tell Todd."

"Here's the thing you don't get," Duncan fired back. "This is war. It's class warfare and there are people out there fighting for a decent livelihood for themselves and their families. Even if I did know something, if Jack himself knew something, we wouldn't betray our troops."

"Even if Jack hangs for these murders?" Ned leaned forward.

"For the good of all the workers," Duncan stated. "That's what we're all about, not ourselves as individuals."

Ned looked over at Louis, who remained impassive. All three of them reacted to the sounds of Jack and Maggie in the back of the kitchen returning from their errand. They could hear them laughing about something and the sound of cans being put on shelves and paper bags being crumpled. None of the three men wanted to move and bring the inevitable moment any closer. Finally, Jack and Maggie came out of the kitchen and into the café.

"What's wrong?" Maggie asked, smiling. "It looks like a funeral in here."

"Sit down, Jack." Louis stood up and pulled a chair over for him. "We need to talk."

"Why? What's happened?" Jack sat down and fussed with the buttons on his jacket.

"Where were you last night between, say, eight-thirty and midnight?" Louis asked him.

"I was here and then went for a long walk around nine-thirty and got back about ten or ten-thirty, and then I read up in my room until about one," he answered. "Will you tell me what's going on?"

"Did anyone see you on your walk?" Louis persisted.

"Did anyone see me? How should I know if anyone saw me?" Jack sounded defensive.

"Did you talk to anyone? What about Gwen Reed? Did you talk to her?"

"What the hell is this all about?" Jack snapped back.

"Last night, around that time," Louis said, his voice very serious, "someone shot Henry Burnham and his secretary to death in his office."

There was a long silence. Jack looked away, and it became apparent that he was making a great effort to keep from crying. "Gwen's dead?" He sounded like a small child.

"Did you have an argument with her last night?" Louis asked patiently. "What was she to you, Jack?"

"She . . . she was my sister!" He blurted it out and burst into tears.

"Oh, my God!" Maggie jumped up and moved her chair next to Jack's. She hugged him and held him until he got control of himself and managed to stop sobbing.

"Did you know this?" Louis looked at Duncan, who responded by shaking his head.

"I can't believe it," Jack said as he took out his handkerchief. "I don't want to believe it."

"You might as well hear the worst of it." Louis looked at him. "They found the murder weapon out in the alley just behind the café."

"So they're going to arrest me again?" Jack let out a derisive laugh.

"They'll probably be here any minute," Louis said to him.

"I couldn't care less. I just don't care anymore," Jack said as he wiped the tears from his eyes.

16

WEDNESDAY

"I **JUST CAN'T** believe she's his sister." Mina shook her head. "I hope he didn't kill her."

Mina and Ned were sitting out on her deck eating breakfast. She was wrapped in her favorite beach robe, and her hair, damp from a morning swim, framed her face in disheveled wisps and ringlets. Ollie was rummaging around under the table looking for crumbs. "It's a shame Grandma left so early this morning," she said as she smoothed the rich, yellow butter over her scone. "She loves your scones. I'll bet you could win a cooking prize with these."

"Are they that good? Maybe I should hire myself out."

"What? I thought you were mine, exclusively," she said, frowning.

"If you're nice to me, Mina." Ned smiled, leaned back, and sipped his tea.

"Do you think that's why Jack made this his home port? Because his sister was here?" As she bit into her scone, she caught an undertone of rum.

"According to Jack's statement," Ned began, "it was the other way around. She's his older sister, and when she found out he was going to make Honolulu his home base, she decided to come here, too. She landed this job at Burnham and Robbins—Jack says she figured out the social setup here pretty quickly—and decided that hiding her relationship to Jack would be to her advantage."

"I'd say she was right about that—up until Monday night, that is."

"Of course Jack didn't like what she was doing, who she was asso-

ciating with, but I guess she gave him money. They had a tough childhood, and he says they were pretty close, always looking out for each
other, until she took up with Burnham."

"I'm sure if you'd always had next to nothing, Henry Burnham's
money could certainly have an effect," Mina mused. "I know I thoroughly misinterpreted what she and Jack were arguing about, but I
have to admit, he sounded pretty angry."

"It's interesting how the same childhood can lead to two totally
different cravings." Ned poured another cup of tea.

"You mean yearning for a rich, glamorous life as opposed to wanting to be the savior of the downtrodden?" She reached for another
scone.

"Speaking of saving the downtrodden," Ned said, "I suggested to
Todd that he run a check on Duncan Mackenzie."

"Why?" Mina asked.

"Well, he made these remarks yesterday about sacrifice and class
warfare, and it occurred to me that he could know more than he's
letting on."

"It would be easy for him," she said, following Ned's train of
thought, "to pretend to be Jack's friend and then set him up to take
the fall, wouldn't it?"

Ned leaned forward and looked her straight in the eye. "You
know, Mina, you are one of the smartest women I have ever met."

"Scones and flattery," said Mina as she smeared butter on the fluffy
scone. "A sure-fire way to a girl's heart." She stopped for a moment
and absentmindedly licked the butter off the knife. "Still," she continued, "Jack's fingerprints were not on the weapon, and there were
no witnesses to the crime. Anyone could have done it."

"They've rounded up a cab driver and an itinerant—sorry, a
bum—who saw people coming and going from the building last
night. Todd's going to interview them today."

"I hope he's invited you," Mina said, just before she took another
bite.

"I'll give you a full report," Ned said, "if you aren't in the hospital
from an overdose of scones."

Just then, the postman's truck pulled into the driveway and

stopped. The mailman got out and asked Mina to sign a paper before he handed her a small parcel. She took it to the table, unwrapped the package, and found another box inside that was gift wrapped, with a white card that read, *For Mina, I could never thank you enough, Sincerely, Henry Burnham.* Mina sat down and had a difficult time holding back her tears.

"In the end," she said, "I guess no one could protect him."

Mina untied the bow on the box, carefully took off the white paper strewn with violets, and lifted the lid. Inside was a beautiful diamond necklace, bracelet, and matching earrings.

The cab picked up Ned and Todd near the University of Hawai'i. Todd wore dark glasses and sat up in the front, while Ned made himself comfortable in the back. The brown leather gleamed, the floor was spotless, and every bit of chrome in the car was highly polished. A rosary hung from the rearview mirror. The faint odor of cigarette smoke and a sweeter scent of some kind filled the interior. Under a cap, the driver's black hair was slicked back, off of his shiny brown face.

"Thanks for meeting us—Mr. Ramos, is it?" Todd asked.

"Joseph Ramos," the man said, "but everybody calls me Jojo."

"I'm Detective Todd Forrest, and this is Ned Manusia."

"Howzit?" Jojo looked at Ned in the rearview mirror.

"It's quite fine, thank you," Ned responded.

"I want you to know, we *will* pay you for your time," Todd said.

"Oh, good." Jojo turned on the meter. "I just no like anybody know I was talking to cops. You never know what might happen to you. So where you like drive?"

"Drive anywhere you want," Todd told him. "Anywhere you feel comfortable."

"So you like know about Monday night?" Jojo asked as he put the car in first gear, pulled away from the curb, and headed up the street into Mānoa Valley. After a couple of turns, Ned recognized O'ahu Avenue because of the streetcar tracks. There were some lovely houses along the street. Tall trees hung over tropical gardens like living umbrellas, creating cool and inviting entryways. They passed several flame trees, alive with their red-orange blooms, and in one yard a jacaranda tree had rained a carpet of lavender flowers over the green grass.

"I guess you know about the shooting at the Burnham and Robbins building," Todd said.

"Everybody knows." Jojo reached in his pocket for a stick of chewing gum. "Big news on the radio and the newspaper today. But yesterday was when the officer came to my house. He talked to everyone who was working from the cab stand, yeah?"

"Yeah," Todd said. "We know sometimes you guys can help us."

"Yeah, well," Jojo went on, "that night, was around ten-thirty, maybe little bit after. I was driving on Merchant Street—I just wen take somebody from Young Hotel down Waikīkī side. I was coming back, and I saw one guy standing across from the building."

"From the Burnham and Robbins building?" Todd asked.

"Yeah, yeah over there," Jojo said excitedly. "I slowed down the cab because, shucks, I thought maybe I could get one rider, because things kinda slow right now, yeah?"

"Did you get a look at the person?" Todd leaned against the door and looked at him.

"Was one haole man, and there was one wahine, too. She was standing more back, so at first, I never even see her. She was holding her hands by her face like she was crying or something, I dunno. I couldn't see her so good." Jojo cracked his chewing gum.

"But did you get a look at the man?" Todd pressed him.

"I told the officer yesterday, I never seen the guy before. But then, this morning, my wife is reading the newspaper. Me, I cannot read so good, yeah? And she goes, 'Oh, look, get the pictures of the dead man and the girl, and his family, too.' So I look the pictures, and I see one looks like the man I saw, and I tell my wife, 'What? That's the dead man or what?' Then she reads under the picture. 'Oh, no,' she tell me, 'that's not the dead man, that's his brother.'"

"Are you sure?" Todd glanced at Ned.

"I think so," Jojo said, nodding. "I think so that was him. And that wahine, I didn't see her face but she get da kine light-brown hair—almost blonde, but not."

"So what happened when you slowed down?" Ned asked.

"The man just wave me on. Then, inside the mirror, I saw they was going by Bishop Street."

They turned down Lower Mānoa Road and passed an old church surrounded by graves and a small cluster of shops. A little past the village the suburban neighborhoods stopped, and the valley opened up into farm and taro lands. Jojo drove on and pulled into the parking area of a cemetery on a sloping hill. He stopped the car and turned off the engine. Ned rolled down the windows and looked out at the steep mountains that surrounded the valley. A breeze blew down from the back of the valley and rippled through the trees around the quiet cemetery. He observed that the tombstones were all marked in Chinese characters. Across the street a horse was tied in front of a small wooden shack, munching away on the grass. Ned recognized the sickly sweet smell of guavas, fallen and spoiling, and was not surprised to turn and see a small stand of the trees nearby. There was a damp, wet feeling in the air back here, so distinctly different from the place they had started from just a few miles away.

"What time did you see them?" Todd looked out his window and surveyed the graveyard.

"Oh, was like I said, around ten-thirty." Jojo took off his cap, smoothed back his hair, and, looking in the mirror, replaced the hat at a jaunty angle.

"That's a big help," Todd said. "Did you see anything else?"

"Nope," Jojo said as he did a quick check of his teeth in the mirror. "You ever been to one Chinese funeral up here?" he asked Todd.

"Hmm, no, I don't think so."

"Funny kine, you know," Jojo said. "They get firecracker, and look, they put food on top the grave." He pointed to a grave with incense and oranges. "Just in case the dead person is hungry for something."

Mina sat in Nyla's kitchen, finishing an apple, as Mrs. Olivera busily polished a silver tea set on one of the counters. After hearing about the shooting, Violet Lennox had called and given Tamiko and Michiko the day off, so Mina and Nyla decided to take the girls out for a little shopping and some lunch. Nyla was still upstairs getting ready, and the girls were outside fussing with Ollie.

"Oh, Mina," Mrs. Olivera said sadly. "It's terrible about those shootings. Makes you feel like it's not safe anymore—with those union agitators running around. They say that those men did it."

"Who says?" Mina frowned.

"People are saying that around town. You don't think so?" Mrs. Olivera stopped polishing and looked at Mina.

"No, I don't think so," she answered, "but I think someone would like us to believe that."

"My friend Betty is very upset. You know, Rose Marie's aunt. She wonders if she should try to call on the children, let them know . . . you know, who their mother really was. What do you think?" Mrs. Olivera seemed to be rubbing the teapot with extra vigor and waiting for Mina's reaction.

"I don't know," Mina said thoughtfully. "I guess if she decides to tell them, maybe she should wait until after the funeral. It might be a shock, or at least a big surprise that they just don't need right now."

"That's just what I told her," Mrs. Olivera said in agreement. "I said, 'Betty, you should wait until things settle down.' Then, she has her nephew to think about, too."

"Who?" Mina asked as she reached for a banana from the bowl in front of her.

"Oh, her nephew. He has some asthma problems, and he comes from Maui to go to the doctor."

"Okay," Nyla said as she waltzed into the room, "you can stop eating now, Mina. I'm ready to go."

"What about Ollie?" Mina looked worried.

"He's a dog," Nyla replied, scolding. "He can stay at home."

"You leave him with me," Mrs. Olivera chimed in. "He knows me and he won't be any trouble."

Nyla was halfway out the door. "Come on, we need to have some fun."

When Tamiko and Michiko piled into the car, they made their way to downtown Honolulu and the shops, parking on Bishop Street and threading their way over to Fort Street. A little intimidated by the busy stores, the girls hung close to Nyla and Mina. They confessed that they had been to Chinatown once or twice with their parents to buy things from the food vendors, but they had never been east of Nuʻuanu Avenue, or set foot in any of the stores where "rich" people bought their clothes. Nyla decided they should start out at Kress, with its speckled stone floors and wide counters full of merchandise. Mina bought each of the girls a wristwatch, and Nyla bought them charm bracelets. Tamiko and Michiko were so overwhelmed with their presents and the store that Mina decided they had to sit down at the soda fountain and have something to drink. The girls twirled in the counter seats as they sipped their root beers and watched the bustling scene.

Then Nyla decided that they should move on to Liberty House. Tamiko and Michiko, when confronted with the big store windows and the mannequins dressed in the latest fashions, said they thought they better wait outside. Mina and Nyla laughed, grabbed the girls by their hands, and marched them into the store. The young women's clothing on the second floor required that they ride up in the elevator. The usually exuberant Tamiko and Michiko became very quiet and clung to Mina and Nyla like shy toddlers. Undaunted, the Beckwith sisters steered them into the young ladies' department, where the saleswoman (who knew Mina and Nyla) greeted them with a smile. With only a discreet glance at the anxious Tamiko and Michiko, the woman assessed the situation and quietly pointed out several areas where the most popular items for girls in their teens were. She suggested they look things over on their own, showed them the dressing rooms, and left them alone. It was difficult to get the girls to start expressing an opinion about what they liked, so Nyla took charge of Tamiko and Mina shadowed Michiko. Nyla and Mina then started by picking things out and making suggestions about what to try on. Soon the girls were able to say whether they liked one thing better than another.

They were a little shy about the dressing rooms, and couldn't believe that they were allowed to try the clothes on. After over an hour, Mina bought Michiko a navy blue polka-dot dress with puffed sleeves and a white piqué collar, a pleated plaid skirt, a white middy blouse and cardigan sweater, and a pair of dark sailor pants and a pullover top with three stars around the neckline. Nyla got Tamiko a pretty plaid sleeveless dress with a wide collar and buttons up the front, a practical dark skirt, a nice blouse with small blue flowers, a blue cardigan, a pair of white pants, and a striped pullover. Both girls simply stood by in disbelief as Mina and Nyla handed the saleslady one item after another and said "we'd like this and this and this." Then they made a stop in the women's department, because Nyla wanted a new hat. Soon, Nyla and Mina were both trying on hats and asked Tamiko and Michiko to help them make their choices.

Next, they went to the McInerny shoe store on the corner, and Mina and Nyla bought themselves and the girls new shoes. By this time everyone was famished, and after depositing their purchases in the car, they headed to the Harbor Grill for lunch. Tamiko and Michiko each had a hamburger, fries, and chocolate malt. Mina decided to have a club sandwich and potato salad, and Nyla ordered the meatloaf special. After lunch, they drove home by way of Waikīkī so that the girls could see the hotels and the famous beach.

"Mina," Michiko whispered, "do you think they'll catch the killer soon?"

"I hope so," Mina said.

"I don't know why people want to kill other people," Michiko added.

"I don't either," Mina agreed.

"They must be crazy," Tamiko joined in. "I hope they catch him soon. I'm getting scared."

Michiko stuck her head out the window. "Is that the zoo?"

"That's the zoo," Nyla said. "Shall we go?"

She was answered by an enthusiastic chorus of "yes" from the other three.

"My teacher said they almost closed the zoo because of the Depression," Tamiko said with concern.

"So we better see it while we have a chance," Michiko said excitedly. "We've never been, you know."

"Michi, you're making us sound like stupid country people," Tamiko complained.

"But we are country people," Michiko snapped back. "That's why we've never been to the zoo."

No one in downtown Honolulu knew where he came from, or exactly when Moxy had first made an appearance on the city streets, but by 1935 he was an established fixture. He had been arrested countless times for drunkenness, vagrancy, or both. When arrested, he always listed his place of residence as Venice, Italy, and said he was just here in Hawai'i while repairs where being made to his villa. As he sat there in Todd's office, stirring a cup of coffee, Ned couldn't help but notice the peculiar odor that emanated from his tattered grey coat, or the suspicious stains on his worn khaki trousers that Ned sincerely hoped were not from urine. Moxy twitched his grizzled head every once in a while, and his smile revealed years of tobacco use and no dental care. But his most startling feature was his eyes, which bulged wide and exposed a large area of white between the iris and his lower lid, creating the effect of a constant, surprised stare.

"Monday night, yeah, yeah," Moxy muttered. "I remember that was the night your boys rousted me from the Bennington building stoop. You should tell 'em not to be so rough. I think they might have sprained my wrist."

"The Bennington building is right across from the Burnham and Robbins building." Todd opened a bottle of cola for Ned and one for himself.

"Everybody know that, boss," Moxy said, and twitched his head to the side.

"Is that a wisecrack, Moxy?" Todd looked at him.

"Oh, no disrespect to you, boss." Moxy smiled his brown-toothed smile.

"So my boys say you saw something that night," Todd continued, "around ten or so."

"I guess I did. I guess I did."

"And what was that?"

"I wandered over there with my little pal of rum-rum, see? Dark rum, that's what ole Moxy likes. And I know it was near ten, because

I heard the church bell, didn't I? And I counted one, two, three, and so on and it stopped at ten."

"Where do you get the money from? To buy this liquor?" Todd shook his head.

"You may not think it to look at me, boss," Moxy said, holding his head proudly, "but I'm a man of means. I have a villa in Italy."

"Right," Todd said, "and I'm Clark Gable."

"Is that a wisecrack, boss?" Moxy twitched again.

"No disrespect to you." Todd smiled and took a sip of his cola. "So what did you see?"

"I saw a Catherine. I saw a Heathcliff. I saw Jane Eyre and Mr. Rochester. I saw a white lady and her gypsy lover." Moxy sipped his coffee and spilled some on his shirt.

"You mean you saw a couple?" Todd asked.

"Yes, boss, a pair of them."

"Would you recognize them again?" Todd took from an envelope a photo of Tessa and Emil that Mina had taken at the Haleʻiwa Hotel. They sat smiling on the front stairs. He showed the picture to Moxy.

"That looks like them," Moxy said immediately.

"Are you sure?" Todd put the photo away.

Moxy nodded. "Pretty sure, boss."

"How about this couple?" Todd produced a photo of Gilbert and Helen Burnham taken at some gala event.

"Nope, never seen 'em, boss," Moxy replied, shaking his head.

"And what was this couple doing when you saw them?"

"They went in and then they went out."

"How long?" Todd began to lean toward him, but then caught himself and leaned back.

Moxy thought for a moment. "Must have been about a quarter of a bottle's worth. I drink pretty fast. By the time it's half past the bottle, I don't remember so good. No, they went in and came out running."

"Running?" Todd looked at him.

"Cinderella broke her shoe now, didn't she? Caught it on the crack in the pavement. Had to take her shoes off and run in her bare feet, like a native, ha, ha." Moxy slapped his knee.

"Is that all you saw, Moxy?" Todd glanced at Ned.

"No, I saw some pink elephants come down the street, ha, ha, ha." Moxy slapped his knee again.

"I think this interview is over," Todd said. "Go with the officer at the door there. He's going to get you something to eat but don't leave town—even if your villa repairs are finished."

Ned watched Moxy shuffle toward the office door. It was hard to tell exactly how old the man might be. He looked as if he was in his sixties, but he could have been much younger. Still, Ned thought, he'd had an education somewhere—all those references to literature and the twisted sense of humor were the mark of someone who'd come down a long way. Todd was busy on the phone as Ned looked out the window at the uniformed officer leading Moxy down the street. He wondered what Tessa Burnham and Emil Devon had done that night. There was certainly more to Tessa than her sincere girl-next-door façade, and Emil, he was a dark gypsy-Heathcliff, perhaps capable of the same ruthless revenge. Ned became conscious of Todd putting down the black telephone receiver. "That was Gilbert Burnham on the phone." Todd looked at Ned and raised his eyebrows. "Seems that his brother had some paid spies informing him on the activities of those who would unionize our islands."

"And?" Ned asked.

"And apparently one of them reported to Gilbert that Duncan Mackenzie held a meeting in 'A'ala Park the night before, and it was all about Shimasaki's supposed murder by Henry Burnham's order. Jack was not present, and apparently Mackenzie got the men pretty riled up."

"I guess you haven't gotten word about his background."

"Not yet, but I expect it soon." Todd looked out of the window.

"He knows everything Jack does," Ned mused. "It would be so easy for him to make Jack a sitting duck."

Mina sat alone on a bench, under one of the tall trees in the zoo. She felt tired. Her shoulder ached, and she had to let Nyla and the girls go on without her. The afternoon light filtered through the branches, making patterns of light and dark that sparkled and shifted with the breeze on the neatly trimmed grass that surrounded her. A flock of dirty white pigeons wandered around, looking for crumbs and bugs, cooing intermittently. From this vantage she could see the flamingo pen. The startling pink plumage of the birds stood out against the green mock orange hedges that encircled the zoo. Their graceful necks curved and twisted in different postures over the rounded mass of their bodies held up by those impossibly thin legs. They looked so vulnerable. She couldn't understand why they didn't just fall over.

She watched as more pigeons landed on the grass, and she had the anxious feeling that it was getting late. It wasn't just the fading afternoon, with its shafts of poignant light. It was a feeling that time in general was running out, that there was something that needed to be finished, that there might not be enough time left before she was cut off and separated from the world. A wave of unexplainable sorrow swept through her, and she felt for a few minutes as if she were lost and far away from home. She sat listening to her own breathing and staring at the white pigeons moving frenetically, almost mechanically, over the landscape. Their cooing seemed much louder and more frequent. As they moved closer to her, the unpleasant smell of their dusty feathers enveloped her, and yet she couldn't bring herself to get up and chase them away.

She leaned back and closed her eyes. *We're all so close to death,* she thought. *I was just spared, but anything could happen to me or to anyone at any minute. Things do happen to people all the time. Look what just happened to Henry Burnham and Gwen Reed. How can we ever be at peace when we have no control?* She thought about the people she couldn't bear to be separated from if she died this very minute—her sister, her grandmother, her father, and Ned. Yes, she knew she would miss Ned and the kind of life she imagined they might have together as a couple, the kinds of things they might share as people who genuinely cared for each other, the kind of future she could have with someone who didn't expect her to be an ordinary wife, or an ordinary anything. Time, how much time was left for them? Mina opened her eyes and became aware of the stillness around her. In the distance, one of the zoo lions roared. The pigeons had stopped their cooing.

They stood, silently tilting their heads. The breeze had vanished and the shafts of angled, golden light glowed over the grounds and onto the bench. She welcomed the warmth of the sun as it spread over her face and arms. Nyla and the girls rushed around the corner in a cloud of fun and laughter, and as Michiko and Tamiko ran toward her, their faces flushed with excitement, the pigeons scattered and flew away in a great, feathery rush.

17

THURSDAY

THE MORNING SUN in Maunalani Heights fell through the windows and onto Nyla and Todd's kitchen table. Ned and Mina had just arrived and were stirring cream and sugar into the cups of coffee that Mrs. Olivera had poured for them just before she went upstairs to sort out the laundry. Ollie had trotted after her, but changed his mind and returned to the kitchen just in time to hear the displeased tone in Todd's voice.

"You've invited them over here?" Todd was about to take a bite of his toast but put it down.

"Why not?" Nyla poured some liliko'i juice in a glass and put it down in front of Ned on the red-checkered tablecloth. "You won't be here, will you?"

Ned and Mina glanced across the kitchen table at each other and smiled.

"She could be a murder suspect!" Todd raised his voice, and Ollie immediately walked over to him and pawed his thigh.

"He wants you to calm down, old man," Ned said with a laugh.

"If she is," Nyla retorted, "it will be all the more interesting."

"Don't look at me, Todd," Mina said as she smeared fig jam on her toast. "I had nothing to do with it."

"No?" Todd frowned. "I don't think I can trust either of you."

"You've just realized that?" Ned looked at Todd with amusement. "It doesn't say much for your detection skills."

"So when will they be here?" Todd asked.

"At tea time. They're coming around three-thirty." Nyla placed a bowl of mixed fruit on the table. "Let's start with this, and then I'll scramble the eggs."

"Maybe you better be here, Ned." Todd made it sound like an order.

"Maybe I'm not invited."

"Oh, you're invited," Nyla assured him. "But Mr. Grumpy is not."

"Mr. Grumpy doesn't care." Todd stuck his tongue out at his wife.

"Does marriage affect everyone's maturity like this, Ned?" Mina asked as she bit in to her overly jammed toast.

"No, only the special couples, darling."

"Mina, you could help me by turning the bacon strips over." Nyla indicated a large cast-iron frying pan full of sizzling bacon.

"No problem," she said, grabbing a pair of tongs and jumping right to the task. "Why does bacon smell so good?"

"Because of the fat," Todd answered.

"And speaking of fat," Mina continued, "does Duncan Mackenzie have a big fat record or not?"

"I'm not at liberty to tell you." Ned pointed to Todd. "You'll have to ask the chief."

"I wouldn't call it fat," Todd said as he stirred his coffee. "He does have an assault charge for which he was put on probation, and several older charges of disorderly conduct, as in being drunk. But the most disturbing thing is that once he was charged along with several others for attempted murder in San Pedro. It was something to do with a company supervisor. The charges were dropped for lack of evidence."

Mina fussed with the bacon in the pan. "Which means he's someone we overlooked."

"What do you mean, *we*?" Todd sounded irritated.

"I beg your pardon," Mina shot back.

"Look," Todd began, "five people are dead. We're dealing with a serious killer here. Now you two are inviting a suspect over for tea. You need to back off and leave this job to the police now."

"We can't help it if we're involved, can we, Mina?" Nyla gave her sister a self-satisfied smile.

"Oh, no." Mina smiled back as she removed the bacon from the pan. "We certainly can't help it."

"We're employed by Burnham and Robbins," Nyla said as she poured the eggs into a skillet. "They're our clients, and now Gilbert Burnham is the head of the company, and he wants me to finish the project."

"He does?" Todd asked.

"Some woman called me from his office when I got home yesterday. That room where the shootings took place? He wants to make it a storage room, and he's going to pick another room for his office that he wants me to fix up."

Todd rolled his eyes. "That's it. Ned is following the two of you around forever."

"You'll have a little respite from these harridans," Ned reminded him. "We're all going to Maui tonight on the cattle boat, remember?"

"Thank God!" said Todd.

Nyla looked at him and munched on a piece of bacon. "Yeah, we're going with Daddy. Grandma Hannah will look after you."

"Hey, where are they, anyway?" Mina asked. "Grandma and Daddy."

"They went to look at a mare," Nyla answered.

"Why would Grandma Hannah want to go and look at a mare?" asked Mina.

Nyla took her sister aside and spoke softly so that the others couldn't hear. "Maybe because that cowboy was meeting Daddy."

"What are you two whispering about?" Todd said. "You look suspicious."

"No," Ned added, "they look guilty."

After breakfast, Mina and Nyla cleared the table, and Nyla insisted that Mina come upstairs and help her decide what to pack for Maui. Ned watched the two of them traipse out of the room, then turned and saw Todd lost in thought. Ned felt he could almost read Todd's mind, and he puzzled for a moment over why Todd had always seemed so easy to decipher. He knew that Todd didn't have the same insight into his thoughts, so what was it, he wondered, that made it so simple for him to know what was going through Todd's mind at this particular moment? Ned reached for the still warm coffee carafe and poured himself another cup.

He knew that Todd worried over the new murders, that he had great concerns for the involvement of Nyla and Mina with the Burnham family, and that he felt responsible and somewhat guilty over initiating more than a working relationship between the sisters and the family. Responsibility and guilt. He could almost feel Todd chastising himself for Mina being shot. He could almost feel his apprehension about what might happen next, about Mina's and Nyla's apparent fearlessness in the face of brutal murder. Then there were the community concerns weighing on his mind, the volatile tension between labor and management in the islands, the anger and resentment of thousands of workers that lay just beneath the surface of their submissive facial masks. He knew Todd had a healthy awareness and respect for that anger.

"There are some situations," Ned said as he stirred his coffee, "in which you simply have to wait for the next thing to happen."

"What?" Todd looked at him.

"You know what I mean." Ned added another sugar cube to his coffee. "And I'll be here when the Burnhams show up, but I have to tell you, Mina may sometimes appear careless about what's going on around her, but she's made of steel and not much gets by her. I suspect Nyla is the same way, but she just covers it up a bit more than Mina does."

"I hate to admit it, but I know you're right." Todd grimaced.

"At any rate," Ned continued, "Nyla is a little more cautious than Mina, and not as likely to take a big risk."

"Let's hope so." Todd shook his head.

"Look, old friend," Ned said, trying to sound confident, "there's the tea this afternoon, and then we're all off to Maui for a few days. I'll make sure they don't get in any trouble."

"Don't kid yourself, Ned." Todd's laugh sounded strained. "Those two could pull our shades down before we even knew it."

That afternoon, as he watched Nyla and Mina playing host to the Burnham sisters and their half-brother, Ned thought about what

Todd had said to him. On their own, the sisters were beautiful and engaging, but together, their combined and purposeful charm could be something more than simply gracious island hospitality, an activity that came as naturally to them as breathing. He watched as they poured tea, smiled, soothed, and most of all listened intently to their guests. They focused much of their attention on Tessa, drawing her out of herself with a nod or a simple word or two at the exact right moment. With ease, they were able to make her feel so comforted and relaxed that he believed she would have told them anything—unless, of course, she was a practiced actress.

Hester had gone out in the yard with Ollie, and every once in a while he could hear her calling the dog. Sheldon roamed around the living room, looking at Nyla's photographs, artwork, and her exquisite family artifacts, both Hawaiian and Western. The late afternoon bathed everyone in its most flattering light, and even though there was only the hint of a breeze, there was still a slight chill in the air, as if the pure warmth of the Hawaiian summer wanted to be there, but couldn't help being a little late.

"I just can't quite believe it's real," Tessa said. She was sitting in a garden chair, with Nyla and Mina on either side. She looked over at Ned, saw that he was watching, then quickly looked away, speaking again to the sisters. "You know, I keep thinking I'll wake up and it will have all been a mistake."

"And how is Hester really doing? I thought she was quite close to your father." Nyla's voice was full of concern.

"Shel and I can't figure it out." Tessa shrugged. "She seems unaffected by it. We're both expecting a breakdown or a scene or something, but she just acts like nothing's happened."

"Sometimes reactions come much later," Mina said.

Tessa nodded. "I know. I'll just have to be on my guard."

"I'm so sorry we won't be here for the funeral," Nyla said.

"I understand," Tessa replied. "To tell you the truth, we all just want to get it over with." She paused and looked at her hands. "Who would have thought that she was Jack Carstairs' sister?"

"It is very strange, isn't it?" Mina commented.

"I guess he's been arrested again, and they think he's responsible." Tessa looked at Mina and then Nyla as if she expected they might have an opinion.

"Well," Mina offered, "I think he's the main suspect, but anyone could have done it. The killer or killers could have dropped the gun in the alley near Jack's residence. Just to make it look like he did it."

Tessa blanched ever so slightly and her eyes opened a little wider. "Do you think that's what happened?" She examined her fingernails.

"I don't know what *really* happened," Mina answered. "I'm just suggesting another way it *could* have happened."

"Where's Hester gone to?" Tessa glanced around anxiously.

"She's outside with Ollie, the dog." Ned tried to sound reassuring. "I'll just go and see if she's all right."

Ned found Hester playing a game of fetch with Ollie in the empty lot next to Nyla's home. She stood there, her hair shining in the sunlight, and threw the ball into some tall grass. Ollie bounded around and nuzzled the ground looking for it. When he found the ball and ran back to her, her face beamed with delight. Looking at her disturbed Ned. She looked so young for her years—too young, as if she were trapped in a youthful bubble, unable to break out. If something didn't change for her as she aged, what was now still a little forgivable would become pathetic. He wondered if her refusal to grow up was a convenience or a genuine inability. She was a strange little creature, so self-contained and withdrawn. What was underneath those glasses, those adolescent braids, and those dowdy flowered cotton dresses? He inwardly laughed at himself and thought perhaps he had read too much Freud. Hester turned and was alarmed to see him standing there.

"Hello." Ned tried to sound harmless and friendly.

"Oh, hello." She turned away and threw the ball again for Ollie. "Tessa says I can get a dog now." She said it without looking at him. "She said she might get one, too."

"How nice for you." Ned marveled at how Ollie seemed to make everyone around him happy. "What kind of dog do you want?"

"I want a German shepherd," she said in a decisive tone.

"That's quite a powerful breed."

"Yes," she responded, "but they're loyal, and he can protect me. I'm going to name him King. Tessa wants to get a miniature poodle. I would never want a poodle."

"Poodles are very loyal, too, and smart."

"Nobody's afraid of a poodle," she said. "They're sissy dogs. But if we get the two dogs together, they'll be friends and we won't have any problems."

"Oh, so you'll be living with your sister?" Ned thought he would push her just a little.

"Of course." She looked at him like he was crazy. "Where else would I live? And Shel said he wouldn't move away now. We're all going to live together in our house."

"I'm very sorry about your father." Ned looked down and watched his right foot skim over the grass. When he glanced back up at her, he had the distinct impression that she was angry. After a punctuated silence, she turned to him.

"At least now he can't marry that little bitch." The word sounded especially vulgar coming from her. "I would never want her living in our house. I'm glad she's dead instead of being my stepmother."

"You knew he asked her to marry him?"

"We found out. We all knew, even Uncle Gilbert. We all wanted to kill her." She blushed and gasped when she realized what she had said. "I . . . I didn't mean we—"

"I know you didn't mean it." Ned's first impulse was to feel sorry for her, but just as quickly he questioned his reaction. "Your sister is wondering where you are. I think she's hoping you'll come in."

"Do you think I should?"

"It would be the polite thing to do."

"Well, I guess I have to be polite." She knitted her brow as she walked toward the house.

Ollie came up to Ned, rubbed his head against Ned's knee, and then looked up at him as if he expected Ned to say something. "That was very good of you to entertain her," he said as he scratched the dog's head. "Now let's go see what Mina is up to."

At the mention of his mistress' name, Ollie gave a little jump and ran toward the house. Back indoors, as the women chatted, Ned found Sheldon near the fireplace mantle, looking at a picture of Mina on the family ranch. It must have been taken when she was a teenager. She was standing in her Western boots up off the ground on the lower rung of a corral fence, in a checkered shirt and dungarees, with her cowgirl hat set back on her head and her dark hair streaming out and framing her face. There was a short lei of mountain ferns around her neck, and she was holding out a carrot to a horse that looked like an appaloosa. The camera had permanently secured her smile of pure and unself-conscious happiness, the kind of look that can make a viewer feel nostalgia for a real, imagined, or yearned-for childhood. Ned could see that for some reason the picture had made Sheldon feel a little sad.

"That's a lovely picture of Mina, isn't it?" Ned said, trying his best to be friendly.

"Charming," Sheldon answered as he ran his finger over the protective glass. "Horses can bring out the best in people."

"Most people," Ned agreed. "But I've seen some owners who were very cruel to their animals."

"There's no reason to be cruel to an animal," Sheldon said flatly.

"I've heard you're quite keen on polo."

"Do you play?" Sheldon brightened.

"I have, but I'm sure I'm a bit out of practice." Ned looked at the photo of Mina and then at Sheldon. "Did you know Mina and Nyla in school? Everyone seems to have gone to school with each other here."

"I didn't know them well," Sheldon answered. "They were a few years younger than I was. It makes a big difference when you're a kid." He paused, and his gaze drifted across the room and out to the lanai to Tessa and Hester. Then he said in a softer, almost faraway voice, "I wish I'd paid more attention."

"Sorry." Ned looked at him quizzically. "I don't quite follow you."

"Oh, nothing." Sheldon turned on his boyish smile. "Certain things, when I was younger, I wish I'd paid more attention to. Then I might have won the heart of the little cowgirl, not you."

18

FRIDAY

FROM THE UPPER deck of the *Humuʻula,* as the ship plodded its way toward Kahului Harbor, Ned saw Maui for the first time. As the morning light began its ritual transformation of darkness, the broad volcanic dome of Haleakalā slowly appeared. The land swept down from the crater to a wide, flat plain and up again to the rain-sculpted West Maui Mountains. Below him, and toward the bow of the ship, the gates that separated the empty cattle pens rattled as the ship rolled with the ocean swells, and the smell of hay and farm animals wafted to the upper deck. He imagined that on the way back to Honolulu the stalls would be filled with cattle. But now there was only a lone pony in the far corner stall. Feeding from a canvas bag, it turned and looked toward him, then went back to its meal as casually as if it were in a barn on a farm.

Ollie bounced up behind him, wagging his tail. He sidled up close and nuzzled Ned's knee in greeting. Mina and her father soon appeared, and they all watched the longshoremen, mostly Hawaiians, tying the ship up to the dock. As Ned stood there he thought about his father, who had worked as a harbor pilot in Apia, Western Sāmoa. This had been his father's life—the docks, the ships, and the ocean. More than once, when he was a child in Sāmoa, his father had taken him out to escort a vessel through the passage in the reef. He remembered the brisk ocean, the smell of salt on the wind, the brightness in his father's eyes, and the way the other men deferred to him. He remembered the excitement of coming through the breakers and the channel into Apia Harbor, with its wooden storefronts and big white churches, and Mount Vaea standing behind and watching over everything. But this was Kahului, not Apia, and Maui's central plain stretched out in a lake of cane that flowed up into the valleys of the West Maui Mountains and lapped at the foot of the majestic Haleakalā.

It was a clear morning, and the long mountain stood silhouetted against the pale hues of the morning sky. They were close to the dock now, and Mina and Nyla were waving to a stocky man standing near a car and an old truck. The man wore khaki-colored pants that were tucked into worn leather riding boots, and a light-blue work shirt with the sleeves rolled up. He had a red kerchief tied around his neck, and a cowboy hat shaded his face. He was leaning against the car smoking a cigar, engaged in lively conversation with a Hawaiian man who was standing next to the truck. When he saw the girls waving, he gave them a big, squinty smile and waved back.

"That's Uncle Jinx," Nyla said, turning to Ned.

"He's your uncle?" Ned asked.

Mina shook her head. "No, not our real uncle. He's our calabash uncle."

"Calabash uncle?" Ned looked confused.

"When someone is very close to your family, not blood related, but close enough to share a calabash of poi with the family, that's a calabash relative," Nyla informed him.

"It's a polite way to acknowledge closeness while distinguishing genealogy," Mina added. "Because we call all our parents' close friends aunty and uncle."

"Jinx's place, Kilakila Ranch, is on the western slope of Haleakalā." Charles pointed toward the mountain. "The ranch stretches up the side of the volcano and borders the park. We'll be staying in a cabin at about four thousand feet."

"Does Uncle Jinx have a real name?" Ned grinned.

"Jonathan Wentworth Montgomery the third," Charles answered, grinning back. "'Jinx' is short for 'High Jinx,' because he was always cutting it up in school."

"A school chum?" Ned asked.

"Jinx and I go way back," Charles said. "Visiting him and his family is what got my father interested in buying a ranch, and what gave me the bug to be a rancher."

In no time the ship's crew had the gangplank lowered, and Ned was following Mina, Nyla, and their father down and onto the dock. Introductions were made and the bags loaded into the old truck, driven by Liko, one of the ranch hands. Mina decided to go in the truck with Liko, as Ollie was to ride in the back with the baggage, and she thought it best to keep an eye on him because she knew he had jumped out of the back of a pickup once before. In the car, Charles insisted that Ned sit in the front seat with Uncle Jinx, as it was his first trip to Maui. Jinx stubbed his cigar out in the ashtray before they got underway, but it didn't seem to matter. Everything in the automobile reeked of cigar smoke and another smell Ned recognized as what his mother used to call a "farmsy" odor. She used it describe the dwellings, cars, and sometimes even bodies of her friends who were avid dog and horse lovers.

Only a few minutes away from the dock they were in the midst of sugarcane fields, with the road beginning to rise up along the slopes of the massive mountain. Soon the cane gave way to grassland. The air felt crisp and cool, and the character of the sunlight softened. Uncle Jinx had a distinct intensity about him, and Ned could almost taste his pointed curiosity.

"So where did you come from, son?" Jinx asked him. "And how did you end up with these oddball Beckwiths, anyway?"

Ned had never quite gotten used to this habit so many older American men had of calling younger men "son." It made him feel uneasy. "Well, I was born in Western Sāmoa, raised in Britain by my widowed mother and my grandfather, and I met the Beckwiths through Todd, Nyla's husband. We've been friends for quite some time."

"Are you a detective, too? Where did you meet up with Todd?" Jinx continued.

"No, I'm not a *real* detective," Ned said quietly, "but I met Todd at a special training session in London that the British government asked me to attend. Todd was still in the military. It was a series of lectures by Dr. Edmond Locard."

"And who is this Dr. Locard?"

"He's a Frenchman and an expert on trace evidence, especially fingerprint analysis. He began the International Academy of Criminalistics."

"But you're not a detective?"

"No, actually now I'm a writer. I write for the theatre."

"I'll bet you're much more than that." Jinx gave him a sly look. "Or you wouldn't have been at those lectures."

"We're all more than one thing, aren't we?" Ned then changed the subject in an affable tone. "I'm sure there's more to you than ranching."

Charles leaned forward. "Jinx could have been a concert violinist. Although these days, he's taken to fiddling for his cowboys, right, Jinx?"

"I still find time for a little classical music now and then. You don't happen to play the piano, do you, Ned?" Jinx gave him a hopeful look.

"He plays way better than I do," Nyla said.

"You play well?" Jinx continued.

"I play well enough to accompany my grandfather," Ned answered. "He plays the cello. He's quite good, too. But I'm definitely not concert material."

"You're in for it now," Charles said, grinning. "Jinx is always looking for someone to play with."

"Would you like to?" Jinx asked right away. "Maybe tonight after dinner? I'll pick some music out when we get back to the house and you can see what suits you."

"I'd be glad to," Ned said.

"And Ned rides like he was born in the saddle, Uncle Jinx," Nyla added.

"A country boy?" Jinx raised his eyebrows.

"The lake district," Ned informed him.

"Well," Jinx said, shifting the car into lower gear as the road got a little steeper, "tomorrow I'm supposed to drive about twelve head of cattle down to Mākena. Charles, you remember Archie Macpherson?"

"Sure I do. He was with Makawao Ranch."

"Yeah," Uncle Jinx went on, "he retired and built a place down there near Puʻuōlaʻi. He grows melons, alfalfa, and squash, and he buys a few cattle from us from time to time to fatten up in his feedlot. How'd you all like to come along? The ranch has a cottage down there. Louise will meet us and we can all spend the night."

Nyla smiled with distinct delight. "Sounds great. Ned, it will be a great ride."

"Then of course I'd like to go," Ned said as he looked out at the breathtaking scenery.

"And Uncle Jinx," Nyla said, leaning forward, "Mina and I are dying to drive up to Haleakalā on the new road. We read all about the opening a few weeks ago."

"Oh, hell," Uncle Jinx replied, sighing. "There was such a big hullabaloo and a long parade of cars with all your Honolulu swells showing off their new clothes. Of course Louise insisted we accept the invitation."

"That must be something, to be able to take a car all the way to the top," Nyla reflected.

"I think it was better when you could only go by horse," Uncle Jinx grumbled. "Now everyone and his uncle will be running around up there. Still, you're welcome to use the car and go while you're here."

"That would be terrific. I don't think we'd have time to go on horseback anyway," Nyla said, "not if we're going to Mākena, too." She gave him a coy smile. "Besides, you wouldn't want me to go back to Honolulu and not be able to brag about how I'd been on the new road, would you?"

"Oh, heaven forbid," Jinx said with a laugh. "That would never do."

Charles and Uncle Jinx then fell into a conversation about bulls as Ned's attention became fixed on the changing view. They had reached a crossroad, turned to the right, and were now skirting along the side of the mountain. Below, he could see the central plain of the island covered in a sea of green cane, and the curve of the coastline to the south. Offshore, in the distance, another island rose from the sea. Groves of flowering lavender jacaranda trees were scattered along the rolling hills, and the shadows of clouds drifted over the pasturelands, forming shifting pools of shade and honeyed sunlight. Ned's response to this landscape was immediate and swift—he felt a surge of unexpected emotion, as if the island were a person, a living entity he had once been intimately attached to, somehow lost, and now had found again. It wasn't the first time this had happened to him in the islands, and he didn't quite understand what it meant. He felt baffled and fascinated all at once by these unbidden emotions, but took comfort in his expert ability to hide them behind a veneer of reserve.

He could see Mina in the truck a little ways ahead of them, and Ollie standing in the back on the flat bed, his front paws on the wheel well, his face to the wind, and his tongue hanging out the side of his mouth. Somehow the sight of Ollie and his dedicated look of pleasure hastened the recovery of his inner calm. It pleased him so much to see Mina with Ollie, as if her attachment to the dog confirmed the innate goodness he already knew she had. He imagined what it might be like to live with her in a big house, in countryside like this, with a stable and horses, dogs, and room to ride. When the car turned off the main road and began an uphill climb on a rutted dirt road, he was bounced out of his imaginary country estate. He looked back at Nyla in the seat behind him and thought she looked a little drawn and worn out from the journey. The road climbed and curved through a stand of eucalyptus trees, then dipped slightly as the ranch house came into view. All of a sudden the car was on smooth ground again, winding around the circular drive and pulling up to the front door.

The entrance to the two-story house faced mauka, and Uncle Jinx ushered everyone in through the wide front doors. The house opened immediately into a sprawling parlor with a rich, wide-planked wooden floor, adorned in places with lauhala mats and throw rugs. In the middle of the right wall stood an impressive lava rock fireplace, flanked by floor-to-ceiling shelves that held Hawaiian artifacts of stone and wood. Above the fireplace hung a large landscape painting of Haleakalā with the sun rising behind it. Sofas, easy chairs, cozy game tables, and a grand piano were all arranged comfortably and with taste. A plump woman with a round, smiling face streamed into the room. She was dressed in a long, flowery muʻumuʻu, and she wore her slightly graying hair in two thick braids.

After giving Mina, Nyla, and Charles each a hug and kiss, Charles introduced her to Ned.

"This is Louise Montgomery." Charles beamed, his arm around her. "Louise, this is Ned Manusia, a friend of the family."

Louise took everyone straight through to the large veranda at the back of the house and seated them around a long table for brunch. Nyla excused herself and asked to lie down for a bit. The view from the veranda swept dramatically down to the central plain and all the way to the West Maui Mountains and included both the north and south shorelines. The horizon line, looking much higher because of their elevation, cut a clear outline across the sky. Ned felt far away and removed from his everyday life. After a superb meal of cheese soufflé, salads, and sausages, Louise served a strawberry tart that she said was made with the first berries of the season from her garden.

An excited Uncle Jinx then showed Ned some sheet music, all of which Ned said he felt sure he could play, but just to be sure, he sat down at the piano and tried it out. Before he knew it, Uncle Jinx had taken out his violin and begun to play along with him. Mina, Charles, and Nyla, who had rejoined them, visited with Louise, half listening to the music. Ned could not help but be impressed with Jinx's skill and sensitivity, and after they had played together for nearly an hour, Ned felt a kind of kinship and tenderness for the rough ranch manager. Uncle Jinx then spirited Charles away to go and look at bulls, and Louise took Ned and the girls on a little tour of the ranch house and grounds. She especially enjoyed showing off her small orchard of plum and apricot trees, as well as her vegetable and flower gardens.

"I have a higher-up garden, too," she added, "where it's even cooler. That's where I grow roses, violets, and things like that. I hope I have time to show it to you."

"Aunt Louise," Mina began, "do you know a family here—I think they live in Makawao—named Rodrigues?"

"That's a fairly common Portuguese name," Louise answered.

"Antone Rodrigues," Mina went on, "and he had a sister named Betty."

Louise thought for a moment as they walked. "Yes, I think I do remember that man. He had a small dairy farm. I went there once or twice with my mother when I was a child. As I recall, he had *two* sisters who helped him, and I think he collected and sold firewood, too. I wonder if his little dairy is still there? I haven't thought of it in years. It was an out-of-the-way place, down a long dirt road."

"Do you remember his daughters? He had two daughters. They were probably about your age."

"I vaguely remember some children there, but it was so long ago. Still . . ." Louise had a faraway look, as if she were struggling to bring back the memory.

"One of them died when she was a young woman," Mina offered.

"Yes, that's right!" Louise exclaimed. "She died in childbirth."

"Really?" Mina didn't want to press Aunt Louise too much.

"Yes, that's right, she did. I think she lost the baby, too. Now I remember; it was something of a tragedy—all these people saying terrible things about her because she wasn't married, and then the poor girl dies."

"That is tragic," Mina said, and she thought about how the family would have wanted to bury her memory. As Catholics, it would have been particularly shameful.

Louise nodded. "Yes, it was. Of course, the woman always gets blamed in these affairs, and the men get off with a little slap on the wrist. It just makes me so mad. No wonder I wanted to forget all about it. Let's think of something more cheerful. Why don't you girls cut some flowers to take up to the cabin?"

Ned helped Mina and Nyla cut flowers. There were so many to choose from, and nearly everywhere they turned, the dramatic view of the island and the sea hung before them like a living painting. The quietness, the brilliance of the grass, the smell of the cool, upland air intoxicated Ned the way anticipating a holiday had when he was a child, and he felt he could hardly wait to be on horseback, riding through the ranch.

In the late afternoon Mina, Nyla, Ned, and Charles drove up to the guest cottage in one of the ranch's trucks. The cottage sat above the house, another one thousand feet higher, in the pastureland, in front of a small stand of pines. By the time they reached the retreat, a flotilla of afternoon clouds was moving in and about to surround them in mist. Mina got out of the truck to open and close the gate that led through the fence and protected the cottage and its small yard from cattle. The cottage was rustic, with green board and batten walls, white-trimmed windows, and a faded red-tin roof. A covered porch ran along the front, and to the side stood a raised water tank. Disheveled but colorful beds of nasturtiums reached up from the ground toward the unpainted porch and the weathered furniture that looked as if it had been taking in the view for many decades. Inside, a faded couch and a couple of chairs surrounded a corner wood-burning stove. A musty smell lingered in the air, and Mina went around and opened all the windows. Along the back wall were a kitchen sink, a food safe, a couple of kerosene burners, and a table with some chairs. On the table were several kerosene lanterns, candles, and a flashlight. Two bedrooms flanked either end of the room.

"There's an outhouse in the back and a shower on the other side of the water tank," Charles told Ned. "But we generally take our clothes and shower at the ranch house before dinner. The water up here is mighty cold."

After Ned settled into the room he was sharing with Charles, the two of them went outside to sort through the wood pile. Charles assured him that they would want to light a fire when they came back after dinner and that they may even want to keep it burning through the night. They hauled and stacked several small logs near the stove, and then Ned said he was going to brave the cold shower out in the back. He found a large, scratchy towel on one of the shelves in the room, stripped down, wrapped the towel around his waist, and walked outside with a bar of soap. The sun was creeping down behind the West Maui Mountains, and although it was still light he could feel the air temperature dropping rapidly. Behind the water tank, he turned on the raised tap, took off his towel, and, facing the tank, stepped under the icy water. Once he was completely wet, he turned off the water and began to soap himself. When he turned the water on again and turned around to rinse himself, he saw three cows standing on the other side of the fence, not six yards away, watching him with devoted interest. One of them began to moo at him, and he wondered whether she was flirting or making fun of him. The uncomfortably cold water made him rinse off as quickly as possible, but once he was toweled off, he felt completely alive, invigorated, and far away from the dark goings-on in Honolulu.

19

SATURDAY

AFTER THEY HAD been riding for nearly an hour, Mina felt the
chill of the dark, early morning and did up the buttons on the
old denim jacket she'd borrowed from Louise. As her horse trailed
along behind the little herd, she thought she could feel the whole
world poised on the verge of a new day. The nearly full moon hung
above the horizon, and before her the Southern Cross lingered in the
sky. She knew that soon there would be a few moments when the
brighter stars and the constellations would stand out like road signs
as the fainter stars were absorbed into the seeping light of the dawn.

The air hung very still and the cattle moved ahead of her in a
warm bundle, lowing peacefully as they made their way in the dark.
She could see the outlines of Ned and Uncle Jinx in the lead. Laulima,
one of the Kilakila paniolo, guarded the makai side of the herd, Nyla
rode on the mauka side, and here she was bringing up the rear. She
remembered the first time she'd ever ridden in a drive. She must have
been seven then, or maybe eight. Nohea, one of the older paniolo
on the family ranch, had always been put in charge of her, and he
explained how the cattle should be moved slowly and calmly, because
it lessened the chance of panic and stampede. He had told her it was
their job to be steady but alert, in case the herd scattered—that the
cattle could sense the calm feelings of the paniolo, but still they had
to be ready. If she wanted to be a good cowgirl, he had said, she had
to practice that peaceful but prepared way of being, and if she had
to spring into action, she better think fast, because she had to let the
horse know right away what to do.

The smell of Nohea's old plaid flannel shirt came back to her—a mixture of hay and castile soap. She remembered how he would let her put flowers in his hat—she'd stick their little stems through the grommet, right where the tie went through, and even though he'd been gone for more than ten years, she still sensed him sometimes, riding beside her when she was on horseback. She imagined him there with her, watching Ned, admiring the way he sat so well in the saddle, and approving of the way he fit so naturally into the rhythm of ranch life. She knew the paniolo on her father's ranch liked Ned, not just because he was Polynesian like them, but because he was respectful and recognized their skills and intelligence. She laughed to herself when she thought about how many times arrogant outsiders had come to the ranch and talked down to the men, how they'd come to regret it when somehow they'd been maneuvered by the paniolo into making fools of themselves. It was very unwise for an outsider to stomp into the ranch in high-and-mighty boots. There was nothing that amused the paniolo more than knocking an arrogant SOB down a notch or two.

She could see that Ned had already enchanted Aunt Louise, and Uncle Jinx, always suspicious of others, was doing his best not to start liking him too much, too fast. When Uncle Jinx had first met Todd, he took Mina aside. "He can't even ride a horse," Jinx complained. "I hope he's not after her money." She could never quite figure out how poor horsemanship led to gold digging, but anyway, no one could ever accuse Ned of either fault.

The trail now turned makai and they began the downhill trek to Mākena. This was the way all of the upcountry cattle used to be taken to market, down to Mākena landing, where the paniolo had to swim them out to the waiting cattle boats. But now, with the improvements to Kahului Harbor, most of the cattle went the other way. The little herd lumbered on as the heavens shifted, and when they were about halfway down the mountain and the first light crept into the sky, the landscape began to transform—from green pastureland to the dry, dusty lowland with its scrubby brush and its thorny kiawe trees. The sea, the islet of Molokini, and the island of Kahoʻolawe emerged from their dark sleep to a morning chorus of birds.

Mina took off her jacket and tied it around her waist. Soon they reached the kiawe groves of Mākena and finally Puʻuōlaʻi, the home of Archie Macpherson. At Puʻuōlaʻi they visited for a while, left the cattle, and headed back along the shore, to the house at Maluaka. Louise and Charles had just arrived by car from the ranch, and with several helpers Louise was opening up the house and getting breakfast together. When everyone was cleaned up, they sat on the porch facing the sea, tucking in to a breakfast of pancakes, bacon, fresh orange juice, and coffee. Jinx and Charles were already planning a fishing expedition.

"We saw the minister on the way in, and tomorrow we're all invited to go to church at Keawalaʻi," Louise said. "There's going to be a baptism and a Hawaiian-food lunch after the service. It would be a nice gesture to the community if we all went."

"I think we'd love to go," Mina volunteered. "It would be wonderful to meet some of the people who live here."

"You won't be sorry," Louise said. "The people here still show visitors heartfelt hospitality. Are you tired? What would you like to do for the rest of the day?"

"Ned and I were thinking of taking a walk and going for a swim," Mina said.

"Yes, the ocean looks lovely," Ned added.

"I'm really tired," Nyla said. "I think I need to go to sleep."

"Why, you've hardly touched your breakfast," Louise said in a concerned, motherly voice.

"I think my tummy is upset from the ride." Nyla yawned. "If you don't mind, I think I'll go and lie down." She got up and went straight to the living-room pūneʻe.

"Hmm," said Mina as she helped herself to another pancake and piece of bacon. "I hope she's not getting the flu."

That evening, after dinner, they all sat out on the lanai and watched the moonlight shining on the sea. They had just finished dessert— a banana bread that Louise had brought from the ranch—and now were all lying around in the kind of lazy poses people take when they've eaten just a little too much for dinner. Mina and Nyla were perched on the floor at the top of the lanai stairs, plucking burrs out of Ollie's coat. He'd managed to run through several clusters of them that afternoon, and they were stuck all over his feet and legs. The moon cast a silvery light across the landscape, and its reflection off the sea was so bright, there was no need for a kerosene lamp. Uncle Jinx had informed Ned that none of the houses in Mākena had electricity or indoor plumbing, and most of the residents still used horses for transportation.

"How many people live out here?" Ned asked.

"I'd say there are about twelve families living around Keawala'i Church and Mākena landing," Jinx answered. "Don't you think so, Lou?"

"About," Louise agreed. "But the families here have very close upland ties, relatives who live around 'Ulupalakua. They come down for the weekends or they all gather for special occasions. You'll see tomorrow at the church and the little party afterwards."

"Over the years the population has dwindled here in Mākena," Jinx added. "The 1918 epidemic took a toll here like it did everywhere."

"Yes," Ned said. "It was particularly bad in Sāmoa. There's hardly a family that didn't lose someone."

"Then," Jinx continued, "lots of the young people want to go to high school, or try for the university in Honolulu, so of course they have to leave. And there aren't really any jobs out here. Most people do a little farming, a little ranching, and a little fishing."

"The people here are great fishermen," Louise went on. "Some of the longtime local families still feed sharks. They believe that they're family guardians, 'aumākua, and there are even places along the coast, shark holes, where certain sharks come to meet their family, to be fed and cared for. They say the sharks sometimes help them fish—although you won't find people talking about it much to outsiders."

"These places," Jinx interjected, "places like Mākena that are remote, are where you still find pieces of old Hawai'i. Families who still do things the old way, people who still remember how things were."

"Things do change fast," Ned said. He thought about Sāmoa and the rapid changes he had seen in his own lifetime.

"A little too fast for some of us, eh, Charles?" Jinx looked over at his friend, who was falling asleep.

"Way too fast," Charles answered, his eyes closed.

"So," Uncle Jinx asked, "are you three kids still set on driving up to Haleakalā on Monday?"

"That would be the best," Mina said as she pulled a big burr out of Ollie's foot.

"The absolute best," Nyla added with a nod.

20

SUNDAY

MINA SAT ON the dark wooden pew in the back of Keawalaʻi Church in her pale yellow lace muʻumuʻu and looked out of the deep window, past the shaded gravestones and over the old rock wall, at the dazzling blue of the Pacific. The surface of the ocean lay glassy and still like a turquoise mirror. In the shaded interior of the little seaside church she could almost smell the stones that had rested in the thick walls, behind the smooth white plaster, listening year after year to the sound of the sea and the singing of hymns. She wondered what it would be like to be part of this intimate little community, to come here every Sunday, to be inside this little church marking all of the births, marriages, and deaths of your family and friends. Ned sat next to her, thumbing through the tattered hymnal for the first song of the service. The faces of the congregation were all Hawaiian, and she felt happy to be tucked away in a little pocket of the island where the Hawaiian people still had a distinct community to themselves, where they weren't pressed on and overrun by everyone else, where they hadn't been "placed" by a homestead act, where many of them lived on family land with roots that went deep into the past. This was one of those special places where families still lived on land that flowed from one generation to the next, with unbroken ties to their ancestors and their spiritual guardians.

The woman at the old piano looked around and then started to play. Everyone stood and began to sing "Jesu no ke Kahuhipa." The hymn singing filled Mina with sadness, as she felt she was listening to something beautiful that was slowly fading away. It was only natural, she told herself, to feel sorrowful about the passage of time and the things that slipped away from the world, and she thought about her mother and how she would have loved being in this place. The last strains of the song hovered for a moment in the air before everyone sat down as the minister began the service. Next, there was the reading of the gospel in Hawaiian, and Mina observed Ned paying very close attention, as if he could almost understand the words. When the reading was over, the piano started up once again for the next hymn.

Mina turned to look behind her, only to see her sister swoon as she stood, dropping her hymnal on the floor. Charles and Louise, who were on either side, caught her just before she fell. Charles deftly swept her up and carried her outside, while Louise and Mina followed. An elderly Hawaiian woman came out after them and directed them to a long, covered pavilion to the side of the little church. Tables were set and decorated for lunch, but over to the side were several old Adirondack chairs and a large lauhala mat. The woman motioned Charles to lie Nyla down on the mat while she took a pillow off of one of the chairs and gently placed it under her head. By this time Nyla had opened her eyes and was coming to. The old woman brushed the hair from Nyla's face and felt her forehead.

"You all right?" Charles asked her.

"Yeah, I think so." Nyla grinned and propped herself up on her elbows. "I just got dizzy for a second."

"You sure?" Charles frowned.

"I'm sure, Daddy," she answered. "You go back inside."

"I stay here with her," the old woman said. "Go, you folks go back inside."

"I'll stay here, too, if you don't mind," Mina said.

"Yes," said the old woman, "you stay, but you two go back inside. It's good for you to be there."

Charles and Louise obediently walked across the lawn to the church.

"You lie down little bit more," the lady said to Nyla. "Sweetie," she continued, turning to Mina, "you go get sister some water." She pointed to a kitchen area off the pavilion.

When Mina returned with the water, the woman was gently feel-

ing Nyla's abdomen and stomach. "My name is Elizabeth Kepau," she
said as she started doing a very gentle massage, "but you girls can call
me Auntie Lizzie like everybody else."

"I'm Mina Beckwith," Mina said, as she put a glass of water near
Nyla.

"And Nyla Forrest," Nyla added.

"You write for the newspaper?" The old woman looked at Mina.

"I used to," she answered.

The lady smiled. "See, us country folks love the newspaper. M.
Beckwith. I heard you were a woman, but I didn't believe it. Now I
know it's true." She winked. "Nyla, you take a little sip of water now,
just a little."

Nyla obeyed and lay back down. Auntie Lizzie went back to doing
a gentle lomilomi. Nyla relaxed and said, "Thank you, that's so much
better. I just don't know what's wrong with me. Maybe I'm coming
down with something."

"No," Auntie Lizzie said with a smile. "You not sick. You hāpai,
that's all."

"What?" Nyla sat up in disbelief.

"I'm never wrong, you know," Auntie Lizzie said proudly. "You
ask anyone here."

Mina sat down in a chair and stared at her sister. "You're having a
baby and you didn't even know it?"

"It's early yet, but I bet you already missed one monthly, right?"
Auntie Lizzie seemed very sure of herself.

"Yes, but—" Nyla tried to defend herself.

"And," Auntie Lizzie interrupted, "your tummy feel little bit sick
in the morning, now it's getting worse, right?"

"Well, yes," Nyla admitted.

"And maybe you think your breasts feel little bit strange to you,"
Auntie Lizzie continued.

"How do you know these things?" Nyla asked.

"Because I deliver plenty babies here. I take care of hāpai women
all my life. I know how to lomilomi them so they don't feel so sick in
the beginning, and then later to make the delivery easier. The doctors
don't like me, but the women know—I never lost one baby! I can

tell early if it's better for the mother to go hospital, and then I tell her—better you don't have the baby at home. And, you know, my lomilomi is better than the medicine for morning sickness, too. That kind is not good for baby, or the mother, I'm telling you. Don't take any of it." She continued to massage Nyla and then told her she could sit up if she wanted to. "You just eat little bit now and then, all day," she instructed. "Don't eat a big meal, and then three months, you feel much better. You live Honolulu, you should go and see Hattie Pa'akai. She's good. She lives down Kapālama. Now let's say a prayer to thank the Lord for your gift."

Nyla and Mina obeyed, and they all held hands while Auntie Lizzie prayed in Hawaiian. Afterward, Auntie Lizzie said she had some things to do in the kitchen to get ready for lunch, and she made Nyla promise to lie down on the mat and rest until the service was over. "It's too hot for you to go back inside," she said.

Mina sat with her sister in the cool of the pavilion. It was a simple building with a concrete floor, open sided and covered by a tin roof, but the kitchen to the side was closed in and more protected. She gazed out at the well-kept lawn, the shade trees, and the stacked stone wall that separated the green church grounds from the dusty road.

"You've always had to do everything before me, haven't you?" Mina looked at her sister affectionately.

"I feel so stupid, not figuring it out for myself." Nyla frowned. "Don't tell the others, all right? I want to tell Todd first."

"How do you feel about it, Ny?" Mina hoped her sister would be honest.

"To tell you the truth, the only thing I feel right now is surprise." Nyla rolled onto her side and faced the sea. "You know, that lomilomi actually made the nausea go away. It's so pleasant here, isn't it? Just lying in the shade, staring up at the trees, and listening to the ocean. I could spend the whole day doing this."

Mina folded her arms. "Well, now you have an official license to do this every day, and I want you to know, if it's a girl, I expect you to name it after me."

"Nope," Nyla said, yawning and stretching. "After Mummy and Grandma."

21

MONDAY

IT WAS STILL dark when Ned and Mina arrived at the top of Haleakalā. It had been something of a hair-raising adventure to drive to the top in the dark on the new road along steep cliffs and twists and turns. There was no one to be seen as they parked a little below the ten thousand-foot summit. Temperatures fluctuated at this elevation from thirty to sixty-five degrees, with the occasional freeze, and even in June it was cold. They were both wrapped up in coats, scarves, sweaters, gloves, and hats. Louise had made sure they were properly outfitted—not only with warm clothes, but with food and hot coffee. Uncle Jinx had told them they may find a surprise at the top of the mountain, but Mina had no idea what he was talking about. She was disappointed that Nyla couldn't join them, but realized that a long and winding ride to the top of the mountain in the freezing cold morning would not be good for a pregnant woman.

They spread a blanket out on the ground, sat down very close together, and wrapped another blanket around themselves. The blankets smelled a little musty, as if they had been sitting on a closet shelf for a long time, but neither of them cared, as the sight of the sky overwhelmed them. The moon had fallen to the west, the luminous ribbon of the Milky Way stretched out across the heavens, and Mina thought she had never seen so many stars in all her life.

"We're being bombarded by starlight," Ned said.

"Do you think it might have any effect on us?" Mina asked.

"It could make our eyes glow," Ned replied, trying to sound serious, "and people will say—what happened to them? They used to be so down-to-earth, and now they're simply starry-eyed."

"Or," Mina added, "we could be starstruck, go mad, and do nothing but chase after movie actors."

"That will only happen if a star falls on us."

"Oh, well then, we might just go on to have nothing but incredibly brilliant and stellar ideas."

"Yes," Ned agreed as he raised a pair of binoculars. "I think that's the most likely outcome."

They sat for a while in silence, and as they huddled together, Mina could feel their two bodies making a small cocoon of warmth against the cold. The stars began to fade out, and in the east there was a faint glow. As the light increased ever so slightly, the outlines of the rocks and little hills around them emerged like gray, shrouded phantoms. Soon, it was light enough to see the wide crater below them, now filled with a sea of clouds. Beyond and above the crater a pinkish light appeared like a long stripe that transformed to a brilliant orange just before the top of the great ball of the sun appeared, and once again the colors shifted into washes of oranges, reds, lavenders, and pinks.

"Louise was telling me the story of how Maui snared the sun from this mountain," said Ned.

"Yes," Mina replied, "because the sun was moving too fast through the sky and his mother, Hina, couldn't dry her kapa properly."

"There's a story like that in Sāmoa as well."

"Really?"

"Yes," Ned went on. "The sun was moving too fast, no one could dry their *siapo,* the crops wouldn't grow properly, people couldn't get a good night's sleep. But instead of snaring the sun with a rope, they sent a beautiful woman."

"And what did this beautiful woman do?"

Ned looked at Mina. "Well, the beautiful woman stood on the eastern edge of the island, on a cliff, and when the sun came up, he fell in love with her."

"So, it was love at first light?" Mina asked, laughing.

"Clever, Mina." Ned brushed her cheek with the back of his hand.

"Yes, the sun took one look at her and fell in love. He promised to slow down if she would marry him."

"Marry him?" Mina cocked her head to the side.

"Well, that's the polite way my grandmother told it, but I'm sure it was if she'd, you know, agree to share his mat."

Mina raised her eyebrows. "Yes, I know."

"So, will you, Mina?"

She looked at him directly and smiled. "Will I what? Marry you or agree to share your mat?"

"Well, both, actually."

"Will you promise to shower me with warmth and light every day?"

"I promise."

Mina put her lips close to his ear and whispered, "I will." She put her arms around his neck and kissed him, then turned to look again at the fiery sky.

"Oops, mustn't forget," Ned said as he fished around in his pocket. "You'll need to remove that floppy red glove from your left hand, darling."

"Ashamed of my moth-eaten finery already, are you?" She laughed and brandished the glove in his face.

He took her left hand and slipped on a diamond solitaire ring. "Here's a much more fitting adornment."

"Where did you get this beautiful ring?" Mina couldn't take her eyes away from the diamond. It sparkled and danced in the morning light.

"It was my grandmother's engagement ring," he answered.

"Ned," she said, frowning, "you didn't ask Tava'esina for her ring!"

Ned shook his head. "No, I didn't have to ask. When I was about to get on the boat to leave, she slipped it in my pocket and said, 'You might need this.' I had to get it resized, of course."

"And how did you know my ring size?" She eyed him.

"It was easy. I just asked Nyla what her ring size was."

"It's so perfect." She looked at the ring and kissed him again. "And I love that it was your grandmother's."

They walked hand in hand back to the car, and with the dawn in full bloom they took out the thermos of hot coffee and opened the basket to find some bread, butter, and honey and several bananas, mountain apples, and tangerines. They had just finished their little feast when Mina saw a man riding up on horseback with two other horses saddled and in tow. He had on a black cowboy hat and a faded denim jacket that he wore over a pullover sweater and an undershirt. His dungarees and boots were worn as well. When he got closer and Mina saw his lean smile and gapped front teeth, she recognized him as a paniolo who sometimes worked for Uncle Jinx.

"Mr. Santos," she called out, waving. "I'm so surprised to see you! I don't know if you remember me. Mina Beckwith."

"I know you, Mina," he answered. "I never forget a pretty girl." He winked at Ned. "And didn't your Uncle Jinx tell you—look for one surprise?"

"Is that you?"

"That's me! I going take you and your friend down inside. I got lunch and everything. You guys get ready so we can go."

"Oh, Ned, isn't it great? We get to ride into the crater!" She had to stop herself from jumping up and down like an eight-year-old.

"That's why your father and Jinx were so insistent that we leave Ollie behind," Ned said.

Mina put her hands on her hips. "I thought there was something fishy about wanting to take him to show to his foreman's family."

"Who's that? Ollie?" Mr. Santos asked.

"He's my dog," Mina told him. "My new dog. He's a Portuguese water dog."

"Ho, Mina! I heard of that kine dog from my father, but I never see one." Mr. Santos was impressed. "I wouldn't mind if you show him off to me. Where you get that kine dog from?"

"I'll tell you all about it on the trail."

"And Mina," Mr. Santos said, squinting, "what's that thing on top your finger?" He pointed at her engagement ring. "Look like one star."

She walked next to Ned and put her arm through his. "We just got engaged. Oh, Mr. Santos, this is Ned Manusia, my . . . my fiancé."

"EEEHA!!" Mr. Santos took off his hat and waved it in a sweeping gesture. "You one lucky son of a gun, Manusia. Come on, hurry up, then, let's go have one swell day!"

As they began their ride down the long switchbacks of Sliding Sands Trail, Mina regaled Mr. Santos with the story of how she had acquired Ollie. The horses walked carefully in the cindery lava that was indeed, Ned thought, a lot like very large grains of sand. The animals were slow but sure of the way, as if they had traveled on this path many times before, and Ned felt free to let his attention wander to the otherworldly landscape that surrounded him. He guessed that it was around eight-thirty or nine, and the clouds that had shrouded the crater from view in the early morning were now breaking. Patches of shade and light swept over the barren, moonlike landscape, with its rising cinder cones and colors that shifted from dark grays to rusty reds tinged with ocher. The farther down they rode into the muzzle of the ancient volcano, the more pronounced the silence, and the sense of being removed and away from reality. Ned recalled all the stories he had heard about the fiery goddess, Pele, and when he looked at the ever-changing, mysterious landscape before him, he imagined that this kind of overwhelming beauty, with its undercurrent of danger and risk, might be a small inkling of what it would be like to encounter a real goddess.

He rode along on his horse, entranced by the view, and when he finally looked ahead, he realized that his daydreaming had left him far behind Mina and Mr. Santos. Up ahead, they had stopped and dismounted. When he joined them, he saw that they were standing near some very unusual plants and realized that they must be looking at the famous silverswords of Haleakalā. Spread along the hillside, not far off the trail, were nearly twenty plants of various sizes, the largest being about a foot and a half in diameter. On closer examination Ned saw that the numerous succulent sword-like leaves that grew out of the base of the plant were arranged in a spherical formation very close to the ground. One of the bigger plants looked to have a flower head or some kind of bud emerging straight up from the center of the sphere.

"This is the silversword," Mina told Ned. "In Hawaiian, it's called 'ahinahina. It only grows here in the crater between around seven to nine thousand feet."

"It's a startling plant, isn't it? But it looks so appropriate for this setting," Ned reflected. "As soon as we get to Honolulu, I'll have to send a telegram to my grandfather. My theatrical productions don't impress him much, but when I tell him I've seen a silversword, I'm sure he'll think I've finally arrived."

"Just you wait," Mr. Santos said, "we going to visit one pu'u where get some plants blooming. Then you really see something."

"These are quite beautiful. And you say they're only found here?" Ned asked.

"This is the only place in the world this species grows," Mina said.

"Yeah," Mr. Santos added, "almost all the plants wen die, too, you know. In the twenties, no one cared about them. People came up here and pulled them up to take home, just to prove they was here. And some people used to pull them up and roll them down the side of the hill here for fun, or take home for make dried flower arrangements. I tell you, nobody cared they was destroying the plants. But now, they coming back. We trying to tell people—hey, don't just go around destroying things! See, these plants, the roots is shallow, yeah? Right under the ground, so even if you walk up too close, you can damage the roots, see? Oh, and goats, they cause big problems for the silversword, too."

"I heard that the park finally has a ranger now," Mina said as she remounted her horse.

"Oh, yeah." Mr. Santos paused to adjust his stirrup. "Mr. Lamb, he's counting all the silversword plants this summer. I help him, because if I see some in a place he doesn't go, then I tell him how many."

When they reached the crater floor, the clouds began to sweep in above and around them. Their surroundings quickly changed, and the floor of the volcano was now cloaked in mist. It swirled around them in slow motion, forming and reforming in wraith-like shapes. They rode without speaking. There was little wind, and the only sounds in the stillness were the occasional cry of a bird and the rhythmic crunch of the cinders beneath the hooves of the horses. Mina turned back once to look at Ned, and it seemed to him that in this unpredictable place she had become more alive and animated. He couldn't deny that he felt some of that same energy, as if he had somehow come into himself a little more, and even though he couldn't see them, he had an acute sense of the volcanic walls of Haleakalā enclosing them in a fortress of silence and seclusion. He thought for a moment that he could actually feel a heartbeat coming from somewhere underneath them, but the sensation passed, and he let the thought go by without questioning its reality.

They approached several puʻu that were clustered near each other. The dark cinder cones rose like a child's drawing of a volcano— smooth, angled, and cylindrical. Their tops looked as if a giant hand had reached in, taken out a scoop of cinders, and patted the depression down so it was finished and neat. The trail wove between two of the puʻu, and Mr. Santos guided them up to a section where several of the silverswords were blooming. The plants grew slowly, Mr. Santos informed Ned, from a seed to a mature plant in fifteen to fifty years. At the end of its life the silversword sent one beautiful, tall stalk straight up from its center that then burst into flowers. The stalk closest to Ned looked to be nearly five feet high, and he gave up trying to count how many blooms there were when he realized it would be in the hundreds. They resembled small sunflowers except for their striking color, which on this plant was a deep, rich maroon. He couldn't remember ever having seen anything like it.

"Once," Mina began, "I saw this picture of these hikers in the crater. They had pulled up the silverswords and were holding them on their laps like balls, and a couple of the men had them up on their heads."

"What a waste." Ned shook his head. "I would love to think my grandfather might see this one day."

Mina smiled. "Maybe he will."

"Yeah," Mr. Santos chimed in, "if he can ride horse, he can come down here. You just tell me."

They rode on, circling one of the puʻu, and came to a hole that sunk into the ground, the remains of a volcanic vent, where they stopped for a lunch of tuna sandwiches, potato chips, apples, and cookies. After lunch Mina wandered off to explore. Mr. Santos and Ned sat together talking, and Ned asked him if he knew the Rodrigues family.

"Oh, yes," Mr. Santos said, "I knew Antone Rodrigues. He was a tough man. Good-hearted man, but very tough until his daughter died. Then, just like he broke."

"We heard about the girl's death—that she died in childbirth."

"Antone was so mad with her when he found out she was hāpai, and then she wouldn't say who was the father. He even came after my brother because he went to the movies with Marie Teresa a few times years ago. My brother swore on the Bible he wasn't the father, to make Antone believe, but still he didn't, not until Marie Teresa told him my brother wasn't the man. She never told nobody who was the real father, and no one could guess because she kept to herself and was never seen with anyone. People thought maybe some man forced himself on her and she was too shame or too scared to tell. Antone was mad, I tell you, but then she dies and you never seen a man so sorry. He cannot take back all the things he said to her, all the names he called her, sad, you know."

"What happened to the child?"

"Oh, the aunties took the baby. Say, you lucky to catch a nice girl like Mina, you son of a gun." Mr. Santos broke into a big smile. "I like you, Manusia," he said, slapping him on the back. "I think you going make Mina one happy girl."

It was nearly two in the afternoon when Ned and Mina said good-bye to Mr. Santos and began their long drive down the mountain. Ned related what Mr. Santos had told him about Antone Rodrigues.

"So Louise was wrong," Ned said. "The baby didn't die."

"That's right." Mina turned to him. "Mrs. Olivera mentioned something about Betty Perreira's nephew having asthma. I wonder if that's him."

"So Amanda's children have a first cousin they don't know about, too."

By late afternoon they found themselves in the little town of Makawao and parked in front of a store at the town's one and only intersection. While Ned went into the store in search of a snack, Mina got out of the car to stretch her legs. She was standing in front of the store, near a wooden bench that had seen better days, looking at a notice for an upcoming rodeo, when she heard a car pull up to the stop sign and the intersection. She turned around just in time to see Sheldon Lennox sitting in the back of a truck as it pulled away, heading up Olinda Road.

"Sheldon!" she called out, and waved.

Sheldon looked very surprised as he waved back. Just when the truck pulled out of sight, Ned emerged with two colas and a bag with two cone sushi.

"I hope this is enough to keep you happy until dinner," Ned said.

"Hmm." Mina gave him a wry look. "I hope when we're married you won't be too tight with the grocery money."

"How about if I just buy you your own grocery store," Ned said as he sat down on the bench. "Then you'll always be happy."

Mina sat next to him, took out her cone sushi, took a bite, and then took a sip of her cola. "Guess what? I just saw Sheldon Lennox."

"Where?"

"He just went by in the back of a pickup. He seemed surprised to see me here."

"I'm sure he was. Doesn't he have polo ponies here?"

"Yep." Mina took another bite of her sushi.

"That must have been some fight between Henry and Gilbert that Sheldon stepped into."

"It certainly was," Mina recalled. "I can't believe how Henry Burnham reacted when it was over. He just went right on to the next thing."

"The next thing?" Ned cocked his head.

"Yeah," Mina said, nodding her head. "He just continued on with his business like nothing happened. He came out of his office and started yelling to Gwen about some report he had to have from Island Trust about his wife's affairs."

"Some men have a talent for tossing off whatever is inconvenient or embarrassing."

"He didn't skip a beat, even though Sheldon was bleeding in his reception area." Mina took the last bite of her sushi.

"Sheldon is going to be one of your many disappointed admirers," Ned commented while brushing away a grain of sushi rice that had fallen on his pants. "Now that you're engaged to me."

"How do you know that?" Mina laughed.

"He told me himself. He said he was envious that I'd gotten the cowgirl." Ned paused for a moment. "If I were a woman, I wouldn't think 'cowgirl' was a very nice word."

"Poor Sheldon," Mina said with a sigh. "I wonder if he'll ever grow up."

"From what you've told me, it sounds like his mother didn't encourage it," Ned remarked.

"I'm sure she didn't. You know, I'd like to drive around Olinda and see if we could find the Rodrigues house, maybe their old dairy."

"Mina, that would really be intruding on their privacy for idle curiosity, for no real reason."

"We don't have to go to their house or anything; we could just drive by. Come on, Ned." She took his arm and started for the car.

"Thou hast more of the wild goose in one of thy wits than, I am sure, I have in my whole five."

Mina gave him a confused look.

"Shakespeare, darling," he said as he opened the car door to let her drive. "Just lead the way."

22

WEDNESDAY

MINA WOKE TO Ollie's excited barking. It took her a moment to remember that she was at home in her own bed, and not on Maui. They had all come home last night around eight. She remembered that she had taken a shower and gotten into bed, and knew she must have fallen asleep quickly, as her lamp on the bedside table was still turned on. She clicked it off and got out of bed to see why Ollie was fussing.

Todd was outside in his car with the motor running. Ned came out of the house in a hurry, all showered and dressed, got into the car, and they drove away. Mina glanced over at the clock, which said seven a.m., and realized she had slept for almost ten hours. Why, she wondered, had Ned run off so early with Todd? She decided to get dressed and call her sister. She was sure that Nyla had told Todd about her pregnancy, but she and Ned decided to keep their engagement a secret for the time being, until they could make a semi-formal announcement. Mina hoped it would be soon so she could wear the gorgeous ring. She went to her jewelry box to look at it and make sure it was right where she left it last night. Then she went into her kitchen and was just pouring a cup of coffee when the phone rang. It was Nyla.

"Did you eat?" Her sister didn't even bother to say hello.

"I just got up."

Nyla laughed. "Come over for breakfast. Mrs. Olivera is making a coffee cake."

"Oh, because now you're eating for two?" Mina stirred some sugar in her coffee.

"I hope it's only two," Nyla said, sounding concerned, "but it could be more, couldn't it?"

When Mina opened the door to her sister's kitchen, the smell of sugar and cinnamon filled the air, and a round yellow cake sat in the middle of the kitchen table, set for two. There were bowls of fresh fruit and a steaming pot of tea. Nyla was seated, staring at the cake. Ollie rushed over to Nyla and put his head in her lap while his tail wagged wildly at the other end.

Nyla moaned. "It looks so good. What if I can't keep it down?"

"Do your best," Mina suggested as she sat down and cut a big piece for herself. "And don't worry about what you can't control."

"Okay." Nyla cut herself a piece. "I'll try."

"Are you up to your rehearsal tonight and the performance for the theatre members' reading tomorrow?" Mina asked.

"I mostly feel sick in the morning," Nyla said as she took her first bite of cake. "But I'll do it no matter how I feel."

"You're a real trouper, Ny."

"No, I just love your boyfriend's work."

"Todd came to take Ned somewhere this morning," Mina said, between bites. "Is something up?"

"If there was, you know he wouldn't tell me," Nyla answered. "Especially now."

"Is he happy about the baby?"

"He's ecstatic. But he's trying to get me to quit the decorating job. I told him I couldn't back out now—when it's almost finished. You know what his solution was? 'Ask your sister to do it for you.'"

Mina stopped eating for a moment. "I would if you wanted me to."

"Don't be ridiculous. I'm pregnant, not sick. By the way, the paintings are all hung, and most of the furniture is in place. We still have to sort out that terrace. Finding the right outdoor pieces will be the trick."

"Right! Hey, where's Grandma Hannah?" Mina looked around.

"She's upstairs planning out a baby quilt." Nyla laughed and caught some tiny cake crumbs that fell from her mouth.

When Mrs. Olivera entered the kitchen, Ollie ran over and sat down in front of her, waiting to be petted. "Oh, you sweet boy," Mrs. Olivera cooed. "You are a very lucky dog."

"I didn't tell you, but on Monday, when we were on Maui"— Mina had finished her cake and was eating her bowl of fruit—"I saw Sheldon in Makawao."

"I don't think so," Nyla said.

"I did. I saw him," Mina insisted.

Nyla shook her head. "No, because Tessa just called me and she mentioned eating dinner with Sheldon on Sunday.

"So? He could have gone the very next morning."

"Oh, right." Nyla's face looked a little wan, and her hands went to her stomach. She leaned forward and whispered to Mina so Mrs. Olivera wouldn't hear, "I can't believe I let you talk me into eating the cake; I feel positively nauseated." She then stood up and rushed out of the room.

"Poor thing," Mrs. Olivera said, watching Nyla go. "It's like that in the beginning. Well, I hope you can enjoy the cake, Mina."

"It's delicious. Why don't you sit down for a minute and have some, too?"

Mrs. Olivera turned away from the sink and sat down with Mina. She cut herself a piece of cake, took a few bites, hesitated for a moment, and then said, "Mina, I hope you don't mind, my friend Betty Perreira would like to speak with you this morning, if you have time. There is a favor she wants to ask you to do. It has to do with Rose Marie's children."

Emil Devon looked very uncomfortable sitting on the old sofa in Todd's office. Tessa Burnham sat next to him in a poised pose that Ned thought looked as stiff as her starched white collar and tailored gray suit. She refused to look at him or Todd, and instead turned her head and stared to one side. Emil exuded an even darker countenance than usual, with his furrowed brow and dark, downcast eyes. Todd sat across from the couple, and Ned hung back near Todd's desk, doing his best to be unobtrusive.

"Thanks for coming in on your own," Todd began in a comfortable tone. "I understand you both have something you want to tell me, is that right?"

"That's right," Emil replied in a low voice. "It's about the night of the murder. We want to come clean about it."

"Come clean?" Todd acted a little surprised.

"Yes," Emil went on, "you see, when you talked to us before? We both—well, we both—"

"Lied." Tessa stated without turning her head. "We both lied."

"We didn't tell the truth," Emil said quickly, "because we were scared."

"Well, what exactly is the truth?" Todd asked.

"We went to see my father together the night he was murdered," Tessa said.

"But they were both alive when we left. We swear to that," Emil added.

"What time would that be?" Todd asked.

"I think it was a little after ten." Emil leaned back.

"And why did you go there?" Todd continued.

"We went there because we knew he was thinking about starting this organization of businesses, the Management Alliance League, an anti-union organization. We told him that we had some evidence, that there were people who had seen Lars Bruhn take Mr. Shimasaki into his car before he died, and we would convince them to come forward unless he gave up the idea."

"I said that I would repeat in public the things I heard him say on the phone," Tessa half-whispered.

"Why would you do that?" Todd asked Emil. "To get even with him for your father's death?"

"Maybe." Emil looked at Tessa. "Maybe that was part of it. But the truth is, I'm trying to help the trade unions. I tell them things, anything I can learn, and Tessa helps me. I got interested in trade unionism in college. I sympathize with the working class, and so does Tessa. Right?" He turned to her.

"That's right," she replied, although it was obvious she was trying not to cry.

"So would you describe yourself as a socialist, Mr. Devon?"

"It's not against the law," Emil shot back.

"And what did Henry Burnham do when you told him this?" Todd tried not to sound as surprised as he really was.

"He was furious, of course, but he laughed at us, too." Emil worked to suppress the anger that accompanied the memory. "He told me I could look forward to being unemployed and that Tessa could get out of his house and support herself."

"He called us terrible names." Tessa sank into the sofa.

"He dared us to bring the witnesses forward," Emil went on. "He said he had enough money and smart lawyers to discredit anyone who crossed him. He said if that didn't work, there were other ways."

"I'd never seen him so vicious," Tessa said. "He told me I had just disinherited myself, and he never wanted to see me again."

Unable to control herself, she began to cry. Todd got her a tissue and everyone fell silent for a few minutes until she stopped.

"The important thing," Emil stated, "is that when we left, he was alive and so was Gwen. She was out in the reception area fiddling around with some papers."

"She smirked at me when we walked out." Tessa wiped her eyes. "I know she'd been listening at the door."

"And you say that when you left it was a little after ten?" Todd asked again.

"I think so; maybe ten-fifteen or ten-twenty," Emil answered.

"And what did you do after that?" Todd folded his arms.

"We went to my place and got a little drunk." Emil paused. "And there's something else we think we should tell you. The day that Amanda died, I wasn't with Tessa. She was in her room, but I went out because I was supposed to meet Jack. We were supposed to meet alone, and I waited for him, but he never showed up."

"Where were you going to meet?"

"On some cane road, not far from the hotel." Weariness had crept into Emil's voice.

"Do you play poker, Mr. Devon?"

Emil looked a little confused, or caught off guard. "Once in a while," he answered.

"And did you ever play with Lars Bruhn as part of your . . . your fact-finding missions for the trade unions?"

"A few times," Emil answered.

Silence hung in the air for a moment before Todd spoke again. "Is there anything else you want to tell us?"

Emil just shook his head. Todd stood up and thanked them for coming in, and he and Ned watched as they walked out the door without exchanging any polite good-byes.

"I'm glad you remembered about the poker," Ned said as he stood and looked out the window.

"I still don't get why you wanted to know that." Todd joined him at the window.

"I don't quite know myself," Ned replied. "That was a painful little confession, wasn't it?" They could now see the couple leaving the building and walking away down the street.

"Do you believe it?" Todd asked.

"I don't know," Ned replied. "Of course, it could be a half-truth. They could have gone there, and then he could have come back later and killed them both. He has a bit of a temper, don't you think? And she's just the type to go along with him, because she thinks he's suffered and needs her love and understanding."

"You mean he needs her bleeding heart?"

"I've nothing against bleeding hearts per se," Ned said. "I only object when they enable the wrong people or when they bleed themselves to death."

"Let's not forget," Todd added, "her father can't change his will and disinherit her now that he's dead."

"No indeed," Ned echoed, "and let's not forget that he can't fire Emil Devon, either."

"Well, now, who do you think would like us to stop by his office if we could spare the time this afternoon?" Todd turned to go to his desk.

"Haven't the foggiest." Ned sat down on the sofa.

"Mr. Gilbert Burnham."

"Do think he'll have a different tale to tell?"

Todd grinned. "I think if he doesn't, I might sit on him a little."

"Well done, chief," Ned said, grinning back. "Any word on Jack?"

"He's taken his sister's death pretty hard. He's not eating, and they're thinking of hospitalizing him."

"I feel very sorry for that boy." Ned shook his head. "I should try to speak to Louis and see if there's something I can do."

After making her phone calls, Mina tossed some clothes in an overnight bag and headed for her car, still stunned by the story Mrs. Perreira had told her in the cozy Kaimukī cottage only an hour ago. It was hard for her to think that it all could be real. It was like a story or a play someone one had made up, full of drama and secret relationships. Things like that weren't supposed to be the stuff of real life. Was she shaking inside? Was it fear or excitement? It didn't matter. She had just been handed this lead, and right now she was determined to follow it to its end. She got in the car, slammed the door, and looked at her watch. *This is no time to sit around and take stock,* she told herself. If she wanted to catch the only plane back to Maui today, she would have to step on it.

"Yes, thank you, Gladys." Gilbert Burnham cleared his throat and swung around in the chair behind his desk. The serious, middle-aged woman who had shown Ned and Todd in from the front desk left the men alone. "I appreciate your coming," Gilbert said to them. "Please sit down."

Todd and Ned took their seats in a room that looked as if it had been used for storage and was recently cleared. It was big and empty except for a pile of rubbish in the corner, Gilbert's desk, and the two chairs they were sitting in.

"I apologize for the state of things here. I shut up my brother's old office. I'm going to consult with your wife, detective, about redecorating this place. In fact, I just spoke to Nyla a few minutes ago to set up a meeting." Gilbert seemed to be working at being cheerful. "I just thought I would check in with you and see if there's been any progress. I know you have Jack Carstairs in custody, but is that the end of the investigation? Are there any more suspects?"

"Well," Todd answered in a very measured voice, "we haven't arrested anyone else, if that's what you mean."

"So you're sure you've got your man?" Gilbert asked.

"I didn't say that," Todd answered. "There are several other lines of investigation I'm following up on. I'd hate to see an innocent man go down for something he didn't do, just because I didn't do my job."

"Oh, of course," Gilbert agreed. "Do you mind if I ask what some of these 'lines of investigation' are, or is that privileged information?" He swiveled his chair from side to side ever so slightly.

"Well, there was that meeting. The one you told us about where Duncan Mackenzie was getting the men riled up about the death of Shimasaki," Todd said. "We are doing some follow up on that, because Jack Carstairs apparently wasn't involved in the meeting."

"From what I heard the men were very angry, and that Mackenzie fellow made some very inflammatory statements." Gilbert looked concerned. "It's not that I'm insensitive to the needs of labor," he said, "but violence, talk of class warfare—I can't condone violence. I don't think it serves anyone. Do you think he might be behind my brother's death?"

"It's like this," Todd told him. "There's a murder, and I see certain possibilities like arrows pointing out from the crime, and I think I should follow every arrow until I'm satisfied."

"I see." Gilbert tapped a pencil on his desk.

"And the answer is yes, Mr. Burnham." Todd leaned forward and put his elbow on the desk and cupped his face in his hand while looking straight at Gilbert. "We do know that you and your wife were here on the night of the murder. That's what you're fishing around to see, isn't it?"

Ned smiled to himself and thought that there were some very good reasons his friend had been made the chief of detectives.

"How do you know that?" Gilbert frowned.

"We have a witness that placed you here around ten-thirty."

Gilbert said nothing for a minute or two, as if he were calculating what he should do or say next. "Yes, all right, we were here," he finally said. "We came around ten-thirty but left about fifteen minutes later, and Henry was very much alive and as cantankerous as ever."

"What were you doing here?" Todd sat back in his chair.

"I came to talk about our family estate on Kaua'i. I thought if I brought Helen, he would be more civilized. He's always had a little soft spot for her." Gilbert sighed. "I came and said I wanted to buy the estate myself. I told him I couldn't stand to see it go out of the family. I told him how much it meant to me. I reminded him of the clause in our mother's trust about family having first right of refusal before selling. He got mad. He told me I was a sentimental fool. He said he had no intention of letting me ruin his plans, and that he would take me to court for as long as it took if I decided to challenge him. There isn't much more to tell. Forgive me if I leave out the personal insults."

"Where did the two of you go afterwards?"

"We went to our car," said Gilbert, "and talked about what a bastard he was all the way home."

The buzz of Gilbert's intercom interrupted them, and he quickly pressed the answer button. "Yes?" He spoke in an irritated tone.

"Sorry, sir." Gladys' voice was all business. "But the boy from Island Trust is here for the document return."

"Come right in," Gilbert said into the brown box, and then turned back to Todd and Ned. "Sorry, where were we?"

"Well, I'd say we were finished," Todd answered, "unless there's anything else important you haven't told me."

"Not that I know of," Gilbert said.

Just then, Gladys entered, and Gilbert handed her a brown manila envelope without even looking at her.

"Island Trust," Ned said. "Good firm, are they?"

"I use Bishop Trust myself," Gilbert replied as he stood up and shook their hands. "Those were some papers Henry wanted to see about his wife's affairs, I think. I didn't really have time to look over them," he added. "They were stashed in his secret drawer. We had a helluva time finding them."

Out on the street, as Todd and Ned walked back toward Todd's office, Todd asked Ned about the Island Trust business.

"If I were you, I'd go to Island Trust and ask to see those papers," Ned said.

"Why, what's the angle?"

"I don't really know." Ned sounded vague. "It's something odd that Mina said about Henry Burnham."

"In other words, it's a long shot."

"Right, a very long shot."

"I don't know about you," Todd said, shaking his head, "but I think Mr. Gilbert Burnham is just slick enough to have bumped off his brother."

"Bumped off," Ned repeated.

"Are you making fun of my vocabulary, sir?" Todd looked sideways at Ned.

Ned grinned. "Sounds like some naughty practice."

"You artists need to keep your minds out of the gutter." Todd jostled him playfully.

Suddenly, Ned stopped in his tracks and, with a quizzical look on his face, turned to Todd. "I've just had an idea! It's another long shot I feel compelled to check out. I think I'll run over and make a call on Uncle Wing."

"If you say so, pal." And Todd, equally puzzled, watched as Ned turned away and sauntered off toward Chinatown.

"I think we might be in for some rain in the next few days," Uncle Wing said as he poured Ned a cup of tea. "The wind is shifting and coming from the south. Please, Ned, I want your opinion on my *pain de genes*. I've made mine in tea cakes. I know you've most likely tasted it in Paris, and I'd like to know if mine measures up."

Ned took a bite of one of the tea cakes and tried to chew it with a thoughtful look on his face. "Best I've ever tasted," he concluded. "No question about it. You could have quite a patisserie if you wanted, Uncle Wing."

"Don't give him any ideas." Cecily had just entered the room and went straight to the plate of *pain de genes,* plucked up a tea cake, and continued, with her mouth full, "He just might do it."

"Aren't you supposed to be working?" Uncle Wing scolded.

"I know you bring out the goodies whenever Ned stops by," she said, "so I thought I'd take a little break. How are you, Ned?"

"I'm quite well, thanks," he said. "And how are the wedding plans?"

"Going great." She winked at him, and he wondered if Mina had spilled the news about their engagement.

"I hope we can all get together before too long," Ned said.

"You know," Cecily mused, "I've been dreaming about a summer picnic."

"That sounds like a splendid idea," Ned agreed. "Maybe near a beach."

"Yes," said Cecily, "with shade trees and little sandwiches and strawberries and champagne."

"And a game of croquet," Ned added.

"And Pops can make the dessert."

"Only if I'm invited," Uncle Wing grumbled. "Now shoo, Cecily. Go back to work. Ned and I want to talk."

"Okay," she answered, grabbing another tea cake. "Tell your secrets. See if I care. Bye-bye." She gave Ned a little kiss on the cheek and vanished. Ned watched her leave. "I'm sure you'll miss her when she's married and gone."

"Gone?" Uncle Wing said with a laugh. "There's another section of the building, almost as big as this apartment that we use for storage. She's trying to get us to agree to let her and Tom fix it up to live in."

"Will you?"

"When she and her mother gang up on me, it's useless to say no."

Uncle Wing shrugged and sat down. "But you didn't come here to discuss parent and child relationships, did you, Ned?"

"No," he said. "I have a hunch, and I know it's asking a lot of you and your contacts, but it might just be a missing clue that connects some things."

"Before I considered using my contacts again," Uncle Wing said, refilling Ned's teacup, "you'd have to divulge your theory."

Uncle Wing listened attentively, and when Ned finished, he said, "Even if that were true, it still leaves the question of how the murders were actually committed."

"But," countered Ned, "it certainly shows motive."

"Yes," Uncle Wing agreed, "motive and malice. And of course you knew by telling me that my own curiosity would be aroused."

"I hoped so."

"Well, wait here while I make a phone call or two." Uncle Wing got up and left Ned in the kitchen with his cup of tea and the plate of *pain de genes*.

Ned sat in the oversized kitchen and looked up at the shiny pots and pans hanging about. He could hear the steady ticking of a clock that he couldn't see. The large gas stove gleamed, as did the deep sink that looked like it belonged in a cafeteria. The room stood quiet and expectant, almost like a dog waiting for the return of its real master, and when Uncle Wing did return, it was with a grim look on his face. He sat down at the table and poured himself a cup of tea. The tea was still hot and a little steam rose from the cup. He took his time adding the sugar cubes and stirring them until everything was dissolved. Then, he took a sip and looked at Ned. "It seems you have the gift of intuition. It was just as you suspected."

"Oh, dear," Ned said without thinking.

"Yes," Uncle Wing said. He took another long sip and placed the cup carefully back in the saucer. "Oh, dear, indeed."

23

THURSDAY

"**O**F COURSE I was worried about you," Ned said as he started up the car and drove away from John Rogers Airfield. It was midday and the bright sun at the airfield made him squint. "I couldn't believe you just went flying off like that."

"I tried to call you at Todd's office, but no one was there." Mina didn't sound very apologetic. "Then there was no time if I wanted to catch the plane."

"What exactly were you chasing after?" Ned looked at her and then downshifted as he pulled up to a stop sign. "Your sister wouldn't say a word last night at rehearsal."

"Oh, no, rehearsal." This time she did sound apologetic. "Did you find someone else to read the stage directions?"

"Johnny did it."

"I really am sorry about that," Mina said. "And tonight is the members' reading, isn't it?"

"Don't tell me you forgot that, too?" He sounded exasperated. "Everyone will be there—the Burnham clan, of course, and Louis is sponsoring the post-reading dinner. Duncan and Maggie are catering with their chowder and bread."

"I wouldn't forget your reading." She frowned. "Listen, Ned, going to Maui was a big breakthrough. I think I know how it all could have been done. I just don't know why."

"Well, I wasn't idle while you were off on your jaunt, darling," Ned said. "I think I know *why* it was done but not *how*."

"Hmm," Mina said, "maybe we should have a little one-on-one."

"Without your brother-in-law?" Ned asked.

"I'm starved," she said, moving closer to him. "Let's go to the Harbor Grill and tell each other first, then we'll go to Todd. Hey, where's Ollie?"

"He's still at your sister's house, and he's probably very upset with you."

"Why, because I left him?"

"Not only did you leave him, but he got muddy last night, so this morning Mrs. Olivera gave him a bath *and* a haircut."

The sky was moving into its evening colors when Mina stepped out of the car in the theatre parking lot. She took Ned's arm as they walked toward the back of the theatre and the stage door. Near the front entrance she could see two white tents decorated with paper lanterns, and beneath one of them was the setup for a bar. Under the second tent Duncan Mackenzie and another man were placing long serving tables, while around the tent other men set up round eating tables with red-checkered tablecloths and white folding chairs. Maggie had a tray of candles in red glasses, and she carefully centered one on each table.

"This members-only reading looks like a pretty fancy shindig for the theater," Mina commented.

"Shindig," Ned repeated. "I guess they're only held in America."

"It is a strange word," she said with a laugh. "Sounds like something football players do. So, do we have to go out before the reading and mingle with the patrons of the arts?"

"That's the general idea," he said, "in hopes that our sparkling, artistic auras will cause an outpouring of financial generosity."

"What do you think," she asked with a twinge of resentment, "about Todd responding to our discoveries by ordering us to leave things to him now?"

"Look, darling." Ned stopped her before they reached the stage door. "First of all, we may have made him feel a little inadequate, finding things out that he couldn't. Second, although he feels he needs a bit more evidence, everything is going to get more dangerous from here on in. And third, he represents the police and the law, and we should do exactly what he asks of us, whether we like it or not. End of sermon." He kissed her on the forehead.

"Edward Manusia," Mina said as she looked into his eyes, "you are so damned persuasive."

"Very good," he said as he swung open the stage door. "It might come in handy when I'm a husband."

Inside, in the green room, Johnny was thanking Louis Goldburn and his wife Doris for their generous contribution of a catered dinner by Duncan and Maggie Mackenzie.

"You're entirely welcome," Louis said. "This is the first time a community organization like this has invited me to participate in anything."

"Oh, that's because everyone thinks of you as that pinko lawyer," his wife Doris said with a deadpan look.

The remark and delivery sent Johnny and Louis into gales of laughter.

"Comrade," Johnny said with a fake Russian accent, "I would be glad to assist in the infiltration of this bourgeois organization."

Louis matched his accent. "Yes, yes, you will start with the staging of the *Three Penny Opera* and then *Saint Joan of the Stockyards.*"

"Yes," Johnny continued, "and this Hollister fellow will sponsor and star in both of them."

They burst into another fit of laughter.

"Really, boys," Ned interjected. "Bring the cell meeting to a close before the real Mr. Hollister shows up. The playwright wants him in a good mood and in tip-top form."

"And speaking of tip-top form," Louis said, "shall we all step out for a cocktail?"

Johnny wagged his finger. "Remember, actors are sworn to having only one drink before the reading."

"And the playwright is minding you," Ned added.

"While he's getting smashed?" Mina poked at him with her finger.

"Playwrights are allowed to get smashed," Ned informed her. "Actors are not."

Outside, the audience had begun to arrive for the preshow cocktail hour, and Mina saw Christian Hollister and Lamby Langston headed for the stage door, to check in, as they had, with Johnny. While Ned went off to circulate, Mina ordered a gin and tonic. She did not really feel like socializing and found an out-of-the-way bench to sit on. She had a lovely view of Waikīkī when she turned in one direction, and a birds-eye view of the reception when she looked in another.

She saw Emil Devon come out of the theatre and go straight to the bar, where he met up with Tessa and Hester. He ordered a drink, spoke to them, and then went back into the theatre, leaving them standing there, wondering what to do. Tessa gave Mina a little wave and looked relieved to see a familiar face. She walked toward the bench with Hester in tow.

"How are you doing?" Mina greeted her.

"We're all right, aren't we, Hess?" Tessa took a sip of her drink.

"I'm getting a puppy next week," Hester reported.

"I know it's soon for us to be out at a function like this after Father's death," Tessa said, sounding somewhat embarrassed, "but we just had to see Emil."

"And Sheldon," Hester reminded her.

Tessa nodded. "Of course, and Shel. Why, look, Hester, there's Uncle Gilbert and Aunt Helen." She had spotted them coming up from the parking lot. "Let's go say hello."

"You go," Hester said. She watched her sister walk away and then fussed with a button on her dress. "She's so gaga about that Devon guy."

"Don't you like him?"

"He scares me," Hester whispered. "Sometimes when he's at our house, he just sits on the couch by himself, and he looks so mad, like he wants to kill somebody."

"Yes, he does look mad quite a bit."

"Who's mad?" A voice came from behind them.

"Sheldon!" Hester exclaimed.

"Hello, Shel," Mina said, not wanting his attention and hoping she wouldn't have to talk to him.

"I'm always so late to everything," he complained with a boyish grin. "I suppose it's because I'm unorganized. Drink?" he asked Mina.

"Got one." Mina raised her glass and tinkled the ice cubes.

"I guess I better grab one while I've got the chance," he said, before he bounded off.

Hester pouted. "He didn't ask me. I'm old enough to drink."

"Yes, you are, aren't you?" It surprised Mina to remember.

"I am and I will." Hester stood up and marched off to the bar.

Mina watched as Tessa spoke to Gilbert and Helen Burnham. Gilbert soon moved off, leaving the women to talk as he wended his way through the crowd, shaking hands, dishing out pats on the back, and kissing the powdered cheeks of the ladies with the expertise of a seasoned politician. She wondered what he felt like right now, having exactly what he'd probably always wanted—control of the family business, control of his family estate, and no competition. Mina got up, strolled over to the bar, and ordered a ginger ale. She moved to the fringe on the other side of the crowd and saw Duncan Mackenzie and his men setting up. She saw Duncan stop his work to stare at the crowd, and she thought she could guess what he was thinking about these gussied-up theatregoers with their jewelry and their fancy cars. Class envy, she reflected, would always be a consequence of an unfair world. She thought Duncan seemed affable enough when she'd met him, but was he one of those socialists who believed that the ends justified any means?

"If she's lost in serious thought, it must be Mina Beckwith." Cecily Chang roused Mina from her reverie.

"Cecily," Mina said, hugging her. "I didn't know you were coming."

"Pops and Mom have been members forever," Cecily said. "They're over there with Tom, fawning over the playwright with a dozen other people."

"I'm keeping out of the way." Mina took a sip of her ginger ale. "Are you staying for the chowder dinner?"

"Mmm, of course," Cecily said. "They make the best chowder in town."

"Could you save me and Ned a seat? We'd love to sit with you."

"Will do." Cecily looked around. "Say, where's Nyla?"

"She's probably inside," said Mina, glancing at her watch, "where I should have been about ten minutes ago. I'll see you after, okay?"

"Break a leg." Cecily hugged her and watched as she disappeared into the theatre.

Once inside, Mina decided to freshen up in the lady's lounge off the lobby, since it was much nicer than the backstage bathrooms. She opened the door to find Nyla ensconced on a large couch, reviewing her lines.

"You're hiding," Mina said.

Nyla looked up from the script. "I just don't like socializing before I perform."

"You didn't miss anything, except for Cecily, but she and Tom are staying for dinner so you can see them later. Where's Todd?"

"He's wandering around in a state," Nyla answered, without looking up. "Last time I saw him, he had Tamiko and Michiko cornered and was quizzing them about something. The girls are going to watch the reading, and then clean up a little backstage. They begged me to ask Johnny, so I told him I'd reimburse him for their services."

"Let me do it, Nyla," Mina insisted. "And if they really want more work, they can come to my house and pull weeds."

"I'm sure they'd love it. Are Grandma and Daddy outside?"

"I didn't see them," Mina said as she checked her lipstick in the mirror. "They'll be here. They probably didn't want to go to the cocktail party."

"Where's your shadow?"

"He's in the car, with the windows rolled down. Ollie, that is."

"You terrible girl," Nyla said, chuckling. "Oops, we better get backstage. I think they're about to open the house."

Once the reading began, Mina was swept away along with the actors into the world of the story. Every so often in those next two hours she was aware of being part of Ned's creative consciousness, remembering that he made this all up, alone, at his typewriter. She could sense that the audience was transported as well. They responded with a laugh, a sigh, or complete stillness, as if they were punctuating the script. The telltale "theater cough," a sure sign of boredom, was not to be heard. The reading ended, and there was a long silence before the audience rose to its feet, clapping and shouting for the author. Ned stepped up and took a bow just before the curtain closed.

"You should be an actress, too, Mina," Ned whispered in her ear. "You have stage presence."

"I don't think I'm cut out for it," she whispered back.

"You could be."

On the lawn, the tables stood beautifully set, and as people sat down, they were served bowls of steaming chowder and substantial pieces of fresh bread and butter under the stars. Ned and Mina sat with Cecily and her family. At another table Mina could see her father and grandmother flushed with pride, not only in her and Nyla, but in Ned as well. Her father looked over at her and blew her a kiss. She knew he would be nothing but happy to have Ned as a son-in-law. The dinner was in full swing, with loud voices, laughter, and clinking glasses. Ned was lost in conversation with Tom, Cecily's fiancé, about some Shakespeare festival scheduled in Oregon for July that was doing the *Merchant of Venice.* She'd never even heard of Ashland, Oregon. During dessert, which was a wonderful mango tart with vanilla ice cream, Mina saw two police cars, with their headlights turned off, pull up on the shadowy side of the street just outside the theatre grounds. Unnoticed, she thought, by anyone but her, Todd went over and spoke to them. He then returned to the theatre party, made his way to the Burnhams' table, and whispered something in Sheldon's ear. As Todd and Sheldon walked into the parking lot, Ned and Mina both excused themselves from the table.

"I wish you would go back and sit down, darling," Ned said to her as they stood in the shadows, watching Todd speak to Sheldon.

Mina folded her arms and shook her head defiantly. Although she couldn't hear their voices, it was obvious, because of their gestures, that the discussion between Todd and Sheldon was getting heated. She saw Ollie's head pop up, alert to possible trouble, from the back seat of her car, which was parked very close to where the men were arguing. To her dismay, the dog leapt out through the open window and was pacing anxiously back and forth and eyeing the men. Mina saw Sheldon turn away in anger and then suddenly turn back to Todd with something in his hand.

"Oh, my God," Ned shouted, "he's got a gun."

With a powerful swing of his right hand, Sheldon brought the butt end of a revolver to Todd's right temple. As Todd slumped to the ground, Ned took off after Sheldon, and the police officers who were parked out on the street jumped out of their cars and raced across the lawn.

Sheldon ran, with Ned giving chase. They were near the back of the theatre when Sheldon whirled around. Ned stopped in his tracks, no more than ten feet behind. With a sinister smile on his face, Sheldon took aim, but just as he pulled the trigger, he was slammed by the fifty-pound body of Ollie, who had taken a racing leap and hit him squarely in the chest. A loud report echoed off the back wall of the theater, but the bullet missed its mark, and Ned was safe. Sheldon rolled twice across the pavement, then got up and dashed for the backstage door.

Mina raced inside through the front door of the theatre. She ran across the lobby and into the auditorium. She stood in the dark, looking at the dimly lit stage. Tamiko and Michiko were sweeping up with big push brooms. There was a flurry of shouts and noises in the wings before Sheldon ran out from stage left with a gun as two policemen ran on stage from the right. Sheldon fired his pistol. Tamiko, who was sweeping downstage and to the right, dropped her broom, jumped off the stage, and ran into the auditorium, but Michiko stood frozen in the center of the stage, afraid to move. Sheldon ran over, grabbed the frightened girl in a headlock and held his pistol to her temple.

"Stay back or the kid gets it," Sheldon screamed in a high, panicky voice.

"Give it up," said a voice from the wings. "There's nowhere you can go."

"Then she's coming with me, wherever I go," he spat back, and started backing off the stage.

Mina intercepted a terrified Tamiko and told her to go outside and stay with Grandma Hannah. When she saw Sheldon had backed completely off the stage, she ran down to the apron and climbed up, hiding behind the black curtains of the left wing. She watched as Sheldon dragged Michiko into the green room, the gun still pointed at her head. She calculated that he would try to escape with Michiko as his hostage through the door in the green room that led outside. She ran to the green-room door, and just before she opened it, she heard a policeman shout at her, but she opened the door and entered anyway. Once inside, she locked it and turned toward Sheldon, her back against the door. He was edging to his escape when he saw her.

"What the hell are *you* doing here?" he shouted. She could see droplets of sweat on his brow and temples. "Don't come near me or I'll shoot her, do you hear me?"

"Sheldon—"

"Maybe I should shoot you first." His voice was bitter. "If you had said yes to me that night on the beach, none of this would have happened."

"Sheldon, that is *not* why this is happening."

"It is. It is. You should have said yes." He was shaking.

"Oh, Sheldon, please." Mina couldn't disguise her compassion. "Please give Michiko to me."

"Why, why should I do anything for you?"

She could see that he wanted to cry. "Because," she said, "you'd like to be a good person."

"Shut up," he said. "Just shut up!"

"That's why you care about me, isn't it? That's why you care what I think of you."

Now she could see tears in his eyes, and beyond him, through the windows, she saw the figures of police officers shifting in the shadows.

"Please, Sheldon," she pleaded.

Staring at Mina, he slowly released his grip on Michiko and then gave her a hard shove toward Mina, who quickly positioned the girl behind her.

"Thank you, Sheldon," she said, "for giving me this girl's life because I asked. I won't forget it."

"Get out of here," he said in a low, serious tone. "Just get out of here before I change my mind and kill you." He waved the gun at her.

Then she turned swiftly, clicked open the lock, stepped outside with the frightened girl, and shut the door behind her. Ned stood right there with Ollie by his side, waiting to sweep her and Michiko to safety. As they hurried away across the stage, they were jolted by the sounds of gunfire.

24

FRIDAY

N **ED LOOKED AROUND** Todd and Nyla's living room, where everyone had gathered. It was nearing four in the afternoon and Todd had not yet returned, so it was decided to get underway without him. Emil Devon sat very close to Tessa, with his arm around her, as if he were protecting a child. Hester sat next to her sister, stiff and staring at the floor until Ollie came into the room. When the dog walked over to her and laid his head on her lap, she relaxed a little and responded by petting him. In their simple black dresses they looked like orphans from a children's book, pale and vulnerable. Ned was sure what they were about to hear wouldn't heal any of the scars, but as Grandma Hannah had said, a clear understanding of what had happened might be good for them. Helen Burnham was perched on an easy chair with her legs folded up on the side, while Gilbert sat in front of her on an ottoman. In another easy chair, Violet Lennox clutched at her cane, and every once in a while she lifted it and put it down, making a knocking sound of impatience. Grandma Hannah sat near her in a koa rocking chair moved in from the study. Louis Goldburn took up the piano bench in front of Nyla's baby grand, while Mina and Nyla sat on the rug next to the coffee table on two *zabuton*s.

"Thank you all for coming," Ned began. "It's useless to pretend that these killings aren't painful to all of you in one way or another. But we thought some of you might want an explanation of the tragic events, so we invited you here, to tell you as best and as gently as possible what happened, especially as there are some things we discovered that may make a difference to you, Tessa and Hester, and I hope to you, Mrs. Lennox. Please, Mina, you start first."

"I tried to think," Mina said, "how to tell this story—I mean, in what order so you would understand, and I came to the conclusion that it would be best to start at the beginning. And the beginning was a very long time ago, way before I was born, anyway. It started with two sisters, identical twins in fact, just like Nyla and me. These twin sisters lived up in Olinda on Maui, the daughters of Antone Rodrigues, a dairy farmer. And just like in the fairy tales they were beautiful, and one was a little naughty and the other one very well behaved. Well, we know what naughty girls do when they get to be teenagers, and one of them got so naughty that their father decided to send the good one away to the mainland before she got naughty, too.

"Then one day, when she was about eighteen or nineteen, the sister who stayed behind went to work temporarily as a maid to a house in Kula. The house belonged to some very wealthy people from Honolulu who used it for vacations, and there she met and fell in love with their handsome son. This handsome son was more than a little spoiled and reckless, and to the horror of his mother he had a penchant for working girls—girls not from his own social class. He and the dairy farmer's daughter began a passionate and secret affair. As you can imagine, this was no small feat, keeping an affair in the islands a total secret, but somehow they managed to do it. The poor dairy farmer's daughter was very much in love. She was faithful and true to him, and selflessly, she never asked him for anything, accepting whatever time and attention came her way. Did he love her? This we don't know, but certainly he knew he could never marry her, and certainly he knew he'd always have to hide her from his mother."

Violet Lennox shifted in her seat.

"Now, imagine his surprise when one day," Mina continued, "the handsome son goes to San Francisco and sees an exact replica of his beautiful dairy farmer's daughter. But instead of an Olinda country girl, the replica is sophisticated, glamorous, well spoken, a lady in every respect, running with the San Francisco elite, a woman he could proudly take home to his mother and to Honolulu society. The lovely replica tells him she's alone in the world, that her parents are dead, and that she's making a living for herself as a fashion model. And he never, ever tells her that he knows exactly who she is and where she's come from. He never tells her that her sister has told him all about her twin who disappeared from the home of her mainland guardian. I wonder, did he think it was a big joke? Did he think it was some kind of coup on his part? Did he love one of them and then the other or both at the same time? Well, he married his fashion model, and shortly after the couple arrived home, both the bride and the dairymaid became pregnant by the handsome son. And nine months later, nearly to the day, they each had a baby boy. Unfortunately, the beautiful dairy farmer's daughter died shortly after childbirth, but before she died, she told her aunt the truth about her baby's father. The aunt told her sister, and the two of them never told anyone until they told me."

"Winston hinted that he had a child out of wedlock," Violet said. "It was once when he'd had a little too much to drink, but he would never tell me any more." She was trying to keep from crying. "I didn't have any idea where the child was."

Ned continued the story. "But Sheldon found out. We don't know how they met, but somehow Sheldon discovered David Rodrigues, the shy and sheltered boy raised by his grandfather, Antone Rodrigues, and his great-aunts, Genevieve Rodrigues and Betty Perreira. Although how much he *really* knew about him other than the fact that they looked alike, we won't know. The two boys were the same age and, being the sons of twin mothers by the same father, looked like twins themselves. When he was on Maui, Sheldon secretly cultivated a relationship with David. He invited David to his little ranch in Kula and got him interested in polo. They spent hours playing polo together, and Sheldon gained his trust." Ned paused before he began again. "Now Sheldon, besides having a penchant for secrets, had some very bad habits. He spent money that he didn't have, and he was addicted to gambling at poker. He was in debt and ended up borrowing money, lots of money, from someone who most certainly would not have hesitated to damage him socially *and* physically if he didn't pay up. We think he might have appealed to his mother, and though she may have bailed him out before, this time she refused.

And that's when he concocted a very wicked and elaborate scheme. You see, Amanda had a secret, too. She had a trust that Winston Lennox had set up for her, a trust that would one day go to Sheldon. It was modest when she was newly widowed. But then she married Henry Burnham, and she never spent any of the money in it, so over the years it grew into a small fortune. Of course, Sheldon must have known about it, and being desperate for money, he decided to hurry along his inheritance.

"He wrote threatening letters to Henry, making it seem like a union supporter was out to get him. We think that Gwen, who toyed with Sheldon even as she set her sights on Henry, had let slip to him the business about Mr. Shimasaki. On the trip to Hale'iwa, Sheldon pretended he was going back into town to play polo, but he returned, disguised as Orsino Hood, and went into a bar looking for someone to take the fall, and who should he see but one of the people Henry hated the most, Jack Carstairs. It was an unbelievable stroke of luck. It was so easy to sucker Jack into his plan, to get him drunk, lead him on a wild goose chase through the brush near the hotel to plant his footprints, drug him, dump him in his room, return later, and leave the weapon on him.

"All along, we were led to believe Henry was the target, that the assassin killed the wrong person by mistake. But it was no mistake. It was Amanda Burnham who Sheldon meant to kill. He talked his brother, who had come to Honolulu to see a doctor, into going to the polo field, convincing him that he needed the chance to play in a real polo game, assuring him that no one would suspect a thing. He created the perfect alibi. A crowd of people who didn't get too close to David or speak to him thought they saw Sheldon at the exact time of the murder.

"Next came the killing of Lars Bruhn in a hit-and-run accident. Bruhn was the loan shark he owed so much money to. Why not get rid of him, too? Sheldon had someone, a female, call and set up a date, and then call and tease him away from the poker game." Ned looked around the room and rested his gaze on Hester.

Hester twisted in her seat. "He told me he was playing a joke on someone. I didn't know what he was doing."

"He left our rehearsal," Ned continued, "and said he would meet us after he got some petrol for his car, but instead he ran down Bruhn on the street and then walked into the Harbor Grill, ordered teriyaki steak, and told us a story about a long delay at the petrol station. Of course his car was never checked, because he wasn't even a suspect. Then, we come to the last murders. But to make those clear, we have to go back to the day that Gilbert and Henry had a fight in Henry's office. Sheldon ran in heroically to break it up and got punched in the nose, but while sitting in the reception area, being nursed by Mina, he heard Henry shouting for some papers from Island Trust and realized they were documents about his inheritance. He panicked. He thought Amanda might have told Henry about his gambling habit. Sheldon was afraid Henry was about to discover what Amanda had always kept secret—the huge assets she intended to transfer to him.

"Henry was smart, a bully, and he already had it in for Sheldon. Sheldon couldn't take the chance that Henry would put two and two together, so he decided Henry had to die as well. Conveniently, his brother David was due to come to Honolulu again, and Sheldon insisted on meeting him for a night on the town. Sheldon lent David some evening attire and told him to meet him at a nightclub at a certain time at a certain table. After our rehearsal, while the brother was at the club, Sheldon killed his stepfather and the secretary who had helped him and with whom he'd once had an affair. Then he changed into evening clothes that matched the ones he lent to David. He called the nightclub, asked for himself, then told his brother he couldn't make it. He knew that David, who doesn't like drinking and is extremely shy, would leave right away. He watched while David left, and then went back into the club and stayed there until all hours— another clever alibi."

Louis looked at Ned and then at Mina. "I don't understand how you found out all of this."

"Amanda's father did try to contact her once, when she first came back as a bride, but was severely rebuffed," Mina explained. "So although the father and aunts knew who she really was, they never revealed her secret to anyone and never approached her again. But when Amanda died, one of the aunts felt compelled to be at the burial.

The aunt just happened to be a friend of Nyla's housekeeper. We met them at the burial, and she told us that Amanda was her niece. But it wasn't until Wednesday that she told me about David. You see," Mina said, looking at Tessa and Hester, "she was hoping that you would want to meet him. They've tried to protect him all these years from shame and scandal. But now she's worried that after she and her sister pass away, he'll feel like he has no family, and when she saw that you had lost both of your parents . . . well, she asked me to talk to you about him."

"Of course we want to meet him." Tessa sat up a little straighter.

"What about me?" Violet Lennox frowned. "Didn't she think I would want to meet him, too?"

"As for the trust fund business and the gambling debts," Mina continued, "I'd have to credit Ned's intuition and persistence."

"But," Louis persisted, "why wasn't he arrested or brought in for questioning when you first got back from Maui? Why this delay that put that young girl in danger?"

"You need to ask Todd about that," Ned answered. "We're not the police, and we don't make those decisions. But in Todd's defense, I think he was hoping for some tangible evidence before he approached Sheldon."

"Which was what?" Louis folded his arms, and Ned thought the lawyer would be a sharp opponent in court.

Ned had to stop himself from smiling. "Well, it actually came from Tamiko and Michiko. By chance, Todd asked the girls, who had been moving some of Sheldon's things into his grandmother's cottage, if they'd seen anything out of the ordinary. At first they said no, but then they started giggling. When Todd asked them what was so funny, they said that they were moving a suitcase and it suddenly opened. Out of the suitcase fell something they thought was a dead rat, and so they both screamed. When Fumi came in and scolded them, they saw it was a pelt of false hair, and they saw some makeup, too. Then they wondered if wealthy men wore makeup like women. Fumi, who I'm sure was perplexed by the objects also, just put everything back in the case and told the girls to go back to work. But of course it was a wig, a fake mustache, and some stage makeup. Stage makeup was a talent Sheldon learned in high school, and he used it to create Orsino Hood. And in case you want to tie up every loophole for your client, Louis," Ned added, "Sheldon admitted he was guilty before he died, in front of more than one witness. He knew he was dying, and he said he didn't want Jack blamed for the killings."

"Even after all the terrible things he'd done," Mina said to Tessa and Hester, "Sheldon still had a corner of good in him."

"Thanks for saying so, Mina." Tessa shed silent tears and leaned into Emil's shoulder.

Grandma Hannah comforted Violet Lennox, who was also overcome, and everyone sat without speaking for several minutes, until they were all aware of the sound of Todd's automobile arriving and the closing of car doors. Nyla got up and went to the front door to welcome Betty Perreira, Genevieve Rodrigues, and their nephew, David, into the gathering. They were all struck by David's startling resemblance to Sheldon.

"I hope you don't mind," Nyla said, "but we thought this would be a good time for everyone to meet."

As if on cue, Mrs. Olivera and Mina began to lay out refreshments on the table. There was coffee, hot and cold tea, and lemonade, along with an assortment of cakes and cookies, including a bowl of warm scones. Ned had prepared the batter in advance and trusted the baking to Mrs. Olivera. Nyla took the Maui family around and introduced them to everyone.

Tessa and Hester, after their initial reservations, were quite taken with David and tried to draw him out by asking him questions about his life on Maui. Mina observed that although David looked like he could have been Sheldon's twin, he had a completely distinct and discernible presence. He was awkward and self-conscious, and he appeared to be working very hard to be sociable. He had all the hallmarks, Mina thought, of a boy carefully raised by his grandparent's generation. Grandma Hannah tried to entertain Violet as best she could, but Mina noticed that although Violet appeared to be paying attention to Hannah, she kept thumping her cane and looking over in the direction of David and the girls. Finally, as if unable to contain herself, Violet burst out, "Now, you girls, I don't think it's fair to monopolize the young man's attention. I'm sure he wants to spend some time with me. I am his grandmother, after all."

David stood up and moved a chair next to the old woman. "I'm very sorry, Grandmother," he said. "I didn't mean to neglect you."

Violet took his chin in her wrinkled hand and turned his face from side to side. "Why, anyone with two eyes could see you're a Lennox through and through," she exclaimed with emotion.

Mina found Ned sitting in the kitchen talking to Louis while Mrs. Olivera bustled about.

"And how is Jack doing?" Ned was asking.

Louis shook his head. "His sister's death is a big blow to him, but he's relieved, of course, that all charges are dropped. I told him that this would never have happened if both of you hadn't been convinced from the beginning of his innocence."

"What's more important is that Todd thought he was innocent, too," Ned reminded him. "If anyone else had been in charge of the investigations, I don't think things would have turned out this way."

"Well," Louis said, chuckling, "I guess sometimes the law *is* on our side."

"Is he eating?" Mina asked.

"Yes," Louis replied, "and in fact I'm going to the hospital right now. He asked me to come and tell him everything I learned at this gathering. Duncan and Maggie are anxious to know, too."

"In that case," Mina said, "I think I better make you a little plate of goodies to take. I'm sure he needs some fattening up."

After everyone had left, Nyla went to lie down before dinner, and so did Grandma Hannah. Mina cleared the living room of dishes while Ned brought the leftovers into the kitchen. Mrs. Olivera declared that even though it was a very sad first meeting, it was also a success.

"That Tessa is a very nice girl," Mrs. Olivera stated. "She is going to pick Betty, Genevieve, and David up tomorrow and take them to her house for lunch and a visit. Poor thing, she needs some help through this hard time. I suppose it will be a big scandal in the newspaper."

"I suppose it will be," Mina said. She wondered if she were still at the newspaper, reporting the story, if she would have been able to protect Tessa and Hester in any way. She knew that some of the reporters liked to milk a story for all the sensationalism they could, while others had a more judicious approach. Maybe she could try to appeal to Christian Hollister, although she hated the thought of asking him for anything. Maybe she could ask Ned to approach him. She couldn't imagine what it would be like to find out that your brother murdered your mother *and* your father, even if you didn't feel that close to them.

"Darling," Ned said to Mina, "you look like you're a million miles away."

"I was just wondering what I would do if my brother turned out to be a murderer." Mina's lips pouted a little.

"How is it I've never met your brother?" Ned asked.

"Yes, how is that?" Mina mused. "He always seems to be off on one of his long trips whenever you're here."

"What does he do on these trips?" Ned inquired.

"He looks into the organizations that our foundation has given money to and combines the job with a little sightseeing. He was born to look after money and do charitable work." Mina laughed. "And to the horror of my father *and* Uncle Jinx, he's a real joke on a horse. He always manages to fall off."

"Hmm, my candidacy for favored son-in-law status looks better all the time."

"A shoo-in, I'd say." She poured herself a cup of tea and put a scone on a plate. "Well, I wonder what's next?"

"I was thinking," he said.

"You were thinking?" She looked at him.

"Yes," he said, "of a lovely summer picnic."

25

SATURDAY

TWO WEEKS LATER

NED WINCED AS the crack of Nyla's croquet ball sent his ball roqueting toward the bushes and earned her an extra shot. Then, she expertly used her mallet to drive her ball through the home wickets and smack up against the stake, clinching a victory of two out of three games for the red, yellow, and orange team. He would be able to come in second, but his teammates, Todd and Mina, were just a little too silly and lagged behind Tom and Cecily on Nyla's team. Todd and Mina were laughing because Todd had mistakenly sent his ball through the wrong wicket, and now Cecily was in a perfect position to strike it on her next turn. He could see he'd have to work on Todd's and Mina's croquet skills.

The previous night's play reading at the Hale'iwa Theatre had drawn a small crowd, and the audience proved warm and appreciative. Mina and Ned had invited all of the readers to this Saturday afternoon picnic, along with their friends and family. Thanks to Nyla and Todd's new membership in the beach club, they had reserved the hotel for their guests for the weekend. Many of the readers had decided to stay over for the party and a day in the country.

It was nearing one in the afternoon, and Tamiko and Michiko were laying out the food on tables covered in white and decorated with roses and lilies that Grandma Hannah had insisted on buying and arranging. The old Hale'iwa Hotel stood bravely in the background, and the turquoise summer sea reached peacefully toward the

297

horizon. More guests wandered out from the hotel as the croquet game ended. Some were arriving by car, and as the gathering grew, the Saturday afternoon picnic on the grass commenced. Ned surveyed the group and couldn't help but feel pleased that Christian Hollister had had to decline the invitation. *Years from now,* he thought, *when I remember this day and the people who have come, the memory won't be burdened with Hollister's envy.* Of course, Ned wished that some of his own family could be here, but there would be time enough for other celebrations.

Grandma Hannah sat in the shade with Kaiwi, Puna, and her old friend Hinano, whom she had summoned from the Big Island for this occasion. Charles Beckwith had also flown back for the weekend. Ned knew that Uncle Wing Chang was busy in the kitchen, probably enjoying comparing cooking notes with Tony as he concocted a surprise dessert. He wasn't quite sure what it was, but Michiko, who enjoyed giving him intermittent reports, said that Uncle Wing had hired someone who was now turning an ice cream maker in the backyard. She also told him that Mrs. Shimasaki was helping in the kitchen and that she was very nice, a good worker, too, and could cook pretty well.

Mina's favorite trio of Hawaiian musicians arranged themselves under the trees and were tuning up their instruments. Ned was surprised that Mina had picked this location for the picnic—surprised, and yet today it seemed so appropriate, as if by being there they were all embarking on a new season and leaving behind the darkness of the last few weeks. Perhaps that's what Mina meant to do. Very early this morning he awoke to the muted sound of chanting moving through the hotel itself and out over the grounds. At first he thought he was dreaming, but after a few minutes he recognized that the sound was actually coming from outside, drifting through the hall and the downstairs rooms and finally out to the grounds. It seemed to go on for a long time, with more than one voice rising and falling in deep, shaded tones just as dawn was breaking. Later, over breakfast, Mina told him that Grandma Hannah had asked Kaiwi and Hinano to pīkai the hotel and the grounds. She explained that it was a ritual, using ti leaves, salt water, and, of course, the right words to cleanse and clear things from anything bad. It was like an exorcism and a blessing rolled into one.

The musicians were beginning to play, and Michiko, Tamiko, and Mrs. Shimasaki arrived with trays of filled champagne flutes and began dispensing one to each guest. Uncle Wing, Tony, and Masami appeared from the kitchen, and Charles stepped up near the musicians as they finished their first number. He called for everyone's attention and asked for Mina and Ned to come forward. He announced their engagement in a simple and dignified speech, but was unable to disguise both the joyful and sad emotions he felt. He then placed a fragrant maile lei on Mina and another on Ned and asked everyone to raise their glasses in their honor. Following the toast, the couple was immediately swamped with embraces, kisses, and congratulations, and it was some time before they got to sit down and enjoy the scrumptious feast that had flowed from the kitchen.

The afternoon took its time passing, as if it wanted to make every drop of summer light last as long as possible. By four o'clock the picnic guests had dwindled to mainly those who were staying at the hotel. Those who had driven out from town had already left, so that their long drive would end before the dinner hour. Cecily and Tom had begun another round of croquet, and it seemed to have degenerated into an exercise of silly fun under the influence of the champagne and wine punch.

Mina and Ned, tired out from so much attention, moved a little apart from the group, taking a lauhala mat to one of the shade trees down near the river. She had just finished a second helping of Uncle Wing's dessert, which had turned out to be crêpes with a delicate frangipane filling and a sprinkling of melted chocolate. They were perfectly complemented by the creamy vanilla ice cream. Ollie lay on the grass at the edge of the mat, anxiously hoping he might be allowed to lick the plate, and although Mina knew it was not good precedent, when she was finished she put her dish at the edge of the mat and didn't scold him as he edged toward the prized remains. Ned lay staring up through the network of tree branches and green leaves at the blue sky and floating clouds. Mina stretched out on her back, using his stomach for a pillow, and joined him.

"Did you think announcing our engagement would be so exhausting?" Mina asked.

"Never," Ned responded. "Although it was a lovely affair."

"Maybe we should run away and get married. A big wedding might really do us in."

"Where do you think we should run away to?" Ned asked, yawning.

"Hmm." Mina tapped her lips with her forefinger. "Somewhere east of the sun and west of the moon."

"I hear there's quite an artist's colony in Bali now. We could go there."

"I've always wanted to see Ceylon for some unexplainable reason. They have a parade of elephants in August."

"I've always wanted to see Tasmania," Ned said. Ollie came around by Ned and tried to lick his face. "Your dog is awfully forward with his affection."

"Ollie, stop," Mina said firmly. "We're trying to determine our wedding location. So far we've only picked islands." Ollie left Ned and began to nuzzle Mina's ear. "Ollie wants to walk down to the bridge and watch the fish."

"I think I could do that for the dog who saved my life."

"I can't believe I finally get to wear the ring," Mina said as she stood up and admired the jewel on her finger.

"I still can't quite believe you agreed to marry me." Ned took her hand as they walked along.

"Taking a bullet can give you a new perspective," she said, looking out at the horizon and then back at him. "Do you believe in mermaids?"

"Mermaids?"

"Well, any kind of water spirit. Kaiwi told me about a moʻo—a kind of a water spirit. She watches over this place."

"To tell you the truth," Ned said with a chuckle, "I've always believed in things like that—that those kinds of beings are around, but we just can't see them."

"I think she could be watching us right now," Mina said.

They sat on the driftwood bridge, dangling their feet above the clear river as the long afternoon shadows spilled over them. Ollie lay contentedly at their side, tracking the fish with his eyes, and behind them, while the softening daylight wrapped the grass, the trees, and the sea in a dreamlike glow, the old hotel creaked and yawned and fell into its own summer slumber.

ACKNOWLEDGMENTS

Mahalo nui loa to my editors at the University of Hawai'i Press, Masako Ikeda for her steady encouragement and enthusiasm, and Cheri Dunn for her dependable and congenial support. I thank the University of Hawai'i Press for choosing to publish this book and each and every person on their staff who have helped in the process. Many thanks go to Susie Corrado for her kind and careful attention to the details of the manuscript and to Kara Smith for her expert proofreading. I would like to extend my gratitude to Craig Howes at the Center for Biographical Research for his valuable advice and to his assistant Stan Schwab for always being so helpful. To Gaye Chan, a thousand thanks for a wonderful cover. To my friend Molly Giles I offer my heartfelt appreciation for the time and consideration she has given to my writing. And my aloha endures for Philip D. Haisley Jr., who is always there, rain or shine.

ABOUT THE AUTHOR

Victoria Nalani Kneubuhl, the author of *Murder Casts a Shadow* and *Hawai'i Nei: Island Plays*, is a well-known Honolulu playwright and writer. Her work has been performed in Hawai'i and elsewhere in the Pacific, the continental United States, Britain, and Asia. She is presently the writer and co-producer for the television series *Biography Hawai'i*.

Production Notes for
Kneubuhl / Murder Leaves Its Mark

Design and composition by Josie Herr
with Garamond text and display in CG Gothic

Printing and binding by Sheridan Books, Inc.

Printed on 60 lb. House White, 444 ppi